ACCLAIM FOR CHARLOTTE BINGHAM

The Kissing Garden
'A perfect escapist cocktail for summertime romantics'
Mail on Sunday

Love Song
'A perfect example of the new, darker romantic fiction . . . a
true, 24-carat love story'
Sunday Times

'A poetic and poignant love story'
Sunday Post

The Love Knot
'The author perfectly evokes the atmosphere of the
era . . . An entertaining Victorian roma
Woman's Own

'Hearts are broken, scandals abound. It's tota   ive,
the sort of book you rush to finish – then wis   dn't'
Woman's Realm

The Nightingale Sings
'A novel rich in dramatic surprises, with a   st of
vivid characters whose antics will have y   ally
turning the pages'
Daily Mail

To Hear a Nightingale
'A story to make you laugh and cry'
Woman

'A delightful novel . . . Pulsating with vitality and deeply
felt emotions. I found myself with tears in my eyes on one
page and laughing out loud on another'
Sunday Express

www.**booksat**trans**world**.co.uk

Television Drama Series with Terence Brady:
TAKE THREE GIRLS
UPSTAIRS DOWNSTAIRS
THOMAS AND SARAH
NANNY
FOREVER GREEN

Television Comedy Series with Terence Brady:
NO HONESTLY
YES HONESTLY
PIG IN THE MIDDLE
OH MADELINE! (USA)
FATHER MATTHEW'S DAUGHTER

Television Plays with Terence Brady:
MAKING THE PLAY
SUCH A SMALL WORD
ONE OF THE FAMILY

Films with Terence Brady:
LOVE WITH A PERFECT STRANGER
MAGIC MOMENTS

Stage Plays with Terence Brady:
I WISH I WISH
THE SHELL SEEKERS
(adaptation from the novel by Rosamunde Pilcher)

DISTANT MUSIC

Charlotte Bingham

BANTAM BOOKS

LONDON · NEW YORK · TORONTO · SYDNEY · AUCKLAND

DISTANT MUSIC
A BANTAM BOOK : 0 553 81387 0

Simultaneously published in Great Britain by Doubleday,
a division of Transworld Publishers

PRINTING HISTORY
Doubleday edition published 2002
Bantam edition published 2002

1 3 5 7 9 10 8 6 4 2

Set in 11/13pt Palatino by
Phoenix Typesetting, Ilkley, West Yorkshire.

Bantam Books are published by Transworld Publishers
61–63 Uxbridge Road, London W5 5SA,
a division of The Random House Group Ltd,
in Australia by Random House Australia (Pty) Ltd,
20 Alfred Street, Milsons Point, Sydney, NSW 2061, Australia,
in New Zealand by Random House New Zealand Ltd,
18 Poland Road, Glenfield, Auckland 10, New Zealand
and in South Africa by Random House (Pty) Ltd,
Endulini, 5a Jubilee Road, Parktown 2193, South Africa.

Printed and bound in Germany by
Elsnerdruck, Berlin.

To the character actors and actresses of 'The Profession' whose voices can fill a theatre unaided, their art brings a play to vivid life

Purposes of accuracy require that the first part of the book reflects the theatrical usage still in vogue in 1950s England. For a modern reader possibly the most muddling of these is the word 'producer'. In the old days the *producer* had the same function as the *director* has now. Much of this terminology has changed, as is reflected in the book, since the lines between theatre and television became less defined.

Charlotte Bingham
Hardway, 2001

People used to say that the theatre was a marsh light, leading you on and on, success and fame seemingly always deceptively close, yet in cruel reality never even within reach. Others would tell you it was like a beautiful sound to which you long to draw closer, the better to hear the music, but which, for all but the few, remained always and ever distant. Whatever the truth, for those whom the theatre calls, there is no other world.

DISTANT MUSIC

PART ONE

THE ORCHESTRA STRIKES UP

So beautiful and strange and new! Since it was to end so soon I almost wish I had never heard it . . .

Kenneth Grahame, 'The Piper at the Gates of Dawn'
from *The Wind in the Willows*

Chapter One

'It is up to you, Elsie, to restore the family fortunes, up to you entirely, you know that!' Dottie declaimed, banging down the iron.

Elsie nodded absently, too busy reading that week's copy of *The Stage* to look up. As was their habit they had lit one of the gases on the stove to keep the kitchen warm, so the windows of the small, kipper-smelling kitchen were steamed up and dripping with small rivulets, which dashed and chased each other down the window panes. When she was little Elsie used to bet on the drips, imagining each emerging droplet to be a racehorse, and herself a rider. Nowadays life was too serious for any such imaginings, too purposeful for anything but hope.

Elsie and Dottie, her maternal grandmother, had lived, for some many years now, together with assorted lodgers, in a tall, thin, crumbling Regency house, exactly like the other tall, thin Regency houses that made up an equally crumbling square, in a Sussex seaside town which, like the Richards family, had once seen better days.

Cheek by jowl though they lived, however, Elsie never *quite* knew when Dottie would come up with her favourite line about the loss of their family fortunes and the need for Elsie to restore them, but whenever she did, it hit home as nothing else did.

Ever since her grandfather's death when she was four years old, and their subsequent removal from the outskirts of the seaside town to a tall terraced house, their lodgers had been a permanent feature of life, as well as a source of fascination to Elsie. Fortunately Dottie, having herself once been an actress, knew all about 'digs' and how to make your house a well-known stop-off for actors and actresses on tour. More than that, she knew all about what it took to become a famous theatrical landlady.

It took wit, and staying up late, it took tolerance and a great deal of cocoa, it took sympathy and a good breakfast. The result of this knowledge was that when she took over the lease of number twenty-two Kings Square, the role of confidante and mother, humorous friend and understanding companion – in other words the role of the ever sympathetic landlady – was most definitely a part which Dottie knew could have been written for her.

Having reached the age of seventeen without having been made homeless, Elsie was appropriately grateful to her grandmother for both her pluck and her fighting spirit, for without it she had always known that they would have years ago had to join the dole queues. Elsie's mother, Benita, having become an alcoholic, had long disappeared over the horizon.

'Missing presumed dead,' was the clipped pronouncement that Dottie always made when people asked after her daughter, which neatly summed up the condition of a young woman who had run off and left her daughter to be brought up by her parents.

Left alone in the world, it had been necessary for Elsie and Dottie to weld themselves into a partnership that was bound with the indissoluble ties of the need for survival. They understood each other as no one else perhaps might or ever would, although of course they never said as much.

Born at the beginning of the twentieth century Dottie was an Edwardian by fact and by nature, and the Edwardians, even Elsie knew, were not in the habit of showing their feelings to each other in a slushy way. Since Elsie was knee-high to a grasshopper Dottie had shown her that she loved her by one means and one means alone – her constant encouragement. Any moment when Elsie might have faltered in her struggle to get noticed at Tippy Toes, the local stage school run by Miss Tippy Morrissey, was immediately dismissed by Dottie with expressions such as *lacking in gumption* or *oh dear, feeling sorry for little me, are we?*

At home, where Elsie really might have been tempted to feel sorry for herself when she was forced to run up and down the steep stairs of the house with trays of food or refreshments for the lodgers, her feelings of tiredness or despondency were put to the sword by a single withering look.

'Oh well, you'll just have to get on with it, like the rest of us,' was Dottie's inevitable comment when Elsie failed an audition, or a ballet exam.

So that was just what Elsie learned to do. She got on with her dancing and her singing lessons, the latter provided by a Miss Belmont who had for a time occupied one of the front rooms on the first floor of their house. She got on with her dancing classes at Tippy Toes. She got on with her ballet shoes, into which, from an early age, she had learned to sew ribbons and elastic tape. She got on with the washing-up and the drying-up, with the boiling and the brewing; she got on with everything that came up, and some things which, like jobs in the theatre, did not come up, but had to be sought out.

And in the process of doing all this, quite inevitably, she grew old before her time, which was probably what her grandmother wanted, because since *she* was alone in the world, and had no one to whom to turn except Elsie, it was better for both of them if most of the time they just pretended that Elsie was the same age as Dottie.

Of course there was an unspoken acceptance between them that because Dottie had been frustrated in her ambition to be a great actress, Elsie had to become one in her place.

Happily Elsie was a beautiful enough child for it to be entirely understandable for her grand-mother to push her towards the stage. She was tall for her age, and slim, with long, slender legs, waist-length wavy blond hair, a tip-tilted nose, and a mouth that turned up at the corners, so that even when Elsie was actually feeling miserable she still looked as if she was smiling.

Unfortunately for Elsie her worst feature was her eyes which although of a beguiling green protruded slightly, something which they both felt would definitely affect her film chances, if she ever had any. Whenever the subject raised its distressing head Elsie would merely shrug her shoulders and say to her grandmother, 'Don't let's think about that yet, Dottie.'

It was a feature of their relationship that not only had they somehow ironed out their familial relationship by first-naming each other, but they never hesitated to disagree. They told each other exactly how they felt, at all times, and in a strik-ingly truthful fashion; until, that is, the kitchen door opened, or the front door, or some other door in their tall, thin house, and one of their lodgers appeared, at which point they automati-cally became as warm and charming as any auditioning actor.

Indeed such was the cordiality of their manners to their lodgers, such their humour and kindness, that Elsie sometimes thought that being with the lodgers had taught her more about acting than even the famous Miss Tippy Morrissey. It did not matter what the complaint, how difficult the demand, Dottie and Elsie smiled and laughed, cajoled and sweet-talked their lodgers until the kitchen door closed again, after which they instantly fell back into their usual professional talk, devoid of any bothering with charm or flattery.

'It is *not* Jack and the Beanstalk this year, thank God, it is going to be Cinderella, so Miss Belmont got *that* wrong.' Elsie looked up from her paper as Dottie nodded down at the washing-up, carefully pouring a hot kettle from the stove into the old butler's sink with its one cold tap.

'You haven't been in Cinderella since you were a dancing mouse, oh, must be eight years ago – or was it a mushroom?'

Elsie frowned down at the paper, willing it to be going to yield a part in the panto for her. 'Never ever know with panto, do you, that is the trouble?' she asked of no one except herself. 'André Gillon is the management. Or so it says here.'

'I sometimes think with panto they take out more than they put in. Nothing but specialist acts and conjuring at the expense of the story,' Dottie agreed. 'Still, Miss Morrissey might know. I think that André Gillon could be an old friend of hers. Yes, he must be, because he choreographed her in Peter Pan before the war.'

Elsie was not listening, too busy trying to think where she, at seventeen, and with an already developed figure, could fit in to the forthcoming panto.

'Are the rats in Cinders always boys, Dottie?'

'Can't remember. Not always, I don't think.'

Elsie sighed. She was good at ballet, and being slim could possibly still play an older kind of rat, if she taped her bust. She sighed again, and turned the page of the newspaper. It was always the same. The gap between what she could do, what she wanted to do, and what was on offer was about as wide as the English Channel that their seaside town and pier faced so bravely, night and day.

'You going up for it, then? Going up for the panto, then?' Dottie turned briefly from the sink as Elsie nodded.

'Yes, because Mr Dimchurch on the second floor, he knows André Gillon too, except not for some years, but he said that he thought there might be something in the minor parts and to go and call, and whatever happens, to mention his name.'

'Yes, but you don't want to go up for nothing, not when there's a bus fare involved, dear. Going up for nothing, spending sixpence and then you don't get the part, you don't want that, do you?'

Elsie nodded in agreement. It was true, she did not. Just the word sixpence was a very emotive one for Elsie, because once Dottie had lost a sixpence under the sitting room sofa, and it had taken hours and both of them pulling up a floorboard to find it. Elsie never forgot that day.

Even though she was only very young it had scared the livers and lights out of her, seeing that look in Dottie's eyes, a sort of mixture of determination to find the coin and fear that it might prove lost for ever. It was then that Elsie had realised that life was not just all about not losing money, not just about not spending money, but about making it, because Dottie had said, over and over, 'It's taken hours to earn that, Elsie. Hours!'

So now, knowing more than ever what it took to save up much needed money, Elsie said with a note of impatient reassurance in her voice, 'Don't worry, Dottie, I will walk.'

Dottie nodded at the frying pan she was busy scrubbing.

'Probably best, dear. "Tides permitting", of course.'

It was pouring with rain, so Elsie, having brushed and combed her long blond hair and placed her Alice in Wonderland black velvet headband across it, pulled on her velvet two-caped coat and her fur-lined boots and started the long walk to the seaside theatre on the promenade in a necessarily philosophical mood. As she battled her way along using her small child's umbrella as a buffer against the elements she murmured lines from speeches that she liked to rehearse when walking, finding the realisation that she was word perfect as reassuring as the weather was not.

Elsie never liked to dwell on her next ordeal, and it was not in her nature to anticipate good fortune. It might bring on false hope, and she had enjoyed enough false hope in her short life to last her for a century. Instead, as she walked along, she let her mind wander ahead, not to the possibility, or not, of being able to audition, but to the other advertisement she had seen that morning in *The Stage*. It was for a young actress to join a repertory theatre. *Female juvenile lead to start immediately*. That was all right as far as it went. And it made no mention of exact age, so that should not be a difficulty either, because she had a feeling that she might be able to pass herself off as being older than she was, given her height, and the sophistication of her conversation. The problem was in the wording of the advertisement, which ran *Own wardrobe, costumes, hats (day), own evening dresses*. No one, not even Dottie, could say that Elsie was the owner of the kind of extensive wardrobe that would be considered suitable for twice weekly repertory. Most of her clothes were still sadly and rather strangely old-fashioned, which they would be, considering that most of them had been cut down from old costumes once belonging to her mother.

It occurred to her that she might be able to hire clothes more suitable for such an engagement from the seconds shop on the corner of the square, but the cost of the hire of so much might far outrun her salary. She knew that she would be all right at the interview, because thanks to Dottie she could talk theatre better than people almost twice her age. She could talk with supreme authority about performances that she could not possibly have seen, because she *had* seen them; she had seen them recreated by Dottie, in a special solo performance, in their small, overheated kitchen.

As the heat from the old gas stove steamed up the windows, as the rivulets ran down the insides of the old panes, and rain poured down the outsides in ever greater torrents, through all the winters of Elsie's growing understanding, Dottie had acted out the greats of the theatre for her granddaughter, until there was hardly a number sung by Maisie Gay, or a speech taken at rattling speed by Noel Coward, or tragic role acted by Sybil Thorndike or Peggy Ashcroft, that Elsie herself could not perform. Most of all she could assume the inside knowledge, the know-it-all air, of the thorough professional.

This, more than lipstick, more than mascara, could and did give her a veneer of theatrical sophistication, and she knew it. It was because of what she could pretend to have seen or heard that other people in the profession always assumed that Elsie was older than she was, even now she was seventeen. Mind you, she was still prepared to use a bit of lipstick and a few of Dottie's hankies tucked into her brassiere where it mattered to help confirm the impression, if necessary.

But not today, not this afternoon. This afternoon would be different, because, after all, she had no idea if there would be anything *for* her.

Dottie was inclined to encourage Elsie to go up for too much, and sometimes anything, in the sublime belief that it was all good experience. More often than not, therefore, Elsie found herself going up for auditions just to please Dottie, whereas left to herself she would not have bothered.

Nowadays, it all too often turned out to be a wasted journey, and Elsie would be turned away after some long bus journey with the terse words *too old* or *too tall* or worst of all *dunno why your agent sent you, dear, there's nothing in here for you!*

The truth was – and it was this truth more than anything that preoccupied Elsie to the point of obsession – she was currently going through that most ghastly of all ghastly moments in a professional actress's life: she was changing categories. Realistically her days of being considered for children's roles were now over, and there was nothing she could do but hope that very soon she would prove acceptable for girls' parts. It happened to everyone in the theatre, and all the time, Dottie said, but like everything that Dottie said, it was said far too often and far too loudly for Elsie's liking.

Dottie also said that it could not be *got* over. She said that rather often too. Elsie had therefore always been horribly aware that she would be very lucky to survive this caterpillar-to-butterfly phase, and yet survive it she *must*, for Dottie, and for herself, and even for the lodgers, who, for some reason that she could never quite understand, seemed, like Dottie, to think that Elsie really would, with just a little effort, become a big star quite soon, at any minute, and in the not too distant future.

Mr Dimchurch on the second floor, who had once played Polonius at Twissingham Repertory to the young John Sisley's *first* Hamlet, and always maintained that he had appeared in a film before the war with Marissa Huntley, also insisted that he had high hopes for Elsie.

'You have *something* dear. I always know, you know. You are a natural star. Just something inside you, over which you have no control, really, something very special. The temperature, as Noel Coward always says of the stars, the temperature goes up when you come on, so whatever happens, do not let anyone put out your inner light, dear. People can, you know, they can put out your light. Just snuff it out, like that—' Here he always snapped his fingers. 'And it can't be relit. So guard it, dear, whatever you do, guard it with your life. Your light, your beautiful light must never be allowed to go out as mine has done.'

Since most of the time Dottie opined that Roger Dimchurch was an untalented old fool, Elsie found it difficult to listen to him with as much reverence as was perhaps his due. Nevertheless he had his uses, always coming up with some contact or other, someone he had known before the war, always ready to help Elsie in any way that he could, because, as he kept maintaining, he really believed in her.

'Next, please!'

'Before I begin, Mr Gillon, Roger Dimchurch told me to say that he sends his kind regards to you.'

'Mr Gillon is no longer producing this pantomime. He has been replaced by Mr Donald Bourton.'

Despite this gloomy piece of news, and silently cursing that she had even mentioned Roger Dimchurch, Elsie smiled beautifully and charmingly into the darkness. The darkness not responding to this polite greeting, she quickly looked over to where the accompanist at the piano was seated, impatiently flattening Elsie's music with two ancient hands, and at the same time peering at it as if the notes were not music, but ancient Hebrew. The cardiganed lady looked too old to even attempt to play the piano, and what with its yellowing keys and battered woodwork the piano looked too old to respond to anything but a can of petrol and a match.

Elsie could sing the well-known number from *Oklahoma!* not just with gestures and slight innuendo but in her sleep, and frequently at auditions felt that this was exactly what she was doing, she had performed it so often. But today, perhaps to wake herself out of her usual trance-like state, she executed a small routine tap dance after finishing her song, ending with both a curtsy and a bow, which she thought, in a confused way, just might make the point that she could dance as both a boy and a girl.

There was a small silence broken only by one of the two men below in the stalls lighting up a cigarette with a match.

Elsie waited for the short sharp 'Thank you' which so often spun back across the footlights signifying an end to her chances, but today, instead of the usual gunshot of words, a voice from the darkness said, 'Can I hear you in something from a play, please? If you could oblige us with a *short* excerpt from something.'

'A speech from *Antigone* by Jean Anouilh, *voyez-vous?*'

Again the response to this announcement was silence, complete and total, but then Elsie was used to that, as she was used to most things that did, or did not, happen at auditions.

France and all things French were all the rage in English theatrical circles at that moment, being currently very fashionable with managements and critics, and Elsie had learned several speeches, albeit in English, from plays by French playwrights such as Jean Anouilh. She also had a good supply of French phrases learned, not from Mr Dimchurch on the second floor, but from Mr Labell on the ground floor. Mr Labell had, he always said, had a French grandmother, which was why he was so proficient in the language with which the whole of theatrical England was so enamoured. Over the years of lodging with Dottie he had taught Elsie to say a great deal in French;

short useful phrases only, but in the proper manner, not as English people usually pronounce French, but full of rounded, guttural sounds.

'Always remember when attempting French, dear, to start as if you are clearing your throat of something rather nasty.'

It was because of Mr Labell that Elsie had just said '*voyez-vous*'. It was also because of him that she had become so good at audition speeches from the plays of the still fashionable Jean Anouilh. Mr Labell had helped her to understand that to absorb roles written by French playwrights it was no good remaining in your heart of hearts a shy little English flower, you had to absorb the intelligence, the vibrant defiance, of the French nature. The French were much more intelligent than the English, Mr Labell had always insisted, which meant approaching the parts they wrote in a completely different way.

'Could you come through to the stalls, please?'

Elsie slipped out of the pass door and down into the auditorium. There was one working light on. The two men seated in the stalls looked taller now that she was standing on the same level as them, as people in managements always seemed to do.

'What part were you auditioning *for*, by the way?' The smaller and older of the two men was the first to speak. His companion seemed happy to stay silent.

'Cinderella's friend, or one of the rats in the kitchen ballet.'

Elsie improvised quickly and efficiently, knowing that the final form of a panto was never, ever fixed, because of last-minute bookings, not to mention last-minute cancellations. Stars were always walking out of panto at the last minute in a fury over their billing or their money, or just because they happened to be feeling a bit umpty.

'Cinderella doesn't have a friend in this version, I am afraid, and nor is there, I fear, a kitchen ballet, at least not at the moment.'

'Cinderella always used to have a friend, most particularly, as you no doubt know, in the 1938 production at His Majesty's Hippodrome, Blackmouth,' came back the tart reply, followed by a small pause after which Elsie continued, 'and I myself danced in the kitchen ballet as a mushroom in Cinderella's kitchen in a production here, eight years ago. So I know it was there. But of course,' here Elsie sniffed disdainfully, 'of course, if you have lots of novelty acts and so on planned, you will never have time for the normal *va et vien* of the panto, as so many managements nowadays do not.'

Elsie was artlessly parroting Dottie, chin up, eyes cool, determined as always not to be frightened of managements. You always had to show them that you knew a thing or three, and were not going to be intimidated by them, which was the reason why she now slowly lifted a slender wrist and sighed as she saw the time on Dottie's best wrist watch.

'Oh dear, look at the time. So hideous, quite

hideous. But if you have finished, which doubtless you have, I have to be off.'

Dottie had always taught Elsie to be in too much of a hurry to wait for any verdict from any management, whoever they might be, and however illustrious-seeming; and not only that, but to make sure to give them the impression of both supreme indifference and supreme impatience.

Whenever she was off out to an audition even Mr Labell always called out to her from the door of his rooms, 'Give them the full *froideur* dear. Always remember, artistic arrogance at all costs!'

'You must speak to producers as if they are beneath you. It is the only thing they understand,' Dottie herself always said.

And it was true. Even if you were not suitable for the role you were up for, you had to pretend you had been offered something else much, much bigger, and you had only really come along for a lark, and for the experience, and not because you really, really wanted the role.

It was a game, but it was a game that worked. Elsie had noticed this most particularly over the years. The young juveniles who did not play the game, the ones who ignored that advice, so freely given, and so often, by Dottie to their mothers or grandmothers, their aunts or elder sisters; the ones who settled for looking as they felt inside, humble and polite, who never yawned or sighed or looked at their watches, who did not tap their feet impatiently, as Elsie was now doing – they were the ones who ended up out of work.

'You are quite tall, but not too tall.'

Elsie made sure to nod absently. It was true. She was tall, but not so tall that the inevitable small height of so many of the male actors could become a problem.

'Twirl, if you would.'

Elsie shook her head, her expression changing from slight disdain to total contempt as she looked at the men from the management.

'I do not twirl. I never twirl, twirling is . . .' she paused tellingly as Roger Dimchurch had taught her, 'twirling is – common.'

As she said this however she curtsied instead, and then for good measure did several pirouettes up the carpet away from the two now thoroughly silenced men. Eventually, his breath perhaps rather stopped in his body by her mixture of arrogance and daring, one of them spoke.

'Miss, er – Elsie, is it?'

He glanced down at his notes, but Elsie was quickly on to him, not letting him get away with such a lack of professionalism.

'Not *er*, and not *Elsie*. Elsie Lancaster. *Elsie Lancaster*. Remember that. You both will do well to remember it, because I am going to be terribly famous. Please, watch this space, *voyez-vous*.'

After which she curtsied again, and turning on her heel started to walk away, up the red-carpeted auditorium, towards the front of the theatre and the doors to the fresh sea air, of which she now felt strangely in need, because whatever everyone at home said, determinedly braving managements always left her feeling both hot and dry-mouthed. In fact it was her experience that braving managements required more acting than acting itself ever did.

'Miss Lancaster. Please, wait!'

The taller of the two men now cantered up the carpet after her, putting out a not unfriendly hand to arrest her exit.

'Excuse me, sir, I must be on my way. I am, you see, like the white rabbit in Alice, in a terrible hurry.'

He nodded in complete understanding.

'Of course you are, but so are we! We are in a terrible hurry to sign you up for Cinders.'

Elsie's eyes, large and slightly protruding, became if anything more of both as she stared at him.

'Which role do you have in mind, did you say – was it Cinders? Did you say Cinders, Mr *er* . . .'

Taking the sarcasm of her tone as the reprimand that he knew it to be Mr Cosgrove did have the grace to blush, but even so Elsie had the feeling that he was actually laughing at her.

'Portly Cosgrove. Yes, I – that is we, Mr Bourton and I – we both think you will make a perfect Cinderella for us. You have the height, the looks, you can sing and dance, you have everything.'

Elsie stared up at him. Of a sudden from being a rude old man of at least twenty-four or five years of age, and of no possible taste, Portly Cosgrove had been transformed for Elsie into a tall Adonis with a discerning eye for talent. No rat turned into a coachman, no pumpkin turned into a coach, could have undergone a more efficient or beautiful transformation than Portly Cosgrove at that moment.

'Who is your agent, Miss Lancaster?'

Elsie's grandmother was her agent, of course, but it would never do to say so to Mr Cosgrove. It would give a far too homely impression, and bring Elsie's salary tumbling right down.

'Dorothy Temple is my agent, Mr Cosgrove.'

Although the family name was Richards, Dottie always operated as an agent under Dorothy Temple, which was fine except on those occasions when Dorothy *Richards* was being represented by Dorothy *Temple*, putting herself up for some role in which, humiliatingly, she would then not be cast; as a consequence of which, on more than one occasion, Elsie had heard her berating some producer in the wrong name, thereby bringing the agency, and therefore Elsie, into disrepute. Producers were notoriously thin-skinned when it came to taking offence. They had long ago changed Elsie's surname from Richards to Lancaster, which they both thought had more ring to it.

'And Miss Temple's telephone number, Miss Lancaster?'

Elsie gave it quickly and clearly, as she always did. Ever since they had moved into the house they now thought of as home, Dottie had made sure that they had a separate number for the agency. The number belonged to the telephone in the hall, and when it rang Dottie answered it for everyone in her official agent's voice. She always said, 'Hallo, Temple and Mead, Theatrical Aaa-gency.'

'Good. I am glad you came to see us, Miss Elsie Lancaster.' Portly gave Elsie a sudden and bright smile. 'Do you know I really think we were just beginning to despair of ever finding our Cinderella?'

Being the hardened little professional that she was, Elsie made it clear that the brilliant smile from the tall, handsome young man did not cut any mustard with her.

'Mr Cosgrove,' she said, pausing to give a small sigh, 'because nothing is as yet signed or sealed I have to tell you that I am shortlisted for another role, as it happens. At Tyningham Repertory Theatre, so if you want to sign me this week, I would say that you are going to have to get your skating boots on and telephone Miss Temple, and as soon as may be.'

Of course Elsie was not shortlisted for anything, not even for a piece of longed-for but rarely tasted Fullers cake, but since she was at least hoping to go up for an audition at the repertory theatre she was happy to be ruthless. She knew managements only too well; they were quite happy to promise a girl a role in the morning, and by the afternoon find that they had changed their minds when they saw someone else. They had no feelings, had management, and the best, the only way to treat them was as if you had none either.

'We will telephone through to Miss Temple at once, you may be sure of that, Miss Lancaster.' Portly shook Elsie's hand, but as she turned on her heel once more he called out to her, 'Are you sure I can't show you to your motor car, Miss Lancaster?'

Elsie turned back, and for the first time she smiled as she drew her caped coat tighter around her neck.

'No, thank you, Mr Cosgrove. I have sent my car home. I always like to walk after auditions. I find it clears my mind – for the next one.'

After which she walked off with determined insouciance, strolling through the various sets of doors confronting her, until she was out in the open once more and opening up her child's umbrella, and starting to battle against rain so fierce that it took all her concentration not to let it soak her.

As a consequence it was only after she reached home that she remembered she had in fact been promised the leading role in the pantomime, which, if it came off, meant that she would be able to buy Dottie and herself more than a turkey for Christmas, she would be able to buy everyone in the house presents, and a cake – everything.

Back at the theatre Portly Cosgrove turned to his business partner, Donald Bourton, and shaking his head, sighed with sheer pleasure.

'How about *that*, Donald?'

Donald, a jovial-looking, round-faced man in his early forties, soberly dressed but with a habit of holding a smoking cigarette and rolling it slowly and methodically backwards and forwards between his teeth, now also shook his head.

'I know, how *about* that!'

'A star is born.'

'It certainly is, Portly, it certainly is.'

They stood on, staring vaguely ahead at the place where they had last seen Elsie as she vanished through the swing doors at the top of the auditorium.

'It is all *there* already, Donald, did you notice?'

'I did. And as always we do not have to do a thing, not a thing. Just costume it, put it on stage, and watch the audience taking Miss Elsie Lancaster to their hearts. How about that, nothing to do.'

'Yes, nothing to be done at all. Just put her up there. Magic.' Portly snapped his fingers, still smiling, and at the same time shaking his head in wonder. Donald Bourton too smiled.

'It's the first time it has happened to you, isn't it?'

'Yes, my first time.' Portly nodded, also serious for the first time, the realisation hitting him of a sudden. 'Yes, this is the first time it has happened.'

'You never get over it, always remember that.' Donald said this matter of factly, in the same way that he might announce the price of fish and chips in a café. 'The first time it happened to me, you know, was the young Harris James. He came on stage, recited a piece from *Henry V*, and then promptly sat down on a chair to the side of the stage and proceeded to yawn fit to bust, looking if anything not just bored stiff by the whole audition procedure, but bored to ribbons by everything that was happening. Never mind it was John Sisley's production company putting it on, and starring the great man as well; it was of no possible interest to young Harris James. It was quite obvious to everyone that he just wanted to go home and listen to sport on the wireless. Outrageous! He was only seventeen, or perhaps sixteen – no, seventeen, anyway something like that, but already with the looks of a young god. Old Plum Loughborough turned to me as soon as Harris had finished galloping through *Once more unto the breach, dear friends* – I was producing at the time – and said, "What can one say, old boy? Except sign him at once." That was the marvel of it, do you see, even sitting on stage yawning you could not take your eyes off him. Really, you just could not take your eyes off him. It is as simple as that, Portly, it really is. They have either *got* it, or they have *not* got it, and that young lady has got *it*.'

'I will telephone through to her agent.'

Portly Cosgrove hurried off back up to his office on the first floor of the building, while Donald Bourton sat down and called, 'Next please!'

He liked to think that he was a kind man, a man

who would not, as it were, willingly hurt another, and the undeniable fact was that he really hated this next bit of the audition process. Having to sit through singing and dancing, recitation and movement while all the time knowing that the part in question had already been assigned was a form of torture for him, yet it had to be done, because, after all, Elsie Lancaster might not be lying, she might really be thinking of signing on at Tyningham Repertory Theatre.

Having reached home and battled her way through the front door Elsie shook out her little plastic umbrella and wiped her face with a handkerchief.

The rain had made her hair turn a little too frizzy, which was never flattering, so she went quickly to her room on the ground floor – overlooking the pavement and the street lights, rather than the garden with its few shrubs and its iron bench at the back – and hung up her coat and rubbed her hair dry. No good presenting herself to Dottie, at any time of the day or night, in any less than starry condition. Even a button undone on her blouse, or a muddy shoe, would gain a reprimand. As far as Dottie was concerned, if you wanted to be a star you got up as a star and you stayed as a star, all day and all night, even in your sleep, if necessary. Anything else was simply not tolerated.

'Doors do not open to nondescripts with their hair messed and their clothes muddied. Doors do not open to actresses without glamour. Doors do not open, ever, to those who are careless of their appearance,' she would intone with the measured voice of an Eastern holy man calling the faithful to prayer from a minaret.

So it was only when Elsie was once more completely presentable, once more the potential star, that she climbed down the stairs to the basement kitchen that was the engine room of the house, and Dottie's power base. And it was only when she was about to push open the kitchen door that she realised she had actually been offered the *lead* role in the pantomime for the coming season.

For one single solitary second Elsie's heart took off and seemed to sweep all normality out of her body, and against all the rules, against everything she knew to be the facts of theatrical life, she let it. For what seemed like a single glorious second she let herself feel thrilled, full to the brim with the singular happiness, the ecstatic realisation, that she had been offered the role of Cinderella.

It would drive her arch rival Jane Buskin *potty*! It would drive Jane's mother Mrs Buskin *mad*! It would make everyone else at Tippy Toes *furious*!

All this went through her head for the one second that she allowed herself to enjoy the moment, before reality set in and she began to wonder how best to approach Dottie with the news.

It was never a good idea to announce anything to Dottie in a *big* way. If you did that she would always deflate you with some crushing remark.

Not was it a good idea not to tell her as soon as an offer had been made, because if Dottie picked up the telephone and was surprised by someone, charming though she might be to the caller she often lost her temper with Elsie afterwards, and then there was hell to pay, not to mention a mound of the lodgers' ironing to do by way of punishment.

No, Elsie had to think of a way to approach Dottie that would make sense of what had happened, and at the same time prepare her to negotiate for Elsie.

Elsie loathed the whole process of being bargained over, simply because it always made her feel like a pound of old plums on a market stall. The grander Dottie made Elsie sound, the more she demanded for her, for some reason the worse Elsie found she felt, and this despite knowing that, of course, Dottie was right.

And of course she *was* right. If Dottie was doing her job she had to make the people hiring Elsie Lancaster feel grateful, and humble, but most of all she had to make sure that they paid up, on time, and the right amount. All this took being tough and difficult and demanding, and not having the famous wool pulled over your eyes.

If the offer was going to go through from Portly Cosgrove, Elsie knew that it would begin with Dottie slamming down the telephone, declaring in a raised voice to the empty hall above them that all managements were unmentionables. Just as, if an offer was being considered but had not yet been agreed, Dottie would shout at the silent telephone to ring – damn it! All this, and many other patterns of behaviour that Elsie found draining and humiliating, had to be endured, somehow, before she could even begin to consider that she might have landed a part, or, as in this case, *the* part.

As it was the telephone in the hall was ringing even now, and she still had not told Dottie the news.

Elsie doubled back up the stairs, and having prepared herself for a few seconds by slipping into the character of a charlady, such as she had seen depicted many times on the films and at the local repertory theatre, she picked up the telephone and said, 'Temple and Mead, Theatrical Agency, could you please ring back in five minutes? Miss Temple is negotiating on the other telephone. Thank-ah yoooo!'

After which, knowing that it had been Portly Cosgrove on the other end, she shot down to the kitchen and told Dottie everything, but not as herself, that would have been a mistake. Instead, cunningly, she told her grandmother everything that had happened at the audition in just the same way that her grandmother might have told *her*. In other words, as if their roles had been reversed. This did the trick, as it always did, because quite apart from anything else, as Elsie herself was well aware, she was not just good at *playing* her grandmother, she was excellent. She should be. She had studied her enough.

Elsie therefore embarked on her first speech to Dottie with a particular form of cold, detached, but for her, familiar, artistic energy.

Everyone at the audition had been a *silly ass* or a *proper pansy* or a *complete clot*. Dottie nodded her head in satisfaction at this. It was just how she saw everyone with any power over their lives. Not in simple black and white, but in roles as colourful as any being currently cast. As to the management, Elsie made sure to make them sound not as even she herself had been forced to appraise them, as being rather more gentlemanly than the normal run of producers, but as if they were a right pair, and more than likely to be going to try to double-cross them.

She took especially great care not to mention that Mr Cosgrove and Mr Bourton had proved, also most unusually for a provincial management, really rather polite, if not gentle and charming to an inordinate degree. Dottie would not have understood that; far from understanding it she would have been vaguely appalled, certainly shocked. Managements as far as she was concerned were out to *do* you – one of her favourite words – and it did not do to regard them as anything less than criminal.

Satisfyingly, as she drew her account of her audition to a close, Elsie could see that it had pleased Dottie no end, for it portrayed the world in which her grandmother had failed to succeed in a way that Dottie understood. It made no sense of her own failure if there were any nice guys out there. They had all to be black hats, otherwise she might have to contemplate the idea that the reason she had not succeeded as an actress had nothing whatsoever to do with the Mr Cosgroves and the Mr Bourtons of her generation; but everything to do with Dottie not having had *it*.

So much had Elsie's account pleased her that by the time the telephone in the hall was once more ringing, Dottie was positively purring with pleasure at the idea that she was going to have to deal with the usual double-crossing so-and-sos that made up management. She sprang up the back stairs and into the hall.

'Temple and Mead, Theatrical Agency, good afternoon.'

The voice at the other end was the pleasant voice of Portly Cosgrove, but as far as Dottie Temple was concerned it might have been Satan himself speaking to her on the telephone.

'I am so glad you liked Miss Lancaster, Mr Cosgrove, but as you are no doubt aware the Tyningham Repertory Thee-*ay*-ter is after her for *Salome*, and the *Importance*, not to mention the young Queen Victoria in an original musical.'

After she had announced this Dottie winked at Elsie, her spiky black mascaraed lashes seeming to open and close like those of an expensive china doll. Elsie smiled back, whilst at the same time feeling the colour draining from her face. It was not unknown for Dottie not just to get her better salaries than everyone else at Tippy Toes, but also to lose her jobs.

Of course, when Dottie lost a job for her through too much boasting and overpricing, she always justified it with, 'Well, you didn't really want to do it, anyway, did you, dear?'

This was never true, because Elsie always wanted to do *everything*, if only so that she need have nothing to do with the lodgers and their trays, or Dottie's washing and ironing, because that was Dottie's bargain. If Elsie worked, then she gave Dottie her salary to bank, but she got off the housework. If she was not earning, she was swiftly sent back to being the maid of all work, which, as Dottie said, 'soon gets your ambitions stoked up again, my girl!'

Nevertheless, whenever Dottie did negotiate the hell out of a situation and lose her a job, Elsie knew that she always, always had to smile and nod, before absenting herself quietly to her room where she would spend some minutes battling with tears that always seemed to turn to gulping hiccups in her efforts to send them back to where they belonged – deep down in a place that not even she cared to visit.

This time, however, she took care to peel off to her own room and switch off any feelings that she might or might not be having as efficiently as Dottie switched off *Music While You Work* on the wireless. She had not been seated pretending to read an old edition of *Autumn Crocus* for very long when Dottie flung open her bedroom door.

'Well, of all the so and sos I have ever had to deal with on your behalf,' she intoned, 'Mr

Cosgrove of Cosgrove and Bourton is the wettest yet! Wait till you hear this. He has only agreed to everything, but everything, that I have ever asked for, and *more*!'

As Elsie allowed her mouth to drop open in a most unbecoming manner and at the same time stood up as if royalty had entered the room, Dottie struck off each of her demands for Elsie on her once elegant fingers.

'Miss Lancaster will require a taxi to take her to the theatre every evening; a dresser, naturally; fifteen pounds a week for a salary; her costumes cleaned twice a week – and two sets of those, thank you very much. She will require one per cent at the box office, and hairdressing and make-up paid for.' There was a small pause as Dottie frowned and tried to think of what other out-rageous demand she had made which had now been agreed to, but then, not being able to recall exactly what else she had spelled out to Cosgrove and Bourton, she finished by saying in a helpless tone, 'He's mad of course. Quite, quite mad.' There was another pause. 'Oh, and the dresser to act as chaperon, someone to sit in the dressing room and make sure of everything. That too he agreed. I tell you, he is potty. Needs his brains examined.' There was another pause. 'That's another thing. He says not that you have the making of a star, but that you *are* one! Just like that. He thinks you're a star.' Dottie paused again. 'A star. You!' Yet another pause. 'Well, we'll see if he comes through, but all in all, if he does, you're on your way, young lady, and about time too, if you ask me.'

She nodded at Elsie as if to dismiss her with 'That's all for now', but instead of Elsie it was she who left the room, and Elsie, after a few seconds, sat down very suddenly at her dressing table and stared at herself.

Mr Cosgrove had said she was a star.

Was it true after all? Were several of the lodgers, not just Roger Dimchurch, right in their predictions that she would one day become a famous actress?

Elsie went to her mirror and gazed at her reflection. This must mean that Mr Cosgrove did not mind her bulging eyes – her eyes that were not as other people's eyes and that Dottie was always on about. He could not even have minded them. She stared into their great green depths. Of course the bulging did not show up so much on stage. She knew that because Mr Labell had told her so, only to reassure her of course, and only because she had actually asked him once, when he had come to see her in a summer tableau.

Now Elsie found herself pacing her small bedroom, the realisation coming to her little by little. She must not think about it. She must not even dream about it, she must just float on the top of the waves of her life, as she saw the little crabs doing sometimes when the high tide came in. Just floating, as seemingly careless of their future as Elsie was always at pains to pretend that she herself was, just lying back and waiting for the offers to come in.

But now one had, and it was a *big* offer, and she would no longer have to battle down the seafront hiding behind her child's umbrella, or stand in a queue waiting to buy cheap, stale, day-old bread which could be toasted for the lodgers. Once she had been Cinderella, she need never do those things again. She could go to the ball of life.

Once she had been Cinderella it might even come about that not even Dottie could make Elsie do the ironing or the washing, or run about with breakfast trays. There would only be theatre, theatre, theatre.

She crossed to her small bed, and having gently pulled back the pre-war satin cover she removed her shoes and laid herself carefully under it. Although she did not feel in the least bit tired, very soon she was fast asleep, dreaming of the sea beyond the windows, of the tides that came in and out, of long days to come when removing stubborn egg stains from cold plates under a cold water tap would be as dim and distant a memory as any dream that ever vanished on waking.

Chapter Two

Oliver Plunkett stared at his father. He had never had the slightest wish to irritate or disturb John Plunkett, and yet he knew that not only had he just managed to do so, but he had, very probably, always done so. Perhaps it was the fact that he was the youngest child, or perhaps it was the fact that his father had only ever seemed to look to Oliver's older brothers to represent the family honour, but Oliver had always had the definite feeling that his father had one son too many. One son too many to have to pay for, one son too many to have to keep an eye on, morally and spiritually; one son with whom he could make no possible connection other than acknowledging that he *was* his son.

It was, Oliver always thought, as if Oliver had come in the back door and decided to attach himself to the rest of the family, trailing along behind, trying to convince everyone that, though he was undoubtedly a very different kind of creature, nevertheless he was still one of *them*.

Even now the expression in his father's eyes

was one of a man pushed to the point of irritation. There were a thousand things that his father would rather be doing around his small estate than talking to Oliver about his future, his father's eyes told Oliver.

But, worse than that, he was now preparing to talk to his youngest son about a future that John Plunkett would not just despise but loathe his youngest son for even contemplating. He would be thinking that Oliver was about to pull the family name through the mire. He would be wondering why God had sent this third boy to him, and he would be supplying the only possible answer: to make him – John Plunkett – *suffer*. Oliver was his father's mortification, his hangnail, his unreachable itch.

And so much so that by the time Mr Plunkett Senior went to open his mouth they were both only too keenly aware that this younger son, this young man called Oliver, was his father's sacrificial lamb. But while Abraham had unquestionably suffered at God's hands when asked to sacrifice his son Isaac on the altar, Oliver had always felt that in Abraham's shoes John Plunkett would have been only too happy to oblige. In fact he would probably have hurried proceedings through at such breakneck speed that he would no doubt have greatly impressed the rest of Israel.

What Oliver had actually just said, clearly enunciated, the Ts proudly crossed, was – 'I want to be an actor, sir.'

His father, being a Plunkett, the owner of a

small estate in remote Yorkshire, a man known by all to be resolutely virtuous, unflappable in the face of the greatest adversity, and a member of a family that had survived many centuries of fluctuating fortunes, had not reacted to this simple statement with the usual, and only to be expected, paternal 'You *what*?' He had proceeded to the drinks tray, and after pouring them both a whisky had merely turned to Oliver and asked him in even tones, 'Water or soda?'

Perhaps, Oliver thought, as he stared at his own immaculately polished shoes, some people might be reassured by this cool self-control. Perhaps they might even have been lulled into thinking that John was not after all the kind of man to object to his son's taking to the boards. But Oliver, little as he knew his father, was nevertheless only too aware that the older man's quiet was the next man's storm.

Oliver knew that the quieter Plunkett Senior became the worse his wrath, the deeper his disgust. A quiet John Plunkett was a person to be avoided for the next few weeks, if not months.

'So, you want to be an actor, you said.'

'Yes, sir.'

'I see.' His father sat down, but did not cross anything. He sat down neatly. It was almost as if he had folded his limbs into the old leather library chair in exactly the same manner his valet would fold his clothes at night, and of course Oliver could not help observing this, noting it for possible use in some yet to be written role in the

55

future. 'And how long has this been going on?'

Oliver stared across at the pale, greyish face of his parent and wondered at his phrasing.

How long has this been going on? made it sound as if Oliver had been having a never-ending, raging affair with the theatrical profession behind his father's back, which of a sudden Oliver realised might just be the truth.

'I – er – well, sir, I have always wanted to be an actor. Ever since I was quite small, I am afraid, sir.'

'Did Mummy know of this?'

Oliver did not want to say 'Yes, Mummy did know of this' because, although Mummy had run off with one of the hunt servants some few years before, her youngest son was nevertheless loath to get his adored mother into trouble, even in retrospect. He felt he would rather die than do that. His mother had not done the right thing, obviously, but he was not in the market for blaming her for something that was after all not exactly due to her unquenchable and overwhelming desire for a handsome, strapping six foot Welshman with a rare ability to communicate with hounds.

'Mummy always knew of this, yes, I think she did, but it was not her fault. It was mine. I just have always wanted to act, ever since I was five years old, and you took me to the pantomime in Lodbury.'

With this piece of extra-curricular information Oliver hoped that he had now shipped at least some of the blame for his acting ambitions and left it fairly and squarely at his father's door.

56

Unfortunately, however, adroit he might have imagined this move to be, his father was up to the challenge.

'*I* never took you to the pantomime in Lodders, your nanny did. I took the older boys, but not you. You never went with me, not to my knowledge, not to Lodders. That would have been Nanny, not me.'

'Well, at any rate . . .' Oliver paused, determined not to notice the relief in his father's voice. 'As I say, that was when it happened, when I went to the pantomime. I just knew that I wanted to get up there, on stage.' He did not add, which was the truth, 'for the rest of my life', because to do so would have been far too upsetting to his poor father.

'Yes, it would have been Nanny,' mused the older man. 'She had more to do with you than anyone, not that I remember *her* ever showing a liking for the theatre. Seemed more interested in the wireless, if I remember rightly.'

Nanny was now obviously being revealed to be fairly and squarely to blame. Which was all right really, because she was known to have long ago, and most piously, ascended into heaven. At least it was not Mummy – whose entrance into paradise, when the untimely moment came, would not, Oliver imagined, perhaps take such a direct route as Nanny's had probably done.

'There is no money coming to you from your grandfather's estate, you know that of course?'

This was another way of his father's saying,

You go into this acting thing, and you will not get a
penny of support from me.

'No, I realise that.'

Not for the first time Oliver felt downcast by
the idea that relationships between parents and
children seemed to be totally governed by the
cheque book. Do your best to please, and you
might be granted a penny or two. Take up acting
and you were on your own for evermore.

'No, there has been no provision made for you
by any of your grandparents or godparents. Your
mother, of course, might have done something for
you.'

They both knew that Mummy's new life had
absorbed every penny, and rather more, of her
private income, and that her new husband, being
the kind of man he was, not content with living off
her, was more than happy to part her from her
personal funds at every turn with the result that
she could hardly afford even to hunt any more.

There was a long silence following this statement. From Oliver's point of view this was
because he simply could not think of anything to
say, and from his father's point of view, because
he obviously had no more to say on the subject
anyway.

To fill the verbal void they both sipped at their
drinks in silence for a few seconds.

'Of course, if you don't mind, I would rather
you did not drag the family name through the
newspapers. People in the acting profession

always do seem to attract a great deal of press attention. On reflection, as you seem determined to pursue this course of going on the boards, I would rather, if you *do*, that you changed your name to something other than Plunkett.'

Oliver nodded and stared ahead. What Plunkett Senior was actually saying was, 'Do not, please, drag me through the mire with you.'

But it was also undeniable that actors did feature in the newspapers. For once he could see his father's point of view. And yet his sense of disappointment was nevertheless acute. He had grown up always secretly hoping that he would see OLIVER PLUNKETT in lights over some theatre in Shaftesbury Avenue.

'Yes, of course. I perfectly understand. Daddy.'

His replacing of the more usual *sir* used in deference to their parent by all three brothers for the nursery *Daddy* made his father wince involuntarily, and his grasp on his glass of whisky tightened perceptibly, as if it was a strap on the London Underground.

For himself, Oliver, at his most devil-may-care, knew that his father hated being called 'Daddy', and always had, but there was very little he could do about Oliver's addressing him as such, because, when all was said and done, much as he would like to deny it, he was after all, as far as they both knew, Oliver's father.

'So what will you change it to, do you think?'

His father turned his pale blue eyes on his

youngest son, and stared at him. It was a moment of sublime power for Oliver, and they both knew it.

'I expect I will think of something.'

'Perhaps you might feel that your – ahem – mother's maiden name might be appropriate? Quite easy to say, and so on?'

Ah ha!

In one blinding flash, a flash as bright as the press photographers' flashlight bulbs of which it seemed Plunkett Senior was so in fear, Oliver saw it all. It was all right for him to drag his *mother's* family name through the mud, but not his *father's* name.

'I don't think Lowell is a very good stage surname, Daddy, really I don't. No, I shall probably take my own name – Oliver – and put a first name to it. Something Oliver.'

'That could be quite good,' his father agreed rather too quickly, and then he yawned suddenly, the matter, as far as he was concerned, seemingly over.

'But, no, now I come to think of it, I think you are probably right, Daddy.'

His father stared at him, his face a picture of disappointment, his reluctance to continue talking about Oliver's stage name more than obvious.

'*Oliver Lowell* will be quite splendid. Not too far down the alphabet either, not too far down the billing.'

His father continued to stare at his youngest offspring.

'If, in the theatre, you have a surname beginning with, say, zed, you are the last name on the
billing, which is never very good. If they decide to
go for alphabetical order, that is.'

'Really.'

Oliver smiled. His father's *really*, as usual, took
not a question mark but a full stop. Still, there was
no doubting his preference for his son's using the
name Lowell. It was a good solid English sort of
name denoting neither one sort of person nor
another, unlike Plunkett which, on account of the
famous English martyr Blessed Oliver Plunkett,
after whom Oliver himself had apparently been
named, brought with it more than a whiff of
incense and Popery.

'So that is settled then. If you go ahead with
this affair, you will do so *not* under the family
name.' His father stood up and nodded. 'Goodbye, Oliver.'

'I am not off quite yet, sir.'

'Are you not? Well then I will see you anon. Oh,
by the way, will you be going to arr aye em aye
dee, did you say?'

'The Royal Academy of Music and Drama? Yes,
as a matter of fact I will, sir.'

'You have obtained a place? As I remember it
one of your cousins went to one of those academies once, and left shortly afterwards under a
cloud. I think he found it difficult to fit in, coming
as he did from this kind of background. Let's hope
you fare better. Things have changed though, I
hear, since this John Eastbourne chap, and so on.

61

Noel Coward and that sort of thing no longer make the running, so I have heard.'

Oliver immediately coloured for two reasons. The first was because he realised that his father was implying that he would doubtless fail as his cousin had, and the second was because in Oliver's reply, inevitably, would be contained, as they both knew, the revelation that he had already applied to several theatrical academies without telling Plunkett Senior.

'Yes, sir. I went up for auditions to the – er – various academies when I was last in London, staying with Howard Hampton's daughter, remember – Coco Hampton? I often stay with her – have stayed with her – at her guardian's flat.'

'Coco Hampton. Oh, yes. Sparky little thing, she was, but I expect she's turned out a handful, coming from that kind of background. When did all this take place? When did you stay with Coco Hampton and her guardian?'

'I – er – can't quite remember the exact date.'

Oliver cleared his throat, and at the same time adjusted his tie, which was one better, he supposed, than nervously jangling the change in his pocket.

'Some time ago, I suppose?'

'Yes, sir. Some time ago, I think that was it, can't quite remember, not exactly.'

'Good. Well, as long as you have a place at arr aye em dee aye, or somewhere, then you are at least on course, are you not? At least you have that satisfaction, a good start, before the long periods of resting set in.'

John Plunkett walked quickly out of the library, leaving Oliver staring at nothing in particular as people do when waiting in banks or post offices for their turn to come.

He had not thought that his father would be exactly overjoyed at his intention to become an actor, but even so he had hoped for a little more. A little more reaction, even anger or impatience, a few more questions about how he planned to embark on his career, what roles he might be thinking of playing, not just a quick enquiry or two before scurrying off like a rabbit to its burrow.

Oliver had even prepared a few impassioned speeches about the need for people like himself still to enter the noble profession of David Garrick and Laurence Olivier. Speeches about how he thought that people like him could bring fresh blood to acting in this stark post-war era. But he had been give no opportunity to deliver them, and was not now, he recognised all too clearly, ever going to be.

His father had quietly and efficiently closed the door on the matter of his younger son's becoming a member of the dreaded profession, an actor, a strolling player. Happily his other two sons were everything that they should be, fine upstanding members of the Plunkett family, not in the least bit interested in the *demi-monde*, the raffish, classless world of the theatre. Obviously, judging from John Plunkett's acceptance of the situation, he had long ago made up his mind that he would have to make do with the first two and forget the third son, wipe him off the slate, take his name out of the family bible, or – as he had perhaps just done – simply shrug him off.

As far as he was concerned Oliver was now a closed book, a skeleton in the proverbial cupboard, and, satisfyingly, a *Lowell* – and *not* a Plunkett. Oliver realised that he had been lured into the change of name as quietly and efficiently as his father had exited from the room, and that he had given his consent without much protest, which was a little humiliating. He now wondered, rather too late in the day, whether his mother too would be upset.

Not that anything much upset his mother nowadays, except Charley the former hunt servant, but even so she might have misgivings, however much she pretended otherwise. He pushed this thought quickly away from him. There was nothing much he could to about it now, and, he realised, with a growing sense of maturity, there was nothing much that he would ever be able to do about his mother. She was after all now someone else, not entirely his mother, and yet not entirely *not* his mother either, but someone quite different, as people who run off leaving their responsibilities to be taken care of by everyone else always seem to be.

Oliver was still staring at nothing when the library door opened once more and his father was yet again revealed, of a sudden, and quite incongruously, reminding Oliver of the famous painting of Jesus with the lamp that had used to hang in the corridor outside his nursery, and one of his brothers had broken when they had been playing indoor cricket on a rainy day.

'By the way, in view of – your announcement. I have been thinking it over, and I have to tell you that I think it will be as well if I have Father Bill say a mass for you on the first of every month.'

At long last Oliver had found something suitable at which to stare – his father's face. Disconcertingly his father stared right back, at the same time giving a sharp nod, as a priest might give an altar boy when he was too late with the water and wine, or otherwise remiss. Realising that clearly something was expected of him, some form, if not of penitence, at least of gratitude, Oliver said, 'Thank you, sir.'

'Good.'

Another sharp nod and John Plunkett was gone, and Oliver sank thankfully down into one of the much worn brown leather library seats. If he had not known that due possibly to having three sons, not to mention a butler cum valet, it was his father's nightly habit to measure the amount taken from the decanters, Oliver would have poured himself a much, much larger whisky. Instead he contented himself with draining his glass and staring at the chimneypiece.

He was going to be prayed for by Father Bill once a month, in the family chapel, doubtless with all the locals and friends of the house joining in.

He was going to be prayed for, because it was that serious going into the theatre.

It was that dangerous.

It was that shocking.

Oliver closed his eyes momentarily, of a sudden experiencing a sublime feeling of danger ahead, as if the theatre was a dangerous motor bike, or a sports car with its speedometer fixed to travel at a certain frantic pace. If the whole family and their dependants were going to pray for him, Oliver's life must, truly, be going to be one fantastic roundabout of colour and excitement. After all, if it was not, they would not be going to pray for him, would they?

'Yes, do pray for me! Pray for me to be a big star, sir,' Oliver called out suddenly and mockingly to the various ancestors staring down from the library walls, a few minutes after his father had left the room. Of a sudden, as if, as always, from nowhere, Clifton the family butler stood at the open library door.

'Of course, Master Oliver, we all will,' he replied smoothly on his master's behalf. 'We will all pray for you, and your success. Meanwhile, if you don't mind putting me in the picture, Master Oliver, are we leaving for arr aye em aye dee today, did you say?'

Oliver sprang up. Clifton always listened at doors, and Oliver for one could not blame him. It saved so much trouble, made for a sort of short-hand, kept him quickly in touch with all the family politics.

'Ramad?' he asked, pronouncing it the way all his friends did, as opposed to the refined Plunkett family delivery. 'Am I leaving for London today, Clifton? Well, not *quite* today. Have to see Hopkins and prise a few pennies out of him first, perhaps – um – ten pounds, if I'm lucky. But after that, yes. I am.'

'Mr Hopkins has already been apprised by me, and you will find the result on the hall table in your name. But I expect you have yet to find lodgings in London, have you not, Master Oliver?'

Before Oliver could reply Clifton produced a card from the pocket of his striped waistcoat. The card was small and cheap, but the writing on it was quite clear.

'Try Mrs Beasley in Tavistock Street, sir. Always sure of a good warm bed and a nice hot cup of cocoa there. Very important, that. Actors need to keep healthy when they are resting, and good plumbing and dry sheets will help you do that.'

'I hope not to be *resting* very much, Clifton, but thank you anyway.'

'The day has at last come, then, Master Oliver. How I envy you! But there you are, it was not to be. Mother never wanted to leave Yorkshire, and I never wanted to leave Mother. So, as we both know, it just was not to be.' Of a sudden Clifton hummed '*An actor's life for me*', only a short bar, but surprisingly tuneful. 'I shall look forward to coming to London to see you as Hamlet, Master Oliver. You have the legs for the tights, I always think. Bit difficult now though, Hamlet, after

Laurence Olivier's film, but nevertheless, it must be tackled anew in your generation, I would say. Every generation must struggle with a Hamlet or two, as you know, and I would like to see you as just one of those, at least. Although how you find a new and original interpretation is going to be something of a struggle, I would say.'

'Tell me, you do – I mean, you actually do go along with Olivier's *Oedipal* interpretation, don't you, Clifton?'

They were both leaning against the library shelves now, which was their wont on rainy days since Oliver was quite small, and following his mother's flight from the family home, Clifton had been revealed to be the only member of the family to take an interest in matters artistic. The older boys having grown up boasting that they hardly ever opened a book and dreading the day when they might be forced to start, Clifton had been a godsend.

'Of course I do, Master Oliver. The Oedipal interpretation is very intelligent, if you listen to the lines. After all, Hamlet has no liking for his mother's new marriage. But then—' He stopped. '*You* would understand that, wouldn't you, Master Oliver?'

Once again Oliver found he was reddening, but all the same he nodded.

'Quite right, Clifton, I should know all about that.'

'But what you have to remember, Master Oliver, if you don't mind me saying, is that as far as *your* parents are concerned, they have *never* known what I like to call "marital union". That is true for everyone. Although all parents must have done, of course, they have not, as it were, ever known marital union, not in the minds and imaginations of their children – not *ever*.'

Oliver stared at the butler, torn between laughter and astonishment at Clifton's honest analysis.

Clifton was quite right, and it was true. The thought of his mother and Charley together was not just terrible, it was unthinkable. So that was how Hamlet must have felt, Oliver realised with a jolt. He felt as Oliver felt when trying not to think about his mother and *Charley*.

However much Oliver loved his mother, which he did, he could never think of her like *that* – having marital union with a hunt servant. No, he could not, ever, and did not want to, ever, think that she and Charley might have what Clifton called 'marital union', not ever, not even once. In fact, now he came to think of it, he had once seen Charley ruffling his mother's hair, and he had not liked it one bit. It had made him feel a bit sick and faint, like church when it became too hot.

Oliver grinned suddenly and almost delightedly at the butler.

'Quite right, Cliffie, quite right. Fathers and mothers don't have marital union, not ever, do they?' He patted the butler on the arm, as if he had just hit a six at the village cricket match, which Clifton very often did. 'Parents don't do it!' he continued, now quite thrilled with the notion. 'No, they don't do they, Clifton? So that is poor Hamlet's problem. His mother's love life turns his stomach but only because everyone's mother's love life turns their stomachs. Parents *never* do it!'

'Never, Master Oliver. That is what I mean about Hamlet. It just might be that he loves his mother in the normal way, but just doesn't want to think of her having *union*, if you see what I mean? Poor Hamlet's no different from the rest of us, whatever all the Freudian scholars might say, at least not to my mind. The way I see it, he is just all the time avoiding the thought of that marital union, while at the same time being in that perilous state we know as mourning. A state when, as we know, even the sound of a loud voice, of a door slamming, is like a dagger in the heart, a bullet through the head. So perhaps the Oedipal interpretation is a little far-fetched.'

Once more Oliver smiled suddenly and brilliantly, a trait of his, which Clifton hoped the youngster would not fail to use effectively when he was on the films.

Of course what the boy did not realise, could not be expected to remember – and it was something which his father's ex-batman now butler would never point out to him – was that it was Clifton, of all people, who had nurtured the seeds of his fanatical interest in the theatre and artistic things, sown by the pantomime production at Lodbury, after Oliver's mother the Honourable Mrs Plunkett had bolted with Charley.

In Clifton's opinion, Master Oliver had always been a mite neglected by the rest of the family, due to childhood asthma and the age gap between him and his brothers.

Not that Mr Plunkett would ever have disowned his youngest son. That would not be his way. Whatever he thought of his quite different, brilliantly handsome third son, he never, not even for a second, let his feelings show. It was just not *on*! Clifton knew that would be how his master would think of it.

It would not be *on*.

He had sometimes said to Clifton, in his quiet way, 'Master Oliver is a throwback to my wife's great-grandmother, Clifton, I always think that. Hence the blond hair, and the green eyes. If you go to the landing you can view a portrait of her. And you will notice that Master Oliver is just like her in every way, you know Clifton? Quite a throwback, but then that's nature, wouldn't you say? She likes to spin the coin differently, and sometimes irreverently, every time.'

Once, feeling that he perhaps should take up the hint, Clifton had actually gone up to the wide landing of the old Elizabethan house and, amid the many paintings of the family ancestors, he had found just such a portrait. Stare as hard as he could, however, he had not been able to find any possible similarity between the lady in question and Mr Plunkett's youngest offspring, beyond the fact that they both had fair hair. It had rather moved him, though, that Mr Plunkett had gone to such trouble to find someone to whom his younger son *could* be compared. But then that was Mr Plunkett all over. He might be a stickler, but he was a gentleman.

'I shall remember that, Cliffie, what you just said about Hamlet, when I come to play it. Now what about Lear? How do you see him? While we are on the subject.'

'Very annoying, Master Oliver. Yes. As I see it, King Lear asks for – and gets – everything that his character demands of his circumstances. You see, Lear, as I see it, is a very *selfish* man. We know this because of his attitudes, because of his treatment of Cordelia: he is a *very* selfish man. And while no one wants to see him wandering the heath, yet, pity him though we do, we can see it is his vanity and his intransigence that puts him there. No, if I was going to play King Lear, I would play him as a proud old general, someone you can admire in his prime, even though you wish that he would just, if I may say so—'

'Come off it a little?'

'Yes, exactly, Master Oliver. Come off it a little. Lear is not what I would call a nobleman. He is a king, but not a nobleman. You can be a king or an emperor without being in the least bit aristocratic, in my opinion. And it is his foolish, kingly vanity that leads him to believe that he can act without sense. He should know his daughters better than he does. Trusting those two older ones when he must know that they are less, in truth, much, much less than the youngest.' He stopped, realising of a sudden that the story of King Lear might prove too close to home for comfort for the youngest Plunkett son. 'At least, that is what I think. I might be wrong, Master Oliver, but that is what I think. He asks for it, if you like, but that doesn't stop us pitying him.'

If Oliver saw that there was a parallel between himself and his two brothers and John Plunkett, and King Lear and his three daughters, he did not seem to be in the mood to dwell on it at that moment, only patting Clifton on the arm again and smiling his brilliant smile once more.

'Tell you what, Cliffie, why don't you go to the Academy, instead of me?'

'I would love to, Master Oliver,' Clifton replied simply. 'But I can't. You see, I am not talented. Whereas you, Master Oliver, are. You are a very talented actor, you always have been.'

Oliver stared at him and once more found himself blushing like a girl, this time at the sincerity in the butler's voice.

'Ever since you were a little boy, Master Oliver, I have always thought you were a born star. There is no doubt about it, not to my mind at least. You have It. Neither of your brothers has it, but you *have* it. You have *It*. And as the Bible says, you must make the most of your talent, really you must, or it will grow in on you and tear out your insides as the fox tore out the innards of the little Spartan boy in the famous Greek myth. There is no worse a personality, in my experience, Master Oliver, than one who has not developed

73

their talent as they should, and, as you know, Our Blessed Lord commanded us that we should.'

'I want to be a big star, Cliffie. Just to show my father that I am not just a wet. You know – what do the other two always call me? *Willie Wet Legs*?'

'We all know what the others have called you, Master Oliver,' Clifton agreed hurriedly. 'And I dare say we can all remember the many ill-timed jests in bad taste that have been made about you, but there is no need to go back into that, not now that you are leaving for the bright lights.'

'It's all right, Cliffie, I don't mind, really I don't. No, truly, I am grateful to my big brothers for making fun of me, because it has made Master Snivels, Master Willie Wet Legs, Master Lily Liver, determined to become a star, if only to show them. Just you watch, Cliffie. I shall show them.'

'I am going to, Master Oliver. Never going to take my eyes off you, Master Oliver. Anything less and Clifton will want to know the reason why, believe me.'

They both stared at each other, and there was a short silence, the realisation at last actually dawning.

Everything they had ever talked about was here, now, not tomorrow any more, but now. There was no time left for laughter and conjecture, for wondering if or how, or what might or could be. With the arrival of his acceptance into the Royal Academy of Music and Drama the gauntlet had been thrown down, and now, with John

74

Plunkett's quiet acceptance of his youngest son's determination to join the acting profession, the gauntlet had been taken up.

The road ahead seemed of a sudden, to both of them, just a little long, and just a little hard; and the courage it demanded all too necessary, as it must seem to a general before a battle, or a surgeon before theatre, or an actor before his stage entrance. This was it. This was the moment that Oliver, and Clifton in his different way, had worked towards, the moment when Oliver would leave Yorkshire for London's West End.

'And remember what I said. Whatever else you don't do, do make sure that you have a decent wardrobe of shoes, Master Oliver. Well heeled and soled, and not about to come apart at the slightest bit of weather. As I understand it . . .' Clifton looked suddenly and almost biblically solemn. 'As I understand it, they are a dire necessity in the acting profession, are shoes, or so I have been told by many of my friends.'

'Providing I can get Hopkins to advance me a tiny bit of the pittance that is my living allowance, I will invest in as many good shoes as possible, Cliffie,' Oliver promised.

'Yes, Master Oliver, but you'll be lucky with Mr Hopkins; he does so hate to give you money from your trust, albeit it is yours, legally. And another thing; as I understand it, actors, members of the profession, they wear out a lot of shoes doing the rounds of the agents' and managements' offices – yes, doing the rounds as they call it, calls for a great many pairs of shoes, and it can be very dispiriting if they let in water, the shoes I mean.'

'I didn't think you meant the actors, Cliffie!' Oliver laughed, turning away, not really seeming to take in very much, such was his excitement.

Clifton could see that now the dreaded interview with his father was over not only had Master Oliver returned to his usual boyish carefree manner, but his face was already set towards London, towards fame, and fortune, but most particularly fame, because money would never mean much to Master Oliver.

'Meanwhile I shall try to find someone who can recommend lodgings in Crewe, Master Oliver.'

'Why Crewe, Cliffie?'

'It is a place which I believe you will get to know a great deal on tour, or so I have been informed, Master Oliver. Everyone in the profession is always changing at Crewe, but sometimes, most unfortunately, the change is delayed, or missed, so a recommendation, a basic knowledge let us say, of good comfortable lodgings at Crewe is particularly essential.'

Oliver laughed, showing healthy white teeth. 'Cliffie, you are a guinea a minute, do you know that?'

'Yes, Master Oliver. Now however you had better go and pack, and don't forget your evening dress for the drawing room comedies, and I have put a cigar box for the Leichner make-up on your bed, and a nice jar of Carmine make-up remover. As we all know, only amateurs use tin boxes bought at theatrical shops, and we don't want to look like that, do we? Amateur. Oh, and one other thing, Master Oliver. Never tell anyone where you come from, will you? Stick to our plan, won't you?'

'Cliffie! Would I dare do anything else?'

They were now climbing the beautiful old wooden stairs to the third floor room that Oliver had occupied since he was a small boy.

Here, far above the rest of the family rooms, Oliver had grown up with Nanny and Cliffie for company, always hearing, never really seeing, signs of the other two children growing up ahead of him, far below, already grown and strong while he was still small and frail.

The little that he saw of his elder brothers, on his few ill-timed sorties from the rocky fastness of his and Nanny's rooms to the public rooms below, so often ended in disaster and ridicule that even now Oliver could hardly bear to think about them.

Once, cringingly, he had even tried to enact a play of his own making for his father and brothers, but with such dismal results – playing to three bored male faces – that he had quickly retreated to his infrequently heated and sparsely furnished rooms with a leaden heart, vowing silently never to attempt to entertain the elders of his family again.

If it had not been for Clifton and Nanny, who, some days later, had eventually persuaded him to run through his precious play again, just for them – if it had not been for them, cheering him with their response, lauding him to the skies afterwards, trying desperately to make up to him for his first opening night disaster, Oliver truly thought that he might have killed himself, such was his despair at his family's lack of reaction.

Of course, being so different from the others had eventually put iron in Oliver's soul and made him realise that he had to stand on his own two feet, make doubly sure of his ambitions. But he also learnt to keep quiet about those same ambitions, vowing never, ever again to try to amuse the older boys, or his father; never, ever again to risk that kind of hurt. He was determined to keep his yearning for everything theatrical a terrific secret. From then on it was something that only he and Clifton, once Nanny had left, knew about, only they talked about, only they relished.

As soon as they had recognised where Oliver's ambitions truly lay Clifton began to smuggle the young boy in copies of *Plays and Players*, a theatrical magazine that as far as both Oliver and Clifton were concerned might have been produced on pages of beaten gold, such was the extreme reverence that they showed towards its arrival in their lives every month. After a while they developed the habit of looking at the pictures together before they settled back and Oliver read the articles aloud to Clifton. This was not because Clifton could not read, but because he liked to stop Oliver at certain moments, and discuss some particular points that had arisen from its pages.

The photographs alone were enough to arouse

intense excitement. The world as viewed through the theatrical photographers' lenses became, from an early age, Oliver's world, and not just *his* world, the *only* world. It was meat and drink, washing and cleaning, it was comfort and cure. It was everything, and even on his announcing his ambition to be an actor, even should his father have taken him and thrown him bodily from the house, Oliver would not have minded, which was perhaps why his father, recognising that any attempt at dissuasion would be useless, had walked from the room, psychologically washing his hands of him, leaving only his announcement that Oliver would be prayed for once a month in the family chapel as witness to the anxiety of his true feelings about his youngest son's future.

'There we are, Master Ollie! Off you go now, and no coming back, no telephoning through to me, nothing, until you have some *proper* news. And don't forget, no mention of your family background. Not ever. Puts people's backs up, if they think you're a nob. Just keep quiet, and keep your ears and eyes open, do you hear?'

'I'll try, Cliffie, but you know how it is with me – I've always been a bit of a bigmouth.'

Clifton ignored him. 'See, Master Ollie, it's just as I have always told you. New places, they always want to pigeonhole you, so keep quiet, whatever you do, most of all at first, because that is often when you can give the game away, in the opening weeks.'

Clifton stared up at Oliver, hoping against hope that he would listen to him. It was not a particularly cold day for September, at least not in Yorkshire, but nevertheless he was busy moving from one foot to the other on the station platform, looking up and down the length of the train with an expression of vague disapproval, as Oliver leaned out of the window and chatted to him.

'I've just thought, actually, Cliffie. How about if I do you, Cliffie? You know, then no one will put me down as a nob, will they?' he asked, ruthlessly. 'I mean, how about if when I get to Ramad I talk with ever such a slight Yorkshire accent, like you? I can get you right, because I know you so well, see? And then no one will spot me, will they? Because I've always done you almost as well as you, you always say!'

'Not a bad idea, Master Oliver, but whatever happens, whether you do or you don't—'

'I know, don't mention the dreaded background!'

They were both going over and over the same old ground to take their minds off the moment of departure.

'Don't wave, Master Oliver,' Clifton called, as the train gave every indication of moving off at last while the expression in Oliver's eyes became, of a sudden, panic-stricken. 'Someone told me that it's bad luck in the theatre to wave goodbye, in case it is for ever. It is always au revoir – see you again, never adieu – never goodbye.'

'I know. So. See you again, Cliffie, and don't

forget to write every now and then – tell me about the place, and how Mrs Piglet is, and everything. I'll swallow the letters once I've read them, of course.'

The expression in Oliver's eyes was now that of a tall young man pretending he was not feeling like a quite small, homesick boy. He leaned out of the window and wrung Clifton's hand, putting as much emotion into that one gesture as he dared, thanking him for a lifetime's affection, and devotion.

'And don't you forget to write too, Master Oliver.' Clifton cleared his throat and nodded curtly, after which he stood watching the train pulling out. Always such an excitement, a train pulling out of a station: all the muck and the cinders flying about, all the passengers pretending that they couldn't care less whom they were leaving behind, but everyone, in reality, wondering if this might, by some awful chance, be the last sight of their loved one.

Clifton turned away, determined not to become sentimental. Master Oliver was going to have a few rude shocks when he reached the famous acting academy, and of course he would eventually forget to write to Clifton. After the first few weeks of loneliness, the letters would inevitably dwindle, until they stopped altogether. Clifton knew that, and it did not bother him, not for a second.

What did bother him – and this was the big 'but' in Clifton's mind – was that much as he hoped he had prepared Master Oliver for the theatre and all its pitfalls, he was afraid there would be a great many more shocks for which he had *not* prepared him. It was not just the implicit dangers from both sexes in a raffish profession, as far as a handsome young man such as Master Oliver was concerned; it was the humiliations. He could never be prepared for those; it just was not possible. The missed opportunities would be bad enough, but the endless battering of his young ego would be worse. It was the conniving, the plotting, the subterfuge; these would be the difficulties.

But still, if he was strong enough, he would survive, and if he was not, well, he could always come back to Yorkshire. Although, and here Clifton as he drove slowly back to the old house somehow knew that he had hit upon the truth as far as Master Oliver was concerned, he would never, ever do that.

The Master Oliver that Clifton knew would choose the theatre over *everywhere*, but most especially over life at the Hall. The sickly young boy escaping from his illness into other people, and now the tall handsome young man, was set to hide behind other characters for the rest of his life, if only to escape from the ruthless mockery of older brothers.

Clifton parked the pre-war Riley in one of the old, now hen-clustered stables and started to walk towards the house. He would miss Master Oliver, and never more than during the long, long Yorkshire winter that lay ahead. It was a fact, as much a fact as that he would not miss the older brothers if he never, ever saw them again. No, with Master Oliver gone there was now no one with whom to share his *Plays and Players*, no one with whom to talk over their collection of plays in the old French's acting editions, no one with whom to declaim the big speeches, no one, most of all, with whom to feel different, one of a separate tribe, recognisable only to each other in their solitary reality, making the rest of the household feel vaguely uneasy in their presence.

'Clifton!'

'Yes, Master Richard?'

In the hall, with its stags' heads over the fireplace and its long oak settles placed for feasts that were never held, Clifton stared up the staircase to the eldest of the Plunkett boys. Here before him was one of the other kind of human being, one of the kind for whom the lowering or raising of the curtain meant no more than the opening of their own bedroom curtains in the morning.

'Where the hell are my evening shoes, Clifton?'

'Your evening shoes, Master Richard?'

'Yes, Clifton, my evening shoes. Brand new, you know. And a pair of my walking shoes, both gone.'

'I expect the new boots' and gardener's boy put them in the wrong room. He's only just started, Master Richard. I will see to it.'

'Yes, do.'

Clifton walked along to Master Newell's room,

and having duly searched his cupboard he bumped into him on the way out.

'Ah, there you are, Cliffie. Seen my new black shoes? Spanking new they are! But not in my cupboard where I left them.'

'No, Master Newell, I am afraid I haven't. I expect the boy put them in the wrong cupboard. I will see to it in a moment.'

'Yes, do, Cliffie. I want to wear them, d'you see – in about ten minutes, once I've changed.'

'I will do what I can, Master Newell.'

Adopting his most sphinx-like public smile Clifton disappeared up to his rooms on the third floor, and having taken off his outdoor coat and hung it in his cupboard he proceeded to put on his butler's uniform once again. Having put off the moment, just fractionally, he then went to his own shoe cupboard and slowly opened the door. He would not have been human had he not experienced a feeling of relief that all his own shoes were still neatly present and correct.

'Not your size, and not to your taste, eh, Master Ollie?' he asked his favourite photograph of Oliver, bequeathed to Clifton long ago by a departing nanny. The butler shook his head and laughed at the handsome young boy in the photograph. 'You always did have the last word, didn't you, you rascal, and doubtless – knowing you – you always will!'

Dear Cliffie,
Well, here I am in London. The landlady is a dear,

and I am having a fine time getting used to her cocoa (worse than old Nanny's actually). The train journey was long and boring, really, so I learned Prospero (ha, ha)! Want to hear my interpretation? Well, I think he was as naughty as Lear in his way, but of course much, much more charming. I would say that he would have to be played with more than a touch of naughty magic. I feel bursting with new-boyness and full of the joys of autumn, and only one day left until enrolment day. Can't wait, in a way, and in another way I am dreading it. All that acting at the start, I mean, about not being me, and etc. – you know, what you keep on about. Not being me! Will I bring it off? I draw the line at too much modesty; it has never suited me, as you know. Do hope the Brothers Grimm found their best shoes missing. What a boon that nature gave us the same size feet – but different sized hats. If my head was quite as small as theirs both are I would not be able to learn lines!!!

A jolly manly cheerio for now, Cliffie, and give Mrs Piglet a pat and don't let Cook take her for cutlets, will you?

<u>OLIVER LOWELL</u>

(I say, lookes quite good, doesn't it, Cliffie?)

Clifton stared at Master Oliver's new name, neatly underlined. It did look *quite* good, as he said, although not as good as the family name, in Clifton's view.

Still, it was better, nowadays, not to have a name that sounded too snobby. It was all

85

changing out there; even people as far away as Yorkshire knew that, and could feel it. All the free health services and the free schooling, and the free school milk that had happened after the war was over, it was all going to change everything for the future. Most of all it was going to change everything for the generation that had grown up during the war, battling their way through the rationing and the bombs, and all that. They were exploding on to the scene, wanting to change things, in the same way that young people always did want to change things, but more so. The beat, beat, beat of the tom-tom was as nothing compared with the jungle beat of the new generation of actors and writers, marching towards London from the provinces, determined to have their time, now.

Where all this would put OLIVER LOWELL, Clifton did not know. His saving would not be his background, that would already be a handicap, as they both knew. His saving would be his intelligence, his quick thinking. It could, if he survived the first onslaught, put him ahead of the game, but the first test was the acting academy.

Could Oliver Lowell really keep Oliver Plunkett under cover, as he had promised Clifton?

Oliver had been so worried about not being late the first day that he had actually walked to the Academy and back again, timing the walk, determined to arrive not just on the dot, but five minutes beforehand.

As he walked along now he was glad that he had taken this particular precaution, but strangely it did nothing for his nerves, as well it might not, for, all through the previous days as he crouched in his digs, he had worried about one thing and one thing alone: how did he *dress* as Oliver Lowell?

It was all very well for Clifton to command him to keep his background under wraps, but how, he wondered, should he dress? He could not wear winkle-pickers and arrive on a motorbike, as some students, he thought enviously, would be doing. He would be arriving on shanks' pony and trying not to look posh, which in his father's old British warm, and a pair of cord trousers – albeit teamed with a navy blue polo neck sweater – was just laughable, but not in the right way.

The realisation of all this had led him to dash to the shops and buy himself a navy blue duffel coat, and then to spend the rest of the time trying to age it so that it did not look too new.

This procedure involved alternating between stamping on it in his brother's new shoes and rolling it up into a little ball, and, for some peculiar reason best known to himself, slinging it into the corner of his room. At last, satisfied that it no longer looked pristine and quite evidently fresh from Selfridges, he walked about Oxford Street in it, attempting to try out different characters.

Eventually he settled for 'lower middle class and shy from somewhere near York' which was a little like a secret wartime address.

So it was in this character, which he felt he had fairly moulded to himself in a pretty secure fashion, that he rolled up with all the other students on his first day at what his father and Clifton insisted on calling *arr aye em aye dee* – in the precise same way that they pronounced AA or RAC.

So there he was, a totally new character, in his own mind anyway, and wearing his carefully roughed up duffel coat, when a girl's voice behind him muttered, 'What's a snob like you need to come to a place like this for?'

He turned round in horror, knowing at once to whom the voice belonged. His best friend in the whole world, Coco.

'I am sorry, I don't think we have met?' Despite the shock of seeing Coco of all people, Oliver stuck determinedly to his new character, using Clifton's slight Yorkshire accent: lightly smoked, but not heavily flavoured.

For perhaps a split second Coco's large brown eyes registered what Oliver was saying, taking in his soft Yorkshire accent, his nearly new duffel coat (although she definitely felt that no one could or would be deceived by it until it was at least a little more faded), before she said, laconically, 'I say, I *am* sorry. I thought you were someone else.'

'Oliver Lowell.' Oliver extended his hand to her, and smiled.

Coco took the hand and she too smiled. 'Coco Hampton, as in Court. I say, would you care to walk down this corridor a little?' She indicated the way. 'I mistook you for a friend of mine, from somewhere quite other, and perhaps it might be just as well to straighten everything out. I mean, the mistaken identity and so on, and so on, could lead to confusion.'

They made sure they were both standing well down the corridor, away from the rest, before they resumed their dialogue.

'What are *you* doing here?' they both hissed at each other at once.

'I got a scholarship—' Oliver boasted quickly, because years of growing up with Coco had taught him to get in first.

'Everyone here gets a scholarship, that's nothing to go on about,' Coco told him dismissively. 'Just about everyone you've ever heard about has won some sort of prize from here. The Bourneton Cocoa Best New Actor's Feet prize, the Alderborough Ham Prize for the Crossing of Verbal Tees and Hissing of Esses, the—'

'I don't think we should be talking like this, not on our first day anyway,' Oliver said reprovingly, interrupting Coco and already shocked, if unsurprised, by her irreverence. For him, with his ardent attitude towards acting and the theatre, it was as if she had remained seated during the National Anthem. 'We have to at least give the place a try.'

'Yes, a try, but wise up, Ollie. People like you and me . . .' Coco looked around them with a cynical expression on her face and lit a cigarette. 'We, people like us, don't have a chance, not now,

89

not with the way theatre is going. We come from the wrong side of the tracks, darling. Quite the wrong side, so you're right to put on the Yorkie accent, but you'll have to age the old duffel coat just a wee bit more, or someone will smoke you out, for sure.'

Coco shook out her thick, shining dark hair, and her large amber earrings rattled as she did so. She had always been incredibly assured and arrogant, and always, like Oliver, theatre mad – but never ever prepared to call anything but a spade a spade, for which, until now, Oliver had always adored her.

Their families had been friends when they were small – at least, they had both gathered, quite separately, that they had been friends, until Oliver's mother had bolted, when the parents' friendship had necessarily been put on ice. Somehow, because the guardians with whom Coco lived, possessed a large, comfortable flat in London, and Oliver was nothing if not totally ruthless, Oliver had, with Clifton's active encouragement, kept the childhood friendship going.

As far as Oliver was concerned, this was solely so that he could spend some of his Christmas and Easter holidays with Coco in the only way that made either of them happy. In their letters to each other from their dark grey, spartan boarding schools, they called it 'seeing the plays'.

It was unbridled bliss, total happiness to both of them, to scramble up to the Upper Circle early early on, long before the rest of the fashionable audience arrived, and stare down at the Dress Circle, never letting their eyes leave the row upon row of seats below.

Somewhere below, they passionately hoped, there was going to be an empty seat, perhaps even two empty seats – and sometimes, alas for the management, there were many, many more – and long before the curtain rose young Oliver and Coco determined that those seats were going to be theirs from the first interval onwards.

So as the lights were lowered, and just before the curtain rose, both of them hung out of their seats and duly marked out the vacancies below for their own future use, once the lights in the auditorium went up on the first interval.

Coco, being Coco, small, slender and deter-mined to be outrageous, had always made sure to bring with her a pair of her guardian's mother-of-pearl opera glasses. As she said, 'It makes bagging the seats below ever so much easier.'

Once of course, and inevitably, they had most unfortunately bagged the seats of the sort of people who saw no harm in arriving at an interval. Being a born coward Oliver had immediately fled, embarrassed to saturation by having been found out, but not so Coco. She had – at the expense admittedly of a very dull drawing room comedy – set about arguing vociferously with the late, and shamefully drunk, arrivals, finally sending them back to the box office with a flea in their ear, not just for not checking their tickets, but for having arrived disgracefully late for the performance, which, Coco had maintained grandly, was an insult to both the author and the actors.

After which, with a curt, and despising nod to Oliver to reseat himself, Coco had gone back to disenjoying the dull little play, but revelling in their nice comfortable seats, the thick carpet below their feet, and the fact that, unlike the so-called 'gods', the Dress Circle smelt only of Chanel No. 5, and not of Jeyes disinfectant.

'Don't you think you went too far?' Oliver had asked Coco afterwards, shocked, but totally admiring of her brilliant dismissal of the quite legitimate holders of the seats.

'People like that should be shot!' was what Oliver suddenly remembered Coco saying, in just the same way as she was saying exactly that now, as they both watched a handsome young man arriving in a brand new sports car. 'No one going into the theatre should start off *rich*. What a twit, arriving in that way. Everyone will hate him. We all should start off poor and equal. What does he need to earn his living for? He obviously has one already!' Coco continued in withering tones.

'By the way, Coco, I didn't know that you were going to put yourself up for all *this*. I mean, I thought you wanted to be a designer. I thought that was what you wanted to be – a designer, not an actress.'

Oliver stared down at Coco, who jangled her amber bead bracelets on her slender wrists for a second, in the manner of a percussionist who has quite suddenly and unexpectedly been asked to play the bells.

'I still *am* going to be a designer, Ollie,' she told him in her most sophisticated and tired voice, which implied that despite their having not seen each other for at least three months, he really should have known. 'I still am going to be a designer, but I so hated art school, I just could *not* stay. All those humourless teachers with their grandiose notions. Really, you would honestly think that not even the Impressionists had happened! *Oh dear me, Miss Hampton, not finished your drawing already? A bit scrambled, isn't it?* Just as if facility is a dirty word. Do you know, Ollie, it is a little-known fact that Michelangelo did the Sistine Chapel not in months and years but in days and weeks, but they have to tell everyone that he spent practically his whole life on his back, because speed and facility are frowned on in art? So pathetic! As if labouring over something ever made it better!'

Coco took out a large silver compact from her strange-looking handbag and stared at her mouth in its mirror, but instead of redrawing her mouth with a lipstick she took out a small, red handkerchief and wiped the lipstick off.

'What are you doing *that* for?'

Oliver stared at her, as always fascinated, mesmerised, and adoring. Coco was in so many ways like an artistic elder sister to him, always a little ahead of the game, and always a little despising. And yet they had everything in common, their reactions to everything having always been identical, almost as if they shared one voice.

'Doing *this* for?' Coco demanded, her tone rising slightly. 'I am doing *this* so that I can appear younger, Ollie, that is why. I don't want to be given all the old ladies' parts, which, with my looks, I know I will be, and lipstick in case you have never noticed, which knowing you, you probably haven't – lipstick and jewellery ages one intolerably, *dahling*.'

She peeled off her earrings and her matching bracelet and put them with the compact in the strange-looking hold-all.

'Why did you wear them here, then?'

'Because I would never be seen on a bus or the Underground without them, *dahling*. Why do you think?' She looked around at the rest of the chattering students with a suddenly bored expression. 'You know this is all going to be a complete and mammoth waste of time, don't you?'

'Oh, I don't know.'

'Well, you wouldn't, really, because you are, as we both know, fairly pathetic, Ollie, but then you always were.'

She looked at him with sudden and familiar fondness, as his brothers never did, but knowing that Oliver would not let her off some sort of explanation she quickly decided that now was the time to produce the real and valid reason for her sudden, and quite inexplicable, enrolment at the Academy.

'You see, I had to get in *somewhere*, Ollie, or else

I couldn't stay in London. I had no excuse to stay in London. *Comprenez?* Had to. The guardians have moved to Norfolk, for ever, and, poor old ducks, they didn't want to take me, and I didn't want to go – can you imagine, me – in Norfolk? Ha. Not bloody likely! They haven't even a phone there, *figure-toi*? So after I was chucked out of art school for too much facility, I came here for an audition, mostly for a lark actually, didn't think I had a chance, but then bloody hell, I only got in. *Me voilà*, my deah!'

There was a small silence as they both stared at yet another shoal of their fellow students, both of them helplessly and hopelessly wondering where the competition would lie.

Would it lie with the tall girl with the plaits on top of her head? With the boy with the dark hair and the glasses? With the large, fat girl – character parts only probably, but never mind. *Who* was going to prove to be the best, the fairest, the starriest of them all?

'Yes, but what good will it do, I mean what good will acting be to you, if you really want to design, Coco?'

'Well, I can design at night and in the hols and all that,' Coco said, suddenly serious. 'But apart from not just wanting to leave London, I thought it would be good to be in plays, to find out what's needed, you know? And also, where the old hat ideas are still hanging around gathering dust needing new modes, new brilliance, and et cetera. And to find out how the costumes feel when they

95

are on. That *will* be useful, I thought. You know, find out how the clothes *move* and what an actress or actor wants from them. And then of course there is getting the feel of the plays, that is important. Don't worry; it will not be a waste of time. Far from it. I shall probably louse up all the plays I am in, or get chucked out or something, but on the way I shall learn. Most of all I will be soaking up the atmosphere, staying in London, meeting people, learning all the time. That's what it is all about, Ollie, learning. I don't want to design costumes like Leonard Bakst or someone, you see. I want to design them like me – Coco Hampton. That's what it is all about. It. I. Me. My face for the world to see. All that. And it is all, Ollie dear, about to begin.' Coco dropped her voice and rolled her eyes before saying in sepulchral tones, '*Act One, Scene One: the Acting Academy.*'

Oliver looked at her, but he did not laugh, being too deep in thought.

In some ways he was sorry that Coco was going to be with him at the Academy, because she was so impossibly, impishly irreverent, and in other ways – so many, many others – he was quite thrilled. They could be a kind of team; that is, if Coco was not, as she had just said, chucked out. They could be an unholy alliance the way they always had been when they were growing up together, talking, talking, talking, theatre, theatre, theatre.

'Come on, love,' Oliver told her, suddenly

exaggerating his Yorkshire accent to make her laugh. 'Time to roll up t'sleeves.'

Instead of her sleeves Coco rolled her eyes, all mischief, as she always was, and probably always would be. 'Curtain *oop*?' she asked mockingly.

'I am not actually playing it as definite as that, actually. I am playing it like Cliffie. Just a light smattering of Yorkshire. I will only let myself down if I try too much.'

'If you haven't already – *dahling*!'

Oliver stared at her. 'How do you mean?'

'Those *shoes*!'

Coco attempted to suppress a laugh, and failed, as they followed the rest of the students forward and Oliver stared down at his feet. Coco had an obsession with clothes, always had. Not surprising really, since she wanted to be a designer.

'*What?* What is wrong with them? What is wrong with my shoes, Coco?' Oliver stared in despair from his feet, moving towards enrolment, to Coco, now bursting with ill-suppressed mirth.

'Pure cavalry officer, *dahling*! I mean, do tell me – were you in the Eleventh Hussars or the Household Cavalry?'

Oliver closed his eyes momentarily. He hated Coco so, so much – quite as much as he loved her, which was so, so much – but no good would come of contemplating either emotion at that moment, because now there were not one but two people laughing far too uncontrollably, tears pouring down their faces, and in danger of holding up the moving body of students.

Coco was so right.

Oliver's feet, now that he bothered to look at them, did not belong to him at all, in fact they looked ludicrous, especially when teamed with his horribly new duffel coat. His feet still belonged to his elder brother, Richard. They were pure army, and nothing to do with him, nothing to do with Oliver, the thespian younger brother.

'Oh *Gahd*! Teach me to pinch shoes from Richard and Newell!'

Chapter Three

It was no surprise to anyone, let alone Elsie Lancaster, that Cinderella was a sell-out. After all, despite the growth of television audiences, despite the success of commercial television, despite the weather and the government, families still wanted to take themselves and their children to that all-British institution, the Christmas pantomime. The pity was that to hear Dottie talking about it, you would have thought that the production had been an all-time failure, not a huge success.

The ghastliness of the costumes, the vulgarity of the producer, the inefficiency of the scene changes, the awfulness of Elsie's shared dresser, they were all aired as news-making items, not weekly, but nightly, when Elsie returned home in the unheard-of luxury of a station taxi.

And all this despite the fact that Dottie had not been to anything except the first dress rehearsal.

'I'm not coming *back* for the first night, not to see that *tat*, never. They should be ashamed of themselves, in this day and age, coming up with a standard of production like that. Anyone would think that the war was still on, really they would.'

And nor did she attend the first night, and nor would she any night, Dottie maintained, loudly and long, every morning, every afternoon, and presumably, although Elsie was never there to hear, every evening too.

It seemed that on principle Dottie *refused* to be a witness to such a disgrace, would not be party to the kind of unprofessionalism that gave theatre a bad name, and as a consequence made people admire anything and everything that was on television. According to Dottie the pantomime was filled with dancers who were overweight, played for by an orchestra that was half asleep. Like everything that Dottie had witnessed in the theatre since the war, it was professed to be appalling.

'Please tell me where standards have gone?' she would ask their lodgers, who were usually unable to supply an answer. 'Do not ask me, not ever, not at all. But gone they have, down the tubes, down the drain. And today's managements! Well, when they're not *doing* the artists, they're doing the *public*. Pulling the wool over their eyes, making believe that just about anything will do. They think the public doesn't notice, but they do! And that is all before we get on to that wretch John Eastbourne, and what he and his like have done to thee-*ay*-ter! What have they done to our darling thee-*ay*-ter? Where the great plays, where the great actors? What since the war – besides

Oklahoma! and *The Deep Blue Sea* – have we to admire? The verse play? Do not even speak to me of the empty seats engendered by the verse play! And now we have these others, these Palace Court scribblers, chest scratchers, dustbin men as heroes, and the like! Please. Just tell me, what is there to admire any more? Where Congreve? Where Wilde? Where anyone of worth? Even Coward, would be better than these . . . *dustbin* dwellers.'

'Don't, Dottie dear heart. Don't ask me. I don't understand what's going on any more, really I don't.'

This was the standard reply of any permanent or temporary lodger, always known collectively, despite their age, as 'Dottie's boys'. But whoever among them happened to be present, they knew that this was the only possible, the only acceptable and standard response to Dottie's passionate diatribe of nightly disgust against the ghastly changes in the theatre.

No such reply came from her granddaughter.

It was Elsie's sensible practice to keep quite quiet during her grandmother's tirades. Quite apart from anything else, she was usually too tired to do anything else, but then there was also the generally accepted fact that no one, ever, interrupted Dottie and lived to tell the tale. When she entered into one of her long diatribes against the fashionable theatre, as Elsie well knew, no one was required to speak, and all the regulars of Dottie's lodging house knew this. What they were required to do was to sit in admiring silence as she launched her personal rockets at the critics, at the new style of theatre, at television, and now, also – despite the success of the pantomime – at Portly Cosgrove.

Portly Cosgrove had become one of Dottie's newer targets.

It was quite clear to everyone who saw Dottie from day to day, and knew her, that Portly Cosgrove had mortally offended her. How exactly he had caused such offence, Elsie had not yet quite managed to ascertain. Generally speaking, since he had employed Elsie and what was more paid her every week and on time, it was puzzling. Eventually, Elsie, who puzzled over this manifestation as much as anyone, was forced to come to the conclusion that having gained his agreement, in every respect, to every one of her demands for her granddaughter, Dottie had finally settled on hating Portly for *not* arguing with her, for robbing her of a unique opportunity to best him.

Portly Cosgrove had taken the ground from under Dottie's feet. He had denied her the opportunity to win points against him, to score triumphs, to walk up and down the hall saying things like *Now then, Mr Cosgrove, get out of that Mr Portly Cosgrove* once she had replaced the telephone receiver.

It seemed unreasonable, but it was the only possible conclusion that Elsie could reach as to why Dottie had her knife in Portly Cosgrove.

Mr Cosgrove would never, ever be able to do anything right because he had bored Dottie. He had acceded to her outrageous demands, immediately, at once, giving in to everything that she had demanded for Elsie, however seemingly unreasonable. From then on his production was bound to fail, bound to appear shoddy, ill managed, ill conceived, and in bad taste.

As far as Dottie was concerned he was like a tennis player who had come on court, taken one look at the opposition, laid down his racket and conceded victory. Dottie only liked and understood conflict. It did not matter where the conflict lay: with the government, in the house, with the ironing; she had to have conflict the way the old people of the town had to have sea air. She had to have it in order to be able to feel that she was the only person on the planet who saw things in the right way. Without conflict Dottie would have to give in to other ideas not just about the world, but also about herself. If Portly Cosgrove was a nice reasonable man, the notion that Dottie was an ambitious woman making unreasonable demands might have to be entertained. Therefore Portly Cosgrove, having denied her the right to indignation and conflict, must now be proved to be second rate. It had to be. There could be no other explanation.

And so it was with the success of Cinderella.

Never mind that the local critics had boomed it to the skies, begging everyone to book to see the production, lauding Elsie to the rafters, and congratulating Donald Bourton on his exquisite production, full of shading, and with the newest and best of everything on show.

To Dottie it was not a patch on, could never come even near to, *Stuart Blaine's 1928 production in the old Hambra Theatre at Beckhampton, using the 1924 Bakst-type costumes from Sleeping Beauty, and Max Little's sets from Ophelia. Now that was the definitive Cinderella, and of course Laura Piper was discovered in it, too. She was the definitive Cinders, No one sang or danced with more grace than Loo Piper, really they didn't!*

Still, despite everything, Elsie was determined that she would not allow Dottie's attitude to her own first real success to influence her optimism. Apart from anything else, there was no real reason to. After all, if she had been about to be cast down by Dottie she would have given up years ago, of that there was no doubt. Instead she continued as she had always done, to go to the theatre, to do her job, *to learn the lines and try not to bump into the furniture*, as the very tired, very over-used theatrical saying went.

But most of all, she made sure to keep as quiet as possible in front of just about everyone. More than anything that was what her childhood in the theatre had taught her, and that was what she had learned to do over the years, perhaps better, she often thought, than she could either sing or dance, or act.

Keeping quiet meant that Elsie could get into

character, and stay there, for even though some might consider Cinderella a stupid part she was determined to make Cinders real, determined to put depth into her characterisation, make Cinderella the sort of person that Elsie understood – someone who had endured all sorts of domestic humiliations, but had come through with her head held high.

Long before being cast in the star part in the pantomime, Elsie had never been tempted to stand around gossiping with the rest of the cast, or passing on scandal, or becoming the least bit interesting to anyone else. Time, and listening to Dottie, had taught Elsie that was for the birds. Quite apart from anything else, it used up all your energy. Elsie always made sure to keep all her acting energy bottled up, waiting to fizz, only uncorking it once she left the wings and walked on stage. Then her dynamic energy was allowed full rein, only to be promptly recorked once she returned to the wings.

Although she had never had one before, even her inexperience in this field did not mean that Elsie would be tempted to gossip with her dresser. Always known backstage as the Dame, for reasons that Elsie had never found out, Tinker Butterworth could say what she liked, when she liked – which she did, and all the time – but could expect to receive no replies from Elsie.

Of course Elsie listened to her. After all, she could not exactly block her ears in front of this old hand from both Variety and the legitimate theatre, but she was more than careful never to add anything, more than aware that, as with Dottie, the lightest remark would be seized upon, exaggerated, told again slightly differently, and finally, without any seeming effort on anyone's part, turned into one of those apocryphal stories that make the theatrical rounds for years and years.

Sometimes, indeed, they made the rounds *for ever*, being printed in one of the many, and often interminable, theatrical memoirs that graced Dottie's bookshelves.

So, just as someone living in a country peopled by secret police will make sure not to see or hear anything, backstage, Elsie smiled, and said nothing. So much so that they were not long into the run before Tinker Butterworth put it about that Elsie Lancaster might be a sweet young thing, but she was also characterless and boring, with nothing at all to say for herself.

Of course Elsie knew this, as she knew everything that was said about her or anyone else, not because she actually heard the Dame saying it but because, growing up on the fringes of provincial theatre, she knew everything that was said about people who did not play the *game*. They were always 'boring'. Or 'terribly sweet, darling, but nothing *up* there, if you know what I mean?'

As it happened Elsie was quite happy with being thought dull and accepting. Along with so much else she was determined to keep her

106

thoughts on the matter in the privacy of her head. She had never grumbled when she was growing up, partly because she was not allowed to, but also because there was no point. Neither was she, at this stage in her career, prepared to give any indication to her rivals that she was anything except a tall, quite talented girl, with her eyes firmly set on the future. Any more would be to show her hand, a hand that she was intent on keeping close to her chest.

And so it was that, as the run of the pantomime drew inevitably to its end, and she contemplated a jobless future, and a list of presents that, as the star, she knew that she would have to present to the rest of the cast, not to mention the Dame herself, Elsie was surprised in her dressing room by Portly Cosgrove.

Of course he knocked on the door, as courteously as he had knocked on it many times before, allowing Elsie time to slip into a robe especially chosen for receiving callers, but this time there was a difference. This time, he asked the Dame to leave them alone.

'You sure?' Tinker's androgynous face peered down into Elsie's now unmade-up one.

'Yes, Tinker, please. It's all right. You can leave us alone. Although . . .'

Tinker turned expectantly. She was after all, according to her old friend Dottie, also *meant* to be chaperoning Dottie's granddaughter, whatever 'chaperoning' might mean, when it was at home.

'You could take some of those parcels over

107

there and wrap them in that pretty wrapping paper, if you don't mind, Tinker.'

'Oh, very well. But remember, the station taxi will be here any minute, and tonight is not the last night. There are no favours from anyone to anyone tonight, love. Still another performance to go before liberty, dear.'

Exit Tinker with a disapproving look to both Elsie and Portly.

'Wonderful old character, isn't she?' Portly asked in a raised voice, and with an accompanying laugh, knowing that the old dresser would be sure to have paused as long as she dared, to listen outside the dressing room door.

'Yes, Tinker is wonderful.' Elsie too had raised her voice and for exactly the same reason. 'She is an old friend of my grandmother's.'

'Known the family for years, has she? A grand old character, salt of the earth, that sort of thing, is she?'

'Oh, yes, Mr Cosgrove. I could not do without her, and that is certain.'

'May I sit down?'

Portly had lowered his voice, and Elsie now nodded, and lowered hers too. 'Yes, do,' she said, sounding more normal, as they both listened for Tinker's footsteps on the cold stone of the corridor outside the dressing room door to die away.

Elsie handed Portly her chair and she sat down on the old ottoman, the statutory fitting of every post-war so-called star dressing room.

'I have been having a talk with Donald Bourton, about you.'

Elsie took care to look polite but disinterested, but then, sensing that they might not be alone, she sprang up suddenly, went to the dressing room door and quickly wrenched it open, stepping outside to make sure that there was no one within listening distance of its exterior. Which, she was happy to say, there was not, just the sound of another dressing room door quickly shutting as Tinker disappeared inside it, safe from discovery.

Watching this action – or, as he had already learned to call it using stage terminology, this *piece of business* – Portly realised at once that he might be dealing with a quite young leading actress, but he was certainly not dealing with a quite inexperienced one. Elsie Lancaster was obviously no amateur.

An inexperienced player might have been tempted to grumble about Tinker Butterworth, or be led into telling some anecdote about her – and if what Donald Bourton had told Portly was true there were enough of them goodness knows – but only a pro would go to the door and make quite sure that they were truly alone. But then, from what he had seen of her, everything about Elsie Lancaster was professional, from the way she checked her props to her choice of the more modern, less ridiculously heavy stage make-up that she took care to wear. She might look like a kid, but she had the strange air and ways of someone quite old in her ways.

Portly smiled suddenly. 'I will start again, Elsie, if you don't mind.'

Elsie said nothing in reply to this, only waiting, allowing nothing to betray her true feelings, not a fidget, not an easing of herself on the ottoman, not a shaking out of her luxuriant blond hair. She remained quite still.

'As I said, Donald and I have been talking about *our* future, which we very much hope could, or might be, wrapped up in *your* future. You are, as you have no doubt gathered from the reviews, a very, very talented young actress, and we don't want anything to spoil this. Not a thing. At the moment you are just on the cusp, *we* think, but we also think that your talent could go either way. Either it could go to drama school' – at this he placed his hands together in front of them both, as if he was holding a parcel – 'or, it could *not*.' The hands moved to make another parcel. 'In our opinion if you went to drama school at this point in your life, you could become completely ruined by second rate has-beens teaching you to speak properly and hold your knife and fork as you should – which you do anyway – in other words, putting you through, as Donald calls it, "the usual drama school rot". *Or* you could sign yourself up with Cosgrove and Bourton Productions, on the understanding that we guarantee to find appropriate vehicles for you over the next two years.'

Still Elsie was determinedly silent, and very, very still, and she took great care to be so for the

110

very good reason that she did not want to betray her inner feelings of accelerated excitement.

If Portly Cosgrove could see her heart racing, or hear how hard it seemed to her that it was beating, or look into her mind and guess how she was already seeing her name up in lights outside the theatre, any theatre, in Shaftesbury Avenue, he would take her to be what Dottie called a pushover, or worst of all an amateur, which was the very last thing that was needed at that moment.

'I have thought about it, and the last thing I want is to go to drama school,' Elsie told him, eventually, noting that if she did not show any willingness to plunge ahead verbally, neither did he. 'I do not want to go to drama school, because,' she continued, not realising that in her anxiety to remain outwardly cool her speech patterns were becoming over-emphatic. 'I – will – not learn anything there, I do not think, that I do not already know.'

'No, you won't,' Portly agreed, and he took a cigar case from his pocket. He was only twenty-five, but appeared to be much older possibly because he wore an older type of tailored suit and white shirts with dark ties. He lit the cigar, slowly and appreciatively, and smiled at her. 'So we are in agreement about that, at least. But, now, if you are not to go on to drama school, what about signing a contract with Cosgrove and Bourton?'

'That will be a lot more difficult,' Elsie admitted. 'My agent is very particular.'

'So we have gathered.'

'She will not want me tied to a contract for a great length of time. She will see it as wasting opportunities. She will not be kept hanging about while better offers have to be turned away.'

'I perfectly see that,' Portly agreed, puffing hard on the Havana and filling the small dressing room with the agreeable smell of a freshly smoked and very expensive cigar, 'but I am sure, given the right terms, she might change her mind.'

This meant, as they both knew, *given enough money*. There was a short silence during which Portly managed to get his cigar going even better, and Elsie stared at him, her face expressionless.

'Let us face it, it is not going to harm you, not at this juncture of your career, is it? To be signed with Cosgrove and Bourton. It is not about to ruin your chances – not, that is, if we can come up with the right play for you.'

'No,' Elsie agreed, reluctantly, because she could already hear Dottie's protests, her insistence on Elsie's turning away any form of contractual commitment. 'If you could come up with the right play for me, the most suitable, it would be all right, but my agent would have to approve of the vehicle before we signed. Yes, I would say that is the way that she would see it. She would need play approval, I think you will find.'

A silence fell in the dressing room, and then Portly smiled his large, warm smile. It was the smile of a young man born to try to play at entertaining the world with confections of his own making, the smile of a young man who wanted to surprise and astonish audiences, to send them home with a little bit of magic tucked into the pages of their programmes, so that in years to come whenever they held those same programmes again just the feel and look of them would make them sigh and say, 'That was a wonderful evening, unforgettable really, truly unforgettable.'

Finally Portly said, knowing very well that at least his dazzling smile had won Elsie over, 'Do you know, Elsie, I don't know why you bother having an agent – you're pretty good at representing yourself.'

Elsie smiled, but it was only a small smile, and it was not accompanied by a laugh, which, Portly realised of a sudden, was not really very surprising, because he had never ever seen Elsie Lancaster laugh, at least not off stage. On stage she had a most accomplished laugh, something that he realised was very difficult to achieve, but off stage she hardly ever even smiled, let alone laughed; just as, he now realised, it was her habit to listen to people intently, although she herself rarely spoke. It was as if she heard what went on around her but it meant little to her; as if in some strange way real life meant nothing to her, and it was only once the stage lights found her that she came to life. And then, of a sudden, she was there, *Elsie Lancaster*, star of the future.

'You're hiding, aren't you, Elsie?'

'I beg your pardon?'

'Please don't. I was merely making an observation. You are hiding, aren't you, from the rest of us? Just waiting, all the time, to start acting.'

Elsie stared at him. It was true. That was exactly how she was. Always hiding, perhaps from Dottie, or others like her, just waiting to go on stage to become someone else, someone that not even Dottie could find.

'Yes, I think that is true.'

She stood up quickly as if Portly's small observation about her was going quite far enough, and as if of a sudden she did not want him to stay any longer in case he came up with another more uncomfortable one.

'Good night, Mr Cosgrove.'

Portly smiled. It was always and ever *Mr Cosgrove* with her, just as it was always *Elsie* with him.

'Good night, Elsie, and tell your agent that I will be in touch with her in the morning.'

Elsie did not have to say 'Good luck, you will have a fight on your hands' because, after all, it was something that they both knew already.

And so the agony started again, the whole awful drama of Dottie and her protestations, or her telephone calls, now taken in a sitting position, a new chair for the hall having been bought by Elsie and placed expressly by the telephone for her particular, argumentative use.

'Who these people think they are I don't know,

really I don't. They take us all for mugs, really they do. Just idiots. Tie you to a two-year contract, my foot. And without sight or sound of a play too! They take us for idiots.'

'No, Dottie, you have that wrong. There is a play, and it is about to be posted.'

Dottie looked up from yet another mound of ironing, but Dottie never listened to good news, it was not her way. She was not interested in good news, any more than she could think well of any-one or anything to do with managements. They were all, to a person, dastardly.

'Managements, Elsie,' she went on, using a falsely over-wearied voice, 'have *always* got a play in the post. That is what they *always* say, and that is what we *know* they always say. Let us just see sight and sound of it, and if we do I promise you I will eat my hat.'

At that moment the doorbell rang and Elsie promptly flew up the stairs to answer it. No one knew how eagerly she had been waiting for that sound, that great and glorious sound, the doorbell ringing to announce the postman and a parcel.

Dear Miss Lancaster,

On Mr Cosgrove's instructions, I am sending you a copy of The Light in His Head *translated from the French by Timiny Morel. Mr Cosgrove hopes that you will enjoy reading it and will get back to him as soon as possible to tell him what you think. It is proposed that you should consider the part of Francine.*

The letter was signed on behalf of Portly by his secretary, but even so Elsie knew at once that by sending the manuscript directly to her, by having the secretary write to her, rather than Dottie, Mr Cosgrove was silently signalling to Elsie that she should read the play herself, and make up her own mind, and never mind her agent. The secretary's letter, the parcel, was all in theatrical code to her, and she appreciated this as much as she knew that Dottie would not appreciate it.

'What was that, Elsie?'

'Nothing, Dottie. Just a parcel for the first floor. A radio script for Bill Langley; you know, the one he was talking about last night.'

'Tripe. He does so much tripe,' Dottie called up, before retreating back to the kitchen. 'I keep telling him he must hold back, wait for better quality, but does he listen to me? Never. You simply can't help some people, because they just don't listen.'

Bill might not listen but Elsie did, intently, and as soon as she heard the dull thud of Dottie's old iron slapping down on the ironing board she zipped off to her room, quietly closing the door, and locking it.

She stared at the manuscript. It was not a promising title, but then very few plays or films translated from the French ever managed a good title. If however it was a comedy, which judging from the weight and look of it it might be – she quickly flicked through the pages – well, it might, just might, have a suitable part in it.

As it turned out, it did, but – how to tell Dottie?

Elsie took care to post the manuscript back by return to Cosgrove and Bourton in London, to get it out of the house as quickly as possible, before turning her thoughts to how to get her own way.

As Elsie saw it that was what life was all about: how to get your own way. Everyone trying to get their own way, and sometimes achieving it, sometimes not. She simply could not understand anyone who did not see life in this way. More than that, she had no time for people who could not see that it was *their* struggle against *her* struggle. She even pitied them. Life was all about winning, no matter what, winning through so you did not have to have lodgers, or clean up after them, or press their clothes for them. It was about pushing on and on until finally there was no more of doing the things you loathed, and plenty more of what she saw other people in the newspapers and magazines enjoying – fine clothes and fine cars, fine food and fine friends.

'Oh, Bill, there is a wireless play come for you from the BBC – Elsie took it up to your room earlier.'

Happily Elsie overheard Dottie calling out to Bill Langley as he let himself back into the house. So, dashing out of her own room and making sure to bump into Bill in the upstairs hall by-mistake-on-purpose, Elsie quickly stretched out and lightly touched his sleeve with one elegantly manicured hand. She mouthed, 'She made a mistake,' nodding down the stairs to Dottie in the kitchen, all the while pointing a finger at her temple and twisting it round and round to indicate that Dottie was not as reliable as she would like the rest of the world to think she was.

'I understand,' Bill whispered. 'It was just the same last time. Script arrived from the BBC, not for me, though, for Ralphie on the top floor. She will not wear her specs, will our Dottie.' He paused, sighing. 'It would have been too good to be true, anyway. I haven't done a steam radio in months, love, not in months. But thanks for telling me anyway.'

Feeling horribly guilty when she saw the look of patient resignation on the old actor's face, Elsie at once, and in an instant, tried to think of some part in the play that she had just read for which Bill could be considered suitable. Realising that there was one – the character of an old man-servant – she quietly made up her mind that she would most definitely put him up for it. Then, leaving the house, and him, as quickly as she could, she went out for a walk.

It would not be very long before Dottie found out about Elsie's having read the play without Dottie's approval, and then there would be trouble. And a great deal of it. Big trouble. Probably the worst trouble that Elsie had been in, ever, in her whole life. Even if she wanted to do the play, which she now did, quite desperately, she knew that, despite everyone and everything, Dottie would not let her.

She sat down on the bench and stared out to the sea. It was a bitterly cold day and her thin tweed coat was not really very adequate, but somehow because she was so fired up with the idea of doing the play, because she had already seen herself in the role, she was not aware of the cold, or the wind, or indeed of anything, really. All she could see were those words on the page. She knew that she could make a hit in the part of Francine, just as she knew that she could sing and dance Cinderella better than anyone else. It was not a question of conceit – she was not a conceited person – it was just a fact, in the same way that the sea pounding up the pebbled beach in front of her was a fact. In the same way that the old man who was passing her with his small Scottie dog on the lead was also a fact. It was just getting by Dottie that was going to be the hardest fact of all.

A few minutes later found her battling her way along the front to a telephone box.

'Can I speak to Portly Cosgrove, please?' It was the first time that she had called him this, and now there was to be another first. 'Portly? It's Elsie!'

Portly sounded, as he always did, rounded and affable, and yet somehow excited too, full of a sort of suppressed excitement that transferred itself to Elsie. Of a sudden they were conspirators. He now knew, she realised immediately, that she had understood why he had sent the play and the letter to her, and not to Dottie, because they *both* knew that Dottie was the wardrobe blocking the door through which they both wanted to go, needed to go, but someone or something had to remove the wardrobe.

'Hallo, Elsie Lancaster, and how are you?'

'We must meet.'

'Yes, I know, we must.'

'But where? You are in London, are you not?'

'In a few hours I could be driving out of London, and we could be meeting at Fullers for tea. And you could be telling me what you think about the play, and we could be eating some of their delicious sponge cake.'

'Yes, we could, could we not?'

Portly was no longer 'Mr Cosgrove' but some kind of older brother, or a younger uncle, someone whom, for the first time in her life, she could trust.

'Four thirty, and don't be late or I will have eaten all the cake, mine and yours, and everyone else's.'

'I, for one, do not mind.'

There was a small sound. Portly stared at the wall opposite his desk. It was only a small sound, but it was unmistakable. It was the sound of Elsie laughing.

Fullers tea shop, just like Dottie's kitchen, was warm, and welcoming, and because it was a cold, blustery, rainy day the windows were all steamed up, like Dottie's kitchen, and the customers' happy and carefree expressions, their cups of tea, and their generous portions of cake all reflected the general feeling that they were lucky to be inside in the warm, lucky to be able to afford tea at a shop, lucky to have everything they wanted at that moment and, most of all, lucky that it was all they wanted.

To Elsie, to eat tea in a shop was not just a treat, it was a solemn and special moment. Dottie never allowed treats of any kind, and never had, the inference always being that it was treat enough to be brought up by her. No tea in a shop, no lunch in a café, ever. It had never been known, not the whole time that Elsie was growing up. She had never, ever been in a hotel, except once when a foreign manager of a production company had invited all the cast to have ice creams after a first night which had gone particularly well, but since he was Italian, everyone had treated it as the particular and spectacular exception that it undoubtedly was.

Now as Portly arrived, a little after Elsie, she could not help bubbling over with the excitement of the moment, all her reserve forgotten as he ordered tea and toast and cakes of all kinds in that particularly conspiratorial manner that belongs to people who know not just how to enjoy life, but how to appreciate it too.

'So you love the play?'

Elsie cut her toast, and put some strawberry jam on it. She nodded, but did not allow her eyes to leave the jam, the toast, the cup of tea. 'I love the play.'

'And you want to play Francine.'

She nodded again, her mouth now full. Being a man of exquisite manners, Portly quickly popped his own jam-covered toast into his own mouth, and they both chewed silently, and then sipped tea while dwelling on this announcement.

'So you will sign? With Cosgrove and Bourton? You will sign.'

'Yes.' Elsie's eyes strayed to the cake. The sponge looked so soft, and the filling so pink, she felt she was eating it before she even took a mouthful of the delicate confection. 'I will sign, but my agent will not.'

'No, I thought as much.' It was Portly's turn to nod. 'She is a bit of a stickler.'

At that moment, her mouth full of the best cake she thought she had ever tasted, Elsie thought she did not really care what Dottie was, not just at that moment, but seconds later, after she had discreetly swallowed the confection, she too nodded her head.

'She is a stickler, and worse.' Portly took a bite of his cake and Elsie continued, 'She does not like your standards of production, I am very much afraid. She thinks they are not up to scratch.'

'I thought as much when she didn't come round on the first night. It *is* only a local pantomime.'

'I am afraid you do not understand. She does not like *any* standards of production – not since the war. In fact she hates all managements, and loathes everything that has happened since 1945, except *Oklahoma!*

'Ah, so we can do no good, whatever happens?'

'No, and I am seventeen, Portly, not twenty-one.'

'You may be a minor in age, but you are a major in talent.'

Elsie wrinkled her nose. 'Touché,' she said, for no better reason than that Bill Langley said it, and she always thought it sounded rather sophisticated.

'It was meant to be a compliment, Elsie. *Touché* is for when people score off you. You say *touché* the way, as it were, you would say "fair enough".'

Elsie coloured. 'Oh, I thought it meant "how touching".'

They both stared at each other, and then it happened for a second time, but now Portly could actually see it, the sublime and heart-warming sight and sound of Elsie laughing.

'What shall we do, Portly? It is a moot point, is it not? I mean, how can we sign me to your company if me, being I, cannot sign for myself, being a minor, *voyez-vous*?'

'There must be some way we could buy your agent off, mustn't there?'

'No.' Elsie shook her head. She was talking about her grandmother now, not her agent. Dottie was not the kind of person anyone could buy off; it was not a possibility. The truth was that Dottie could not be bought off by anything, because she liked how she was, in fact she adored how she was. She liked the difficulties, the awfulness of the theatre, the lodgers and their hopelessness, she enjoyed it all.

'Does she own her own house?'

Elsie nodded.

'Does she have a car?'

'She would not want a motor car.'

'Nothing then?'

Elsie looked up of a sudden, before embarking on her second helping of the delicious cake.

'There is something. But I don't know, I don't know whether it is possible, whether it would work, but we could try it.'

Dottie stared at her. It had been years since she had acted, and they both knew it.

'Cosgrove wants me for the part of the house-keeper?'

Elsie nodded. 'Yes, yes, he does.'

'But he has never seen me act.'

'No, but his uncle did. Remember his uncle was in management, before the war – Cosgrove and Barraclough, it was in those days.'

'Don't remember that.' Dottie looked momentarily suspicious. 'Don't remember him, not at all.'

'Well, you would not. Most of their productions were north of the Watford Gap. They really only did plays for the north, what they called brown soup plays, trimmed and tailored for a specific audience. They did very well, apparently. Always full, at the seaside resorts of course.'

'Do you know Brighton still had forty theatres, even a few years ago?' Dottie asked, from nowhere, and for no reason she picked up a saucepan and examined it.

It was Elsie's turn to stare at Dottie. This was her grandmother at her most awkward. Bad enough, Elsie knew, that Elsie had been offered the lead, but for Dottie to be offered the important part of the housekeeper was almost worse. What would happen to Mr Cosgrove now? What would he become? Obviously he could no longer be a man of hideous taste since he was offering Dottie an acting role. Nor surely could he be a man of shoddy standards, for the very same reason.

Elsie now watched her grandmother with the cold discerning eye that is reserved for those who hear and see too much from too young an age. She watched while Dottie struggled with her emotions like a fish on the end of a line. Vanity and flattered pride now struggled with realism and fear. She had castigated Portly Cosgrove for so long, reviled him throughout the pantomime season; now that he was offering her a chance to tread the boards once more, what would she do?

'I will read the play through again, and then see.'

Elsie phoned Portly a few days later to report on progress.

'She is reading the play through, yet again.'

'This must be the fiftieth time.'

'She wants to make sure that she is right for the part, and that the part is right for her.'

Portly groaned. 'Of course she's right for the

part. Why else would we have offered it to her?'

'Because you want *me*, remember?'

'Oh, yes, I know *that*, but – but I don't think that is the point, Elsie. I mean, she hasn't worked for years, has she?'

'No, she has not.'

'Well, then, I would have thought that she would have fallen down on her knees and thanked God. I am, I thought, manna from heaven.'

'It is *because* she has not worked for years that she has to think about it so hard. You know, I think she is frightened. I think that is at the back of it. That she is terrified. She is rusty. She must be, having not acted for so long.'

'Supposing she says no, we really are up the famous alley.'

'Do not worry,' Elsie told Portly in her clearly enunciated way. 'Please, do not worry. I know she will say yes.'

'How do you know?'

'Because,' said Elsie, 'I do.'

She quietly replaced the telephone, and went in search of her grandmother.

Dottie was ironing, as usual.

Elsie sometimes thought that the iron was attached to her grandmother's hand, so much had it become a part of it. She also thought that Dottie's oft-declared aversion to a particular and very famous new play was because one of the main characters was always, like Dottie, at the ironing board with a depressed expression.

'I suppose that was Portly Cosgrove, yet again?'

126

Dottie did not look up as Elsie came into the kitchen carrying a large basket of her own ironing.

'No,' Elsie lied, quickly and adroitly. 'No, it was not Portly Cosgrove, it was Dimitri Becq, remember him? He wants me for a tableau in the summer, but I said no. Unless *you* want me to do it, of course?' she added, ingratiatingly.

'Of course I don't want you to do it,' Dottie said, looking up for the first time. 'That man is an absolute crook, really he is. I don't know how he looks at himself in the mirror in the morning.'

'He probably wears a beard for that reason.'

Dottie gave her a quick look, but seeing that Elsie had made a joke, and quite a good joke, she merely looked away as if she had said nothing.

'I don't know what to do about this wretched part, Elsie, really I don't. I mean, going on tour at my age – I mean, what will it do to the lodgers, to my boys? I mean really, I don't think I can leave them just like that. They won't be able to cope.'

'Of course they will. They are all grown men, and besides, you know you can get Queenie to come in and run the whole caboodle for you, just as she does when you go to London to see plays. There will be no real problem there, Dottie, really there will not.'

'I know you say that, Elsie, but supposing there is? Supposing they are miserable while I am away, supposing they walk out? Then my whole livelihood, the whole business that I have built up here, will all be wiped out, and I will have no more security.'

'Very well, then do not take the part. Say no to Portly Cosgrove. It is quite simple.'

'But you said he will not do it without me, which means he will not give *you* the part. I don't want to sacrifice your hopes just because *I* don't want to do it.'

Elsie had been waiting for this, and now at long, long last she saw it rising up in front of them all, the great, grand Let Out for Dottie.

The whole implication having settled comfortably around her, Elsie, if she could have, would have run around their small garden giving great whoops of joy. If she could she would have made Red Indian noises – *whoo, hoo, hoo!* – but as it was she could not, and so she stayed, quite still, as was her habit, staring at Dottie with interest. She was always able to stand back from her grandmother, regarding her with the same cold eye that she had used on her ever since she was quite small and Dottie had first beaten her for trying to mend a clock, and then laughed at her when she cried out in terror and pain. Dottie had not been a kindly relative, she had not been warm and soppy; she had been just as she was now – Dottie.

But at that precise moment Elsie had a feeling of exultant power, because she knew, absolutely, and without any doubt, that she had Dottie where she wanted her. Dottie was in a cul-de-sac. She would now be forced, willy-nilly, to go forward through the stage door, where Elsie wanted her to go, and from there on to the stage itself.

She would now do the part Portly was offering

her, no matter what, because she had found the *excuse* that she needed. *Elsie* would be her excuse.

No matter what the performance she turned in, no matter how she fared in the role of the house-keeper, Dottie now had her emotional get out. She had only taken the part for *Elsie's* sake. Had not she agreed to go on stage her granddaughter would never have been given the part of Francine. She *had* to accept, for Elsie's sake.

Elsie could hear her telling her 'boys' this, could see the steam on the kitchen windows, hear the sound of the iron banging down on the ironing board as she repeated her cry.

I would never have taken the part if it had not been for Elsie needing the work, really I wouldn't. But they just wouldn't do it without me. It was not my part, but I had to do it for her, she wanted me in. I didn't want me in, she did, so I had to do it!

'So, for your sake, and you must understand that, Elsie, I will go back to acting. I will do the part, I will take on the tour, but whatever happens, please do not – *never* put me through this again. It is too much, at my age, to expect a whole production to ride on my shoulders. But, for your sake, I will do so. You understand? Just for your sake, I will do it. But only if the terms they offer are all right, only if, Elsie. Not other-wise. If they do not offer the best terms, if I can't pay Queenie to took after the place out of my salary, and if my boys are made miserable, then that is it. I will not do it. And I will have to have a one-week get-out clause. You understand that,

Elsie? One week get-out and no mucking about.'

'I am quite sure that Portly Cosgrove will give you just whatever you want, Dottie. I know that he wants you more than he wants me.'

Dottie nodded, not really paying much attention to the compliment, accepting it as her right. The right of an actress who had been deprived of the great roles, and so now could and would accept compliments in the same way that Elsie imagined she doubtless would have accepted rave reviews and bouquets long, long ago, had she ever become a star.

'You had better start learning the role straight away, Dottie,' Elsie said, suddenly and shrewdly. 'Because if you do not, you know what it is, you will land yourself in trouble with the management. They like the cast to be word-perfect before rehearsals start.'

'Of course I shall be word-perfect.' Dottie looked furiously at the departing Elsie. 'I know that!' she told the closing door. And then to the iron she said, 'I am not an amateur. Of course I shall be word-perfect before rehearsals begin.'

She banged the iron down on one of her boys' shirts and waggled it over the material in a strange zigzagging sequence all her own.

'As if I would not be word-perfect by the time rehearsals started!'

And she was, she was word-perfect by the time they all met in the kind of dreary drill hall, Elsie thought, looking round it with her usual sense of wonder that only managements always seem to be able to find without any problem. It was as if the flea-infested halls were opened only to, and for, particular kinds of penny-pinchers.

Small places of former worship down dreary side streets that no one else had ever heard of, or would ever know of, ever again. Places so obscure that, should you stop to ask the way from passers-by who had lived in the town for their whole lives, they would look at you astonished, shaking their heads, quite mystified. Small, unheated stone buildings with vague marks on the old, wooden floors that were relics of some equally unknown, no longer practised activity, some vital part of war-time work that no one any longer even spoke about.

Since the play they were rehearsing was a comedy, the atmosphere was one of determined courage, and the cast, wearing various degrees of temporary rehearsal costumes, started blocking the moves for Donald Bourton, who was producing it, as if they thought he was brilliantly talented, while all the time, as is normally the case in a comedy, feeling quite the opposite – all, that is, except Dottie.

Dottie, as she had boasted, had taken care to learn the lines before she came to rehearsal, and she was indeed word-perfect. She knew the lines as if she had written them herself, but the only trouble was, perhaps because it was so long since she had actually trodden the boards, it seemed she had completely forgotten how to *act*.

Elsie found her fascinating to watch, in a macabre sort of way. Dottie could sit and read the play all through, without a single hesitation, she too, like Elsie, having a photographic memory. What she could not do was speak the lines and move at the same time, and, as they all knew, this was actually what acting was all about.

Happily, Elsie was now contracted for the run of the play and thoroughly enjoying herself, so she cared less if Dottie was making an idiot of *herself*. Indeed she quite enjoyed watching her, and, for her sins, without a shred of guilt. Dottie had, after all, taken on the part, and of her own volition had undertaken to show everyone just what she had imagined, all these years, *she* was actually made of. And this was it. She was not made of brilliance. She had not been endowed with a golden talent, thwarted by marriage and childbirth, as she had, for year after year, loudly maintained – it became abundantly clear from day one that Dottie was made only of the stuff of amateurs.

Her gestures were mechanical to the point of hilarity, her sense of timing entirely absent, and her voice (a voice that she had always told her 'boys' was her greatest asset) a landlady's voice. It was the voice of a woman who had spent too much time complaining and haranguing. Worse than that, it was, actually, when Elsie listened to it with her usual detachment, the voice of a crotchety woman who having had her own way for most of her life was now being tested, given a chance and failing – and, worst of all, knew it.

'What shall we do about her? I mean, she is your agent, isn't she?'

Portly frowned. The whole spectacle of watching this old woman ruining a large part of the second act had long ago stopped being funny and become torture not just for Donald who was producing the play, but for all of them.

'Sack her!'

'But she's only been rehearsing for a week. We might get her better.'

'No one ever gets anyone better.'

'Donald thinks he can get her better—'

Elsie looked at Portly, and he was amazed to see the expression in her young eyes was one of light derision.

'That is just producer talk. No one ever *gets* anyone right, Portly. They can either act, or they cannot act. It is just a fact, isn't it? And obviously, Dottie can't act, poor soul, can she?'

Portly raised a hand. 'Thank God. At last! Now. That is how you must talk from now on.'

Elsie stared at him. 'How?'

'Like that. Stop enunciating the way you do, stop saying "I do not" and say "don't".'

Elsie coloured. 'Oh. Do I do that?'

'Yes, you do, and I wish you wouldn't. You make yourself sound *too ladylike*! Just talk

133

naturally, and all will be well. Talk naturally,' he repeated. 'You have a very pretty voice, you mustn't worry about crossing every t and essing every s.'

He put out a friendly hand and touched her on the arm, not wanting to hurt her feelings, and at the same time knowing that he must have, and not caring at all because it was for her own good.

'Oh, fine. So I – won't say "will not", I will say "won't", is that right?'

Portly nodded. The point having been made, he now only wanted to get back to his problem, their problem, of how to get rid of Dottie.

'So I sack her, and she takes you down with her?'

'She can't, not now I am contracted, can she?'

Portly stared at Elsie, suddenly realising, with no small sense of wonder, that she must have known all along that this was going to happen, that Dottie was going to be hopeless, that she would fail, but that it would matter less than a hill of beans, because Elsie would remain contracted.

'But – isn't she some sort of relation of yours? I mean, as well as being your agent?'

'No,' Elsie lied to him airily, and then, seeing he did not believe her, she added, 'at least not any more! Anyway, she will be pleased to get back to her other work.'

'Prefers being an agent, I expect.'

'Exactly.'

'I can understand that.'

'So, who will do the sacking?' Elsie stared up at Portly, smiling sweetly.

'Donald had better,' said Portly, just a little too quickly.

'How will he do it?'

'Oh, you know, in his usual way, take her out to dinner and tell her she is too good for the part, tell her it is all his fault for miscasting her. And then send her on her way with a pay-off and a promise of a *much* better part, very soon.'

'That sounds just a little bit better than calling her out of rehearsal and throwing her coat and handbag at her.'

'People don't do that, do they?' For a moment Portly lost his affable expression and managed to look appalled.

'I once saw a leading actress – Colleen MacNaughton – remember her?'

'Of course I remember Colleen MacNaughton.'

'I saw her having her handbag and coat thrown at her by the producer and not at the end of rehearsals – mid *line*!'

'That must have been quite something,' said Portly, quickly switching off as he always did when people talked about other people's shows. 'Now do you want to *know* about all this?'

'Of course not! I shan't know *anything*. No, when she tells me I will be indignant on her behalf. I will consider handing in my notice, and all that.'

'But not quite furious enough to do so, I hope?'

'Definitely not.'

Elsie found her mind wandering to the scene ahead.

Dottie would not cry at the reversal of fortune that was about to be meted out to her, because Dottie did not cry. What she would do was become angry. After which she would set to work on Elsie, pointing out that she too must be miserable in the production. She would tell her that Donald Bourton was a hopeless producer, that the rest of the cast was appallingly untalented and dragging Elsie down, that this was no way for her to make her grown-up debut in a straight play, and that no good whatsoever would come of the play anyway. The vogue for France and French plays was sure to pass, and it would be much better for Elsie to look for work in a musical where there would be more money.

Elsie was sure that was exactly what Dottie would do, but as always, Dottie confounded her.

Chapter Four

Coco Hampton had not been christened Coco. She had been christened Marjorie Mary, but within a few years of arriving at her dark grey boarding school she had been nicknamed Coco, although for what precise reason even Coco had now forgotten. The name had stuck because it suited her, and she had kept it for the same reason, so much so that she imagined that by now not even Oliver remembered what her real Christian names were. She had made sure to put herself down for registration at Ramad as Coco Hampton, realising that Marjorie Mary, while obviously genteel to a degree, would not be in the least bit suitable for someone who wanted to play about with a bit of acting before moving on to design costumes and sets.

The Hamptons, Coco's parents, had been the participants in a very public, and therefore shocking, divorce; the result of which had been that they had both to agree that neither of them was particularly suitable to bring up Marjorie Mary, the still small, but perhaps happily unique product of their brief union. As a result of this Coco had been handed over to guardians who lived in London, and being childless, were only too grateful to bring her up.

Quite apart from anything else, Coco had not liked living in the country, so being handed over to Frank and Gladys had been nothing but a huge relief. Even as a very small child she had hated ponies and riding and country life, longing only for the bright lights and fashionable environs, the cinemas and theatres of which she had occasionally heard her mother speak with such longing. She therefore had never, not even for an instant, blamed her mother for divorcing her Squire Toby father and shortly afterwards leaving with her new husband for an ambassadorial post in Paris.

What she did sometimes blame her mother for, however, once she had fallen in love with French fashion, was not bothering to try to fight for custody of her daughter just a little harder. Coco longed passionately to go to Paris and see for herself the wealth of beautiful clothes, not to mention the women who wore them, but she quite understood that the last thing her stepfather wanted was to have an over-active stepdaughter running about his embassy demanding to be taken to the fashion shows.

Her mother did send cheques, however, although to Gladys rather than to Coco herself; one always arrived somewhere round about the time of Coco's birthday – never quite on the day

– and another just before Christmas – a date which even she could not manage to ignore.

Gladys seemed to look forward to the arrival of the cheques (always signed by Coco's stepfather) quite as much as Coco.

'Ooh, look, Coco, fifty whole pounds,' she would breathe, flashing the cheque in front of her charge, and within a few minutes they would both be dressed in their best coats and, if it was Christmas, fur hats and fur muffs and fur-lined boots, and stepping out into the busy metropolis, hearts and minds set on visiting Harrods and Fortnum & Mason, or Woollands and Harvey Nichols, in short visiting all the shops that might have clothes suitable not just for Coco, but for Gladys too.

Because that was part of the strange pact that Coco and Gladys had made, at some point in the distant past, that if Coco was sent money, some of it always rubbed off on Gladys.

Not that Gladys lacked clothes, or anything else. She had everything that most fashionable women would want, and could possibly ever want. No, Coco shared her money with Gladys because Gladys could not bear anyone to spend money without her spending some too, and if Harold had put an embargo on any more spending, which he usually had, Coco knew that Gladys felt horribly bored and depressed. So, pity for her, and guilt, always forced Coco to invite Gladys to choose something for herself too. And guilt made Coco happy that Gladys was always

139

able to find something that she liked, so that both of them would be able to return home satisfied that the cheque had been shared out in the best possible way.

'You shouldn't have, really, you shouldn't,' Gladys would say every time, but the happy look to her, the many glances that she gave to whichever mirror she happened to be passing, always told Coco that, really – Coco *should*.

Now that she was studying the strange art of acting, of how to best become someone else, Coco thought of Gladys a great deal. This was partly because she missed her effervescent guardian with her too great passion for fashion, but more because Gladys, of all people, was the person who had most encouraged Coco to go into the theatre, to fulfil her ambitions. She had encouraged her in a way that was kind and well meant, but also insistent and persistent.

'You don't want to be dependent on a man for your money, not the way I am, Coco, really you don't. You want to have your own life and your own money, and make sure that you stay that way, with your own money and your own life, no matter what. You don't want to end up like me, always and ever dependent on the say-so of a man. Can't buy a pair of stockings, or a new handbag for spring, without going, cap in hand, to *Frank*. It is appalling. Turns one into a sort of servant, really. *Please sir, could I have some money for clothes!* What a thing. But nothing to be done now, not for me. Whereas for *you*, Coco, there is something that you can do. You can go out there and make a name for yourself, become somebody, just so that no one can ever, ever turn you into *no one*. That is what I have been turned into – no one. The person who goes along with Frank. His wife. A nobody. Honestly, I sometimes think that if I dressed up Mrs Gage instead of myself, if I dressed up my daily help as me, same dress and coat, same hat, no one would even notice, least of all *Frank!*'

So now, when required to stand up, say, in improvisation class, Coco would think of either Gladys or Mrs Gage, and she would become them, and to her astonishment, and sometimes to her derision, she gained praise, and was even singled out.

'Do you know not one girl in my class speaks to me – except to bag a fag off me? What have I done – *what*?'

'Trust you, Coco, you've put everyone's backs up, that's what.'

Oliver sprinkled brown sugar over the foamed milk top of his cappuccino coffee and they both watched with some interest as it gradually sank to the bottom of the cup.

'How do you mean, "trust me"? Oh, I know – you mean the opposite.' Coco blew out a puff of smoke and watched it making its lazy way towards the new modern lighting in the coffee bar. 'You mean "I can't trust you". People always seem to use phrases like that in the opposite way, if you notice. For instance, take Gladys. She is always saying "Don't you love it?" when she means quite the opposite.'

Oliver stared at Coco. She was like his sister. She could have been his sister, if he had had one, but since he had not he could only presume that she had been sent as a stand-in. Today she was wearing an outrageously large black hat, which she had pinned to her head with an Art Nouveau hatpin such as only old ladies seem to sport. Of course Coco looked so much the thing that it was difficult not to find yourself wondering if everyone should not wear such an outrageous outfit.

'Why don't you wear what all the other students wear, Coco, then they might be nicer to you? You stand out like a sore thumb – you know? None of them dress like you.'

'Maybe I don't want them to be nicer to me?'

'Maybe, but if it is of any interest, which knowing you it will not be, I would say your trouble is that you look too much the art student and too little the actress. That is what the trouble is with you, the way you look.'

'I know.' Coco smiled and stayed smiling as she pulled yet again on her cigarette. 'That is my trouble. It's not "the trouble with me"; it is my trouble, full stop. I never want to look like everyone else, not ever, not anywhere, and I just don't know why. Of course you are right, I should look more like an actress and less like an art student, but I just cannot bring myself to look so – well – *actressy*!'

They both laughed.

'You've made a name for yourself already – at least there's that, everyone knows who you *are*.'

'There you go *again*. What you really mean is what you said before – I stick out like a sore thumb. Perhaps I should just fling the towel in and forget about Ramad altogether?'

'Why? You're teacher's pet, you and that older student who does everything like Richard Burton – you know – Hugh Hughes or whatever he's calling himself at the moment.'

Coco's eyes wandered. They both knew that the true reason why Coco had brought up the subject was not that she had any intention of leaving the Academy, but simply that she wanted to talk about herself. That was why they had lunch together every day: they wanted to be sure that they had someone to listen to them talking about themselves, and as Coco now maintained, this was a great deal easier if you had known someone – as she put it – *for ever*.

'OK, Coco, we have fifteen more minutes until we have to go back, so now it is time to drag *me* on, love.'

'*Must* I?'

'Yes, you must. It's not fair otherwise.'

'Oh, very well. Your turn for *us* to talk about *you*.'

Oliver leaned over the table and tapped it. 'Should I – do you think I should grow a beard and stop washing, that kind of thing? I mean, so I can go up for more of the character parts?'

Coco considered Oliver's looks. He was actually too handsome for the character juvenile leads.

'It might be a good idea, for character parts, yes.' The expression on Coco's face was solemn. Sizing up her childhood friend with a cold eye, she went on, 'You haven't a chance as you look now. You look too chocolate box handsome. But on the other hand, it is no good growing a beard and stopping washing if your character remains as it is. That has to change too.'

'What is wrong with my character? I'm always nice to you.' Oliver smiled and stared in the mirror behind Coco's head.

'Stop looking at yourself in the mirror.'

'I can't.'

'Yes, you can. You can stop. It's an awful habit.'

'I'm so worried that I'm ugly – I keep having to check.'

'No, you're not. You're just terrified that you're not as beautiful as when you last looked!'

They both laughed.

'So, since it's still my turn to talk about me, what parts do you think are for me, will be best for me? For which I will be utterly perfect?' Oliver asked, at his most droll.

'Hamlet, obviously.'

Oliver looked sceptical. 'With my legs, I'm not so sure.'

'But Clifton is always raving about your legs. Anyway, Richard II – but we've been through this before, Ollie. You know the parts you are suited

144

for, it's just a question of having enough talent to do them.'

'Oh, I think I have the talent all right. It is just whether or not anyone else will ever spot it. If I don't make it Cliffie will be so, so disappointed in me. I don't know what he'll do if I don't make it.'

Coco, who was not as hard-hearted as she loved to pretend, promptly put out a sisterly hand and covered Oliver's with it.

'It's not fair, really. I mean, I am here, at this peculiar establishment, just for a lark, but it's very serious for you, and I keep forgetting that.'

'I don't,' Oliver told her gloomily.

'No, I don't suppose you do. By the way, did you know that – Yorkshire pudding is my favourite, favourite dish?'

This was Coco's new secret signal to Oliver to switch to his Yorkshire accent.

'Mine too. Yorkshire pudding, all golden and crisp.'

Oliver's light Yorkshire accent was instantly and securely back in place, as they both watched a fellow student passing their table, and then smiled. They had been using secret codes since they very first met as children.

'Did you know that Harold Liskeard – you know the film producer? He's coming round this afternoon, apparently. He's a friend of Bertrand's and they're having lunch together, and then coming to take a peek at us all, lucky old us.'

Of a sudden Oliver's eyes clouded with a

mixture of anxiety and ambition. He could see himself being chosen, of course, which they both knew was a distinct possibility. He was certainly the handsomest of all the students in his year, his looks standing out in every class that he attended.

'So now is your opportunity to gather stardom while you may, Oliver Lowell. There is, after all, no doubt in anyone's mind that you are the most likely to be chosen for a film, I mean with your looks – and don't look in the mirror!'

'Oh, I know, but *film* acting, love? I'm not sure it's me at all, really I am not.' Oliver lit a cigarette and puffed out his smoke too noisily.

'Much easier than acting on stage, *love*, really,' Coco told him in her best off-hand manner, at the same time standing up and moving off. She herself had no interest in being a film star but she could see that Oliver would, or could, make it straight away. They had surely only to point a film camera at him and the lens would fall passionately in love with him?

Later, as Harold Liskeard watched and listened in on their classes, as Coco had predicted, everyone could see that he had quite fallen in love with Oliver's looks, but Oliver was not chosen.

As Liskeard said later to the principal of the Academy, his old friend Bertrand, 'Oliver Lowell – is that his name – yes, he *would* have been perfect, but we're looking for a southerner, a public school type, and the Yorkshire accent –

well, it just won't do, and there isn't time, now, to iron it out. On the other hand, the girl with the crazy clothes.' He ran a finger down the list in front of them, looking for the name. 'Ah yes, here she is. Coco Hampton, that's her. She will be fine as the flighty Wren who falls in love with the admiral. Perfect, in fact. Typecasting, I should say. Can I get my people to get in touch with you?'

'Of course. She hasn't got an agent, but we can soon fix that up. How many days will she have on the film?'

'About three weeks, probably, not more. And then you can have her back.'

'I don't think we will want her back, not after a film. They're never the same after a film, Harold, you know that. They acquire two fatal drugs while doing a film.'

'Namely?'

'Ideas, and salaries. The sole purpose of the Academy is to accustom them to the notion that they are destined for the theatre and starvation, nothing more and nothing less. A film, even one, ruins all that.'

Coco stared at Bertrand. He was a tall, bespectacled man with a line in old suits that she felt sure just had to be old costumes from parts he had once played, because of course, like so many who ran classes and academies to teach the ever changing, never changing art of drama, Bertrand had once been an actor.

'Why does Harold Liskeard want *me*?'

'I gather he thinks you are typecasting, dear. Wants you to go along to see him, tomorrow afternoon. Don't get your hopes too high. If his director and all the rest don't like the look of you, you can still be turned away. But you know, don't worry too much. There's nothing much to film acting; just hit your mark and say the words, and gesture above the waist. Most of the time you'll find you play cards and gossip, eat breakfast, lunch and tea from early morning to cocktail hour, and generally try not to get into too much trouble on Sundays, when you're not required for filming. That's all.'

Coco stared at Bertrand. She could not, dared not tell him that she never wanted to act, that she still did not want to act, that she had only gone along to audition for entrance into his academy so that she could have an excuse to stay in London and not go to Norfolk with her guardians.

'What about Oliver *Lowell*?'

Coco always over-emphasised Ollie's new surname to remind herself of the change.

'*Oliver* Lowell? Oh, you mean the *Yorkshire* man? Oh yes, Harold was quite taken with him. With his looks, he could have been perfect, but he has the wrong accent. Shame, because he would have been ideal for the part of the fallen hero, apparently.'

Again Coco could not tell Bertrand that Oliver had put on his father's batman cum butler's accent for the sole reason that he wanted to be accepted at the Academy as a nice working class

148

type, and not get typecast as a public school twit.

'Oh, but he *can* do the public school officer type. I have heard him, you know.'

'No, no, my dear.' Bertrand shook his head. 'I am afraid not. No, you have to be born to it. He has not been here long enough to learn how to speak properly. I mean, I can tell, believe me. He is a Yorkshireman through and through, and nothing wrong with that, but not right for the film, not at all what he is looking for, although he may well be soon. That is why young people come here, among many other reasons, to be taught all that. How to handle their knives and forks correctly, and all that type of thing. No, it is obvious, he is a Yorkshireman through and through, I know. I should do, since I was born in Yorkshire.'

Coco went to open her mouth and say something, and then closed it instead. What was the use? There was nothing *to* say.

'You, on the other hand, are, apparently, just what Harold Liskeard is looking for. You are a very lucky girl, Miss Hampton, do you know that? Only a few weeks here, and cast in a film role already. How people will envy you! So much so, in fact, that if I were you I would not bother to come back to the Academy after this.'

'But I want to. I mean, my guardians, they want me to, they will want me to. They have paid for me to come here.'

'Your guardians? I see, and what do they do? Are they in the theatre?'

'No, antique English oak furniture, actually. At least when last heard of.'

'Well, there you are then.'

'Where, exactly? I mean, I don't understand.'

'If your guardians were in the theatre, they would say exactly what I have just said to you, Miss Hampton. Never darken the doors of this academy again.'

'But why not?'

'Why not? Because, Miss Hampton, no one will speak to you. It will be as if you have measles. Believe me. It will not be worth the agony.'

Coco stared at him. She could not pretend that she would miss the classes, which she was already finding more tedious even than art school, but she would miss the lunches with Ollie, the gossips in the coffee bars, lining herself up against other hopefuls.

'Do you think the other students might be jell-jell? Is that what you're saying?'

'Jealous? Miss Hampton!' The ex-actor turned principal paused and then smiled wearily before continuing, 'Miss Hampton. You are clearly from a privileged background, you have just landed a part in a film – no matter what kind of film, or whether it will be a huge success or never seen or heard of again, it is a *film*, and you will have a small part that you will undoubtedly register in; you will be quite well paid, not brilliantly, but quite well, and you are asking me if the other students will be *jealous* of you? Have you left your brains at home, Miss Hampton? They will be ready to kill you. If you care for your life, you leave the Academy now.'

'I see.' Coco paused for a minute, seeing his point suddenly, and then thinking of actually being paid she quickly became businesslike. 'I haven't even got an agent. Could you recommend an agent to me?'

'Of course. My wife. She is an agent, and she will look after you as if you were her very own child, the direct offspring of her loins.' He produced a card. 'Go and see her.'

'When?'

'Now. Straight away. As far as I am concerned you are a back number. And . . .' He smiled for the first time. 'Good luck, Miss Hampton. Not that you will need it.'

Bertrand shook Coco's hand, and the expression on his face was one of envy mixed with solemnity. He might have been handing her some select prize for best voice production, or best dramatic performance, so serious was his expression, so grave and sad the look in his eyes.

'I have to tell you, Miss Hampton, that at this particular moment I would do anything to be your age and cast in my first film. That time of *my* life was taken up with the war. How lucky you post-war students are, to grow up as you did after the war, and how fortunate. May *your* young years never be snatched away in the same manner as *my* years were snatched from me, and those of my friends and colleagues too. May that never happen to you, or your friends.'

Coco tried to look solemn, but only partially succeeded. She hated older people reminding her of the war and how lucky her generation was not to have fought, and all that. After all, try as you might, you could not be them, and feel sorry as you might you could not roll the years back and give them a bit of your luck. It was not after all like sharing a Mars Bar, or a pile of Marmite sandwiches.

And besides, even mention of the war made her feel hugely guilty, as if she had inadvertently been the cause of it. As if her generation, having insisted on being born, had somehow *made* the previous generation fight, for *them*, for all those babies they had produced in the war. As if, had her generation not been born, something better might have happened, or someone might have thought of doing something sensible, to save all the bother, like shooting Hitler or poisoning him, or something.

'Goodbye, Mr Bertrand, and thank you very much.'

'You've only been here a fortnight.'

'I know, but just think, if I had not been here a fortnight and Mr Liskeard had not been in the army with you, and then at the Shakespeare Memorial in the old days, been one of your friends, you know, I would not have been cast, would I? I mean, it is all due to you, really.'

Coco was being a creep, and she knew it, trying to make up to Bertrand for the fact that she was young and perhaps going to be successful whereas it was all over for him, he just had his academy, full of people younger and luckier than himself.

Bertrand sighed, but since he looked as if he was about to remind Coco, yet again, of how terribly lucky her generation was, how grateful they must be to life at all times, she quickly fled the room, snatching up her coat and ramming her outrageous hat on top of her head but still feeling, despite everything, somehow completely to blame for everything that had happened to him, or – perhaps worse – not happened to him.

Oliver on the other hand was furious, but at least he had the grace to show it.

'Trust you, Coco!'

'Stop saying that, Ollie, really, stop saying "trust you"! It is just so damned irritating.'

They were back in the coffee bar, and Oliver was looking not just both angry and morose, but even more as if he now had to take the great decision of his life and not only look and be angry, which was after all fashionable, but also grow a beard and become fascinated by tramps and things.

'And I suppose the great Phyllis Brandon has now signed you up to the agency? I suppose Bertrand's wife, the great Miss Brandon, has signed you on, I suppose, has she?'

Coco nodded. 'Yes, Ollie. What do you *think*? Of course she has. I've got a job, haven't I? Agents always take you on once you're working, you know that. It's when you're out of work and need a job that they don't want to know, love, *savez*?'

'Oh God, and you've got an agent too! God, how I hate you, I can't help it, Coco, I really hate you.'

Oliver leaned forward and banged his head on the coffee table in front of him, narrowly missing his luncheon omelette.

Coco watched him with her usual detachment. He was such a clodhopper, such a great bungling twitto, such a total lumbering fool, and he always had been, but nevertheless she was in no mind to stop him making a fool of himself with his anger and envy, because it was obviously much healthier for him to carry on as if he was having his toenails pulled out, get it out into the open, let his ill feeling flow all over the coffee bar, than to bottle it all up.

'Why *you*, Coco? I mean you don't even *like* acting! You don't even want to be an *ahctress*, *dahling*? It is just so *unfair*. So unfair. *So* unfair that you should be chosen while I who am passionate about acting are – is – completely ignored. It is – are – unfair. And I hate you.'

'Yes, it is – are – unfair,' Coco agreed, eating her own omelette as fast as she could, because she knew that in the mood he was in it was perfectly possible that Oliver would suddenly stick his fork into her food and finish it before she could. For a moment she experienced a twinge of guilt as she remembered that it was she who had encouraged Oliver to cultivate his Yorkshire accent, thereby losing the film. 'But life is unfair,' she reminded him. 'If it wasn't you would have been born *ugly*, instead of divinely handsome, and so on and so on. You just have to get on with it. I may be cast today, *you* will probably be cast tomorrow.'

'But you only enrolled at Ramad for a lark. Your heart's not even *in* acting.'

'I know, but that is the whole joy of the situation, because if you think about it, I shan't be *doing* any acting, Ollie. If you think about it, acting is the last thing I will be doing.'

Oliver straightened up, his eyes suddenly brightening. 'You mean you've turned it down, you've turned the film *down*?'

He looked quite excited at the idea.

'No, I mean, film acting is *not* acting. If you ask me all film acting is is just standing still and thinking your feelings. I shall be being, not acting, that is what I shall be. I shall not act at all, not in front of a camera, I shall *be*.'

'Who told you that?'

'No one. I just thought it up.'

'They haven't even *screen* tested you yet,' Oliver moaned. 'They don't even know whether you will be any good.'

'I know,' Coco agreed cheerfully, 'nor they have. But apparently, Bertrand's missus told me, when I went to see her yesterday, Harold Liskeard always *knows*. He has X-ray eyes or something, knows straight away whether someone has It or not, whether they will read on camera, and all that baloney.'

'It's not baloney! Coco! Wake up! This is you up there on screen, fame, success, everything, it is you.'

'I just hope they offer me a decent fee,' Coco said, having bolted her omelette and now viewing her empty plate with some satisfaction. 'I mean, I hope they don't scrimp on the payment.'

'A bit tricky, isn't it, I mean if Bertrand's wife, Liskeard's friend, is your agent? It doesn't leave you much room for manoeuvre, does it, *dahling*?'

'No, apparently she gets good fees for all her people, no matter who her husband is friends with. She is quite, quite ruthless.' Coco lit a cigarette and because Oliver had not finished eating his double cheese omelette she blew the smoke into the air.

'I just think it's so *unfair*! You getting a plum part like that, and the rest of us who really, *really* want to be actors, don't get near it. Not even within a half a mile of it, so unfair!'

Coco wanted to say, 'Well, if you hadn't been such a complete twit and swanned about pretending to be Clifton you would have been cast too.' But since Oliver was carrying on like one o'clock she felt that this was neither the time nor the place. So she smiled instead, even though she did not feel in the least bit sorry for him, or guilty about being cast.

After all, she had not put herself up for the part.

She had been chosen by Liskeard for no better reason than that he thought she would be right. If films and acting people were that superficial, what was it to her? Why should she care? Besides, she needed the money, whatever it was going to be. She wanted to buy herself a car, any car, so she could dash about the countryside, go to auctions, and buy up old costumes and clothes, that kind of thing. As far as she was concerned parts in films were only a way forward to another more interesting, less limited, future.

Still, since she loved Oliver, although strictly only as a brother, she put out a comforting hand and touched his arm.

'Look, Ollie, I know it's tough on you, me getting a part and not you, but don't worry, you'll get there soon, and I will be out on my ear – sure to be – after the first day's shoot, because as you say it doesn't interest me. I shan't be any good, I'm sure, so don't worry. I will be a flop, for you.'

But Oliver's eyes told Coco that he was refusing to be comforted by her flippancy.

'No, you won't, Coco,' he said, the look in his eyes one of complete, if accepting, defeat. 'You see, Liskeard is right. You *have* got star quality.'

Coco stared at him, her large, round eyes quite disbelieving. 'Get on.'

'No, it's true, really it is. You have got the most enormous star quality. Why do you think the rest of the girls in your class hate you, *dahling*? Not because old Liskeard chose you, because they hated you before that. No, it's because you have

157

It. They may have beauty, you have It. That elusive something that makes you stand out.'

'It's just my funny clothes—'

'But your funny clothes are all part of it, *dahling*. All part of the whole great quality thing that sets you apart from all the rest of the boring Brigitte Bardot or Sophia Loren lookalikes that are crowding this place with their spiky eyelashes and beehive hairdos. You are you, Coco, and you always have been, ever since we first met. I could take the *you* bit of you, and set it out in the middle of Kensington Gardens, or wherever we were – the Classic Cinema, the Comedy Theatre – and say "That girl is going to be a star of some kind." Even when you were a little girl people always picked you out, always turned round and took a second look when you passed them.'

'No, Ollie dear, that was *you* they were taking a second peak at, not me, you fool.'

But for once Oliver would not be diverted from what he wanted to say, not even to talk about himself.

'To tell you the truth I didn't really want you to be at the Academy, because I knew it would take away from *me*! And yet another part of me did, because of, because of – just that. Because of the fact that there is no one else like you, Coco Hampton. You are and always have been totally yourself, whereas the rest of us are nowhere near anything like we should be. We settle for being pale grey and shadowy, too damned afraid to let it shine out, the bit of us that is unique, but you do

158

that, you let it shine out and eclipse the rest of us. And the beauty of it is, you don't even know it, and if you did, it would probably go.'

Coco stared at Oliver, and lit another cigarette.

She was determined to remain completely unflattered by Oliver's speech, and disbelieving. What was more, she thought she knew exactly why Oliver had made it – he wanted to put her off. He wanted to compliment her so largely, so unexpectedly, so fulsomely, that once in front of the cameras she would freeze up. Luckily she had known him for so long that she had taken care not to hear him very well, and certainly not to take in what he was saying, so instead of looking moved and pleased she nodded at someone else coming into the coffee bar and muttered, 'Yorkshire pudding.'

'Thanks, but I hardly need to bother. None of the other actors in this place ever listen to a word anyone else says anyway.'

Oliver sighed and looked ungrateful at the same time. He was beginning to be fed up with going around being Clifton; it was beginning to get him down.

'So that is you taken care of, going to be a great glamorous film star. What about *me*? What will I do now that you are going to be a film star and I am going to be lumbered in this place with no Coco to have a laugh with me? I mean to say.'

'Mmm.' Coco smiled, her eyes half closed, loving the moment. Oliver, the coffee bar, the possibility of money coming in, the lovely warming reality of it was suddenly washing over her. 'You know that old actor I used to know, Ollie? Percy Howard? You know, the one that was a friend of Gladys?' As Oliver nodded, looking round the coffee bar, not in the least bit interested, she went on, 'Well, he told me there were two things that you should never do to an actor. One was give him an intonation, and the other was compliment him. Yes, that was what he said. Two of the most cruel things you could do, he said.'

'Mmm.' Oliver had caught sight of himself in the mirror once more and was wondering if he really should grow a beard, or just sideboards. He was sure that he needed something to 'rough' up his image.

'Yes,' Coco persisted. 'Yes, that was what he said. You must never compliment another player, you know, like saying *I love that thing you do with the pipe in the second act, darling*, that kind of thing, because then, whatever they were doing with the pipe that might or might not be terribly clever, well, it goes away, and never, ever comes back.'

Oliver stared at her. 'What do you mean?'

Coco smiled again, but this time it was a sphinx-like smile.

'Just that,' she told him, her face at its most innocent. 'Thought it might help you. Little bits of wisdom from older members of the profession, passed down through the ages, treasured traditions of how to go on.'

'I just can't believe you getting a part in a film after only a fortnight at drama school. I should really hate you, I feel that most strongly, that I should really hate you, but I am damned if I do.'

'Don't worry, Ollie, I expect you soon will!'

Coco laughed and Oliver smiled back wanly, stroking his chin, thinking to himself that, yes, really, he might grow a beard after all.

Chapter Five

Dottie was crying. It was the most miserable sound that Elsie had ever heard. It was not like stage crying at all, no great wailing and snivelling, just a quiet, controlled, sad sound, the kind of sound that could be passed by and not noticed, if you were not related to it, or did not think yourself in some way the architect of it, a crumpling of tissue paper sort of a sound, seeming not to last long, but held in the air in some way, just as the sighing of the wind through an old house can stay in the consciousness of the listener long after it has ceased.

Elsie tiptoed back to her bedroom, horrified. She had never known Dottie less than irritated; she was nearly always furious. Certainly Elsie had never seen her more than momentarily buffeted, and now she was crying. Elsie closed her door as quietly as she had ever closed it, facing the ghastly truth of that sound. It was, it had to be, because Donald Bourton had finally done the dirty deed: taken Dottie out to dinner and sacked her.

Having quietly shut the door, Elsie stood for a

moment in the middle of her bedroom as if she was waiting for a producer's voice to come from the stalls to direct her next move. Then, lifting the old blackout blind that still hung at her window, she peered out into the spring night of the old seaside town.

Portly had assured Elsie that Donald would be very kind, that he would be more than reasonable, but now that Dottie was crying, something that was in itself utterly unbelievable, it seemed to Elsie that the producer must have done or said something quite horrifying for Dottie to have returned home in tears.

Momentarily distracted, she found herself watching an old man making his way drunkenly home, sitting first on one bench overlooking the seafront before rising unsteadily and continuing to the next. As she observed him by the light of the old-fashioned lamps it occurred to her that no actor she had yet seen had captured a drunkard's walk accurately, always seeming to miss the desperation that lay behind the determination to try to appear sober, just as she, at that moment, was desperately trying to pretend that she could not still imagine that she could hear Dottie crying, if not in actuality, but in her head. That sound, slight but persistent, that was causing Elsie agonies of guilt.

Elsie climbed into bed again and pulled the pillow over her head. 'It is not all my fault that Dottie has been sacked, is it?' she asked herself in the darkness of her bedclothes.

Of course, it was certainly her fault that Dottie had been cast, but not that she had been sacked. It was not her fault that Dottie had been so bad, that was Dottie's fault, surely? Where lay the blame, and if there was blame, did it matter? Dottie had been so, so bad that it had finally proved impossible for anyone to look at her. Not just Elsie, but none of the other actors could watch her stilted performance, first the words and then the gestures, and last of all the feet. She had even counted under her breath as she moved. 'One, two, three, the table, four, five six – the door.' It had been excruciating to watch, positively sweat-making.

Yet, Elsie asked the bedclothes, should she go to her? Was that where her duty lay? To go and attend to her grandmother?

She sat up in bed. She knew that she should, but she also knew that Dottie, whose pride came before everything, would not want Elsie to see her crying, or to know that she had been upset. Determined to try to alleviate her own guilt, but not knowing quite how to do it, she finally decided to knock on the door, risking her grandmother's fury, while at the same time using as an excuse that she was not feeling well, or something like that. She would also make sure to make a great deal of noise to warn Dottie of her coming. However, it seemed that was not now going to be necessary, because the sound of the torn off, tightly held in sobs appeared to have ceased.

Elsie knocked gently on the door to Dottie's

sitting room, relieved to hear the old wireless playing, and at the same time the sound of Dottie blowing her nose fiercely.

'What was that? Who is that? Was that someone? Is there someone there?'

She had obviously turned down the wireless to listen, so Elsie knocked again, this time a little louder.

'It's only me, Dottie. I have a headache and can't sleep, so I wondered if I could get us both a cup of Horlicks or cocoa, or something?'

'Nothing, nothing for me, Elsie,' Dottie called in a shaking, tearstained voice. 'Nothing at all.'

'Are you all right, Dottie?'

Bravely Elsie stood on, finding she was staring at the door as if it was indeed the spirit of her redoubtable grandmother, as if she was in fact standing in front of her.

'No, of course I am not all right.'

Of a sudden Dottie flung open the door and stood before Elsie in what Elsie knew to be her best evening dress, a sequined pre-war top, a long black crepe skirt, about 1935 probably, Elsie found herself thinking distractedly, not looking at the mascara streaks her grandmother was busy wiping from her face.

'And how you, of all people, can come knocking on my door at this time of night, when you know what you know, I do not *know*. How you can sleep at night, I know less. How you can even talk of sleeping at night is even more a mystery, you little *viper*.'

Elsie lost all colour. She did not need a mirror to know that she had lost all colour because she was sure she could actually feel all her colour draining from her and seeping away. So much so that she would not have been surprised if she had looked down and seen it flowing off down the corridor, a stream of colour, trickling off back to her own room.

'I don't understand, Dottie!'

'Oh yes, you do! You double-crossing little *bitch*!'

Elsie felt her mouth going dry, knowing at once that someone must have double-crossed her, but not quite knowing who it could have been, because she imagined that she trusted Portly Cosgrove more than any human being whom she had ever met.

'Dottie, what do you mean?'

'Oh, come off it, *Elsie Lancaster*, I know what you agreed to, I know everything. Donald Bourton told me. He told all, Elsie. He said *you* were un-happy with my performance, that *you* thought it was too much for my health, that *you* had suggested I should be removed and given some-thing less strenuous, that I had heart trouble, or something. And since *you* are his precious little star, he is replacing me, on *your* suggestion!'

Elsie opened her mouth to say something about Donald Bourton, about his perfidy, and then the cold reality of caution struck.

She had never yet known Dottie to tell the 'so help me God' type of truth, not ever. She had never yet known her not lie, in some way or other. Not creative lies as in *I was once a great star*, no, Dottie told small, twisted, furtive lies, lies that laid blame somewhere else, absolving her of guilt. It did not matter if it was a napkin she had burned while ironing, or a pair of stockings she had snagged on a piece of furniture, there was always a reason why it was not her fault.

If that wretched Mr Labell had not barged in and talked the hind leg off a donkey, I wouldn't have left the iron on . . .

Elsie realised, almost instantly, and certainly happily, that this might easily be just such another occasion: that the story of Donald Bourton blaming Elsie for Dottie's dismissal might well be one of Dottie's endless fantasies, fantasies that if she laid them end to end would very likely stretch the whole length of the sea front outside the window; and some of her colour started to return.

Dottie would never, ever blame herself for her amateur acting and rusty technique; she would have to quickly find someone else to blame. Naturally, within a very few minutes of Donald Bourton's giving her a diplomatic and merciful release from the play, she would have alighted on the idea of blaming Elsie, but not in the way that Elsie had first thought she would: not for persuading her to do the part in the first place, but landing poor old Donald Bourton in it by making out that *he* had placed the blame for Dottie's removal from the cast firmly at Elsie's door.

'I shall speak to Donald in the morning,' was all

Elsie heard herself saying, and then she shut her mouth tight, and Dottie's bedroom door with it. Hardly had she done so when Dottie wrenched it open again.

'And there is no point in you speaking to Donald Bourton, Elsie, he is in management. He will never, ever tell you the truth, and if you think he will, you must be quite, quite mad.'

'No, I shall. I shall speak to him in the morning.'

'You will do no such thing.' Dottie stood in the corridor, powdering her nose with a small feathery powder puff and staring aimlessly at herself in an old-fashioned Art Deco powder compact as she busily changed conversational tack. 'As it happens I have no wish to continue in the play. I *was* unhappy in it. Unhappy with my performance, and yours, I may say. No, I shall be quite happy to be out of that wretched play, and away from those shoddy standards that you all seem so happy with. I shall be happy to be back in my own dear home with my boys to look after, my boys who really care for me. But I shall never forget what you have done to me, Elsie, not ever. And you yourself, if you have any conscience whatsoever, will wish to move out of here. Leave. You will leave. At once. After all, if you think about it, it will not, in view of what you said to Donald Bourton, be very comfortable if you stay on here. Besides, you have a job now. You have a tour.' She prepared to shut her bedroom door once again. 'Oh, and get yourself another agent, Elsie. I can't – no, I don't *want* to represent someone as two-faced as you, never again. Just don't want it.'

She shut the door again, quite heartily, and the sound of the small, fractured sobs having ceased, Elsie could hear her turning up the old-fashioned mahogany wireless.

Elsie returned to her own room, and sat on at the window where she had been previously seated, feeling as muddled and at the same time bereft and shocked as she had ever felt.

She did not like living with Dottie, now that she was older, but on the other hand the thought of leaving at once, and finding digs, was not the most entrancing idea she had ever entertained. And then too, finding an agent might be difficult.

And again, had Dottie been lying? Or had Donald Bourton really shopped Elsie? Had he really, after all that Portly had promised, laid the blame at Elsie's door, and therefore, for whatever reason, cowardice or carelessness, made her life with Dottie totally untenable?

'Of course Donald would never say such a thing!' Portly looked appalled. 'Good God, I would trust Donald with my life, Elsie. No, he is not that kind of person, really he isn't. And anyway you must know that it would be ridiculous, that he would know that you wouldn't forgive him for betraying you like that. No, Donald would never say anything like that, Elsie. I promise you.'

Portly looked mature and kind, and at the same time his round, dark eyes looked troubled too. He was genuinely shocked at what Elsie had just told him, and at the same time worried. He did not want anything to upset the person whom he thought of as their brightest young star. He wanted everything to be smooth sailing for her.

'I'll ask him, of course. I'll try and find out, if you like, but really, if my word is anything to go by, no – Donald would never do something like that.'

'No point in asking him.'

Elsie looked across the dingy little side room in which they were standing. Outside in the main hall they could both hear Act Two being rehearsed, and the assured, and for them reassuring, tones of a professional actress playing the part of the housekeeper.

They could also hear Donald laughing, a great, fruity rumble that echoed across the rehearsal hall as the cast, refreshed and reinvigorated, brought more and more invention to their roles.

'Plenty of happiness in there, at any rate.' Portly nodded towards the hall, and for the first time Elsie smiled. It was true. With the arrival of poor Dottie's replacement had come immense artistic relief to all concerned.

'Oh, and by the way, Elsie.' Portly stopped Elsie as she prepared to go back to rehearsal, the matter now closed, since they both knew that the truth, whatever it might be, would never now be discernible. 'How come all the luggage et cetera in the hall outside? None of my business I know, but are you intending to spend the night in the rehearsal hall? Because if you are this is taking dedication just a half-inch too far, I should have thought.'

'I've been chucked out of my lodgings, and – and no time to find any more before ten o'clock this morning.'

Just in time Elsie avoided any kind of reference to Dottie's being not just her agent, and a so-called distant relative, but her landlady too, not to mention her only relation.

'Oh, what a blow.' Portly stared at her. 'Like to move in with us?'

'How do you mean?' Nothing in Elsie's calm manner indicated either suspicion or fear despite the fact that she was momentarily experiencing both.

'Donald and I rent a house further along the coast, five miles out of town. If you would like, you could rent the wing from us? It's furnished, quite cosy but best of all quite self-contained, so you will not be disturbed by Donald's singing at unreasonably early hours. He is a lark, I am afraid, whereas I am an owl.'

'Do you really mean that?'

'If I didn't, would I be asking you?'

Elsie gave Portly a sudden hug. 'You are kind.'

After which she slipped off back to rehearsal leaving Portly head over heels in love with her.

As promised, the house that Portly Cosgrove and Donald Bourton shared was at the top of a short carriage drive and overlooked the sea, which, on an afternoon in early spring, seemed to be a very different sea from the one Elsie had been able to glimpse from her grandmother's house.

This was a free sea. This was a sea filled with the hope of a new play, a play in which she had a starring role, and the admiration of two men who picked her up and dropped her back again outside her own front door as if she was a piece of Dresden china that would break if she was allowed to walk further than two yards on her own. This was a sea that sparkled and shone as soon as the sun came out. This was a sea that was no backdrop, but real and salty, quite unlike the one that she had only ever seemed to notice at the end of a long hard day spent either out trying to get work, or helping with the lodgers. Here was a sea that beckoned beguilingly, an anxious dog always ready to bound up and drop a stick at her feet. And in her new house there were no lodgers, and for all she knew, setting aside her own few clothes, no ironing either, only Portly Cosgrove and Donald Bourton, laughing and whistling, singing and playing records fresh from America. Here at Mount Vernon, as the house was called, Elsie felt that she might, finally, have arrived. And young though she still was she realised that she had at long, long last crossed the tracks, and she had Dottie to thank for the complete change in her fortunes.

It had taken an age to pack up all her things, and of course she had not had enough suitcases.

Dottie had gone out, very noisily, ostentatiously leaving her a note on the hall table, a note that commanded her to be out of her room by noon because there would be a new lodger coming in that afternoon.

Dottie had underlined *that afternoon* in her note, and Elsie had no trouble believing her because, when all was said and done, a theatrical boarding house, or digs, or bed and breakfast, or whatever it was in which she had spent her whole life, never had any real trouble filling its rooms, if it had any pretensions to comfort.

Of course, Elsie, along with all the lodgers, was well used to Dottie leaving notes for everyone on the shabby little hall table. What she was not used to was having to leave the house where she had grown up, for ever, and by noon, as if she was just any old lodger who had offended Dottie in some way.

Mr Labell, looking terrified but resolute (wearing much the expression that Elsie imagined aristocrats in the French Revolution might have worn), perhaps out of sudden pity for her situation, gave her one of his very old small leather trunks, and it was into this that Elsie packed all her childhood and other belongings. Dusted down, and the cobwebs removed, it still looked more like a prop than a private person's suitcase as it was fitted into the back of a station taxi and driven, with Elsie, to rehearsal.

But, sad though she had felt leaving her room and the house, never to return, it was not

173

until Elsie found herself unpacking her few possessions at the Mount that she faced the moment of real truth. For it was only when she saw all her stupid possessions in another room, somewhere completely different, for the first time in their, and her life, that she started to feel the grip of true homesickness, that searing aching pain that seems to be more of a sickness than illness itself.

It was not just that her few things looked really too pathetic for words. Worse than that was the feeling that all around her there was no one else near by. With Portly and Donald occupying the main part of the house, Elsie for the first time in her life realised that she was quite, quite alone. There was no one to walk past the window, below in the street, no one to tread past her door, no Dottie to call impatiently for her, no new lodger to introduce to the old ones, no old lodgers to ask her in for cups of tea or cocoa. No one would stop her on the stairs and ask after her rehearsals as she carried laundry up and down, and there was no sound of Dottie's old wireless turned up too loud. She was quite alone, and at peace, and after only a couple of hours inevitably she found herself wondering if she was in fact dead.

The relief when Portly rang her doorbell and asked her into the main part of the house for a drink was therefore indescribable.

Almost as indescribable was how beautiful Elsie looked when, later, around cocktail hour, she strayed into Portly's part of the house wearing an old-fashioned dress of sprigged muslin supported by stiff petticoats that rustled. The kind of dress that Donald and Portly mutually imagined might have been worn in a drawing room comedy at the beginning of the decade, together with a large straw hat decorated by velvet ribbons which tied under the chin.

'Oh, but you look so pretty, and that is *such* a lovely dress.'

Portly stared at Elsie, intent on keeping detachment in his voice while not bothering to keep the admiration out of his eyes.

'It was given to me. It's actually an old costume, made for Vivien Leigh, but she never did the part, and they sold off all her costumes to help defray the costs, because Patricia Miller who was cast instead was too big for them. Anyway, I saw them advertised, and *me voilà*, my dear!'

Elsie did not, as many another young actress might have done, 'twirl'. Instead, she sat herself down on the chintz sofa near the window and arranged her skirts so beautifully around her that, it seemed to Portly, she succeeded in looking as if she had just arrived on wires from the wings, or on wings from the sea, and settled herself as a bird or a butterfly might, with that particular degree of delicate artistry that only nature seems to be able to practise.

Portly sighed, his head on one side.

'I shall always remember you like this,' he told her. 'I shall always remember this early spring evening, the sunlight on the sea out there, the sun itself sinking down, that sofa, that dress, and

175

even' – as Donald Bourton came in carrying a bottle of champagne – 'and even Donald, I shall even remember him. There.' He shut his eyes. 'It has been painted on my mind. I always carry a sketch book in my mind, you know. It's really because I can't draw or paint, so when the moment arrives I quickly sketch, *et voilà!*'

He opened his eyes again, and they all laughed.

'Portly is such an old queen, isn't he?' Donald rolled his eyes and set the bottle of champagne down on the bar in the corner of the room. 'Don't you love bars in drawing rooms? It has always been my fantasy, to turn a sitting room into a bar, but to have one in the corner of the room is next best really, and not bad, not bad at all.'

Taking some glasses from the shelf he put them down on the bar, and beckoning to the other two he waved to the leather-covered bar stools, and then to the nuts and snacks he was setting out.

'*Asseyez-vous, mesdames and messieurs, je vous en prie!* The Bar Bourton is now open!'

Portly helped Elsie on to one seat and sat himself down on one of the others, and they all laughed as if they were doing something rather shocking, which they were really, because Portly and Donald knew only too well that drinking at a bar led to more drinking, and drinking late when in rehearsal was frowned upon by everyone who was anyone in the theatre.

'I really must go to bed,' Elsie confessed, a couple of hours later, and she went off, kissing her hand to the other two, leaving them still at the bar.

Having undressed and washed, she tumbled into her lone bed thinking only of the luck that had recently befallen her, having for the first time for some hours quite put behind her the fact that her only relation in this world no longer wanted to have anything to do with her.

She closed her eyes and fell asleep, and when she awoke in the morning she found that she could hardly remember that twelve hours earlier she had felt so homesick that if she could have run all the way home to Dottie and the lodgers, she would have done. But, as it was, she contented herself with bathing and dressing herself, while from afar she could hear the sound of Donald singing somewhere around, in a strong baritone voice, and, a little later, Portly's voice raised on the telephone as he argued with someone or other's agent. And all the time, although alone and awake, she did not feel a second of the pain she had felt when she had arrived at the Mount the previous evening. In fact, if she thought about it, Dottie had now become as much part of her past as everyone else in her family. In throwing Elsie out of her life, Dottie had effectively freed her. From now on she would make her way on her own. She would travel alone, by herself, and there would be no one to whom she had to feel grateful or who would expect her to be subservient.

Rehearsals beckoned. She would make the play succeed, whatever happened. She would make sure that the local critics boomed her performance to the skies. She would see to it that everyone who had seen the play in the West End, starring Gwen Leronde, would say that Elsie Lancaster was better, that they had never thought that anyone could be better than Gwen Leronde, but that Elsie Lancaster most definitely was, that she was everything and more in the part than anyone else could or would ever be.

She checked her image in the mirror. She still looked as she had the day before, but she was more than she had been the day before. She was now a grown-up.

The time for the curtain to go up on the first night had arrived. Rehearsals had flown by, as rehearsals for a play that the cast is enjoying always seem to do, and now the audience, that voracious animal, that great chattering set of individuals that seemed to be intent on devouring anyone or anything that displeased it, was busily settling itself, making itself comfortable before dispatching any object of its displeasure within seconds of a sighting. Elsie stared at them through the spyhole set to the side of the stage. The whole town was out front, but no one that she knew, thank God, would be in the audience. That was one of the unending blessings of Dottie's throwing her out of the house. There was no one sent by the great landlady to spy on Elsie, to report back on how the play had or had not gone; no one of whom Elsie had to be afraid, no pair of eyes belonging to someone who knew her, who would sit in silent, unmoved, critical judgement on her.

The very thought was such a relief that her heart seemed to burst with happiness as she skipped back to the number one dressing room. No one but her and a bunch of strangers was a fair contest, and it was a contest that she knew she could win, and would.

Whatever anyone says, a light heart is actually a prerequisite for the lightest of comedies, and so the actual moment when Elsie stepped gracefully on to the stage to speak her first line was for her a moment of joy. She knew that she looked perfect, and she felt assured, happy and relaxed, waiting only for the audience to welcome her into their hearts, take her to them, make her their own, as she had read in so many accounts of theatrical debuts. Nothing could go wrong, the cast loved her, Donald loved her, Portly loved her, and now the audience would too. She was quite sure of their welcome, until she heard the laugh.

It happened as the lights seemed to hit her, and she opened her mouth to say her first line – the laugh, the unmistakable laugh that only Dottie could produce, the long, rippling laugh that she sometimes gave when she was listening to some hit radio show or other. Elsie did not need to look towards the stalls. She knew just where the old devil would be. She would be sitting in the front row, leaning forward, ready to 'fright her' as she always called it, because there were two things at which Dottie was really quite accomplished – besides ironing that is – and one was 'standing people up' and the other was 'frighting them'. She had always kept a little black book in which she wrote the names of those who had offended her, and it was they who became the objects of Dottie's frighting.

'Off to fright old Eddie Griffiths,' she would tell Elsie proudly, before making one of her rare attendances at a theatre. For, to Elsie's certain knowledge, the only time Dottie ever went to the theatre was to pay out some old enemy who, unbeknownst or beknownst to them, had upset Dottie or her husband or daughter in the dim and distant past. Which was why she kept her little black book filled with names, and why she checked them against the cast lists of forthcoming productions coming to town.

Sometimes it was true she would let them off, but only if one of the lodgers told her that the person in question was known to be dying, or something similar. Otherwise, they got Dottie's treatment.

And now Elsie was getting Dottie's treatment, and so she knew, for certain, that her name had been written up in Dottie's little black book, and that it would, in all likelihood, stay there for ever.

Frighting was a perfect way of putting off an actor or performer. So ridiculous, it always seemed to Elsie, from when she was quite small, that it was silly to be put off by it. The action of the perpetrator was quite simple. They merely sat in one of the front rows of the stalls and laughed in all the wrong places, and applauded in the wrong places. However, and this had always astonished Elsie, despite being simple it was always horribly effective. So fragile was the average actor's confidence that it was not more than a few seconds before they were effectively put off, and their performances, however assured, would become something to be retrieved, if not, finally – lost.

Now, however, that it was being directed at her, Elsie realised in an instant why it did put off the most seasoned actor. It was not the laugh itself, or the applause in the wrong place – that served merely as a warning for what was to come. It was the awful sense of anticipation.

Would there be another misplaced laugh, and if there was, when would it be? Would there be a sudden handclap, coming out of nowhere, favouring something that had not yet transpired, and if so, when would that too happen? Cool as the evening was, Elsie could feel herself perspiring as, of a sudden, yet another of Dottie's laughs came rolling towards her as she began her next line.

'It's all—' (loud laugh from the stalls). She tried again. 'It's—' (loud and prolonged laugh from the stalls). She tried once more. 'It's-all-right-Benda-I-will-do-that.'

The only way, finally, to take the line was at the gallop and on one long breath.

Elsie looked at Phil Mander who was playing the butler and he must have seen the terror in her eyes, because he turned and wrote something on a pad laid out on the desk behind him. Obediently, seeing his signal, Elsie allowed her eyes to stray to the pad as she crossed stage left.

TELL WHOEVER IT IS TO TAKE A RUNNING JUMP! Phil had written in large capitals.

Elsie paused. Then, realising that this was the only possible way forward, she went to the front of the stage and shading her eyes said clearly, pointing at her grandmother, 'Someone out there is making a terrible noise, Benda, driving me *dotty*, in fact. Take care of it, would you?'

She turned and looked at Phil who, bowing slightly and keeping an admirably straight face, intoned, 'Certainly madam. Silence out there, please!'

The audience, quickly realising that something was going on but not quite what, responded immediately by applauding, and Elsie and Phil went back to the play as written.

After that the first act became everything that it should be, and as the curtain was about to rise on the second, Elsie, looking through the spyhole to the stalls, was unsurprised to see that no one had returned to Dottie's seat.

'Something the matter, love?' Phil glanced down at Elsie, not quite understanding the expression on her face.

'No, nothing. Nothing, really.'

'Just for a moment I thought you were upset about something. You shouldn't be – the play's taken off, thanks to you. I loved the look you put in at the end of that first—'

But Elsie shook her head, and put a finger to her

lips. 'Not now, Phil, you know that. Not now or at any other time.'

He shrugged his shoulders and, having checked his costume in the mirror to the side of the stage, went on.

Elsie watched him through half-closed lids, her head raised slightly.

What a fool people thought you were. Just because you were young, they thought you were wet behind the ears. Well, not only was she not wet behind the ears, but not even Dottie could win now. She had trounced her. Dottie, the old battleaxe, had tried to fright her, but she had not succeeded. Elsie had frighted her back, and now Dottie's name would be in *Elsie*'s little black book. What was more, she would top the list.

You are done for. You have closed our deal for ever. You have betrayed me, but I don't care, because you are no one now. You tried to kill my performance, but you did not succeed in frighting me. I would see you in hell before you could succeed at that, you witch! Elsie wrote in her engagement diary when she awoke the next day. Unfortunately Portly read it. Quite by mistake of course, but read it he did, and he looked shocked.

'Why did you write that?' He stared at Elsie, his eyes rounder than she had yet seen them.

Elsie coloured. 'Oh, it was nothing. Just someone, in the stalls last night, trying to put me off. So I was writing about it.' She closed the book.

'Elsie. You mustn't feel like that about anyone,

183

really. I'm sure whoever it was wasn't trying to put you off, not doing anything on purpose. They were just nervous for you, that's all. After all, so much runs on your being good in the play, doesn't it? They were just nervous for you.'

Elsie looked at Portly. He had led such a sheltered life she almost felt sorry for him. Never known what it was like to be out there, quite alone in life. She looked at him, not guessing what her beautiful, large, slightly protruding eyes did to his heart, and smiled. Her smile was serene and cat-like and so contained it could have been accompanied by a swishing of the tail.

'Think what you like, Portly, but as far as I am concerned, I never want to see that woman again, not ever. She did to me what she only ever does to her worst enemies, people who have done her harm, people whose names she has written in her little black book. People like my *father*, those sorts of people, and last night she made *me* one of them, and I shall never forget that. I stopped loving her last night, for ever, and I hope she knows it. That is all. I just hope she knows it.'

'I must say I never saw who it was. Donald and I were outside in the street, smoking our heads off!' He shook his head, laughing at the memory.

'Nothing is *too far* for someone who does that to you! Anyway. She didn't stay for more, not once she knew she couldn't shake me. She left. As well she should.' Elsie smiled again. 'No one should do that to anyone, let alone someone they have pretended to love all these years.'

Portly, who hated hearing anything distasteful for more than a few seconds, had lost interest halfway through Elsie's speech. He was already far too used to actors' shenanigans to pay much heed to any surface drama, suspecting as he did that Elsie would probably be reunited with whoever it was within a few days, and all would be tears and kisses, and all that.

'Want to read your reviews?'

To change the subject he at once slapped down a large pile of newspapers on the table in front of them both, and reached into his pocket for his cigar case, smiling.

'Are they interesting?'

'Interesting? Well, yes. You have not been discovered, Elsie darling, you have been hailed!'

And so it seemed she had.

A STAR IS BORN the *Evening Argus* declaimed, showing a picture of Elsie that made her look five years older. THE DISCOVERY OF THE YEAR was a small piece in the morning paper, also showing a photograph of Elsie, but making her look at least five years younger. ELECTRIFYING PERFORMANCE FROM JUVE! was on the front of one of the trade papers.

And on it went, and in such a manner that as Elsie read through them she had no doubt at all that she had arrived. Whether it was to stay or not did not matter in the least. What mattered was that Dottie would be reading at least some of them, and, her granddaughter hoped intensely, grinding her teeth with fury as she did so.

185

'Where from here?' Elsie looked up at Portly, already drawing happily on his cigar. In her own mind she had already played the tour, to packed houses of course, and was now buying herself a flat in London preparatory to storming the West End, as the newspapers always put it.

'Where from here, Elsie?' Portly frowned momentarily. 'All the usual tour dates, Brighton of course, everywhere really. The interest we are getting in the tour at the moment is fantastic, Elsie darling, fantastic. We are going to fill and fill.'

He stared dreamily out to sea at the now white-topped waves. The weather might be changing, but the box office till would be ringing, and the telephones as well.

What a feeling it was too, and nothing to touch it. Just people putting their hands together and cheering at the end of a play, making a kind of magic that was indescribable, but meant that someone had arrived in their midst, a star. Someone with that something that sent the temperatures of theatre audiences soaring, that made people long, long afterwards sigh and say, *Oh, but you didn't see Elsie Lancaster in comedy, did you? Now there was a star!*

And so Elsie left her home town, Dottie, and the lodgers, everyone and everything that was familiar, for ever. Finally, she did so with all the usual regrets for what had happened to her, and to Dottie, but with no idea of how she could ever make anything or anyone better.

186

She realised that Dottie had brought her up, had made her what she was, but that there was no looking back now, because Dottie, of all people, had frighted her. She had done to her own flesh and blood what she had only ever done to her most hated enemies. What she had done was not a quick·frustrated stab in the back, which in the event might be forgivable; what she had done was nothing that could or would be passed off as an understandable *crime of passion*. Rather it had been a planned campaign, conducted in cold blood, and executed in the same way.

One day, Elsie hoped, she would be able to forgive and forget what Dottie had done, but at that moment she turned away from her only relation in the world, remembering only now how hard Dottie had worked her from the time she was tiny, how she had kept her short of money and clothes, even when, as a little girl, she was earning a good salary dancing as a mushroom, or posing for a local cakemaker as a fairy on top of a wedding cake, doing ridiculous, embarrassing things which upset her for days afterwards, things which were stupid and degrading, but nevertheless brought in money. Even when she was doing all that, none of the money – none of it had come Elsie's way.

Dottie had never rewarded her with so much as a new dress, not ever – always sending her out to the second-hand shops to search for her clothes, for dresses and coats, for cast-offs worn by more well-off children, for children's shoes that had been handed in, sometimes happily unworn, by nannies from rich houses who conducted a sideline in the nearly new, or sometimes quite new, clothes and shoes of their spoilt charges, thereby boosting their own meagre wages, and at the same time benefitting the less well off.

Elsie settled back in the train carriage and folded her gloved hands neatly in her lap, and to avoid any feelings of sadness at leaving home she chose instead to go over and over in her mind, with renewed relish, how she had beaten Dottie at her own game, how she had forced her to leave the theatre before the second act, how she had finally kicked her grandmother in the teeth by making such a huge success in her first grown-up, starring, comedy role.

As the train started to pull out of the station towards their first tour date, Elsie stared at the poor homes that ran down by the side of the railway tracks, at the washing that flapped in the early spring breeze, at the strained face of a woman digging at a bed of poor soil, and worse vegetables, but she saw nothing of these, to her, still unfamiliar sights. She saw only the glowing words of her reviews, and how those words would bite, deeper and deeper, into Dottie's soul; how, even as she ironed sheets or moaned to the lodgers, or drank her sweet sherry at night, those words would crawl their way into the heart of Dottie, and, like some fearful desert insect, give her gip for the rest of her life.

And she felt no pity for her.

She felt no pity for her because when, at last, after all those long years of being turned away at auditions, after all those tedious roles, after all the studying and the dancing, after all the singing lessons, and the parts learned, when the moment came for Elsie to succeed, Dottie had responded by turning round and frighting her.

No, Elsie did not feel sorry for her. She hated her.

'Mind if I sit in here, Elsie?'

Mervyn Castle whistled tunefully, and happily, while placing his luggage on the rack above his seat, and collapsing with purposefully exaggerated drama opposite Elsie.

Elsie studied Mervyn Castle with her usual detached indifference. He was the kind of actor that she had come across a great deal while she was growing up, a puzzling kind of man of indeterminate class, small, middling plain to almost ugly. In fact so plain that she often found herself wondering why such men became actors at all.

Sometimes, at a dull moment in rehearsal, she had tried to capture the moment when the Mervyn Castle kind of actor, whilst they were growing up, stood in front of their mirrors, of a bleak morning, and said to themselves as they stood on the bathroom stool, 'Mervyn, you are small with a large nose, small eyes and hardly reaching five foot three. You really should become an actor, for with your looks and height you too could be a great star!'

Well, Mervyn might not ever become a great

star, as he probably knew by now, but he probably did not care, because he was a great character actor. Pin accurate, never fluffing, Mervyn could not, ever, be faulted, not ever. Never *corpsed*, as the expression for laughing at the wrong moment on stage had it, and handled whatever was thrown at him with the kind of faultless aplomb that Elsie already knew came from a dedication and inner discipline which was totally admirable. He was also the perfect gentleman. She therefore did not mind his seating himself opposite her, and settling down to the crossword with the look of a man well used to being not only on tour, but on an endless tour. For that was what actors like Mervyn were used for by managements: to tour endlessly, even sometimes pointlessly, backing up the bigger names that were often precisely the opposite to themselves, inaccurate, unpunctual, careless and unreliable.

'Worked for Portly Cosgrove before?'

Elsie took advantage of a pause in his thoughts as he stared out of the window struggling with some elusive clue.

'Yes, and Donald Bourton. Good team. Pay on time, never let us down so far, number one tours too, which for a young management is quite something, wouldn't you say?'

Mervyn nodded agreeably across the short space that divided them. Elsie stared at him.

'Yes, I would. Yes, but you know, what do *you* know about them?'

'Just that.' He returned to his crossword. 'That,

after all, is all you need to know about management, isn't it, dear?'

Elsie said, 'Yes.'

Like most actors determined to survive, as well as most character actors, Mervyn was a cautious customer. He would not trust anyone not to say at least something *to* someone, to his detriment. Speaking out of turn would not be his style. Besides, he had probably known Dottie, way back, when she was meant to be a star, and the moon was made of green cheese.

'Well, now, that's finished.' He folded his newspaper and nodded at Elsie. 'Want to come for a coffee?'

'That would be nice.'

Elsie followed Mervyn swaying from side to side down the train corridor to the refreshment car, not because she wanted a cup of British Rail coffee, or because she particularly wanted to get to know Mervyn better, but because, for some reason she could not define, she thought she might now be going to learn something new about Portly and Donald. Something else told her that it was not going to be to their advantage.

Chapter Six

There was a beautiful lake. That would be enough to quite fill the eye and mind, but not withstanding that, there was, too, a folly with Gothic windows and in front of it a jetty, and a boat tied up, but not any ordinary boat. This boat was canopied, and had long cushioned seats, and was waiting for Coco to finish in make-up before stepping down into its welcoming pale blue velvet comforts.

Make-up.

Coco had stared at herself the first morning when the gentleman in whose charge she had been put had finished with her. She did not just stare, as a matter of fact, she *gaped*. The reason she had gaped at herself, hardly recognising her own face at all, was because the make-up man, Gus Chester, or whatever he was called when he was at home, had managed to make her look like a pretty good imitation of an old actress friend of her guardians – big red lips, blue eye shadow, rouged cheeks, and worst of all worsts – no eye-liner, just a little mascara on the lashes.

Coco said nothing about the horrendous vision of herself that Chester had achieved until she was in her costume, and then, being Coco, she had marched straight up to the director, and not caring what anyone thought of her, or was likely to think of her, had accosted him with, 'I say, Mr Trimble, I am not altogether sure that a young woman in the Edwardian era would have looked exactly like this, are you?'

After which she had made sure to push her face towards the director until their noses practically touched.

Of course Freddie Trimble had taken one look at her, and burst into fits of laughter. Just as well they had met before they went on location or he might have thought that Coco looked like that normally.

'Coco, darling, you look ghastly. Take it all off for goodness' sake, and tell Gus to give you a *no make-up* make-up, would you? To make you look as fresh as the morning dew, and not a hint of Garbo in the silent era, *please*.'

Telling Gus Chester this was not only not easy, it was perfectly impossible.

He kept saying, with a shrug of his huge shoulders, 'I've been making up stars since before Freddie Trimble was even sucking his thumb! You stay as you are, madam, or else he can come and have it out with me.'

There was obviously no arguing with him, so Coco waited until Chester had moved on to some other luckless individual and then, once his back was turned, had flown at her face herself, removing the ghastly red lips and rouged cheeks, taking out everything except her eyes, to which she swiftly applied kohl from a little supply kept in her handbag. Then she shot off towards the lakeside location before anyone could notice.

As it happened the young actor playing her lover-to-be had already arrived, tall, immaculately made up and costumed in a blazer and boater. They were introduced by Trimble in a quick perfunctory manner, and what seemed to Coco like only a few seconds later found themselves kissing each other in the back of the luxurious craft provided for the scene. Well, to be accurate, as Coco would tell Oliver a few days later, 'Within seconds of saying how do you do he was kissing me passionately on the chin – you know, cheating it, because of the camera angle.'

Of course Oliver would pretend not to be interested, because that was Oliver all over. He never did want to be interested in anything he had not yet done, until he did it, after which he became a perfect expert on the subject, or, as Coco often reminded him, a perfect bore.

But that was all to come. Now all Coco could hope was that her chin had not doubled in size since she had wolfed a large breakfast from the refreshment place, or butty wagon as she had learned that it was called, and that the cheating was working, because whatever Aeneas Mayo was doing to her, it certainly did not feel anything like a kiss. She just hoped that it looked like one.

'Sorry.' Aeneas straightened up, and tried to smile after 'Cut!' 'I haven't had much experience of this. Your first time too, I expect?'

Coco nodded. A silence fell as the camera crew stared up at the sky and down at their light meters, and Freddie Trimble paced up and down beside the lake shore looking every inch the worried director.

'What are you thinking about?' Aeneas whispered as they both watched the crew, themselves somehow frozen into position.

Coco looked from the water where she was now trailing one lace-mittened hand back to Aeneas.

'The money we're earning!' she whispered back.

Their eyes met instantly, and they both tried not to laugh, recognition of their mutuality of approach being so instantaneous, however, that they failed dramatically in their efforts.

'What are you going to do with it? If we get paid, that is?' Aeneas went on, one eye on the green bank and the director muttering to the cameramen, and one on Coco herself.

'I am going to buy myself a car, and I am going to drive very fast in it. An MG, I hope. If I'm not sacked beforehand. And you?'

'The same. An MG. Or an Austin Healey.'

'Yes, or an Austin Healey,' Coco agreed, and another silence fell as they both stared into a future where this might, just might be possible, if they were not sacked, or something.

'Right, let's go again,' Trimble bellowed from

the lake shore. 'And Aeneas? Try to give it a bit more passion, would you?'

Aeneas nodded towards Freddie Trimble with his loudhailer and viewfinder. As he turned towards her to start the scene again, Coco whispered, 'Just pretend I'm an Austin Healey, and passion will flow!'

'Don't – please – I'll only get carried away!'

'Cut! Would you two stop giggling, please? You're meant to be kissing not laughing.'

'Sorry Freddie.'

'Sorry Freddie.'

'We'll be lucky if we earn enough to buy a spare wheel, if this goes on. You know what Trimble's called,' Aeneas whispered, so *sotto voce* that even Coco could hardly hear, as they sank down once more into the pale blue velvet. 'He's called Two-Take Trimble. So if this is take number three this is our lot, Coco Hampton, as in Court.'

They scraped under the wire, with only three takes, and into their next costumes, after which came lunch.

Aeneas Mayo had graduated, if, as he told Coco, that was the term for it, from a rival drama school. He had actually lasted the whole two-year course, and as a result had the worldly air of a much travelled actor, someone who had seen the world, and learned from it. In other words, he had subsequently spent two years in weekly repertory work at innumerable theatres all round the country. He knew Crewe like the back of his hand. He had felt its hard benches eating into his backside on cold Sunday afternoons. He knew about train delays, and missed entrances, both into trains and on to provincial stages. He knew about theatrical landladies who send you down the garden to the privy with the wrapper from the loaf; not to mention directors such as Freddie Trimble who send you up the wall, as well as he knew his own hairline.

Coco, being Coco, was outwardly completely, and determinedly, unimpressed by all Aeneas's experiences.

'I know all about touring actors,' she said airily, as they queued incongruously for roast beef and roast potatoes, or Irish stew, on what was turning out to be an increasingly hot day. 'All about weekly rep.'

Aeneas took his spectacles from the pocket of his costume, held them upside down, and stared through one of the lenses at Coco. 'Oh yes? And how long have we been at Ramad?'

'Two, no, three weeks.'

They both started to laugh.

And then, as Coco said, 'Roast beef, please,' to the caterer, she added, 'No, just four, actually. Then Liskeard came to the college and I don't know why, he cast me. Though he seems to have disappeared, for some reason.'

'Oh, yes, the great Harold Liskeard. He was meant to be directing this, until the day before yesterday, or thereabouts.' Aeneas's expression was laconic. 'But you know how it is.'

'How?' Coco seized her plate of roast beef and vegetables, suddenly ravenously hungry.

'Irish stew, please.' Aeneas nodded up to the caterer. 'Our great star, Richard Lexmark – thank you. Yes, thanks to our great star, Harold has gone on vacation.' He turned with his plate of food, and nodded towards a free table behind them. 'Let's go over there.' As they walked he went on, 'Yes, the great Richard Lexmark.'

They sat down.

'We won't be meeting him, will we?' Coco asked with some relief.

'No.' Aeneas, already all too practised in the ways of the world, looked carefully round to see that no one was listening. 'No, thank God. Do you want to hear the story?'

'You bet.'

'Well, he wanted the starring role like there was no tomorrow. So, you probably know what happened?' Coco shook her head. 'No? Well, he went bald-headed after Liskeard. Holed up opposite his flat, rang him at all times of the day and night, flew at him whenever possible, *must have* just *must have* this part! And once ole Frank had cast him, and he is signed for the role, ole Richard Lexmark, what do he do? Big Star Sexy Lexie make sure to have Harold Liskeard sacked!' He nodded at Coco's amazed expression. 'Oh yes. That is par for the course with stars and directors. There was no way Lexmark was going to have him direct him, not once Liskeard had held out against his being cast. Capiche? Understand? The philosophy is: you didn't want me, and now you have got me I don't want *you*, fruit cake!'

Coco stared at Aeneas, her mouth full of roast beef and potatoes. 'Wow,' she said eventually.

'Quite a big wow, as it happens. But there you are.' Aeneas shrugged his costumed shoulders, his napkin carefully spread across his clothes. 'That is how it is with ye big stars, Miss Coco Hampton as in palace. They get what they want out of you – or you might say they get what they want out of *one* – and after that they throw you overboard. We'll probably be the same, when we are big stars. Just the same, when it comes down to it.'

But Coco was not interested in their future stardom. She was much more interested in Aeneas Mayo's making fun of her.

'Did you just take me *off*?' she demanded.

Aeneas pulled an innocent face, and immediately put on his spectacles upside down to make her laugh.

'No, no, no, it was just a passing *blague*, as in French for joke, see? I just thought you might say *one* at that moment. I mean, you might. Not that you did,' he added hastily.

'Well, I wouldn't,' Coco told him sharply. 'And if I don't make fun of you and your horrid way of holding your knife, you just keep off my accent, OK?'

They both stared at each other. Impasse. No further than this could either of them go, at least not with any confidence. Deadlock. Their eyes met. She could see that she had annoyed Aeneas, and she was glad. He could see that he had annoyed Coco, and he was glad.

After which they both burst into fits of laughter, and Coco asked for Aeneas's help.

'In what way do you need my help?'

'Make-up.'

He stared at her. 'Yes, well, we're both having to go back in, after this little lot.' He cast his eyes down at their now empty food plates, wiping his mouth on his napkin and sighing.

'But that is the whole point,' Coco explained, doing the same. 'That is the whole point, I can't.'

'Why not?'

'I did my own.'

'You did your own? You did your own make-up? You do realise that you are quite likely to cause a strike? That that is enough to have all the plugs pulled, doing your own make-up? You so much as pull a comb out and scrape at your own quiff and the whole set could be left in darkness, you do realise that?'

'Well, no, but I do now that you have told me!'

Aeneas frowned and rubbed his face with the side of his glasses, and then he put them away, frowning.

'Who was it who did you, ole Chester? Made you look like Clara Bow or something out of the silents, I expect?'

'That's the one.'

'OK, so I'll cover for you.'

'Yes, but what will you *say*?'

200

'I'll say . . . I'll say that you are unwell, as in, you know, gone to Matron, off games? And that you will be back any minute, if he asks for you, which he won't, because he's a lazy old devil.'

Diplomatically Aeneas stopped suddenly because Coco had reddened to the point where she knew that any old passer-by could have warmed their hands by her face, so hot had she become. Aeneas put out a cool, and surprisingly elegant, hand, and covered hers with it.

'It's all right, Coco as in Hampton. I am a man of the world, remember. Believe me, two years in repertory turns you into a very grown-up boy.' He smiled with sudden, genuine warmth. 'Look, skip off and hide behind a bush until you're called. Two-take Trimble won't care if you have half your head missing just provided he does the scene in two takes, and Chester won't care, providing he gets off early to see his boyfriend. Really. Just scarper.'

Coco did as she was told, and lived in fear for the rest of the afternoon. In fact everything that Aeneas Mayo had said would be so, came true. She did her own make-up again, Aeneas and she did their scenes in two takes, and the end of the afternoon arrived with the end of the light. No one seemed to care a tuppenny damn if she had orange lipstick on her mouth or, as it transpired, kohl on her eyes.

'That is it for me, then.'

They were on the bus together going back into the centre of London.

'Oh.' Coco turned and looked at Aeneas. Out of costume, in his *usuals*, as he called them – black-framed spectacles, dark hair cut long, suede jacket brass-buttoned, and blue jeans tucked into suede half-boots – he looked every inch what she thought a man should look, good news indeed to her costume-conscious eyes. 'I thought you had some more scenes?'

'No, yet another nameless part, my speciality. I am doomed to be cast as luckless young men found in boats kissing the wrong gels and then sent to India for my sins.'

Coco nodded, expressionless. She would miss Aeneas on set. Might even miss him off set. 'OK. So, hope we work again.' She shrugged her shoulders and stared out of the bus window.

'Is that all you can say, Coco as in Hampton Court?'

'Oh, do shut up about Coco as in Court or Hampton, or anything else. What else is there *to* say?'

'Come for a coffee?'

'Oh, all right.'

She followed him off the coach into Hammersmith Broadway where, for some reason, they were all being ejected.

'Taxi!'

She followed him into the taxi too, but as she did so, and they sat down together on the back seat, she immediately regretted it. She did not want to make time for any Aeneas Mayo in her life. As a matter of fact as she stared ahead at nothing in particular Coco realised that she did not want to make time for anyone, and she never had wanted to either. Love, or attraction, all that, she had long ago set aside, settling for emotional crushes on movie stars or older actors she had met once in the company of her guardians, and was not likely ever to meet again, but whom she was happy to think about, as one had romantic thoughts about Clark Gable, or Dirk Bogarde. There was no reality to them. They were just dreams, romantic notions, nothing more or less, although real enough to keep her happy, and they had nothing to do with life as she knew it had to be lived.

She turned to Aeneas. 'Look, it's just coffee, OK? Because, you know, I have an early night, early call, even if you don't.'

'Of course.' Aeneas looked at her innocently. Too innocently. 'I like your gear,' he told her. 'Great look that. Tight trousers, the bracelets, the ruffled shirt, terrific.'

Coco stared out of the window, her heart sinking. Christmas daisies. He felt the same.

PART TWO

THE WALTZ BEGINS

The beauty of it! The merry bubble and joy, the thin, clear, happy call of the distant piping! And the call in it is stronger even than the music is sweet!

Kenneth Grahame, 'The Piper at the Gates of Dawn' from *The Wind in the Willows*

Chapter Seven

Oliver had made up his mind to ignore the publicity surrounding the casting of a complete ingénue, one Coco Hampton. It was the only possible way not to go mad with jealousy.

However, the sheer horror of seeing Coco, who had never had any serious intention of becoming an actress, being cast in a film after only a miserable handful of weeks at drama school, drove home to him, as nothing else could, the utterly random, incomprehensible methods of the so-called profession into which he had flung not just himself, but all his ambitions, from far too early an age. The reality of Coco's amazing good fortune was hideous, and yet it was somehow so like Coco – to launch herself carelessly into the theatrical world as an actress, when all she really wanted to do was design for the theatre, not act in it. And then to see her cast, just like that, in a matter of moments, in a big budget costume film was bitter stuff.

Of course he had been forced to forgive her for her good luck, because he loved Coco. He always had done. He loved her in a jealous sibling sort of way, in the way that boys and girls love each other when they are growing up together but are not related, and never intend to be. Coco had been what he had so looked forward to in the holidays, not just Coco herself, but her whole world, her awful anarchic sense of humour, her dismissive attitude to him, her *you know nothing* arrogance; they were something he clung to through dreary schooling and bullying classmates, through hearty sports masters, and even heartier house-masters.

Naturally, having had asthma badly as a child, he had got off the army, so that was all right. However, his health had never got him off Coco, and he knew now that he had never wanted it to. She had been the one jolly thing in his life, the light that drove him on. Coco – and Cliffie. And now she was gone from the drama school, and actually starring, for heaven's sake, in a film, and little snippets about her were appearing in the newspapers. Now the film was coming out, and there was even a cover picture of her on the front of two of the glossiest of the glossy maga-zines, she seemed to be receding from him.

Oh God, how he hated her – quite as much as he loved her. Here he was at the end of his second term at Ramad landed with Hamlet, and one of the servants in the Scandal, and all the large parts and character parts, everything that he had always thought he wanted, that his heart might desire in his end of term productions, and yet their importance in his life, the singular achievement they represented, all appeared to be wiped out by the knowledge that Coco was already launched into her second film, and swanning about on some set at Shepperton or Pinewood or somewhere. Meanwhile he found himself walking about Ramad, his upper half clothed in a polo-neck jumper and sports jacket, his lower half in tights and ballet shoes, trying not to feel vaguely ridiculous, trying to keep from imagining Coco sitting in make-up, a certain hush surrounding her, fame just around the corner. There would be Coco enjoying all the accoutrements of stardom and about two lines a day to learn, while there was Oliver swotting up some interminable speech written by one William Shakespeare, and having to sit through music and movement class, not to mention mime, and worse.

And there was worse, too. Worse was a man named Putt, proudly taken on by Ramad's principal, Bertrand, as a witness to his modernity, an ostentatious bow to the East Coast of America school of naturalism, or, as it was thought of by the old guard, the *scratch and mumble school of drama*.

It seemed that Putt was keen to bring all the new American ideas to Ramad. Oliver, among many others, was just as keen not to absorb them. He wanted to improve his range and understanding, make his voice more mellifluous, but Putt wanted none of this. He wanted them all to spend days and weeks becoming tables and chairs, dissociating themselves from their minds and bodies, detaching themselves from their personalities. Inevitably, after spending what seemed like forever lying on a dirty floor becoming a coffee table, Oliver found himself wishing that he had signed on for the Arthur Rank Charm School, or the Household Cavalry, rather than Ramad.

The trouble with becoming a coffee table was that, in reality, it had nothing to do with anything, and they all knew it, but in an embarrassed and somewhat sheep-like way none of the students dared to voice any criticism, outside the coffee bar or the pub.

Oliver knew just why Putt upset him so much. It was because they all knew – and perhaps even Putt knew, for all Oliver knew – that once they got out *there*, in the real world, there would be no *time* for such things in places like twice weekly repertory, or wherever they would be lucky enough to find themselves. Hard enough to learn their roles, and their moves. Managements just would not put up with actors spending hours of valuable rehearsal time lying about becoming pieces of furniture in order to achieve maximum dissociation from their original personalities. It was just a fact. They were all perfectly aware that becoming a table or a chair, even something as select and chic as a coffee table, had as much to do with earning your living as a professional actor as jumping off a roof without a safety harness had to do with film acting. It was a dangerous waste of time. Just as, Oliver was beginning to think, sliding up and down with your back to the wall endlessly repeating phrases like 'think move speak' might also be a dangerous waste of time, as might be so much else that he was doing at blasted drama school.

The terrible truth dawned one day when spring was starting to spread across London, and the bulbs in the parks were beginning to push through the still wet and muddy grass. The thought struck Oliver amidships that his longed-for terms at Ramad just might be one hell of a waste of time.

When, Oliver suddenly asked himself, seated on a bench opposite a clutch of trees, *when* did anyone ever learn anything at drama school that was of any use out *there*?

'End of term productions. That is why you have to stay, old boy. That's when all the agents come in and gawp at the students and seize the opportunity to sign you up, and the next minute you're acting your backside off at Clacton on Sea for two pounds a week, and *no* luncheon vouchers.'

Oliver had gone for private voice lessons to Arthur Melson, an old actor friend of the family. Not Oliver's family, *Cliffie*'s family, but since Cliffie *was* family, so was Arthur Melson.

Melson gave a hearty, rumbling laugh that would have done credit to Falstaff. Still, laugh or no laugh, Oliver attended Melson's voice classes assiduously. Apart from anything else, now that Coco was so busy, it was only in Melson's company that Oliver was able to be himself, not Oliver Lowell, Yorkshireman, but Oliver Plunkett, the youngest son of landed gentry.

'Why do you want to go into the profession?' Melson had asked the first day Oliver climbed down into his basement flat off the Bayswater Road. And then before Oliver could answer he had answered his own question for him. 'You want to go into the profession because for *you* there is no other life, and never *will* be. Never *mind* the poor pay, never *mind* the atrocious conditions; becoming someone else for just a few hours a day, inhabiting another person's world, whether it be Shakespeare's or Terry Rattigan's, is all that matters to *you*. Next best thing is going into a monastery, really, though, isn't it?'

Oliver had started to say something, and then stopped. He had stopped because he had found that it was one of the persecutions of the theatrical profession that everyone in the whole world, including the cleaning lady, knew better than you. However little they had acted, however little their success, the theatre was peopled by know-alls. At least dear old Cliffie, God bless him, had warned him of this.

'Your sainted mother,' he would say. (Oliver's mother, once she had run off with Charley the hunt servant, had always, for some reason, been referred to by Cliffie as 'your sainted mother'.) 'Your sainted mother always said to me "acting and dressage, Cliffie, are the two activities over which no one can ever agree, and equally where, you will find, no one is ever, ever wrong."'

Oliver's thoughts returned to the overheated room with its seemingly endless prints of long-forgotten shows and actors in frozen stances posing in classical roles. Melson was still lecturing Oliver on the benefits of staying at Ramad.

'It is the cut and thrust of your future life in microcosm, it is the long and the short of the theatre in two years. It may seem futile at times, it may seem inane, but it has its purpose. Most of all it is a time when you can try things which will not be open to you once you turn professional, believe me.'

Oliver stared at Melson. His white beard made him typecasting for a silent Lear, but he had a terrible voice, light, thin and sliced through with a suburban whine, which was passing strange for a voice coach. Nevertheless he was actually a brilliant teacher, because he cared so deeply. He saw himself, and possibly himself alone, as handing on the precious torch of Garrick and Irving.

'Humma, humma, humma!'

Once again.

And again.

And again. Oliver intoned the newer voice exercises, thinking how senseless they were, finding that his mind kept returning to his imagined world, a world where Coco was swanning about in beautiful dresses, the kinds of dresses which she had always said that she wanted to design but was in all probability now wearing, posing as, of all things, a film star.

He hated her.

'Humma, humma, humma!'

Warm up for yet more voice exercises.

Relax.

Oliver thought of Putt. Maybe he was right, in some strange way. Maybe that weird man was right, and while Oliver was doing these tedious exercises he should imagine that he was, not a coffee table exactly, but perhaps – a cello? And maybe by taking the humanity out of his psyche he would, as Putt maintained, improve his attitude? And maybe, by an act of dissociation, take the nerves out too? But what would be left? Would there be anything left in the locker after that? He could not, personally, say, but it might be interesting to try, just for a few minutes.

'Why the dead expression, Oliver, dear boy? The last few minutes the look in your eye has reminded me of nothing less and nothing more than a dead cod. Is this something new we are trying? Or is Ramad changing to some new dead cod method of acting?'

Oliver looked at Arthur Melson. Typical. Just as he was becoming a cello the old boy had to home in and make an *ill-timed jest in poor taste* as Cliffie always called it.

'Just trying something.'

'Well, don't. At least, not while I'm teaching you.'

'But Maestro – you just said – now was the time we *should* try things.'

'So I did. But not in my classes, please.'

As soon as Elsie found out just what there was to know about Portly Cosgrove and Donald Bourton, her heart sank. She had heard about managements from all sides, and from every one of the lodgers. She knew all about the floating of false cheques, about phoney names and even phonier bank accounts. She knew about actors who had been foolish enough to pay for their own wigs, or sometimes even costumes, and about scenery that had to stay in storage because no one could afford to get it out. She knew about getting stuck in Scotland with only five shillings in your pocket, and about being stranded in Barnstaple with fifteen pounds owed to you. She knew about managements who had taken off for the States with all the profits, about bank accounts in the Isle of Man where producers lodged money for all sorts of reasons, and other accounts elsewhere opened under false names for all sorts of yet other reasons. And now she knew about Cosgrove and Bourton, too.

It was only a rumour, of course. That was what Mervyn Castle had been all too anxious to say, and to prevent a run on the bank, as it were, it seemed that they, Mervyn and herself, had to keep completely quiet about his suspicions. Still, true or untrue, it made for an underlying uneasiness. Mervyn had said that he would not have said anything, except that he knew that Elsie was carrying the show, and since she was, and he knew that it meant so much to her, it was just as well to be on the lookout for anything suspicious.

'It might just be a rumour,' Mervyn had kept saying as the train hurtled into the darkest of black darknesses in the tunnels and out again into what then seemed like the brightest of bright lights, so that they were only able to see each other intermittently, each thinking solely of their own much needed cheques, of the real need to survive. 'Just a rumour – but if it is not, we could be in for a bad time.'

'Do you think Portly knows?'

Mervyn shook his head. No, he was quite sure that Portly knew nothing, but he was equally sure that neither he nor Elsie should say anything. Simply because it would do no good, and it was only a rumour that he had heard from a friend of a friend who had known Donald Bourton long before he met Portly Cosgrove. He might have changed, after all, but, more than that, Portly might be up to him. He might know, and be prepared to deal with him.

Elsie frowned. Portly was much younger than Donald. Portly might be one of those men who believed in the goodness of people, could see no evil in anyone. Certainly he had been dreadfully shocked when he had read what Elsie had written in her little black book. He had not understood how she felt at all. Had not had a clue why someone who had been frighted should seek to revenge themselves on the person who had done the frighting.

Finally, as the train journey drew to a close, Mervyn and Elsie had made a pact, and in the event a quite admirably simple one. The moment their money was late, or postponed, for whatever reason, they would down tools. If the moment did arrive, they avowed, they, and the rest of the cast, would say, 'That is it, no money, no performance.'

And now the moment *had* arrived, and Elsie was facing an outraged Donald and a deeply hurt Portly with just those agreed words, the only difference being that Mervyn Castle and the rest of the cast were, for some reason, nowhere to be seen. Only Elsie was there making their case.

As soon as she had asked for her money, there and then, doing a good imitation of how she knew Dottie would ask for it, Donald managed to look both shocked and disgusted, as if he had found Elsie hanging around the stage door soliciting. At the same time he shrugged his shoulders and demanded why she could not wait for her money like everyone else.

'No, as a matter of fact, I can't wait for my money, Donald.' Elsie looked neither mulish nor angry. She looked calm. 'As a matter of fact if you look at the date' – Elsie glanced down at the calendar on the office desk, which proclaimed 'Fairburn's Baby Food' to be the best and most nutritious, for infants and toddlers, and carefully turned it towards Donald – 'if you look at the

217

date,' she repeated, 'all our wages are actually more than a week late now. They are a fortnight late, and that really won't do. It causes hardship, especially for the married ones. They have to send their money home, you know. That's hard on the wives and the babies.' Elsie was of a sudden enjoying her role as a modern day Saint Joan, most unusual casting for her. She was taking a stand, and loving it. 'No, I am afraid it is pay up, Donald, or I leave.'

'Well, old love, in that case,' Donald said, glancing briefly at Portly, 'in that case, old love,' he repeated, his normally good-natured voice quite different in its tone, 'you had better leave. If I were you, I *should* leave.'

The words had been spoken. They were there. Incredible, indelible, filling the whole space between Elsie and Donald Bourton with a sea of incredulity.

'You don't really mean that. He doesn't really mean that.' Portly had stepped forward, standing between Donald and Elsie and saying the very words that Elsie had thought but was too proud to utter.

'Of course I mean it!' Donald laughed. 'What is this girl, Elsie Lancaster? Who was she, Portly, until we cast her? No one. Never heard of her! Now here she is threatening us. Ridiculous. There are another dozen of her I can call up at any time. You think anyone will notice in York, or in Blackpool, in Torquay, or in Manchester, who the hell is playing the lead in this? Not at all, they'll be too busy booking their seats to get out of the rain, to sit somewhere warm on a cold summer evening and fall asleep after too many beers, that is what they will be doing. No, Elsie Lancaster, you can go, and quite frankly, good riddance. We can get someone cheaper than you, and better. We are all replaceable, most of all you.'

'I have a contract. You can't do this to me—'

'Yes, and I have a beer belly. But I can. Just watch me.' Donald laughed. Portly stared. Elsie stood her ground.

'You pay me up to the end of the week, in cash, or I will—'

'Yes?'

'Go to the papers!'

'Ooh, will you now? Hark at you! You, Elsie Lancaster of no fixed address with no agent, who is now care of *Spotlight*, you will go to the papers? I say, they *will* be interested, won't they? Go to the papers? Elsie Lancaster, sometime star of an out of town tour, complains about Cosgrove and Bourton paying her a *week* late? Get out of our office, and be sure that if I have anything to do with it, you will never find work with us again.'

Elsie walked, as carefully as she had ever walked on stage, out of the office and down the stairs, and it was only when she reached the bottom that the realisation hit her. She was quite alone. Only half an hour before, Mervyn had said that he, and some others of the cast, would meet her in the office, but they had been nowhere,

219

and she had been landed with the confrontation, opening proceedings in a way that she thought quite harmless, always expecting the others to be arriving. She closed her eyes when she reached the bottom of the stairs. She had been done. Such a know-all as she had been, such a clever clogs, and now she had been done just like some sort of ingénue who knew no better – so unlike her, really. Never had done that kind of thing before, but now, thanks to her own impetuosity, and to Mervyn Castle's doubtless entirely untrue rumour, she was out. Kicked out, and likely to be replaced by the end of the week.

She sat herself down in a coffee bar and stared around her, not really believing what she had just been told. They would go back on it. Donald would revoke what he had just said. Portly would talk him round. They could not replace her by the end of the week. The rehearsal time, all that . . . it would be impossible to replace her.

But of course it was not impossible, it was horrendously easy. The telephone wires sang, telegrams were sent in all directions, and because the tour was already such a success a replacement, a new unknown, was found for Elsie's role: one Jane Buskin, Elsie's old rival from Tippy Toes days. And, no surprise to Elsie, she turned out be Mervyn Castle's niece.

The bitterness that Elsie felt following her dismissal was compounded by the fact that she had only herself to blame. That and the added fact that every hour of every day, and every night, she did not *think* that she could hear Dottie's mocking laughter – she *knew* that she could hear it. After all it was Dottie who had managed to negotiate a contract for Elsie that had a hole in it the size of the Atlantic Ocean, so that Elsie had no comeback against Cosgrove and Bourton, or anyone else for that matter. She was sure Jane Buskin would be doing the role for much less money, saving the management more than she personally cared to think of, because the Buskins were famous for their grovelling. Dottie had always said that the Buskins did not start with the Equity minimum for a salary, since they could not care less what they were offered: the Equity minimum was where they ended *up*.

'They're all the same, those Buskins – don't care what they're paid, just so long as they're working,' was what Dottie had used to say as her iron crashed down on the old wooden ironing board. 'They spoil it for the rest of us, people like that, grateful to be working, always grateful to be working, which means they'll do anything for a ha'pence three-farthings, and do.'

The show duly left town, but Elsie stayed on.

She stayed on for two very good reasons. She had nowhere else to go, and she had found herself a job, working for Fullers, as a waitress. The little money that she had saved for a rainy day now looked terminally small, and she dare not touch it, not for anything, except to pay her lodgings. Fullers gave their staff food, so she was not as badly off as she could have been, and she knew it. It was just the bitterness of it all that was eating at the insides of her, and no amount of delicious cake could block out the reality of that bitterness.

There is nothing so instantly maturing, so character building as the self-induced, brought-about-entirely-by-yourself, form of regret, and the bitter taste it brings with it lasts not for months, not for years, but for a lifetime.

No point in Elsie's asking herself why she had been tricked by Mervyn Castle, no point in trying to turn away from the utterly real sound of Dottie's laughter, no point in hating Portly Cosgrove for not standing up for her, not forcing Donald Bourton to change his mind; the truth was as it had always been and always would be when it came to her career. It was Elsie's fault, and she knew it.

Donald was the producer, so he obviously had to have his say. Portly was new on the scene, or so Mervyn Castle had said, so he would, in his naivety, probably think that he had to play by the rules. She could not imagine that Portly would ever have negotiated a contract to Elsie's detriment, or anyone else's for that matter, Portly just did not seem to be that kind of person.

But, nevertheless, as the days and eventually the weeks crawled by, and Elsie tried to come to terms with her future, ringing round in her lunch hour after theatrical jobs which all seemed to come to nothing, she finally found herself facing the fact that it was not impossible that Portly had not only colluded with Bourton, but had also agreed to dismiss Elsie.

Politics in the theatre, as Elsie well knew, were always a jumble of motivations, entirely and ever governed by the money in the bank. No money in the bank meant that everyone fell out. Plenty of money in the bank and people fell in love with each other, sometimes, unbelievably, for ever and ever, sending each other Christmas cards and remembering birthdays well into old age, never, ever forgetting the glorious time when they were all, for a short time, happy and secure in a glorious hit.

At last an advertisement in *The Stage* sounded desperate enough to accept her, and, when she rang, proved to be just that – desperate. Could she come at once? They knew of her success. They wanted her at once.

Saying goodbye to her friends at Fullers was much harder than Elsie had imagined it was going to be. As she did so, it came to her that the Marys and the Jeans, the Deborahs and the Janets, had become more than just her friends, they had become her supporters, sensing perhaps that Elsie was not destined, as they were, to be for ever pouring tea and slicing cake, waiting on tables and wiping them, smiling at people, hoping for tips, and seldom receiving them.

'You are going to be a big star one day, Elsie, we all know that, and we will come and see you and cheer you, and you will sign our autographs, and it will be so lovely,' one of the Jeans and Janets told her.

Then they all kissed her, again and again, in between laughing and giggling and drinking strong cups of tea, bringing a lump to Elsie's throat because a part of her wanted so much to be what *they* all were, settled and accepting, yet she knew that she could not be. Why, she would never really know. Partly, perhaps, because of Dottie and her ambitions for her granddaughter, partly because of her own feelings. She had to keep on trying to become a big star, not for Dottie now, but for herself. It did not matter if she failed, only that she had tried.

Elsie looked back longingly as she waved to the other waitresses, and they waved back from the door of the restaurant cum café. Working at Fullers for the previous months had proved to be a far cosier existence than any she had previously enjoyed. Nice landlady, regular wages that got you by, no one carping. Perhaps she should have stayed on, she told herself. And then she remembered. She had to go on, for a very good reason, or rather, a very bad reason. She had to continue with her career as an actress not just to fulfil some hazy feeling of destiny, but also to revenge herself on those two Ds – Dottie and Donald.

Vengeance was once more in the forefront of her mind and locked into her heart as she climbed aboard the Green Line coach. Opening her new little black book, she stared in satisfaction at their names. Added now to those of Dottie and Donald was that of poor old Portly.

Poor old Portly her fat foot!

He, Portly, must have been as much a party to her sacking as all the rest of them. Saving pennies, saving his skin; as bad as any of them. Elsie closed her little black book again, and opened her new copy of *The Stage*, always and ever the bringer of both bad and good tidings. Unable to read for very long in either a car or a coach before she started to feel sick, she did not find the relevant item, the item that would make her heart not only pound with joy, but sing with it, until she had checked into her new digs and was preparing to find the rehearsal venue for that good old theatrical warhorse *Rookery Nook*.

COSGROVE AND BOURTON UNABLE TO MEET THEIR OBLIGATIONS.

It seemed that far from filling every theatre and stopping at all the big tour dates about which Donald Bourton had been so happy to boast, the play, without its popular young star, had collected poor reviews for Miss Buskin, and had not filled anywhere. As a consequence the tour had eventually fizzled to a stop.

All alone in her bedsit Elsie started to dance around the room, laughing and hugging her copy of the paper to her.

'Serve them right for putting in Jane Buskin. Can't act her way out of a paper bag,' she told all the pre-Raphaelite prints that decorated the walls. 'Serve them a hundred times right!'

After which she went off to her rehearsals with a song on her lips, and murder in her heart.

She would show them all, she would show the lot of them, she would show them what she was made of. Not only that, but one day she would employ them all. No, better than that, she would turn them all away. That was how big she was going to be, big enough to turn them all down. Now that *was* big.

Meanwhile to her great regret, and very possibly even to his, the delightful Aeneas Mayo had disappeared from Coco's life, as is so often the way with enchanting people. It was inevitable. They had both known it. Why would it not be inevitable when, as everyone in their world knew, work had to come first?

So, when they had enjoyed an hilarious night out together at a new, totally tiled – more tiles than food, Aeneas had said – Italian restaurant, or *Terrazza*, and just as Coco was beginning to fear that she might be falling in love with him, to both their mutual relief and their mutual disappointment Aeneas flew off to Australia, of all places, and for no better reason than that someone had spotted him playing an Australian in a flop revue earlier in the year. Having mistaken him for the real thing, the film company had then decided that he must play the real thing in a small but crucial film role to be shot in and around Sydney Harbour.

'Bye-bye Aeneas,' Coco now always called,

every time she saw an aeroplane flying over where she was filming.

'Who is this lucky Aeneas person you keep calling to?' asked Victor Martin, Coco's leading man on her second film in as many months.

'Oh, no one. Just a joke really. An old friend. Only I promised I would call to him every time I saw an aeroplane flying overhead, until he came safely back to England.'

'You could still be calling to him when you're a hundred. Time to forget about him, and think about someone else.'

Victor Martin was tall and thin, with a pair of startling blue eyes which were almost too beautifully set off by his thick richly dark hair. His dark good looks were quite enough to get him cast as a juvenile lead in the particularly juvenile remake of a so-called classic silent, *The Snow Maiden*, upon which they were all now embarked.

As was now becoming a little too usual, Coco had nothing much to do in the script except sit about looking ladylike and be kissed, passionately, on the chin when the plot required it.

Not that she could have cared less. She was far too interested in saving up for her Austin Healey, now that she had found herself a new and entirely chic flat just off the King's Road in Chelsea.

'Any more films and I shall have to go on a diet.'

Coco stared down at her plate, which was now empty of the paella that had once crowded it. She sipped at her sugary coffee and smiled across at Victor. He was not tall and handsome for nothing.

She had briefly thought Aeneas was just about the best friend anyone could make, but even his looks, which, despite wearing glasses, were considerable, paled beside this epitome of a dynamic young leading actor.

Added to which Victor had that much spoken about, often rumoured, but seldom found quality – danger. She noticed that he even seemed to lend eating Spanish omelette and biting into his bread roll that special quality. As if, did not the roll quite behave itself, he would find a way of biting into it which would render it unable to enjoy life ever again in the same way.

Not that Coco was in the least bit attracted to him, because she was not. As it happened she was not someone who particularly liked dynamic men, always suspecting that they must be tiring. But there was no denying Victor was good-looking, and, on a film set entirely devoted to the noble art of hanging about waiting for a cloud to pass over, or the leading man or lady to deign to appear, that was at least something.

'You're coming out to Spain, aren't you?'

Coco nodded. Yes, she was.

'Good, because I could do with someone to swim with, not to mention – anything else.'

Coco looked away. Oh dear.

She stared up at the sky once more. She wished she was not going to Spain and that Aeneas was not in Australia, not that she missed him particularly – she did not, after all, know him that well – but she just wished that they were both staying in London, going to movies, enjoying themselves in Italian restaurants, walking in the Park arguing, that kind of thing. For the truth was that ever since Aeneas had taken off for Australia, even Oliver had become less of a friend and more of a complete pain.

Devoured by some new messianic devotion to his craft, Oliver spent most of his spare time either at the theatre brooding over other people's performances, performances which he necessarily found either totally riveting or totally devoid of talent, or in the company of his elderly voice coach making strange sounds.

Happily, or rather unhappily, Coco was seeing him tonight.

'It is just so unfair, Coco.'

Oliver appeared at the door of Coco's new sitting room looking unshaven, heavy-eyed, mournful and vaguely unhealthy. Coco stared at him. By the look of him he must be doing a modern drama. Whatever it was, it was quite apparent that drama school was not doing Oliver much good, whereas filming was doing her a lot of good. Well, not her, but anyway her bank balance.

'Do you act to live, or do you act to eat, Coco?' Oliver asked her, of a sudden.

Coco looked at him, trying not to show surprise. It was as if he had guessed her thoughts and decided to articulate them in some way, or start an argument, because he felt that they were in some way now different, which indeed they were. Whether they liked it or not, and in a matter of months, they already represented the two sides of the theatre, in their own minds at least, Oliver being art, Coco being commerce.

'I act to live, Ollie, you know that. I am just saving up, and saving up so that I can afford to give up acting, and become a designer. But as long as I am being paid to muck about on a film set, that will do very nicely thank you, although I doubt that it could be said to be remotely linked to art.'

'That is what I mean, it is just so unfair.' Oliver put his head in his lap in a gesture of overdone melodrama, holding his hands over his neck as he did so, which meant that his voice was coming out smothered and sulky. 'That is just what I mean. You hate acting, and I live for it, and here you are acting in film after film, while I am still treading water at drama school. Mind you, I did appear on the stage of the Royal Opera House the other day, as a singing slave. Did I tell you? And guess who I met there, doing the same thing?'

'Can't.'

'Newell. My brother, Newell. Can you believe it? Apparently it is—'

'I can't hear a word you are saying, Ollie.'

Oliver lifted his head. 'Apparently it is some age-old agreement. The Opera House doesn't just use Ramad as a supply for extras in their productions, but also, of all things, the Household Cavalry. So there we were, the brothers Plunkett,

230

marching on to the stage at the Royal Opera House, and of course their marching was yards better than ours, and didn't we all look silly titties.'

'Did Newell spot his shoes?'

Oliver groaned at the memory. 'He did more than spot them, he took them off me! I would have had to walk home in my socks if I hadn't had my blasted ballet shoes in my zip bag. Oh God. Can you imagine what I looked like to him, to Newell of all people, shuffling home wearing a duffel coat and ballet shoes? He always thought I was a ponce anyway, and now of course he knows it.'

Coco, having handed Oliver a glass of wine, now sat down opposite him. The evening was threatening to become a total washout. She had never before seen Ollie in such a blue funk, and yet she knew, and felt like kicking him for it, that his blue mood, his mean reds, had nothing to do with anything more than that he was eaten up with jealousy because she was flying off to start filming in Spain the following morning.

'Ollie. Why don't you give up drama school, and just concentrate on *films*? I mean, drama school is making you just so mizzy, isn't it? With your looks you could get into films straight away. Why don't you? I mean to say.'

'Because I do not want to *prostitute* myself, that is why, Coco. I am not like you. I am *serious* about acting, I want to play the great roles, really be up there, act my socks off, and everyone else's too.'

'Oh well, I suppose that is a point. No one could

say I have done anything of great interest, except be kissed on the chin and say "My lord, but does my lord think . . . ?" a couple of dozen times. As a matter of fact I have done that a very great deal, not to mention being laced into costumes that are so just so cheap and nasty, just so *nylon*, that it makes me cringe to wear them for even half a day. Still, mustn't grumble. I *am* saving like crazy for an Austin Healey.'

'What?' Oliver looked genuinely shocked. 'What a reason to prostitute yourself! For an Austin Healey, of all things. How shallow can you get, Coco Hampton?'

Coco considered this for a moment.

'I don't know,' she said finally, 'it might have been much worse. Just think, Oliver, it might have been a Ford. And I mean, say what you like, Ollie, but an Austin Healey is a great car. Really. Say what you like, but my money is on the Healey. Should be a classic.' She disappeared to stir the leek and potato soup, and then popped her head back round the door. 'But you, of course, only want to act in a classic, not drive one, don't you, Ollie?'

Oliver stared at Coco. 'Ha, ha, ha,' he told the once more empty room in a flat voice.

In Coco's absence, Oliver stared around him at the stylish new furnishings that his childhood friend was accumulating. It was always the same with actors, Melson had told him very early on in his coaching.

'You starve to do the classics, dear boy, and

232

then, later, things come your way. But you will have to wait, if that is how you want it.'

And a great part of Oliver *did* want it, the part that wanted to show his father, but most of all Cliffie, just what he was made of. But another part of him – at this he put his hand out and stroked the seat of a new leather chair that Coco had just bought for herself – another part of him wanted fine things like leather chairs, and cashmere, and Italian shoes, and steak and salad whenever he felt like it, not to mention an Austin Healey.

This duality of purpose was what was known at drama school as '*a right Edward the Second*'.

Did you starve for art, with a capital A, or did you pay the bills and let the art come around when, or if, it could? Like some maiden aunt who called occasionally to make sure that you were eating healthily, and were changing your socks at regular intervals.

'I say, Coco, when you're out there, on location, in Spain, keep an eye out for anything that might suit me, any recasts, that kind of thing, would you? Know what I mean? Sometimes they change the script on location and they need other actors. So you will keep your ears open for me, won't you?'

Coco smiled. 'Of course. Croutons?'

With this vague agreement between them now settled, Oliver's blues immediately lifted and he was able to wolf his soup and his steak and salad, and smoke the subsequent Gauloise cigarettes with all the élan of a man who sensed that he had come to an uneasy compromise. Not only that, but they both knew that Coco's promise to keep an eye out for him had stilled a little of his envy, and that after all was not nothing. Nor indeed was his admission that he would not object to earning a buck or two on a film.

'Now, how are you getting on with Hamlet. How was it, in the end?'

'I was brilliant.'

'Naturally. And modest with it.'

'Only saying what everyone else said, darling. But Ophelia was a pain in the neck, I can tell you. And Osric stole it.'

'Osric always does.'

'Still, I've already had offers on the strength of it.'

'What to do?'

'Oh, you know. Things.'

'What *things*, Ollie?'

'Television.'

They stared at each other.

'So.'

'Oh come on, Coco, no one decent does television. Bad enough doing films. And no one in England does *those*, unless they're starving, or saving up for an Austin Healey.'

Oliver smiled at her, and Coco found herself catching her breath, while at the same time turning away from the implied insult, because really Oliver had become such an artistic snob, there was nothing to be done about it, at the moment. It was obviously a drama school thing. She herself

234

could not have cared less what anyone thought of her doing films, but even so, of a sudden, it seemed to her that the British acting profession was filled with the biggest bunch of spoiled children that she had ever come across.

What was *wrong* with television, for heaven's sake?

'Know what I think, Ollie?'

'No.'

'I think you're frightened. You're all frightened of television, that's what I think, you're frightened because it's live and reaches so many people. You're scared rigid, all of you. That is why you look down on it so, because if you fall on your face on television, it is live in front of millions of people, and you will never recover from it, like the opera singer who fell into the orchestra pit. You think you will only ever be remembered for your fluffs or your dries, or your mistiming, and that is such a risk. Could kill off your career. That is why you all avoid it like the plague.'

Of course after that, Oliver promptly lost his temper, which made Coco smile smugly knowing that she must have hit a six, scored a bull's-eye, aimed and shot and blown up the target. She was absolutely sure that she was right. Actors *were* all scared witless by the very idea of television, which was exactly why Oliver was being so condescending about it.

Nevertheless, despite her know-all airs, Coco was still innocent of the ways of filming, and film people, and completely ignorant of the old theatrical saying about infidelity – that on location or on tour *it did not count*.

If she was ignorant of the saying, however, she very soon was not ignorant of the fact. Her first day on the set, just outside Malaga in southern Spain, thinking to get away from the crowds of extras being used for the battle scenes of this newest of what seemed to be an endless succession of inane pictures pouring out of England, she climbed up the hillside, taking with her a half-bottle of cold white wine and a plate of food.

She half closed her eyes, wanting to block out both the sound of the people below her on the hillside and the few events that were actually being filmed at the usual snail-like pace. She sipped her wine and ate her food, thinking about Aeneas and wondering how he was getting on in Australia, and whether he had saved enough yet for his Austin Healey, or had ever thought of her again.

'How shallow we are!' she remembered him shouting at her between their mutual bouts of joyous laughter as they compared their ambitions during that first dinner together. 'Why *don't* I want to play Hamlet and wear tights?'

'Because you see acting just as a means to bringing home the bacon. Of course it takes some art and some sacrifice, but basically, it's mostly about bacon rather than Shakespeare.'

Aeneas was so pleased with what he thought of as Coco's *bon mot* that they continued to sign off their subsequent telephone calls to each other with 'Remember – it's mostly about bacon rather than Shakespeare.'

That was the difference between Oliver and Aeneas.

Oliver was serious-minded and looked down on Coco for only wanting to act so that she could have a nice flat and an Austin Healey, while Aeneas on the other hand thought it hilarious that Coco did not mind being frank about her complete lack of depth. What was more, Aeneas articulated his own feelings with admirable brevity.

'If you have to do Shakespeare to bring home the bacon, so be it, but how much better if you can avoid the tights, and those ghastly little tunics that only just cover your family jewels, leaving everyone to wonder why a Prince of Denmark can't afford a longer top.'

Now a voice near to her said, 'A penny for them?'

Coco had an unnatural hatred for people who disturbed other people's daydreams, not to mention people who enjoyed saying something so crass as 'A penny for them'. She opened her eyes – oh so slowly – and half sat up, hoping that whoever it was would buzz off pretty soon.

'Oh, very well,' she said, seeing that it was Victor. 'If you really want to know, I was just wondering if my old mate Aeneas had saved up enough for his Austin Healey yet. We are having a race, to be the first one to buy the car of our dreams, and there's money on it.'

'You haven't come all the way out to Spain to talk about him again, have you?' Victor groaned as Coco shook her head.

'No, of course not. It's just that I'm due to take a few quid off him, that's all. We're only mates.'

'Which is not what that lot are by the looks of it! '

Victor pointed down the hill. It was half an hour into the lunch break for the large cast of extras and they were obviously determined not to waste a minute of their time off after pushing cannons up hill and down dale, not to mention marching endlessly and pointlessly towards the same twenty-yard point and back again.

Coco stared down the hill. It was a film in itself. There was not an extra, anywhere, who was not busying him or herself with another her or him, unless he was busying himself with another him.

'What a – what a – what a sight!'

'Such a pity they're not filming Sodom and Gomorrah, isn't it?'

They laughed in a companionable sort of way, still staring at the sight below them.

'I'll say.'

'Makes you wonder what kind of home lives they have – that they are so frustrated, doesn't it?'

'It certainly does.'

Victor stared into Coco's eyes, and she became uneasily aware that three or four weeks of filming might be going to lead to the kind of trouble she did not want. She carefully lay down in the grass again, of a sudden covering her low-cut costume

238

with a table napkin, murmuring as she did so, 'Must be careful not to get a tan, so out of period.'

But the voice beside her murmured, 'No point in covering them up, Coco, I have memorised them already.'

Chapter Eight

So there it was, at last, the train, bringing Master Oliver back to Yorkshire, and, as the saying went, straight to the bosom of his family. Clifton stamped his feet up and down for perhaps the fiftieth time and blew fruitlessly on his woolly gloved fingers, Yorkshire in spring not being the warmest of places.

He repeated this exercise once more before hurrying forward to where he knew the first class carriages would be stopping. The great engine drew slowly to a halt alongside the platform, looking for a few alarming seconds to be about to outstrip the station itself. Slowly carriage doors started to open, as if the realisation of arrival was only just dawning on the occupants of the train, and then decorously, brusquely, hurriedly, ponderously, the different passengers stepped down and out on to the platform.

As Clifton had expected, the doors of the first-class carriages were the first to open, making it appear to those waiting that even the act of dismounting from their carriages gave the first-class passengers precedence over those in the second- or third-class coaches, after which, slowly following on, came the rest. Clifton stood among the first to emerge, his eyes searching eagerly for his surrogate offspring.

After a minute or so his heart started to sink as he realised that Oliver could not be going to be among this first elite. Turning round he hurried back towards the second-class carriages, walking anxiously along the length of them and peering in at the windows, yet still there was no sign. Finally, as he was beginning to despair, and as the other carriage doors were beginning to be closed by the assiduous porters, and the train engine prepared to leave the station once more, a door reopened and a tall, thin, youthful figure began to crawl down from his carriage and on to the platform.

There, at last, was Oliver.

After his initial double take, a double take which combined a feeling of relief at his safe arrival and astonishment at his appearance, Clifton hurried towards him. He had fully expected Oliver to change in the months that he had been away, but not to turn into a tramp. Unshaven, his hair longer than Clifton had ever seen it, Master Oliver's face was not pale, but grey. And the lines under his eyes were so deeply etched that they could have been drawn in by a theatrical eye pencil. He looked worse than anything Clifton had ever seen, except perhaps on the Pathé News at the local fleapit.

'Master Oliver.'

'Cliffie.'

Oliver hugged him, quite unselfconsciously. Clifton smiled, tentatively, momentarily flattered, while looking around for some sort of suitcase. But Oliver, it seemed, had no baggage that he could see, apart from a bag slung over one arm of his duffel-coated shoulder, and he stank of alcohol.

'Had a couple on the train,' he told Clifton, ingenuously.

Clifton took him by the arm and marched him, not walked him, through the ticket barrier, nodding at his old friend Parker, who was on duty that day, and at the same time raising his own eyes to heaven. Parker responded by not bothering to ask to see Master Oliver's ticket. He knew.

Young men everywhere, his look told Clifton, they were all the same. Send them to London to improve their situation in life and they came back looking like something the cat had brought in.

Outside in the station forecourt, Clifton paused. 'Very well. Straight to the Station Hotel, Master Oliver, but first a stop-off at the chemist's, I think.'

'What for?'

Clifton stared at the wreck that was his protégé. 'What for, did you say? Why, to turn you into a human being before your father sees you, Master Oliver.'

Clifton's mind cast itself back to the old house where the Plunketts had lived for so many generations. Once back there Master Oliver would look worse than a bag of rubbish dumped in the middle of the immaculate drive. There his un-shaven grey skin, his greasy unwashed hair, his shabby clothes and his vague but pungent smell of old stout would stand out against the immaculate presentation of centuries of proper living. The spring flowers in the halls and receptions rooms, so lovingly arranged by Clifton himself, the old silk curtains that could never be cleaned except by a specialist in old materials, and then only along approved lines. The old furniture that could never, ever be polished, only lightly dusted. The dull Charles I silver, the Georgian china, the French enamels, the lightly weighted eighteenth-century silver knives and forks, all of it, every single item, would gang up on Master Oliver's appearance and frowningly reject him – and that was all before Easter Sunday mass in the private chapel, with Father Bill in his centuries-old vestments, vestments made of the palest silks and gold threads, vestments that exactly toned with the candles and the flowers, the incense and the lace.

Clifton booked them into the best suite at the Station Hotel, which although not up to much had the advantage of being not so posh that it would reject the tramp of whom he was now in charge. Once let into the rooms he ran a great tub of water in the en suite bathroom, and, doubting that Oliver could be relied upon to wash himself properly, he threw in some bath salts for good measure. The rich lavender scent rose up towards Clifton as he also threw in a newly purchased loofah and placed a large bar of Pears Soap for Oliver's use by the taps.

'Scrub yourself, shave yourself, and stay where you are until I get back.'

Leaving Oliver laughing helplessly at the whole fandangle, Clifton shot off in his car back to the house, happily not too far away to be returned from by the time Oliver had come to, let alone shaved off his ridiculous excuse for a beard. Up the stairs he ran to Master Richard's wardrobe and from the back, where items of less interest were stored, he grabbed what he could of the older boy's cast-off clothing, a shirt here, a tie there, a jacket, and a pair of cord trousers. Shoes he could not bring himself to steal, since he had noticed that Master Oliver was still wearing a much scuffed pair once worn by his eldest brother.

'Lucky you are away in Africa, Master Richard!' Clifton muttered to the photograph of John Plunkett's eldest son on the dressing table. 'Or else we might be having words by now.'

He shot down the polished wooden stairs again, and out to his motor car, which he drove as fast as he dared back to the Station Hotel where, to his immense relief, he realised Oliver must have finally finished his ablutions, because he could hear him singing in a strong tenor voice a verse of two of the Slave Chorus from Verdi's *Aida*, always one of Clifton's favourites.

Knocking on the door of the suite and letting himself in, he was confronted by a changed man.

Master Oliver stood before him all pink and perfect from his bath, clean shaven, a towel around his waist, his face glowing and bright, and the smell of alcohol quite gone, happily replaced by a light waft of English lavender and clean shampooed hair.

'Clothes.'

Oliver held up his elder brother's old clothes and looked across at his father's old batman, teasing him.

'Not really my part, you know, Cliffie. I have been playing more real characters lately. Hence why I travelled in this manner.' He pointed at his old clothes. 'And the beard and so on. I am just living one of my latest roles, trying to find out what it is like not just to be alienated, but to cause alienation in others. Very interesting too, particularly in the dining car!'

'I know, I know, Master Oliver. I realised you must be up to something, but there is no time for that now.' Clifton glanced down at his watch. 'Tea is in the library at four o'clock, and you know Mr Plunkett does like punctuality.'

Oliver nodded. It was always the same with his father. The memory of the iron routine, never varied or deviated from, came rushing back.

First would come a glance at the library clock – *Where are these people?* – this would be barely one minute after the arranged time of their arrival. Then, two minutes later, *Well, if they're not coming we might as well carry on.* Finally, *Don't they know that to be late is so selfish? The servants have to get*

245

home to their own families. Delay them and you ruin their families' meals. So thoughtless. Really, unforgivably thoughtless.

Oliver started to hurry. Much as he knew that he had changed in the previous eight months, and despite staying in London with only Coco for company at Christmas – and in a valiant attempt at saving money working in a restaurant throughout the whole holiday – let alone playing Hamlet, and winning a prize for verse speaking and plaudits for his acting that had everyone predicting – depending on whom they favoured – that he would be the new Olivier, Richardson, Gielgud, Guinness, or whoever, Oliver wanted to be late for a meal at his old family home as much as he wanted to have his toenails pulled out.

To be late for tea by as much as a minute would be to ruin the whole Easter break.

It was as simple as that.

In the event they both just made it, Oliver glowing from the bath and scrub up, not to mention the shave and the shampoo. Clifton on the other hand, far from glowing, was nothing if not hot and flustered from the whole horrible experience. Happily, however, having shot up the drive and decanted himself by the staff entrance, he was still, somehow, in time to serve tea from the library table, handing Oliver a tier of home-made scones and cakes, and a cup of China tea taken in an old Victorian teacup with precisely as distant an expression as any butler might wear who hardly knew who Oliver might be. There was, therefore, no sign on either Clifton or Oliver's face of the previous little drama. No one would have known from the butler's demeanour that only a little more than an hour before he had been standing in the town's chemist with sweat pouring down the back of his legs while he purchased a razor, a toothbrush, a loofah, soap and bath salts, let alone hiring a hotel suite and risking life and limb to sort out new clothes for Master Oliver.

'Thank you, Clifton.'

They had always kept up the pretence of not really being aware of each other in the presence of Plunkett Senior, and now, because he was very much aware of being an actor, Oliver revelled in this other form of acting, this real life acting, where it was vital to keep his face straight and his manner one of deference and filial piety.

All the world was certainly a stage, and men and women merely players, and never more, it seemed to Oliver, than in the library at the Hall.

So—' his father began.

Ever mindful of his tiny allowance, and on Cliffie's instructions, Oliver had written to his father once a month. His letters were carefully penned to put himself in as good a light as possible, naturally, but never boastful. This was for two very good reasons. First of all his father would not approve of any kind of self-praise, and secondly he would never, not in a million years, understand how thrilled Oliver was at being cast in something, or how difficult it was to win even a paltry cup for verse speaking, how keen the competition, how earnest the competitors.

Nothing like that would interest him, as why should it? He was much more interested in what Richard was doing in Africa with his regiment, or how the trade unions were running the country. These were the real things, and real things, like the price of tractors and people living off the state, or the Army being kept short of guns, were the only things that really interested John Plunkett. Mucking about at drama school would not be something which he would consider of the slightest worth, nor would it be something in which he could interest himself. Worse than that, he would not understand why anyone else would consider it in any other way. To him, drama school and the problems of actors would be like a foreign country that had never set eyes on a British flag. Neither it, nor they, would have any real relevance at all in his world.

So, Oliver had confined his letters, which as a consequence seemed to take for ever to write, to trying to describe London, and minor events that his father might find amusing, news of family friends, and Coco's films: small vignettes, well away from the complications of playing Hamlet, or trying to make sense of this strange character called *Estragon*.

'So, how have you been doing, in London, that is?'

'Quite well, thank you.'

From nowhere, or more accurately from an LP of Coco's that she had only recently played to

248

Oliver, came Gertrude Lawrence's voice in a Noel Coward play. The actress's clear, exact, charmingly precise intonations floated into Oliver's mind and acted as a kind of mental anaesthetic, numbing Oliver against the pain caused by the slow progress of his non-conversation with his father.

There was a line that went

I work in a bank.

Quite high up in the bank, or just sitting in a little cage totting up things?

How strange and marvellous it was that actresses, someone like a hall porter's daughter from Putney, or wherever, actresses such as Gertie Lawrence, should come to represent, more than anyone else, more than the daughters of kings and princes, the elegance and beauty of an age, not just for their lifetime, but for the rest of time.

Perhaps it was art's way of mocking life, that the people who were most remembered as being beautifully themselves, ones whom other lesser mortals longed to imitate, were in fact mere artistic imitations of the real thing, no more real than the scenery against which they moved and spoke, yet somehow a great deal more real to more people than many so-called real human beings.

'I said, "How is the work?"'

His father was obviously repeating a question which Oliver had failed to answer, his thoughts taking off in another direction as the all too familiar and terribly unexciting exchange of dialogue limped along.

'The work is fine.'

'Have you got any?'

'Have I got any what?' Oliver was being deliberately obtuse.

'Work.'

'Not yet. But I have been cast in a great many productions, and one semi-professional Sunday night performance, playing Estragon in—' Oliver stopped, realising that it would be ridiculous to explain that most famous of parts since his father would not know Samuel Beckett from Thomas à Becket. He skipped the next bit and ended hurriedly, 'It was only a one-off, but very interesting, and I am due to play it again, in a student production, quite soon.'

There was a pause.

'I see. I don't know that one.' John Plunkett carefully licked the remains of the Dundee cake that he so enjoyed off his fingers. 'No, I don't know that one, I am afraid. Estragon? Is he a foreign playwright? I suppose he must be with a name like that.'

'Estragon? No, no, he's not the writer. He's a character from *Waiting for Godot*. It's a famous play, by Samuel Beckett. Samuel Beckett is an Irishman who lives in Paris. Probably the perfect combination – you know, being Irish, and living in Paris. The wit and the humour, the warmth, combined with the food and the Left Bank, le jazz hot, and the endless coffees drunk at pavement tables. Perfect really, wouldn't you say?'

Oliver had no idea why he had added all those extra pieces of information. The bits about Paris had nothing to do with anything really.

After that there was a small pause, and then, 'Ah yes, so many of our playwrights are Irish, are they not? Sheridan, Oscar Wilde, Bernard Shaw, and now this fellow. What did you say he was called? Beckett. This play, or what you will, is it a hit? What's it about, would you say?'

Of a sudden, perhaps guided by guilt, it seemed that Plunkett Senior was making a huge effort to understand Oliver's theatrical world. Oliver appreciated this, even felt vaguely moved by it, and yet explaining the nature of Samuel Beckett's most famous play to his father was not an easy task.

'What's it about, this play?' John Plunkett repeated, helpfully.

'What's it about?'

'Yes, what is the plot?'

'The *plot*. Um, yes. Yes, well. It's, er, about, well, it's about these – well, tramps really, and—'

'Tramps?'

'Yes, sort of tramps.'

'Sort of tramps. I see.' John Plunkett reached forward and having sliced another piece of Dundee cake he started to eat it a great deal faster than he would perhaps normally, as if his hunger for knowledge had brought about a more real physical hunger, as if the cake would help him understand Oliver's world better.

'Yes, I suppose you would call them tramps, and they are waiting around for – well, God, I suppose, you would say. Yes, I think they are perhaps waiting for God. Yes.'

Being a religious man Oliver thought this would please his father no end, but if it was meant as a palliative, it failed.

'About tramps waiting for God. Doesn't sound very amusing.'

'No, no, I don't think it is – very amusing.'

Oliver cleared his throat. There was a long silence broken only by the sound of Plunkett Senior emasculating his cake.

Oliver's eyes slid to his wristwatch, half hidden under his eldest brother's old shirt cuff. Still only half past four of a spring afternoon, and there were five more days to go. It was a moot point, out of the two of them, who would be more relieved to find that it was now time for them to part until drinks and dinner – his father, or Oliver. Perhaps sensing the new lull in the proceedings, Clifton once more entered the library and cleared his throat.

'Someone on the telephone for you, sir, in the telephone room, Mr Plunkett.'

His father shot out of the room, barely able to keep the look of relief from his face, leaving Oliver free to escape into the garden and light a cigarette.

For once Oliver had truly managed to shock himself. He was shocked to ribbons at how bored he was in the company of his father. It was like being with a very tedious clergyman who you feared was about to lecture you on some of the finer points of the Bible. Not his father's fault, of course, Oliver hastened to tell himself, it was quite obviously his fault – not his father's fault, he thought, over and over again. But no use denying the fact, Oliver was about as interested in being with his father as his father was in being with him. They had so little in common that really Oliver might as well be a Swahili native, and his father a missionary intent on trying to come to terms with a quite alien culture, trying to stop Oliver going around naked as nature intended, putting his Mother Hubbard on his head instead of around his loins, and all that kind of thing.

Of a sudden Oliver found himself longing for Coco. He imagined himself telling her about the *Waiting for Godot* fiasco. He could see himself imitating himself stuttering out the word *tramps*, and Coco laughing and urging him on to do imitations of both of them. Coco would see just why the whole thing was so funny. Oliver on the train trying to practise alienation. Cliffie haring off for razors and putting him in lavender scented baths; the race to be in time for tea in the library. Coco would find it all hilarious, as Oliver did, really. It was just that on your own there was no one with whom to laugh. He had Cliffie, of course, but however close he was to Cliffie, Clifton was not Coco.

Oliver frowned, staring ahead of him at the still wintry but immaculately maintained garden as some pretty wintry feelings settled around him.

253

How he felt at that moment, with this awful distance between himself and his father, must be how his mother had felt. This must have been how far apart his parents had felt, as apart as anything could be. Good God! No wonder the poor woman had run off with Charley. He felt a warm rush of sympathy not just for his *sainted mother*, as Clifton always called her, but for his father too. Their life together must have been hell.

Huis Clos, an existentialist play written on the theme that hell is other people, fairly sprang into Oliver's mind. His parents must have been caged together, and while perhaps not hating each other all the time, certainly not understanding each other at all, while all the time acting, always acting that they were, in reality, the perfect upper-class couple. Living at the Hall, hunting and shooting, serving tea in the library, being kind in the village, but all the time not understanding, not really understanding a single word that each said to the other.

Of a sudden Oliver made up his mind about something pretty important.

It was at the exact moment that he found himself obsessively throwing away the stub of his Gauloise, while making sure to carefully cover it with earth with the heel of his half-boot, so that one of his father's gardeners would not find it. It was at that precise moment that he made his resolution.

He was never, *ever*, going to marry, not ever. He would not ever subject another human being to the awfulness of existence that his mother and father must have endured for the sake of their three sons. He would never ask another human being to do what he now knew his parents had done, to stick out an unhappy marriage for the sake of society and religion. Everyone did only pass this way once – Oliver had no time for re-incarnation – and that being so it was criminal to expect human beings to soldier on in some man-made living hell, and for no better reason than to keep up appearances.

He turned and walked back to the house. It had to be faced, the only person who would keep his spirits up, the only reason for his returning, was to see not his family, but Cliffie.

'You realise that you have ruined my chances, Cliffie. Jumping on me at the station that way, forcing me to wash and brush up. Now I have no chance, no chance whatsoever, of delving deeper into experiencing that sensation of total alienation that I might have done when confronting my family looking as I did.'

Clifton looked unimpressed.

'Be that as it may, I don't think you should play too many unshaven or whiskery parts, Master Oliver, really I don't. Finally, producers and the like, they can't see the actors for the whiskers, can they?' Clifton spat judiciously into the boot polish tin and carefully made circles with his shoe brush in the result. 'Not if you keep burying yourself beneath them. They won't be able to see your real face for the hair, if you get my meaning, and that is no good. Stars must have faces, unless they happen to be rather plain like Alec Guinness, in which case they have to put on whiskers and make a feature of it. It's just a fact. No, as I understand it, the grown-up moment in a young actor's life is when they know they can abandon the whiskers and play, as it were, naked of face and limb. Make the audience see what is there, without its actually being there. That is the actor's art. Sarah Bernhardt playing to packed houses, already old but playing young girls with such utter conviction, wooden leg and all, that it is said by those who saw her that she was able to convince her audiences that not only was she young, but that her body was whole. Now, *that* is acting.'

There was a pause while Oliver considered this.

'Even so, I bet you're glad you didn't have to see her, Cliffie?'

Clifton ignored this mischievous remark, and Oliver's droll expression. 'She had monarchs in tears even in old age,' he added, his own expression one of almost religious piety.

Oliver looked sulky. 'But I *like* making up, growing stubble and building false noses, and all that. That is so much what I like, about acting, I mean.'

'Humph.' Clifton looked across at his protégé. 'Even so, the day must come when the whiskers go, or you will. Have a humbug.' He passed Oliver the old-fashioned jar he always kept in the pantry, and Oliver took one in much the same manner as he had used to when he was a small boy, popping it eagerly into his mouth and sucking it rather too loudly.

'Well, I suppose you're right, Cliffie. After all, whatever anyone says, there is nothing better than acting bare-faced, as it were. It is the big one, isn't it? The bare-faced acting bit, none of that striding on and hiding behind the nose putty. Oh, by the way, did I tell you? I'm not doing you so much now. I am growing into my new accent, which is to say, I am growing into my old one, bit by little bit – I am reassuming a public school accent, and getting so much praise from my teachers for it. It is really quite hilarious.'

Clifton looked up from polishing, because this, after all, was very interesting. Much as he had inwardly applauded Master Oliver's decision to adopt a working man's accent and attitudes at his drama school, he had always known that it was, however small, nevertheless a risk. People might find out that he was not working class, and there would be sure to be a backlash. They would hate him more for being from a genteel background and pretending *not* to be, than if he had brazened it out in the first place.

'No, you didn't tell me. How is it going, Master Oliver?'

'Really quite well, because the thing is, I am able, now, to do less of you, and more of *me*, improving my accent and all that, because of how well I am supposed to have learned to do a proper

257

BBC standard accent in my voice classes, et cetera. So the classes have been nothing but good cover, and now I don't have to do you any more. That is it. No more Cliffie.' The expression on Oliver's face was impish. *'Do you mind, darling?'*

He uttered his last question in a purposely Noel Coward accent, and even Clifton, who rarely allowed amusement to disturb their talks, smiled.

'So you can be more yourself, then?'

'Yes, but I still have to remember to go back to being you whenever I'm in the coffee bar or the pub, *savez?* Can't let too much show in my lunch hour, or after six o'clock at night.'

Clifton nodded at the finished pair of now highly polished shoes. 'That's better. Not even Mr Richard would recognise them as his own now, they look that good.' Clifton stared at the shoes with justifiable pride.

'You do everything perfectly, don't you, Cliffie?'

Clifton did not reply, but sighed and for a second looked pensive. 'Do you want to do a piece from your Hamlet for me, Master Oliver, just a bit before I have to run on and do dinner? I'd quite like to see a short audition piece, and then perhaps a piece from the Sheridan, that might be nice.'

Clifton made the so-called pieces or play extracts sound as if he was ordering a nice slice of coffee cake, and a bourbon biscuit to follow.

'Certainly.'

They left the butler's pantry and climbed up the

stairs to Clifton's suite on the top floor, and there the former batman listened in solemn silence as Oliver gave him a muted rendition of two of his latest roles.

Muted or not Clifton found himself moved to reluctant tears by Master Oliver's soliloquy from Hamlet. Without Oliver's realising it, it was his youth that moved Clifton. Although his voice was good, and much improved with Melson's lessons too, it was his surrender to the debate of living or dying that was so immensely touching, and all the more so for the speaker's being not yet twenty-one. Seeing Cliffie's eyes filled with tears thrilled Oliver, and having listened to a few notes, good ones at that, from Cliffie, he went downstairs to change for dinner in as happy a mood as he had known for many a week.

His good humour was short-lived, however, and for a very good reason – namely one Captain Newell Gordon Plunkett, who was also home for Easter.

Newell had always been Oliver's least favourite brother since he had a line in laconic sarcasm and needling which made Oliver actively dread any encounter with him.

'Why don't you do any television? That's where the money is, surely,' he asked after only a few desultory exchanges in the library. 'Afraid to sell your soul to the devil, is that it? Too grand! I bet that is it. Only interested in the classics, that would be you!'

'No. I er – I am studying at the moment,

hadn't really thought ahead much. I mean, do *you* know if you want to be colonel of your regiment?'

John Plunkett followed this exchange with the solemn and determinedly disinterested expression of a tennis umpire. The rally continued as the combatants moved from the library to the freezing cold dining room.

'You should have a show of your own, that's what. Get a show of your own.'

'I haven't had time to go up for anything yet. I haven't even got an agent, let alone a show of my own.'

'You should buck up, you should, young Oliver. No good poncing about the stage all day long when you could be selling toothpaste – that's where the money is now ITV is here. You could be starring in your own show, or fronting one of those quizzes. That would suit you, that's what you should be doing, fronting a quiz, like Hughie whatsisname, or whoever.'

Of course Oliver knew what Newell was doing, and quite purposefully. He was reducing his younger brother's future to a few crummy commercials or a quiz show, hating the idea that Oliver might be going to be famous, might be going to be someone, might actually succeed at his acting.

'Oh, by the way, Newell, how did you enjoy being on stage at the Royal Opera House? Quite something, wasn't it?'

Newell reddened, having, it seemed, entirely

forgotten about their encounter backstage at the Royal Opera House.

'Just a lark,' he quickly told John Plunkett. 'We all go on in the chorus, for a lark. Walk on as slaves or whatever is needed at the time. It is the tradition that the Royal Opera House is supplied with extras from the Royal and the Household Cavalry. Rather different supply routes, what?'

Plunkett Senior's face remained unmoved, either by the idea of his two younger sons at the Royal Opera House, or by their meeting there unexpectedly. Perhaps the notion did not interest him, certainly it did not seem to elicit anything more than a wintry smile, the kind of smile that might be aroused by someone nearly spilling a glass of wine, but not quite.

'What do you think of this burgundy, Newell?'

'Splendid.'

'Good. Just as well. I have laid down a great deal of it. Tell me, what do you think of the new anti-tank—'

They started to talk about the army and Newell's regiment in particular with rather less feigned interest than they had shown towards acting, and almost at once Oliver seemed to slip out of their line of fire in exactly the same way that he had slipped out of it when he was young, and growing up at the Hall.

It was as if he did not exist, as if he did not matter, and more than that, as if they had rather that he did not. Once more his mind started to wander, back to Cliffie's room, back to Cliffie

261

looking moved by his audition pieces, and all that. It was the only way to keep the pain at bay, to detach himself, fly above everything like Peter Pan. Except he was more like one of the Lost Boys than Peter Pan, but unlike them he wanted to stay lost, had no wish to be rescued by a belief in fairies, or anything else for that matter.

Nothing much changed at the Hall, Oliver thought sadly, staring at the plate in front of him, and nothing much would ever change, he supposed. Everyone just the same. Hardly worth coming home. Oliver and Cliffie polishing shoes and talking about theatre in the pantry, his father and Newell talking about guns in the dining room.

He had looked forward so much to coming back, seeing them all after all this time. For so many months he had imagined how it would be, but now that he was home he found himself wishing that he was back in London. Anywhere in London, too, doing anything except sitting like a lummox with nothing to add to anything. He would rather be waiting at tables, walking in the Park, going off to his voice lessons – he wanted to be anywhere but where he was, sitting silently in the ancestral dining room surrounded by portraits of Plunketts, none of whom had been bitten by the acting bug. If he had known what it was going to be like he would probably never have saved up the fare to come back. Except for Cliffie, of course, it had been well worth coming back to see his favourite old boy.

'Where are you going, Oliver, if you don't mind my asking?'

'He's retiring with the ladies! Leaving us to our port. Must be all that wearing of the tights, eh, Ollie?' Newell always laughed long and loud at his own jokes, and now even his father could not help.

'Got a bit of a headache. Going to lie down—'

'What did I tell you?' Newell gave another guffaw of laughter. 'A headache. Any excuse, *we* know!'

'Very funny, Newell, I don't think. Sorry, sir. If you don't mind, have to attend to the migraine. Take some tablets. It's a cracker, I'm afraid.'

Oliver backed out of the room and straight into Cliffie who was, as always, listening at the door.

'Come on, Master Oliver, come on down to the snug. I have a grand bottle of eighteen-year-old whisky sent by an old army friend from Scotland. We can really enjoy that, and have a long talk about your plans. You must have some ideas about the future, haven't you? Myself, after what I saw earlier, I would say that you are in line for a Ramad gold or silver medal, I would really.'

Humiliated, and set about by his usual feelings of total inferiority in the presence of the males of his family, Oliver followed Clifton downstairs, glad to be away from the other two, not caring what they thought of his leaving the dining room early, altogether not caring about very much really.

'By the way, how's Mrs Piglet, Cliffie?'

'As well as can be expected, since she is feeding about seventeen offspring at the moment.'

'It just shows you. I had forgotten to ask after her, after all this time.'

'No, you hadn't, you just didn't dare to ask. I know you, Master Oliver. Saint and Francis are your middle names, aren't they?'

Clifton poured them both two socking great whiskies from his special bottle of eighteen-year-old, and smiled.

'Here's to you, Master Oliver. You're going to show them. Just you wait and see, you will show them. All of them.'

They both knew whom he meant by *them*.

Those other two, his brothers. The two men in his life who did not understand how he felt, who did not want him to do well at what he wanted. They wanted him to be ground down, not raised up, by what he did. They thought that people like him were beyond the pale, just flotsam and jetsam.

'Yes, you're right, Cliffie, I will show them, and soon.'

Coco was feeling more and more homesick, which was a paradox, really, if that was the right word.

Really, the longer she was on location the more she should feel at ease, with herself, with her surroundings, with the cast and the crew, with everything, but the truth of the matter was that she did not. Worse, the further truth of the matter was that, despite the much appreciated funds for her long awaited Austin Healey piling up in her bank balance, she wanted nothing more than to fly home to London. Being on location on a film in circumstances which, however much you were being pampered, after only a few days revealed themselves to be completely devoid of the slightest interest was actually very disappointing, however much she tried to pretend that she had not expected more.

In fact, it seemed to Coco that being on set over the last few days was just like being trapped in a lift. The film seemed to be going neither up nor down. At some moments she even found herself praying that the Central Bank of Pima – or whichever unfortunate institution it was that had backed the film – would blow the whole thing apart by refusing to fund it any longer.

But no such luck. Despite seeing what surely must be the most wooden rushes known to man, the bank had, it seemed, happily continued to allow a fortune in money to stream out to Malaga. No amount of costly delays in shooting, or mounting crises with the two perfectly awful stars, who were now, needless to say, knocking each other off, seemed to put them off. The bank continued to sign the cheques with an equanimity bordering on lunacy.

Victor and Coco had, therefore, necessarily, to become friends. Quite apart from anything else there was no one else remotely within their own age group with whom they could pal up, and boy, did everyone need a pal when stuck on a hot location, with temperatures and tempers rising to equally high levels.

Victor had, it seemed, soon got the message that Coco was not in the least bit interested in him, and never would be. She had explained to him, most patiently, that they could be friends, but that was all.

'The famous Aeneas, I suppose?'

He had asked this with a resigned look, and a voice dripping with regret.

'No, no one. I am committed to my career.'

'Ah, we want to be a great actress, do we?'

'No, we want to own an Austin Healey, that is all. Nothing else will do.'

He had laughed at that. 'I like honest people.'

But like so many people who said they liked honest people, Victor liked nothing of the sort. He liked to be complimented, to be told that he was a great friend, that he excelled in his scenes, to be commiserated with, and nothing much else.

Coco went along with this new role of admiring sister/friend, simply and solely because she was on location, and for no other reason. She said things to Victor that she would never say to Oliver, and allowed him a line in flattery that Oliver would never be allowed to get away with – for a start they would both be laughing too much. But with handsome Victor Martin, it worked. And just when she had found that there was a small part going spare, for which Oliver would be all too suitable, and had telegraphed to tell him as much, Coco, from a combination of

266

boredom, homesickness, and drinking too much wine, one hot summer night, gave in, and went to bed with Victor Martin.

Waking up the next morning with a pounding head, and the feeling that she was actually in the Sahara desert and had not been given water for as long as she had been on location, Coco staggered towards the bathroom and drank her fill from a very nasty bottle of water. It was tepid and had obviously been bottled from some sluggish source somewhere that did not bear thinking about, but Coco had drunk it all before she realised that she must be still drunk to have drunk it at all.

'What was I doing last night?' she asked the revolting person mirrored in the glass above the basin. 'Was I mad, or drunk, or what?'

The answer was, as Coco well knew, all three.

Please tell me that I did not just lose IT *with Victor whatever he calls himself, for no better reason than that I am homesick, bored and lonely?* she demanded of her conscience, but being Coco's conscience, the answer came back loud and clear.

You just did. You just lost it.

After that it became a lengthy process of self-justification. As she cleaned up her face and prepared for the day, took aspirin and drank gallons of water, Coco told herself that she must be in love with Victor. It could not be that she had thrown herself away on Victor because she was feeling homesick. She must be in love with him.

They got on so well. That must be what love was: you got on well, laughed and joked, and then went to bed together, and got married, or something. That must the logical process through which everyone went, the procession of normal emotions that eventually led to marriage and children.

'Are you all right?'

Victor stared at her. They had just finished in make-up and were waiting about, as always, for shooting to start.

'If it is of any interest – no.'

'Why aren't you all right, Cokes?'

'Because, again, if it is of any interest, I am more than horrified at what I got up to last night.'

'What did you get *up* to last night, as you put it?'

'The same as that writhing mass of extras on the hill, that's what. And besides, I have a shattering hangover, and I swear I will never drink wine of such a low type, or sleep with such a – sleep with anyone ever again. Why oh why do they call it *sleeping with someone*? It is such a stupid expression, isn't it? Sleeping with someone. You don't sleep with someone, that is the whole point, you stay awake. You sleep when you have not slept, as it were. Pathetic way of describing it.'

'Didn't you enjoy it?'

Coco stared at Victor Martin. 'Not for a second.'

'It gets better.'

'I'd rather not try, actually, Victor. I am too

sensitive for this world. Besides, I rather think that things should, as the song says, have been organised better.'

'No one enjoys their first time.'

'You don't say.'

'Oh, come on, Cokes, you're a beautiful girl, I am a handsome man, we are on location. Why not enjoy ourselves a little?'

'Look, Aeneas – I mean Victor—'

He stared at her, and they both reddened with embarrassment at Coco's slip, but for entirely different reasons.

'That was *not* funny. You wished that it was him, last night, that is what you wished, isn't it?'

'No. As a matter of fact I can't remember last night, so wishing for someone, or not, does not come into it. Now, come on, let's try to get over the whole awful business and concentrate on the scene. Quick rehearsal, please!'

Victor looked shattered, and serve him right, Coco thought to herself, almost smugly. Good God, taking a girl when she was as drunk as fourteen sailors was just not on, but it had happened, and now they just had to get on with it. She just wished that she had not been drunk. It seemed so awful to lose *it* when you were practically unconscious.

'Oh well.'

Coco walked ahead of Victor.

'Oh well what?'

She could hear his anxious footsteps behind her.

'Oh well, I had to lose it some time, so I suppose it might as well be to you or with you, or whatever the expression is.'

'Can't you at least pretend that you're in love with me?' Victor complained from behind her as he tried to negotiate the grass they were traversing without ruining his costume.

'What is the point, Victoire dear?' Coco demanded, becoming deliberately camp. 'It will only lead to complications.'

But, although Coco did not know it, but was soon, unhappily, to discover, complications had already begun.

Oliver stared at Coco.

'But you were only out there five weeks,' he protested.

'Quite enough time to get pregnant, Oliver.'

Oliver stared out at the people walking past the restaurant window. Fresh from coming back from being on film location Coco was treating him to lunch. He had got in first with all his news, long before Coco could embark on any location stories, not giving her time to say much about herself. The principle behind this tactic was, of course, as they were both well aware, to put Coco in her place, but more than that, to make sure that she knew that while she was fooling about on location Oliver had been bent on doing proper, good work, which was not what Coco would have been doing, for all that she would have been paid large sums of money for larking about on location, doing nothing more serious than remembering a line a day, and avoiding a tan, which was not in period for the film.

He had hoped to have fascinated her with all his stories about playing various roles, about all the new gossip, about Bertrand sacking the now infamous Putt and for no better reason than that Putt had enjoyed an affair with one of the students. Finally, Oliver's *pièce de résistance* was his story that Putt had been promptly snapped up by a rival establishment and had taken the girl in question with him to a rival drama school, upon which she too was snapped up – but this time by a film company.

'So you're not the only person to be whisked off to become a film star, Coco love. Putt's bit on the side has been cast as the maidenly daughter of an Anglo-Saxon king. She too will now, doubtless, be saving for her Austin Healey.'

Oliver had just finished spouting his deliberately patronising little speech, which was really meant to make Coco laugh, when she had burst into tears and started to tell him her awful news, as the waiter was putting a perfectly delicious plate of minute steak and chips down in front of each of them. Seconds later, instead of picking up his steak knife and fork, Oliver had found himself staring out of the window at the people outside, slowly passing by, because he was not used to women crying, least of all Coco crying. Coco did not cry. Coco was arrogant, mocking, and confident, Coco did not cry. It was just not Coco.

'Don't do that here, Coco, not here, not in front of everyone, they'll think I'm being cruel to you. I was only trying to make you laugh, really I was. You know, just pretending to be jealous, and all that. That's all, really.'

Oliver's eyes moved restlessly from Coco's distraught face to the minute steaks, and back again. He was starving, and at the same time desperately upset at Coco's distress, not least because it meant that they might be forced to abandon their food and leave the restaurant. His stomach gurgled loudly as Coco dabbed hopelessly at her panda eyes with a paper napkin.

'I am not a film star, as you call me, Oliver.' Coco wiped her eyes with her paper napkin. 'I am, as of this moment, a pregnant *ex*-actress. Oh God, Ollie, what shall I tell the *guardians*? They will have a twin fit. I will bring disgrace on them, and after all they have done for me, all they have *been* to me.'

'You won't. You will say nothing to anyone, least of all your guardians, that would be madness. Just keep yourself to yourself, stay in London, make all sorts of excuses, but whatever happens do not, repeat not, do *not* tell them. It will do no good. Particularly now they are down on their luck, and, from what you told me, eating dog food for Sunday lunch.'

Coco nodded, sniffing. Oliver was right, of course. Besides, she could not bring herself to even imagine the scene. Her guardians so proper, always so kind to her, never blaming her for

272

anything the way they probably should, living in Norfolk, making do on fresh air and brown bread, because of their shares collapsing and all that. What a way to repay them for all their kindness to her.

'Go and see them quickly, before they get suspicious, and then stay in London while you have him, or her, or whoever the baby is going to be.'

'I wish I could, but I am burgeoning already. I can't go and see them, they will guess straight away.'

Coco began to eat her steak and chips, sniffing bravely, and trying to halt the great shudders of emotion that were raging through her.

'I am burgeoning and burgeoning, Ollie, straight off. None of my costumes fitted at the top, and everyone on the set was starting to talk. I tell you, it's true. The costume department can never, ever keep its mouth shut, as you will pretty soon discover. They are always the fount of all knowledge, suppliers of corsetry to the truly enormous of both sexes, or the about to be heavily pregnant, or the merely pathetic. They notice everything from your skin tone to your toenails, judge you on it and then rush off and tell everyone.'

'Who is the father of your baby, Coco?'

Oliver tried to look brotherly, his heart aching for her, despite the basic fact that at least his hunger was being assuaged by the steak and chips.

'This, this actor – Victor – Victor Martin, no,

273

Richards, not Martin, oh I don't know, something like that. He's very good-looking, but, you know, we didn't know each other, don't know each other at all, not really. It was just a drunken moment that we have both tried to forget.'

They stared at each other. The very idea of not being able to quite remember the name of the father of her burgeoning burden suddenly appealed to both of them as being hilarious, and they promptly burst into hysterical and unstoppable laughter. Coco equally promptly developed hiccups, and so between the laughter and the hiccups they finally ploughed their way through their steak and chips, the food bringing welcome relief from the awfulness of Coco's situation.

Afterwards Oliver lit a cigarette and put on his most worldly expression. He had to be a true friend to Coco, had to think of the best way she could deal with her situation.

'I know a convent where you can have the baby, Coco. I mean, it is actually a nursing home, full of kindly nuns and things. They do a great job for the mothers of unexpected babies, apparently. It's a bit of a way out of town, in the suburbs. But once you've had your kitten, they find homes for the little mewlers, nice homes too, goodly couples who can't have mewlers themselves, but will bring them up as if they were their own, and treasure and love them probably more than if they were their own kitties.'

'But you seem to forget I'm not a left-footer like

you, Ollie. I mean, I am not the stuff over which motherly nuns will purr in sympathy.'

'Don't matter, love.' Oliver leaned over the table and squeezed Coco's hand. 'Don't matter a single diddly damn, promise. You just have to be a nice person who won't set fire to the place, and all that, that is all.'

'Is it terribly expensive?'

'No, I think you just pay what you can afford, or something. I don't know why I know – oh yes, I do. One of the actresses in my elocution class at Ramad has a sister who found herself in your situation, and since so many actors are, one way or another, left-footers, she told me all about it. And one of my cousins—'

'I have earned a few bob. I can pay. Oh dear.' Tears welled up in Coco's eyes. 'Oh dear, oh dear. Bang goes the Austin Healey, doesn't it, Ollie?'

"Fraid so, Coco. But don't worry. You will soon be back to rights, and able to get on with your life. You have no idea how quickly nine months can go. After all, even as we sit here, just think, you've only seven and a half left, even now, so that is something, isn't it?'

Coco wiped the tears, yet again, from her eyes with her paper napkin. She had been such a fool, but they both knew there was nothing left now for her to do, except pay for her error.

'I suppose good will come out of bad, if we wait and see, that's probably what will happen. I expect. I hope.'

'Exactly. Now did I tell you, I'm probably going to be auditioning for the Royal Shakespeare?'

'Oh, but Ollie, that is wonderful.'

To her surprise, despite knowing that she was out of it now, however temporarily, Coco felt only delight at this news.

'Yes, someone saw me, and said they would get me an audition. They're not taking on anyone new at the moment, not this year or even next, so I will have time to finish the course at Ramad, and then perhaps go and do a spot of rep. And then bang, in we go, we hope, and on with the old spear carrying, if there is a gap in the ranks, which of course there may well not be, because you know people don't leave the company nowadays. Like hen's teeth when a job comes up there.'

'Well, at least they're interested, I mean, that is something, isn't it? That they are interested in you, that someone has seen you and thinks you're worth seeing again.'

Coco put her hand over Oliver's and sighed. Inside her, deep down, there was such a mixture of emotions, a veritable dolly mixture of emotions, that she hardly knew where to turn next. Oliver stubbed out the cigarette in his free hand and taking out a pen scribbled on a piece of paper.

'Here's the address of the nuns – give the maternity sister my love.'

Coco looked up, surprised.

'I was about to tell you, earlier. The sister in charge of the deliveries, she's a Plunkett cousin.

Brilliant horsewoman actually, but she gave it all up to dedicate her life to God. And babies. In fact I think two of our cousins are in there, both nuns, as it were. They will see you right, so don't worry, eh?'

This made Coco feel better. She had a healthy fear of nuns, but she knew that Oliver's cousins were innumerable and the fact that a couple would be in evidence when she was having her baby was somehow reassuring.

Her baby.

As she left Oliver and wandered in a desultory fashion down the streets Coco said those two words over and over again, wondering all the time why they sounded so right. Her baby. Her baby. And then she realised why it was. And it was quite simple. It was her baby. Whatever was making her burgeon was *her* baby, and what was more it was *only* hers. The father, the Victor Martin or Richards, or whatever Victor's stage name was – oh, God, that had been so funny, the moment when she could not remember his name – anyway the young dark-haired actor who had laid her on that hot night in Spain what now seemed like a hundred years ago was no more the father than Oliver. Victor whatever-his-name might be the instigator, the reason she was having to face this pregnancy, living off her savings, but he was not the real father. No, in her head, she knew who the father was really, and, it was certainly not Victor – *thing*.

*   *   *

Oliver's thoughts at the same moment were quite different.

The idea that Coco would be caught up in her own particular drama and not able to stir up maddened feelings of envy in him for the next seven and a half months should have made Oliver feel spring-heeled, elated, and full of the joys of midsummer, but it did not. In fact he felt oddly depressed.

He loved Coco, and so, of a sudden, as he had kissed her on the cheek, and they had both turned to go their separate ways, the thought that she would have to go through this horrendous child-bearing experience on her own was almost more than he could bear.

He stared morosely out of the bus window. He hated to think that he could be a father at his age, so what on earth must it feel like to be a *mother*? They both knew that Coco would have to go through pain and anguish, and then more of the same when she gave it away.

And yet it had not occurred to either of them that she should do away with the little mite. It was not a religious thing, anyway not with him, but somehow, once there, it seemed that the baby did have some sort of right to carry on trying to make its way into this strange old world. Oliver did not care to think of its not being allowed that right, not once it had been formed and was waiting to become a human being. It was against normal feelings, somehow, not to give it that right, if you could. The worship of life, even just the tiny beginning of life, was part of the human psyche stretching back thousands of years, and the noble tradition of bastards, which stretched back equally far, had always been in existence. In fact the *bar sinister*, displayed in family coats of arms all over England, positively celebrated the bastard line. Whoever Coco's child turned out to be, whatever it was like, of one thing Oliver was quite certain. He would make sure that it was proud of its entrance into this world, not ashamed. He would make that his duty.

Ahead of him that afternoon was fencing, and then music and movement, all of which he enjoyed. Ahead of Coco was nothing but sickness and fatness, having to book herself into the nursing convent, be nice to strong-minded nuns, listen carefully to adoption arguments, and suffer heartbreak of one kind or another. All sorts of things that had nothing to do with being young and enjoying the world as she surely would never ever be able, now, to enjoy it again?

Oliver sighed, of a sudden remembering practically every moment that he had ever spent with Coco. At the theatre, at the cinema, arguing in coffee bars, writing to each other, one minute heartily despising each other's opinions, the next admiring them just as passionately. After all that, all that looking forward, all that hope, what was now in store for her would be sure to change *that* Coco completely. People always changed once they had done what Coco herself was fond of calling 'grown-up type things'.

And almost the worst of it was that Coco had never, ever wanted to be a grown-up anyway. She had always shuddered elaborately when marriage and children were mentioned. Oliver sighed yet again. There was nothing for it but to use the emotions he was currently feeling in his work. Tomorrow, in improvisation class, he would remember the pain he was feeling now, and he would reuse it. That was the only way to cope with it.

He felt a little better after that, as if he now knew that it was possible to tidy up the world a little, to reduce its emotional litter, and so in some small way to make it a better place.

Chapter Nine

It did not take long for Elsie to resign herself to the vaguely amateur if charming ambience of the Stephens Theatre at Tadcaster. As a matter of fact, after a childhood dedicated to the harsh realities of the utterly professional theatre, to Dottie's constant moaning about the conditions of work, or the lack of it, and the ineptitude of the unions to deal with any of the very real problems of the show business population, the gentle amateurism of Mr Stephens's small, surprisingly modern theatre set on the river at Tadcaster was not only reassuring, it was positively life-enhancing.

The show, for which they had been desperately searching for some sort of emergent young musical star, was not brilliant, but neither was it without talent. It was one of those gentle musicals that only the English can produce. Indeed it might, before the First or even the Second World War, have been an amateur production put together at some grand house party where even the servants, if remotely talented, were roped into performing and singing. Where the costumes for the participants were designed and made in the house by the governesses and the ladies' maids, and where the fine musicianship and singing of the family was a long established house tradition, providing after-dinner entertainment for the more refined of the household and its guests, the rest taking refuge in the billiards room.

Tadcaster was a small town with a very large abbey at its centre, where, the fine tradition of music had been carried on for centuries. Walking along the narrow streets of the town in the early morning to buy bread for her breakfast and a paper from the newsagent, Elsie experienced a feeling that she had never truly felt before. She felt content. The fires of intense ambition that had been stoked since she was a tiny child by Dottie's plans for her life still burned and were not damp-ened – no listless smoke coming from damp wood – but, perhaps for the first time in her life, neither did they truly rage. They were, for the moment, content to burn merrily, and as they did so, for the first time since she had come into the world, Elsie found that she could walk along a street and notice how good the world could be. Tadcaster was very much part of that goodness.

Of an early morning, walking along the narrow, winding main street, Elsie could take time to notice all the old buildings from a multitude of different centuries propping each other up, while from the bakery came the unmistakable smell of dough rising in bread ovens, eventually to be delivered into the eager hands of the townspeople by a red-faced baker who shinned up and down the narrow back stairs of his bakehouse with all the agility of a much younger man.

Having bought her bread Elsie would then turn towards the dairy where smart ladies with silk scarves knotted at the throats of their cashmere jumpers sold their husbands' farm butter and cream, and unusual breakfast cereals. Here there were tins of Grapenuts, and jars of home-made marmalade with carefully written labels detailing the name of the farm, or house, where it had been created from home-grown fruit. Life was delicious, and never more so than when Elsie was back in her digs brewing coffee and eating her cereal, cutting fresh bread and spreading it with butter and thick marmalade, with none of Dottie's daily imprecations slicing through her head.

While the quality of her life was being so immensely improved by the goodly citizens and shopkeepers of Tadcaster, Elsie was also experiencing an extraordinary success in the musical. The house was packed out nightly, and Mr Stephens, the widower who happened to own the theatre, had developed the habit of proposing marriage to her, also nightly.

'You must marry me because you are my star. I will change the name of the theatre to yours,' he promised Elsie after the first night, kissing her hand, again and again. 'It will be the *Elsie Lancaster Stephens Theatre*'.

Elsie thought Mr Stephens looked just like a piece of his own pork, but of course she let him worship her, as why should she not? She was only interested in her career, and she would never willingly marry anyone, she knew that, any more than Mr Stephens would ever do anything so stupid as to change the name of his theatre to hers. But the very fact that the short, bald-headed, wealthy butcher was so pleased with the success of his son's musical was enough to give her a new, more settled confidence. That and the fact that, within a very few weeks of the musical's proving to be a sell-out, he signed her up to a new contract, after which they both settled down to try to find a new play or musical, or to arrange some classical revival, that would suit Elsie's talents.

'How about attempting some Coward?'

Bartlett Corrigan, artistic director of the Stephens Theatre, frowned and gazed past Elsie, adjusting his horn-rimmed spectacles. 'Aren't you a bit young for Mr Coward?'

'I can age a bit.'

'Noel Coward is very much out of favour at the moment.'

'Surely then someone should put him on, in that case, defy the trend, make people realise what a fine comedy writer he is? Besides, so much of his work has music, it should keep young Jolion Stephens happy. He can play and score it, and all that. It could be good, *n'est-ce pas*?'

Elsie frowned down at her figure, momentarily assessing it for herself. If she put on a bit of weight she reckoned she could convince their provincial audience that she was at least twenty-five. A bit of weight, more sophisticated clothes, a heavier make-up, particularly around the eyes, and – *voilà* – she would be on her way.

'Well, you may be right, Elsie,' Bartlett agreed suddenly, after a pause. 'After all, if you remember the balcony scene in *Private Lives*, it really depends on an orchestra playing "Some Day I'll Find You" just a little too slowly behind the dialogue. That will be something for young Jolion Stephens to do. I mean, I always think that is what makes the scene so poignant. If you don't have that, you don't have the balcony scene.'

Bartlett fingered the neck of his polo-neck sweater, frowning. He did not want to seem old-fashioned, or out of touch, but at the same time he did have to think of pleasing his audience. Being a confirmed provincial, in his heart of hearts, he did not care much for the fashionable plays of the moment that the London critics so enjoyed. The tramps waiting for someone to arrive, or the ladies sitting in sand bemoaning their lot, in order to prove some existentialist philosophical point. These were the kind of plays that were all the rage in artistic circles, certainly, although rumour had it that they were not filling the theatres to quite the degree that the managements, and the press, would have everyone believe. Bartlett was certain that such plays, all too influenced by the Parisian intellectual élite of the post-war years, were certainly not suited to the tastes of English provincial audiences. Moreover he had always sworn that if he was in charge of running a theatre he would be guided by one firm and unalterable principle: to give good value for money to a loyal following. Making something as good, and therefore understandable, as it could be was his one and only aim.

He therefore went on to tell Elsie that he did not care a whit if Noel Coward's work was not being played any more. More than that, he did not mind a jot if boiling hot oil of artistic hypocrisy was being poured over every single one of Coward's quite brilliant talents. All Bartlett cared about was – could he produce and direct the play the way that it should be produced and directed?

If he could, and with Elsie in the star part he thought that he could, he was sure that they would have another success, and two successes would lead to another, and another. Because once you got the tone of a theatre's productions right, you were on a roll. He had seen it time and time again, the ongoing, successful, seemingly endless roll that was the natural consequence of getting it right.

'OK, so let's go against the trend, let's do some Coward,' he told Elsie, almost casually. 'But who shall we get to play opposite you, do you think?'

Just as his first year at drama school was coming to an end Oliver had found himself an agent. Sometimes he wished that he had not found himself Tad Protheroe, but, frankly, since Oliver was totally unknown and still at drama school, it was any port in a storm, and Tad was certainly any old port.

Tall, middle-aged, and imposing to look at, he had a stable of well-known if equally middle-aged stars who, happily for him, were always and ever *away filming*. This meant that Tad could happily spend his time between the Betterton Club and the restaurants and small gaming clubs that, at that time, littered newly fashionable London.

After Tad had signed up Oliver, Oliver found himself wishing, most heartily, that he had been spotted by someone a little less illustrious in his end of term Easter production at Ramad.

Not that he was not flattered that the great Tad Protheroe wanted to sign him up so quickly, but the fact was that he had the feeling that he was too young for Protheroe's agency, and that the reason Protheroe had signed him up so quickly was purely and simply that he wanted to add a few more actors under forty to his stable of stars. Oliver had, of course, been flirted with by a few of the other agencies, but he had also been turned away by just as many of the same.

Not quite flash enough in looks to be put straight into film, not quite mature enough to be cast in television or snapped up by the Royal Shakespeare, he found, to his chagrin, that he was not quite as marketable as he had hoped. He had quite set his heart on joining one of the permanent companies when Tad Protheroe stepped in and, with one eye on the slender profits to be made from Shakespearean apprenticeships, seemed determined to put Oliver off.

'You can spend your whole life in one of these big companies,' Tad had intoned, 'you truly can, earning no more than seventy-five pounds a week, and that is top money. Oh yes, I know' – he had held up one majestic hand – 'you will play everything, you will be the talk of the town, here and there, but you will, finally, have played them all – and I mean *all* – you will finally find yourself cast aside as too old for this or that, and too young for the truly Senior roles. And so, panic-stricken, you will start to cast around for film and television parts, and having lost the whole of your youth to the pursuit of Shakespeare you will find that the parade has passed you by, old boy, just passed you by.'

Here Tad had paused to hitch up the trousers of his pin-striped suit, which on account of his shape were very large, the legs appearing to Oliver as having been cut in such a way as to be slightly frightening to the younger members of the profession.

Following the judicious heave to the Savile Row suiting, Tad gave Oliver the deep and admonishing look of the seasoned *I've seen them all come and go* West End agent.

'No, what you want to do, old boy, at your age, is to get out to the provinces and play everything *but* Shakespeare. You have done Shakespeare at drama school. Now it's time to get moving on the light comedies, get out of tights and into a suit, do modern plays. You don't want to spend your life washing off body make-up after the performance, rinsing off the old bole before haring off to the Dirty Duck to discuss some poncy review in the *Sunday Times*, only to wake up years later to find you're ninety, do you? No, you want to find out more about yourself, do everything, the Agatha Christies, the – well – you know – do the *other* things. So important, really. To move or not to move from the company, it becomes the obsession of the company actor, and in the end, when they do decide to move, it's nearly always too late, poor dears.'

Oliver had nodded, not believing Tad Protheroe at all, and what was more not wanting to believe him. He had every intention of playing all the great roles, and he did not see himself as being in any way the same as any other actor in the whole world. He was different. He would go straight to the top of any company. He had to, just to prove to his father that he was *someone*, not just Oliver, the youngest, unwanted son.

Besides Tad Protheroe, Clifton too was coming to town to see him in his end of year production at Ramad, which was exciting. Oliver was looking forward to impressing his mentor. His only worry was that he had worked so hard with Melson on deepening his voice that he now felt that every time he opened his mouth it did not really match his bony body, but even so, he felt that Clifton would be impressed.

'Hallo, Dad.'

Oliver had already made an arrangement with Clifton to pose as his son, adding to the authenticity of his so-called Yorkshire background, something to which they had both agreed by letter.

'Hallo, lad.'

Actually it was not that difficult to pretend that Clifton was his father because in all reality, since he was very young, Clifton had been so encouraging to him, so interested in him, that the butler had in actuality assumed the role of, at the very least, Oliver's artistic father.

Clifton stood backstage at the little amateur theatre looking strangely un-Cliffie-like. His neatly pressed suit, perhaps newly bought, looked impressively modern and affluent. Narrow trousers, mohair and silk mix, it was so up to date it might have been made by Dougie Millings himself. Indeed everything about Cliffie at that moment gave off the aura of the prosperous northern father, come to see his son in his end of year production.

'Yes, well, that was really very . . .' he started to tell Oliver's backside as Oliver bent down to wash the make-up from his legs, narrowly avoiding three other actors doing the same thing. He then added, 'But we must discuss the whole thing over a pint, rather than here, wouldn't you say?'

He was cut short by the arrival of other visitors, including Tad Protheroe, who now pressed into the dressing room and boomed at Oliver, 'Well done old boy,' before backing out again with 'Ring you in the morning.'

Cliffie, with an evident feeling of relief, also now backed out of the dressing room and stood against the whitewashed wall outside, waiting. As he did so another party of relatives arrived and gave their names to the stage door keeper. As soon as he saw and heard them, Clifton fled down the corridor towards the stairs down to the theatre basement.

Inside his crowded dressing room Oliver stared at himself with some satisfaction in the mirror. He did not think that he would ever really get to enjoy the *toga parts*, as he thought of them. For a start, he was sure that he had too much sense of humour, but for now, as far as he knew, he could honestly say he had not discredited himself.

He had used his voice as Melson had taught him, he had commanded attention, he had even, he knew, elicited some jealousy from his fellow thespians – because someone had very sweetly, at some point before dress rehearsal, inserted pins in his jar of bole, the body make-up that he used to cover his all too skinny legs and arms. Happily, he had been warned by Cliffie, years ago, of such theatrical practices, and always paused before applying anything or plunging his fingers into a jar. Cliffie had said that the rule was always look first, make sure – and only then apply.

Happily Oliver had seen the pins well before they could inflict any lasting injury. He had

291

thrown the offending jar out and sent for another via the very sweet assistant stage manager who seemed to have an unending, and very boring, crush on him. Naturally, as is the way with assistant stage managers, she had subsequently quite forgotten the commission, and Oliver had been forced to borrow bole from another occupant of the already overcrowded dressing room – possibly, it had suddenly occurred to him, did he but know it, from the very person who had ruined Oliver's make-up in the first place.

All these thoughts flashed through his mind as he stared at his now togaless, fully dressed self, so much so that he did not hear the dressing room door open yet again. He turned at once to see who it was, only to freeze as suddenly. Worst of all worsts – it was his father.

Oliver opened his mouth and shut it again, realising as he did that his reaction could not have been better had he been Hamlet seeing his father's ghost. Making a mental note to remember this he turned to see whether his fellow performers, busy dealing with their own relatives and friends, had also seen his new visitor in his dark grey town suiting. Realising that they had, he managed to follow up his initial reaction with, 'Oh, hallo, sir. I didn't know you were up in London?'

How happily this strangely Victorian form of address now sat on Oliver's lips, and how relieved he now felt that his father was so stuffy. Coupled with the fact that they did not look even

292

the slightest bit alike, it meant they could not be thought to be related in any way.

'Hallo, Oliver.'

John Plunkett's blue eyes looked briefly into Oliver's green ones, and then slid off in the direction of the other parents, all of whom had more in common with Cliffie than they had with Plunkett Senior in his well-worn but impeccable suiting, his Lobb shoes, his old, gold wrist watch, his signet ring, his carefully cut hair, and his hat and umbrella, both carried in a gloved hand at just the right angle.

'Would you like to come for a drink, sir?'

'No, as a matter of fact, I can't come for a drink, Oliver.' His father cleared his throat. 'I have to go on to the Garrick for drinks and dinner with friends, whom I am meeting there. Very good matinée this, though, I must say. And I did want to come round and surprise you at your end of year performance. Tell you how good you are, that sort of thing.'

There was a small silence while both of them tried not to look as embarrassed as they felt.

'Thank you very much, sir. And I am! Surprised, I mean.' Oliver smiled happily, feeling even more relieved that his father was not able to come for a drink, and at the same time feeling massively guilty too. He should want his father to come for a drink with him. God, he was such a bad son, it was frightening.

'Good. Well, that's all. Well done.' His father patted Oliver lightly on the arm. 'Very good

293

indeed. You came across very well, I thought.'

He actually said 'I thought', which immediately gave rise to a ghastly suspicion in Oliver's mind that he might have been with someone, or even several people, who did not share his opinion, but there was no time for Oliver to question him because he had already turned away and left the dressing room. Oliver stared after him, wondering, as he always did, why being with his father always left him with pangs of sorrow and regret, as if they were like two people crossing on a bridge, who, having met halfway, would merely nod as they passed each other, and despite their acquaintance would carry on walking in opposite directions, as if they had not really seen each other.

Clifton returned to Oliver's dressing room imagining that Oliver must by now have gone off for a drink with his father and some of his own friends, but on finding Oliver still waiting for him in the now empty dressing room he kept an admirably unsurprised face.

'Right, *Dad*,' Oliver said, teasing him and using his, he fondly imagined, impeccable northern accent, 'coming for a pint?'

Clifton nodded, wordlessly, still half expecting his employer to appear from behind a door, but the wide-eyed look of innocence on Oliver's face reassured him that Mr Plunkett had paid his respects, and left.

When they were seated opposite their pints in the back of the Salisbury pub, Oliver did not ask Cliffie what he thought of his performance. He was too canny for that. He knew, more than anyone, that Cliffie would come out with his comments in his own time. Instead they chatted about home, about Mrs Piglet, about his brothers, about his father's surprise visit, about everything and anything, until, at last, Cliffie came out with his pronouncement.

This time it had taken so long for Clifton to say anything that Oliver knew, for certain, that something about his performance had deeply worried his mentor. At last he spoke.

'You said it as if you knew it, Master Oliver.'

Clifton pulled his mouth down into an expression of such solemn and sad disapproval that it seemed to the astonished Oliver that he might have been a Roman emperor at some great game, and himself a poor gladiator being given the thumbs down.

'Your voice is good, it has come on a bit, I mean it has deepened, I will say that for it,' Clifton went on, 'but you said it as if you knew it, and that will never do. After all, when we speak, we never really know what we're going to come out with next, do we, Master Oliver? Something nice might be what we *want* to say, but what comes out, all too often, is something that hurts someone else, and all that. So, if I was you, next time you go at it, I should try and surprise yourself. Try not knowing it, take a risk. I mean, I thought that *beauty loving* way of spouting Shakespeare had long gone out of fashion, but doubtless they're still teaching it in these drama school places. Or it might be that it's old Arthur Melson's fault, he's always been a bit of an old ham. But, you know, what's disappointing, Master Oliver, is – what we used to talk about at home, you seem to have forgotten it all.

'I mean, if you take Hamlet for instance, Master Oliver. Take, well, take *To be, or not to be: that is the question* for instance. That is not a speech that he is making, it is a question he is *asking*. Is it worth living, is it worth going through all this toil and moil only to die at the end? That is what the poor young man is asking himself, a question being asked by millions of people of themselves even as we sit here, but they're not *spouting* that question, Master Oliver! They're asking it, even murmuring it.'

Oliver stared at Cliffie, and then he lit a cigarette with a shaking hand. Bloody hell, he had not expected this, far from it. He had expected something, but not this.

Of a sudden he hated Cliffie with all his heart, and with all his soul. All of a sudden he was glad that Cliffie was not his proper dad, glad that his own father had come round and gone away, not given Oliver his opinion about everything. He was a million times gladder than he could say that Cliffie was not his real dad, saying tactless and hurtful things, coming to the Salisbury to make ill-timed criticisms just at a moment when Oliver truly, truly did not need it.

And yet.

296

'You're right, Cliffie. You're quite right,' Oliver said finally, after a long silence, and he stubbed out his cigarette and promptly lit another one. 'And I can't blame old Melson for it, it is my fault. I did say everything as if I knew it, not as if it had only just occurred to me. I mean, really, what a twit. The basic mistake of a bad actor, and I made it.'

Cliffie finished up his beer. He had been truly horrified by Oliver's stilted performance. All that they had worked on while he was growing up had seemed to have disappeared out of the window, replaced by self-conscious drama school acting and a Victorian style of booming voice production.

'And another thing, you came on so pleased with yourself, Master Oliver. You did not need us, really you did not. You had no vulnerability, no humility, nothing. It was terrible. Your perform-ance was terrible. I was ashamed of you, really I was. All this way for me to see you like that, and your father out front too. Really, it was awful. You made a hash of it. Not that you were any worse than the rest of them, they were all awful, but you – you should know better, after all we have put in together, all we have worked on. I was ashamed, really I was, and I would be remiss if I did not tell you as much, really I would.'

Oliver put his head on the pub table. 'OK, OK, don't kick an actor when he is down. It is only an end of year production, you know, Cliffie, it's not Stratford or anything.'

'All this time down here in London, and all you have done is regress. Backwards is all you have gone. Seems to me these drama schools are more about employing the teachers than creating any kind of artistry, if you ask me.'

'Which I didn't—'

'Never mind. You will be fine now, I dare say, now that you've finished your time here.'

'But I haven't finished, Cliffie. I have another two years to go, you know that.'

'Oh no you haven't,' Clifton told him. 'You are not staying another week in this place. You're going to get out there, into repertory, and start learning your craft, Master Oliver. One more week in that place and you will turn into a proper popinjay, and we wouldn't want that, either of us.'

Oliver started to say something, and stopped. It was true. Everything that Cliffie had said was true. He *had* become pleased with himself. He had already been signed up by a London agent. He should leave drama school. It was doing him no good at all. He was bored stiff in most of the classes, and the only real work he had done had been with Melson.

'I don't suppose anyone will have me, I mean any of these rep companies, will they? Not if I don't finish.'

'This one will.' Clifton produced a card from his waistcoat. 'A friend of mine telephoned me a few months ago. He's very friendly with the man who owns it. It's only a small place, mind, but it will give you plenty of the *right* kind of experience.'

Clifton snorted lightly before going to fetch another couple of pints at the crowded bar, and returning with a satisfied look to him.

'They should not be called drama schools, they should be called melodrama schools,' he said, returning to his subject with some relish as he sat down again. 'Anyway, now you have an agent. Next you have a run in repertory theatre, or in this case professionally sponsored theatre, and then we will see. But no more spouting and prancing, and I don't know what.'

Oliver had been taken down so many pegs in such a short time that he now could do nothing but stare ahead of him, misery settling around him like a damp mist on a May morning. He had not thought that he could have been quite as bad as Clifton made out, but he now realised that he must have been, and it was shaming.

For some reason, as he drank his pint, above the hubbub of the busy pub he could only hear his father's cultured voice saying, 'You came across very well, *I* thought.'

That was the worst of it, really, that he had been bad in front of his real father. The man who was having a mass said for him each month had seen him *spouting and prancing*, as Clifton had put it. He had witnessed for himself his youngest son coming across as nothing more than a popinjay. It took Oliver back to the days when he was small, to acting in front of his family in the library, to a resounding sound of silence.

He picked up his beer mug, but this time he did not savour the rest of his pint, he simply swallowed it, and after Clifton left him to return to his hotel, he swiftly followed the pints with a couple of whisky chasers. Little wonder that some time later when he returned to his landlady's house he could not see to put his front door key in the lock. Finding it to be a feat all too far beyond him, he sank down on the doorstep, and putting his head in his hands, he cried his eyes out.

Back at his hotel Clifton told the friend he was having dinner with, 'Only just in time. I tell you, one more term in that place and we would have lost him for ever.'

His dining companion listened appreciatively before agreeing.

'We have to suffer or we cannot become anything, not anything at all.'

'Your table's ready—'

They both nodded sagely before finishing their drinks and going in to dinner.

Coco could not decide on the right clothes to wear that morning. The only thing she did know was that if she was to be examined, it would be better to wear things that came off easily. She did not fancy struggling out of her clothes. She finally opted for a pinafore dress and white shirt together with long white socks and flat shoes. She stared at herself in the mirror. She still could not believe that she was pregnant. Pregnant, and, it had to be faced, quite alone.

Keeping it from her guardians had been tough. She had finally opted for pretending that she was immersing herself in her acting, promising to visit them, even making dates and subsequently not turning up, telephoning at the last minute to say she had an audition, sending them flowers and letters, but never going to Norfolk to see them.

It was an exhausting and very hurtful way of going on, and she knew that she was behaving very, very badly towards them, causing them terrible pain, but it was better than confessing all, telling them that she was pregnant, which she was certain would be a shock from which they would never, ever recover, such was the disgrace of a baby born, as the saying still went, out of wedlock.

Not that whoever she was carrying was visible yet, but since Coco's bosom had, for some reason, shot from thirty-three to thirty-six, and her waist expanded by about the same number of inches, she was feeling both dismal and claustrophobic. She had never given a thought to having a baby, nor would she have ever thought that it would be a good thing for someone such as herself to bring one into the world. So, it had to be admitted, she was now doing the last thing, apart from shooting herself in the head, that she had ever wanted to do. She was having a baby.

Her distress at night was particular. It amounted to staring into the darkness and wondering, over and over again, how she had come to be in such a mess. And in the morning, as she clung to the bathroom basin being hopelessly sick, she wondered again why she had not 'done' something.

But for no reason that she could clearly define, she came to realise that the morality of having or not having a baby was, for her, a strange one. She could not have said why, but from the moment that she had found out that she was pregnant she had been overwhelmed by an intense feeling that not to go through with her pregnancy would be in some way completely immoral.

What she was facing now was her own mistake, but what she would face, it seemed to her, if she did not see her pregnancy through would be compounding that first mistake. She could not go back on her own stupidity, but she could go forward into a future that could make something positive out of it. To do anything else would be to be untrue to herself.

'What was it like then, the old nunny wunny nursing home? They treat you all right when you went along for your interview? They're usually very good, nuns as nurses, or nurses as nuns, at least so Cliffie always said. Quite disciplined, and so on, very clean, very hygienic, comes naturally to nuns to be clean and hygienic, and of course since they can't have babies of their own they're usually rather fond and all that, at least so they tell me. But, you know, it is only a rumour.'

Oliver said all this hopefully, because he wanted Coco, despite showing every outward appearance of being quite miserably unhappy, not to have a bad time. In fact Clifton had never mentioned nuns as nurses to Oliver, or indeed nurses as nuns, not even once. Oliver had made it all up just to fill in time, to cover his discomfort at seeing his oldest friend at what must be, in reality, rock bottom.

Coco looked at Oliver. How could she describe the chill she had felt when she entered the frighteningly pristine nursing home with its nursing sisters in their winged headdresses, and seen the beds filled with what had seemed to her to be an endless line of miserable young girls holding or feeding babies that perhaps, like hers, had been the result, not of careful planning, but only of a hot night in some faraway place?

'Oh, it was all right. Quite clean. In fact very clean. In fact spotless. Yes, you could eat off the floor, if you wanted to. Strange expression, isn't it? When you come to think of it? I mean, who wants to eat off the floor, for heaven's sake?'

'Good. Well, so long as you can if you want to, I mean eat off the floor, that's all right, then. You look well, anyway, Coco. Quite well,' Oliver finished lamely, not being quite able to find in himself anything which he could celebrate in Coco's condition. Although he had to admit her skin did look exactly, but exactly, like a ripe peach on a summer day, there was no denying that.

Yet ever since he had arrived in her flat Oliver had been trying not to look at Coco's burgeoning shape. It had truly shocked him to see how big she had become in the short time since she had made her great announcement to him.

'Yes, it's quite clean. Yes, the nursing home is quite clean.'

Coco sipped at her fruit juice and stared ahead of her morosely. She could not bring herself to ask Oliver about what he was doing, but she knew she had to do just that. She had to face asking Oliver what he was doing. She had to ask him, even though she was fairly sure that if he said that he had been signed up to make a film and was now, in his turn, saving up to buy an Austin Healey, she might scream and throw her fruit juice at the wall.

In the event, and happily for her at any rate, all Oliver had to tell her was that he was going to Tadcaster, to the Stephens Theatre, which had been founded by a wealthy butcher solely, it seemed, so that his musician son could muck about putting on musicals every now and then. Oliver himself was going there to play in a mixed season of plays, starting with a Noel Coward revival and going on from there.

As Oliver started to talk about going up to be seen for a major role at Tadcaster, the wonderful new facilities there, the costume department that made all its own clothes for the productions, the new theatre designs, all the old longing for the way of life that Coco had once so enjoyed mocking returned in a flood of nostalgia. Of a sudden she yearned for the smell of the size, the hollow sound of footsteps ringing on the floors of corridors outside dressing rooms, all the things that she had only just begun to appreciate before she fell, as the saying went, for a baby.

She turned away to search for a handkerchief, desolation welling up inside her like the morning sickness that had, at last, gone away.

The good thing about Oliver was that he knew her so well that he said nothing at all to make light of her problem, because he must have realised just how annoying that would be, and how she would resent it. Nor did he attempt to sympathise with her, or mouth stupid bromides at her to try to make her feel better about something that she knew no one could make her feel better about. He just put out his hand and covered one of hers with it, and lit a cigarette with the other.

'It won't be long, love, and then you will be back in the swing, and having a grand time of it, you will see. You can have the baby adopted and make someone very happy, and be back with all of us before you can say happy nappy!'

They both started to laugh, although Coco was as usual now hiccupping and sniffing at the same time, such was her lowness of spirits, such her feeling that her life was now, irrevocably, ruined.

'I don't know why, but since I got preggers I can't stop snivelling.'

'I expect that's normal.' Oliver gave her a brotherly pat on her back. 'Anyway, as I say, it will soon be all over, and the new-born kitten given to a new and loving home that will welcome it with open arms.'

'There's only one fly in that particular face cream, Ollie. I am not going to have the baby, or the kitten as you call it, adopted.'

Oliver promptly removed his hand from hers, lit yet another cigarette and handed it to Coco.

'Oh my *Gahd*, Coco!'

'I know – I agree. I know. Oh my Gahd.'

For some reason, ever since they were young, besides making pints of Birds Eye custard the moment Coco's guardians had gone out to a cocktail party, they had found saying 'Oh my *Gahd*' exceedingly funny, accompanying the phrase as they had used to do, and now were doing again, with a downward flap of their hands, while at the same time bending their knees.

'But how can you bring up a tiny baby, Coco? You don't know anything about tiny babies.'

Coco pulled a face. 'I dunno,' she said, immediately switching accents. 'But you know, I gotta do it, or else *what*? I mean, the baby will have bits of me in it, and I sort of do know about what it is like to be given away and brought up by other people, and, you know, he or she might be dotty about the theatre and want to make costumes, like me, or act like you. And – just think – the kitten might be brought up by some couple who did not approve of acting and so on, and have a terrible time making its way into the theatre, or something. I mean I keep thinking about that, and it makes me realise that I am not, after all, just having a kitten, I am having a human being.'

'A human bean—'

'Exactly, a human person, not a puppy or a kitten. A human person might be someone like us, Ollie, and they might not want to be brought up by a bank manager and his wife, because however kind and sweet they just would not understand the sort of kooky types that we are.'

'And talking of them, the kooky types I mean, what, I mean to say, what – what about the man who time forgot – the father of the tiny baby?'

'Best forgotten about, I am afraid – I mean, don't you think, Ollie? Best forgotten about, handsome Victor whose surname I couldn't even remember.'

Coco now discarded her cigarette halfway through, leaving it to make a little snake in the ashtray.

'He is not really the father in any way. I mean to say, to be a father you have to really know the person whom you have made fearfully *enceinte*, and, since I can't even really remember his name without a huge big effort, *à quoi bon?*'

'Nil despairing then, Coco. And no good trying to stop me. I am now, quite officially, going to appoint myself the tiny baby's goddaddy and come through the door at Christmas and birthdays with armfuls of wonder goods, and marvels of every kind, so that he or she will finally love me far more than you who have to be quite beastly to him, or her, and make sure that they don't turn into an axe murderer or a theatrical bore who tells long, tedious stories about very old and very dead actors.'

Coco smiled.

It was after all better than crying.

Oliver too smiled, and for just the same reason.

Elsie also felt like crying, not just because she knew that the casting of Elliott had been a fix, but also because she had been looking forward so much to playing in Coward and now she was convinced that she would be faced with some great big unseasoned amateur who would naturally ruin it all.

Some London agent called Tad Protheroe was at the bottom of it all. He had, it seemed, some interest in the theatre, way back when, and had known Stephens the Tadcaster butcher and businessman and owner of the Stephens Theatre for many a long year. Apparently they had been in the army together, something like that. Whatever the actual connection Elsie knew that there was one, and she also knew that Bartlett would be the last person to admit as much to her, or to anyone else. Dottie had used to say that you never could get anyone in the theatre to admit to either of two things – that they had been bad in a part, or that undue influence had been used to secure them a role.

'Actors are such hypocrites!' Dottie would boom over the sound of the wireless, completely forgetting that she was meant to be one. 'Sleep their way to the top most of them, and then turn to God and the vicar and become horribly pious once they become famous.'

This particular morning was the morning of the first read-through of the Coward play. Elsie climbed out of bed and surveyed herself in the long mirror of her bedroom. Did she look as she should? Young, vital, hair long and glossy, eyes bright. Mentally she ticked off the physical list as nerves started to eat at her insides, and outside the traffic started to ease itself down the main street of Tadcaster. To take her mind off her feelings, she found herself looking out of the window. Opposite she could see the woman who owned the hat shop arriving early with a whole lot of parcels.

For a second Elsie found herself envying her. She could quite fancy owning a hat shop. It would be a very pretty sort of shop to own, now she came to think of it, and people were happily wearing hats again, not just for weddings and christenings, but all the time.

As was now her established routine, Elsie went out to the baker opposite and purchased a loaf of springy white bread, and bought a paper. She took longer than usual to complete each commission, spending minutes over the choosing of her loaf, and finally buying a magazine as well as a newspaper. She did so because she was dreading what she knew the rest of the morning was going to bring her, namely meeting the fresh-from-drama-school lummox that the management had undoubtedly cast opposite her.

'Of course you are far too young, and so is he, but I think we can get away with it simply and solely because of that one line *we were so young and so over in love.'*

Bartlett had said this about a hundred times to Elsie, with the result that she had started to see herself as nothing more than totally unsuitable, as unsuitable as the characters in the play had obviously been for each other when they had married first time round.

Elsie now sighed and stared around her flat. She had been very lucky to find a place that was so warm and comfortable, and above a green-grocer's shop with vegetables and fruit sold off cheap at the end of the week. Fruit and vegetables in abundance were deemed not good enough to last the weekend, but they were certainly good enough for Elsie who did not much like meat, probably because Dottie had always kept the lion's share of her larder for the lodgers and herself. As a consequence Elsie had grown up grateful for a diet of grilled tomatoes and fried mushrooms, or the occasional boiled egg, and the equally occasional steamed pudding. She did not particularly like alcohol either because, until people like Portly Cosgrove had offered it to her, she had never been given it, and since it was expensive it seemed quite mad to acquire a taste for it now.

She dressed slowly for the read-through, putting together her wardrobe of clothes with the same care that she was in the habit of putting into her performances. It was not a question of being spoilt for choice, it was simply a question of asking herself which of her three cardigans she should start off wearing. Which of her three cotton dresses would she team with her cardigan? Which of her three sets of shoes would be the best to wear for the first day of rehearsal?

Everything that was going to happen in the ensuing weeks was, in her experience, hinted at, sketched in, and made obvious on the first day. That was why everyone went to the first rehearsal in a state of nerves. They knew that everyone would know by the evening of that day just what the state of play would doubtless turn out to be. Of that there was no doubt at all.

Elsie was always word-perfect before any read-through. It was part of her training. Dottie would never let her attend rehearsal without having learnt not just her own part, but the *whole script*. To Dottie's annoyance this had never been a chore for Elsie, who had been born with a photographic memory. Dottie had found this irritating. She wanted learning a play to be a trial for her grand-daughter.

'Here, you don't know all that!' she would say, snatching some rehearsal script from Elsie, only to find that Elsie not only knew it all, but could tell her where the typing mistakes occurred, and recite the stage instructions off by heart. 'You'll end up as Mrs Memory Woman, if you're not careful! Nothing but a parrot, that's what you'll be if that's all you can come up with. Have to give a performance too, you know. Oh yes, it's not just learning off by heart that gets you to the top.'

Elsie had always switched off during Dottie's longer speeches, the words seeming to flap around her head with the damp washing that hung overhead on the clothes airer. She knew that 'parroting' as Dottie called it would not get her anywhere, but she also knew that her ability to memorise was going to stand her in splendid stead. She had seen too many actors and actresses *um um umming* their way through the dark days of rehearsal, seen too often how some other actor's fluffing caused a cast unutterable misery, not to say senseless delays. So she closed her ears to Dottie's threat that she would turn into a parrot and thanked her lucky stars for her ability to learn a play in less than a day.

She had been so assiduous in her renaming of the unfortunate young actor brought up from London and cast opposite her that by the time she arrived in the empty rehearsal hall Elsie very nearly found herself asking Bartlett Corrigan, 'Where's the lummox then?'

'Ah, there you are!'

From the moment they met it had seemed to Elsie that Bartlett did not just beam bonhomie, he exuded it. Bonhomie was a sort of room fragrance which followed him in and out of rehearsal rooms, in and out of the auditorium, and everywhere he went. No matter how grim the news, how often it seemed to be coming from the left, Bartlett would nod and smile and pat the arm of the messenger, whoever it was, and say, 'Don't worry, it'll be all right, really it will.' Or 'Just you

312

wait, it'll turn out for the best.' Or more often, 'Well, we had better just press on then.'

All in all he was the kind of man of whom everyone else will say, 'Ah dear old Bartles, what a sweet fellow,' and wonder to themselves if he really was as sweet as he seemed – which Elsie had soon discovered, however stern he sometimes appeared – he truly was.

'Elsie, love, come over, come over. Late for you, Elsie, aren't we, love? Elsie is usually here long before any of us, and always word-perfect,' Bartlett told the young man standing by the tea urn at the end of the rehearsal hall. 'Perhaps she has decided not to frighten us this morning? Come over, Elsie. Come over here and meet Oliver Lowell. Elsie Lancaster. Oliver Lowell. I say, I've suddenly realised that Elsie must win on the billing. *A* comes before *o* doesn't it? No, seriously, no, we would not argue over billing, would we, darlings? Of course not.'

Bartlett looked from one to the other. He had been hoping for some sort of chemistry between Elsie and Oliver. Hoping against hope that *it* would happen, and the thing would take off. It did so help, he always thought, if people fancied each other, at the very least a bit, when they were playing lovers in a play. It cut out so much of the director and producer's problems. If they were always squabbling and chewing garlic before their love scenes – all that sort of nonsense – it made everything such an uphill struggle.

Certainly, as he saw Elsie Lancaster eyeing

Oliver Lowell from under her long eyelashes, the look in her slightly protruding eyes one of light scorn, and Oliver Lowell eyeing her right back with one of growing appreciation, Bartlett could see that sparks were going to fly all right, but whether they were the kind that would set a production alight, or the theatre on fire, Bartlett hoped he would not find out for some hours yet.

As it happened, he was quite wrong. No sooner had they sat down at the read-through, with Elsie hardly looking at the text, so well did she already know it, than it was obvious that Oliver Lowell, of the quite brilliant smile, was going to have his hands full. But better than that, more than that, so it seemed, to her growing and quite apparent amusement, was Miss Elsie Lancaster.

Chapter Ten

In all his twenty-six years, Portly Cosgrove could honestly swear that he had never paid much attention to anyone but himself, which was probably, he realised, why he was already famous among his acquaintances for being so relaxed and even-tempered. Perhaps if you did not really listen to anyone but yourself, stayed in your own little world, you could quite easily go about with a serene outlook, because the real problems of earning your living, bringing home the bacon, did not have to be faced.

Now, of course, that he was wishing, most heartily, that he had, it was too late.

The reason why it was too late for him to listen to other people's advice was that he was broke. Bourton had gone off with his money, and not just a little bit of it but all of it, every single penny. He had done this, most effectively, while Portly's mental back, as it were, was turned – or in other words while Portly was in America trying to buy the rights to a play he had seen off Broadway.

Donald Bourton, trustworthy gentleman that

he had pretended to be, had decamped with everything, withdrawn the lot from their business accounts. He had even absconded with the stamp money. That had been quite something. To find that you could not even afford to stamp an envelope to send Donald Bourton a letter filled with invective was, Portly discovered, humiliating to a degree.

It was only now he had his back to the wall that he was being forced into the recognition that, in this new reality he was occupying, he was not in the least bit self-sufficient.

Having been brought up by an affable uncle who had died and left him a small fortune, he had never really thought much about where money was coming from. Money had always been there for him, like the weather, or the news on the radio; a fact, but not a worry.

Staring out at the rain falling from a leaden, grey sky, Portly tried, for perhaps the hundredth time, to work out how he could best start his life again. At that moment his feelings exactly matched the sky, and at the same time he knew that to indulge in such feelings was a pathetic waste of time and energy, and he had very little left of either before he would be joining the tramps queuing for soup at various addresses around the poorer parts of town.

The first thing he knew he had to do was get out of London. London was too expensive for him, and not only that, but in London he was always in danger of bumping into one or other of his friends or acquaintances, all of whom would have heard of his misfortunes, and all of whom would be less than sympathetic, knowing as they would that he had lost everything he had inherited by investing in his one great love – the love of his youth – the theatre.

Once out of town, burying himself in the English countryside, putting up at a cheap pub here, staying in lodgings there, he set himself to try to think how best to redirect his life, and as he settled to this task he started, little by little, to raise himself from the deep depression that arises not just from failure, but from a failure brought about by yourself. Because, for Portly, there was no one *except* himself to blame. He knew, absolutely, that all his current woes had been brought about by himself. He was the sole architect of his own misfortune. Once he had put his hand into that particular fire, he started to feel better.

And, too, once he was out of town there were many reasons for his spirits to begin lifting, not least being that his increasingly shabby clothes, his whole appearance, lined eyes, lank hair, noticed less, out of town, than it would undoubtedly have done in the West End. His shoes, now so down at heel, his old suits now worn and shiny, the newer coats and suits having been sold in the second-hand market, together with everything else of any possible value – his signet ring, his motor car, his Sheaffer pen, his bachelor uncle's Sulka dressing gowns and Rolex watch. Everything had gone in a vain attempt to put

317

together a small sum off which he felt he could not just live, but start again.

However, if there is a silver lining to a crash in fortunes Portly soon discovered it is that, of a sudden, the very stuff of day-to-day existence becomes a great deal simpler, much less complicated; and with it also, of necessity, arrives a deep appreciation of the small joys of life.

Portly had never before imagined, or even conceived of the notion that buying a cup of tea in a café could give him such intense pleasure. Nor that someone else leaving a newspaper behind on a seat on the bus could, as he sneaked into their seat and picked it up, produce the feeling that he had won the football pools.

He was, at that moment, experiencing just such a feeling from the kind smile that the provincial landlady with a back room to let was giving him.

'We pride ourselves here in Tadcaster on offering the best possible kind of hospitality. You will find no newspaper in lieu of Bronco in the toilets here, Mr Cosgrove. No, nor would we condescend to charge for such a small item as a cup of tea – by no means. And while we are on the subject, would you like to subject yourself to a cup of my very own brew? Part China, part Indian, with a small smattering of Lyons? I think you will find, as all my gentlemen do, that it is most refreshing.'

Portly accepted and then gratefully drank the delicious tea proffered, and, such was his hunger, tried not to swallow whole the accompanying scone. His new landlady watched him with intense interest. Part of the fascination of being a landlady lay in the ability to sum up in a very few minutes, by the simple ruse of offering a free cup of tea, the precise circumstances of the new lodger.

This young man, Mrs Graham would swear, was not just down on his luck, he was clean out of it. His shoes, worn down at the heels; his overcoat, a button missing; the state of his hair, unkempt; the state of his mind, doubtless, the same. It was for this reason that, having watched a little colour returning to his cheeks once he had finished not one cup of tea but two, Mrs Graham said, 'We do like our week's rental in advance, Mr Cosgrove, if that is not a trouble.'

'No, not at all.'

To Mrs Graham's surprise, if not astonishment, Mr Cosgrove reached into his pocket and drew out a very expensive wallet – smooth black leather, small gold initials in the corner – and very promptly and without a murmur paid her in clean, crisp one pound notes.

Mrs Graham placed the notes in the front pocket of her best pinafore, having surveyed them first for some seconds with a look of deep appreciation.

'I do like a clean note, don't you, Mr Cosgrove?'

Portly nodded absent-mindedly. 'What? Oh yes, yes of course, so do I. I always insist on them at the bank, as a matter of fact.'

Mrs Graham looked down at the small white

319

space on the smallest finger, or pinkie, of the left hand of her new lodger. It stood out pale against the rest of his hand. He must have once sported a gold signet ring, something expensive which he had been forced to sell for some reason or another. Now, she realised, getting there in one, she understood the man better. He must have just had a financial disaster, and was lodging with her until such time as his luck changed. A part of her immediately became wary as she realised this, and yet another part of her became sympathetic. Most of her customers, or lodgers, were only passing through, some staying for a few days to see the old town and its beauties, others recuperating from some sadness or disaster; yet others, like this young man, wandering from one town to another in search of either a new identity, or a new life.

'If you're in this evening I am cooking Kate and Sidney pie tonight.' And as Portly looked blank she added, 'Or, as you probably know it, steak and kidney pie, Mr Cosgrove. Would you like to join me?'

'No, thank you.' Portly shook his head. He could not afford a full blown meal. A bun at a café would be as much as he would let himself run to, nothing more, except perhaps a piece of fruit bought from some closing shop at half price. 'No, I won't, really. I, er—'

He started to get up, but his stomach rumbled so loud that its insistence on both being heard and reminding its owner of its emptiness stopped him abruptly. As it happened he was not the only person to hear the hungry message being sent up from his lower regions. Mrs Graham too had heard it.

The expression in her eyes was one of some warmth as she leaned forward and touched Portly on the arm.

'It is free, dear, dinner is free, really it is, it comes with the room, really it does, that and breakfast and as much barley water as you want, not to mention cups of tea, it's all thrown in.'

Of course it was not normally thrown in, she had merely said this to try to reassure the young man. She could not possibly afford to give away dozens of cups of tea, not to mention barley water, to her lodgers, except in special circumstances, which, for some reason, she judged this occasion to be.

Portly dropped his eyes. He would have loved to turn his back on such very obvious charity, but the truth was that he was far too hungry, in fact he was faint with hunger. The very idea of a steak and kidney dinner was too delicious for words.

He felt a lump coming into his throat and as he did so, he stood up abruptly, at the same time murmuring, 'Thank you very much, that would be nice,' and left the room in a hurry, quietly closing the front door of the small, narrow, back street house behind him.

Ambling through Tadcaster he wondered dazedly how on earth he had come to find himself there. He had somehow travelled in a zigzag fashion through England, sometimes, now he looked back on it, even seeming to be going in circles. Just keeping on moving, until such time as his money might run out, or his energy; after which he often wondered if he would not, like some luckless person in a Victorian story, head for the river, and an end to it all for ever.

Money worries were, he had discovered, very, very hard to bear. They were most particularly hard to bear if you were not used to enduring them. They were like a yoke which seemed to be resting without ceasing, without any easing whatsoever, on your neck, so that even at night – most especially at night – you were aware of this heaviness, this burden, this unalterable fact: that you were penniless, and hungry, and cold, and wet, and putting newspaper in your shoes did nothing to take away the permanent chill that seemed, like damp in a house, to rise upwards, making your head ache constantly, ceaselessly, forming a duet with the hunger pains in your gut.

Perhaps worse than the physical discomforts that Portly had endured, though, was the bitterness that he felt towards himself.

Bitterness is most particularly hard to bear when it comes to being really down on your luck. The bitterness of knowing how foolhardy you have been, how stupid, how shallow, how trusting, how careless, in every way. The bitterness of knowing, without any doubt at all, that you have no one but yourself to blame for everything that has come about, for all your misfortunes.

Of course Portly had known all these things,

but only in a vague sort of way as he cleared up all Cosgrove and Bourton's debts, as he made absolutely certain to pay back every single pound to every single person to whom he and Donald had owed money. Now that he was done for, skint, the vague unreality had cleared, and he had been forced to bring himself to face the truth of his own character flaws.

He had prided himself on being easy-going when in fact he had been quite simply lazy. He had prided himself on being able to trust everyone, when in reality he could not be bothered to distrust them. He had prided himself on thinking that he had a relaxed personality, when in fact the only person he was truly relaxed with was himself. He had been very like the man at the back of the temple in the Bible, always thinking what a fine fellow he was in every way, trusting Bourton to take care of so much while he, good old Portly, had congratulated himself on being able to see the bigger picture, go in search of the future talent of the age, read the scripts, and steer clear of the boring office work.

What a bighead he had been! Not Portly Cosgrove Esquire, but Portly Cosgrove Clever Dick, that was exactly who he had been. The man who could spot a star from five paces and negotiate with agents, while finding new plays and new backers, and leaving all the office work to his older partner, the well known producer, good old Donald Bourton! It had taken months to make good and pay back the small creditors, to deal with the ever-hungry bank, to sell his flat and everything else, but finally he had, and now he must – he had to – start again, forget about the past, or else he really would find himself ending it all.

He stopped outside a downtown café, trying to peer at the price of egg and chips chalked up on a small board propped against the wall inside the window. He finally made it out to be two shillings and sixpence.

Just the thought of eating a hot lunch was almost unimaginable. Normally he made do with just a cup of tea, but today, in view of Mrs Graham's promise of a free dinner of steak and kidney, he thought he might go mad and spend his day's allowance of half a crown on the egg and chips for lunch.

'Egg and chips, please. No, no tea. Just a glass of water, thank you.'

He stared out of the window towards the street. He had spent months castigating himself, but he wondered now, for the first time, and probably because the sun had just come out, whether the moment had not arrived to put a full stop to the treadmill of bitter feelings that he had been experiencing recently.

But even as he reached down, right into himself, it seemed to Portly that the unalterable fact was still there for all to see: that he himself was now hardly more than an empty vessel. He was, to all intents and purposes, a place bereft of everything. He was an empty room, his personality merely a dustbowl of a landscape with nothing green growing anywhere, nothing worth noting. Portly Cosgrove, nondescript, a man of straw, a person of whom the old Portly would have said, 'Bit of a silly ass, wouldn't you say? Getting taken in by Donald Bourton like that?' And there would have been no one, but no one, who would not have agreed with that other Portly.

Elsie Lancaster on the other hand was on top of the world, as why should she not be? She had opened in the Coward revival, scored a personal triumph, and was now enjoying her first love affair with none other than Oliver Lowell, whom she had nicknamed right from the start, and quite openly, the lummox.

Except now Oliver Lowell had become her 'sweet lummox', her angel, her best friend, her everything. He was tall, and handsome, working-class and from Yorkshire. He was everything she could wish for, and more than that he was funny. He was droll. He liked to dress up and wear odd clothes. He let her wear his shirts in bed, and his jumpers to rehearsal. He insisted on making-up her eyes every evening once the curtain fell, and before they went out to supper together, because, rightly or wrongly, he was convinced that he knew how they should look. He shared his every thought with her, and she shared hers with him.

How it had all come about was quite simple.

Simple because it is all too mesmerisingly easy

to fall in love in the rehearsal room. Not because actors and actresses go into a play thinking about love, or making love – although a great many, it had always seemed to Elsie, did – but only really because of foolish nerves. Nerves, she had often thought, like war, brought people's emotions very close to the surface, and once those feelings were up there, bubbling away, you only had to add good looks and the inevitable youthful longing for romance, and you were away.

Elsie was thinking about all this just after she and Oliver had made love, and were lying in each other's arms. She subsequently thought about it a great deal more as he left her to run a bath for both of them. Soon she would climb into the hot soapy bathwater smelling of their favourite stephanotis, and he would wash her back, dampening her long thick curly hair so much in the process that she would have to spend far longer than she liked, once she was towelled dry, combing it out and drying it.

But if Elsie's nickname for Oliver was the sweet lummox, Oliver's nickname for Elsie was 'Popeye' because early on in their relationship she had confessed to him how much she hated, was all too over-aware of, her protruding eyes.

'Nonsense!' Oliver would have none of it. 'You don't want eyes like everyone else, all flat and *samey*, do you? No, your eyes are large, and the fact that they stick out slightly gives you an intelligent air, as if you are constantly thinking new thoughts, which being so incurably lightweight of course you and I both know that you are not, but that is none the less, darling old Popeye, what you convey. A sort of sprightly intelligence, a sort of strange feeling that you are in control of a great deal more than the rest of us, which of course you are not, but that is why, I am dearly afraid, you are a far bigger star than myself, at the moment.'

Stardom aside, Elsie was also, as they were both well aware, at that moment a far better actress than Oliver was an actor. This was because, they also both appreciated, Elsie had been in the profession since she was knee high to a grasshopper, and was in actual fact so well versed in her craft that nothing much could throw her. This, coupled with the fact that she had a photographic memory, meant that she could be on her feet and acting the socks off the rest of the cast while everyone else was bumbling about getting their lines in a twist.

And once off the rehearsal room floor, Oliver noted, Elsie would wander off to the tea urn, pick up a magazine and start reading as unconcernedly as any window shopper in the street outside.

'You're such a lucky little devil, being able to memorise like that.'

'Yup, I know.'

'Have you always been like that?'

'Yup.'

'Then you are, you are a lucky little devil, Popeye,' Oliver said again, speaking from the bottom of his heart, because he himself had hell learning a part, however small. He always seemed to need to understand the person he was playing first, long before he could possibly learn his lines.

'Don't worry. Once the play is over, I can't remember a word.'

'Oh, get on.'

'No, it's true. A fortnight after we finish this, I won't be able to remember a single speech.'

'What? Not one?'

'Nope.' Elsie kissed the top of Oliver's nose. 'Make you feel any better?'

'Yes, as a matter of fact it does, it makes me feel much better. What about when you go back, when you have to play something again?'

'Oh, yes. I see what you mean. Oh, that's all right. I just pick up the play, read it, and it seems to come back straight away. It's nothing special. It's just how it is, or rather how I am.'

Oliver stared at Elsie in some awe. She was something else.

On stage she was Mrs Hitler, Miss Hard Heart, Blad the Impaleress, the lot, and he was always telling her so. On stage she did not give an inch, not even a quarter of an inch. She knew what she had to do, and she got on and did it, leaving Oliver for dead, and the audience in raptures.

Offstage was quite different. Offstage she was his precious angel, Mrs Temptress, Popeye, Loopy Lu, and whatever else sprang into his mind.

Acting against Elsie had made Oliver realise

that if he was to survive in the theatre he had to avoid confrontation. There was a very good reason for this; he would always lose. Elsie herself seemed quite unconcerned by her own hardness. It was her childhood, she kept explaining to Oliver whenever he remarked on it. She had been born and brought up steeped in the hard-hearted ways of the theatre. She had acquired not just a veneer or a varnish but an impenetrable coating, more like something that would be put on a warship rather than a piece of furniture.

So Oliver gave way. He stepped back and let her take the audience with her from the first moment she put her slim, elegant foot on stage, and then he waited, and sure enough after a while he found that he could edge his way in too. But that was only after he had given his all, while all the time he had the feeling that Elsie was giving very little, that she was, deep down, almost bored by acting, so easy did she find it. The truth was that Elsie could do no wrong with audiences. She was a star. Not in the making, either, but already made. It was an established fact.

When, Oliver wondered, would he acquire what she had?

Night after night, despite the fact that he was wildly in love with her, he struggled against the knowledge that he lacked what they both knew she already had. Star quality.

For some reason that Oliver could not quite fathom, since the play had opened and daily rehearsals had stopped, shopping had become one of their lunchtime rituals. Not ordinary shopping either, but madly serious shopping for some item that assumed a tremendous importance as soon as they realised they wanted it.

After their usual routine – breakfast, making love, bathing – they would scramble into their clothes and bolt off down Tadcaster's main street, intent on buying the most extraordinarily unnecessary things, in which they took an equally extraordinary and quite unnecessary interest. Nail clippers, or black handkerchiefs, ribbons for a dress or a hat, the perfect pair of dark socks for Oliver, a small book of poetry – whatever took their fancy after the first spate of their morning rituals. All these commissions could take hours and hours of strangely satisfying time.

Sometimes, as he walked after Elsie into yet another shop, Oliver would find himself wondering why this pastime had become such an obsession, eventually coming to the conclusion that, like so much that an actor found to do between performances, it was a way of not being part of real life. Actors could not take control of their own lives in any major way, because in a very few hours they would have to slip into character and take control of the lives of those other people, the characters they were playing, and there simply was not room for both. So for the few hours that they were actually themselves, there was no alternative except to tread water, become entirely frivolous, in their case, spending hour after hour in small shops and boutiques searching for items such as the perfect nose scissors, or a comb that could be guaranteed not to scratch.

Unlike Oliver, Elsie did not seem to question why they spent their free time as they did. She had grown up in theatrical circles, and real life, as other people lived it, had not been something that she had either actively pursued or even been vaguely encouraged to take much interest in.

For Oliver the routine of life in the theatre, so new as it was to him, gave him a glorious feeling of at last having joined bohemia, while for Elsie, on the other hand, it was just life. She had never really known what it was like to get up and go to bed at normal times, to have a regular job that paid you regular wages.

'Except for Fullers.' She always said that. 'Don't forget I had a proper job at Fullers, Ollie. I was a waitress and eventually assistant manageress. So you see, I have had a proper job, at Fullers. I have known real life, *bien sûr*.'

Of course Oliver had done his share of being a waiter, and salad chef, and all that. He had done more than Elsie, but because his childhood had not been spent acting, none of these part-time jobs had assumed any great significance for him. They had just been a way of earning money. He did not think of them as a slice of real life, something of which he should be in awe, like working in an armaments factory during the war, which was rather the way Elsie seemed to view her single experience at Fullers.

'Ah, yes, your *proper* job at Fullers, where you made so many friends.'

'I certainly did.'

Elsie stared down at the bead bracelet that the girls in her branch of Fullers had given her for a good luck leaving present. She would never ever take it off, she had told them, and she never had yet. She played with the beads for a second, thinking back to that time, which seemed so very long ago, but was not at all, to the friendship and the camaraderie, both of which she had never, ever known before. Girls of her own age, married girls, normal girls who had never had a Dottie in their lives pushing them forward, again and again, audition after audition, failure a constant reality – never thinking, for a moment, that there was anything else to life except the theatre. Those girls at Fullers had all seemed so kind and so warm-hearted, so wholesome, and most of all so sincere. So much so that for ever after, for Elsie, they would always remain enveloped in a sort of golden glow. She would never be able to see them as normal human beings with faults and virtues. It was pathetic, but it was true: so much had their honesty and kindness touched Elsie that in her mind they would always remain a kind of brilliant troupe of angels, a touchstone to which she could look back from her tougher, more brittle world.

'You always wear that bracelet, don't you? Was it given to you by someone special?'

Oliver looked momentarily jealous, but Elsie, finding any kind of jealousy, either professional or personal, immensely boring, immediately stood up, pushing aside the cup of coffee that she had been drinking. After performing a long and dramatic stretch, she said, 'Come on, Ollie. I want to look for some old-fashioned buckles for my evening shoes.'

'Not buckles for your shoes again!'

'And what are you going to be looking for today, may I ask?'

'Nothing.'

'Come on. Nothing is very hard to find.'

Oliver thought for a little while, and having decided he said carefully, and to his own surprise, 'I'm going to be looking for one of those old-fashioned ink wells. You know, with a kind of quill pen that goes with it. I want one of those.'

Elsie packed her cigarettes and lighter smartly into her stylish shoulder bag.

'What do you want a quill for, Ollie?'

'To write, perhaps?'

'Logical.' She nodded, and began to walk ahead of Oliver, preparing to leave the café. As she did so, she turned back and said, 'Don't tell me you are planning to take up writing as a profession, Ollie?'

'Might be.'

'Why?' Elsie stood still suddenly and frowned at him, while other customers pushed by them.

'Why do you want to write? You're such a fine actor.'

'Yes, I know,' Oliver agreed, 'but you see, Popeye love, a terrible thought occurred to me, and only the other day.'

'Which was?'

Elsie flicked back her long, curly hair, shaking her head to encourage her great mane to drop down her back in ringlets, just as she knew Oliver liked it, and indeed his eyes did rest for a second, most appreciatively, on her hair before he could tell her his all-important revelation.

'This was my thought, Popeye.' He paused, touching her on the arm to make sure that he had her complete attention. 'Someone might never, ever write a part that would be suitable for me again, ever. Don't you see? Or there might not be another one for – say – ten years, by which time I will be too old. So, as I see it, the only solution is for me to try and write one for myself—'

'Good gracious! I don't believe it! My God!'

Elsie had suddenly turned back to the last table before the door.

'It's not that amazing, Elsie love,' Oliver protested. 'After all a lot of actors take up the old quill and start writing to help out with the old acting—'

But Elsie, which was really quite galling, was not being amazed by Oliver's professed determination to try to write parts for himself. She was too busy being amazed by something quite different.

Oliver turned back with her to where a man was sitting at a table just before the door. Tall and shabby, the man was staring at Elsie, white-faced and shocked, just as Elsie was staring back at him, also white-faced and shocked. Seconds later they were in each other's arms, and Oliver was feeling jealous for the second time that day.

Coco had been taken into the nursing home early due to the tiny size of her baby. She had to rest up, the gynaecologist who helped look after the mothers informed her and the nursing sisters. She had to lie back and wait for her baby to catch up, because if she did not the baby would not grow, and that would never do.

Coco had now passed out of the early stages of pregnancy when she would wonder at her own courage at going ahead, facing a future not only without a father for her child, but as far as she could gather without friends or family. Now she no longer cared about herself, but only about the baby and his or her welfare. And so she lay for day after day, surrounded by other young mothers in precisely the same state, staring at nothing in particular, hardly able to read, or concentrate on anything, only willing the baby to grow a little more, for her sake and its own.

Of course as soon as he knew from his cousins that she had been taken into hospital, Oliver wrote to her, ostensibly to cheer her up.

Dear old Coco,
I was very sorry to hear from my cousin Theresa that you are hors de combat *on account of my future*

godchild's being determinedly on a diet at the moment. What a beeswax! Oh Gahd! I mean to say. Still, I expect, knowing you, you are passing the time making hideously beautiful drawings of costumes you are going to inflict on thespians such as myself. Well anyway, enough of that. I am hoping that you will be able to come up and see the Stephens Theatre at Tadcaster as soon as your little bundle is delivered. I say, Coco, it is quite something to be here in the provinces doing the old thesping, and I am very lucky in my new Best Friend and Leading Lady.

Of a sudden Coco stopped reading and put the letter down.

She stared ahead of her, her eyes not taking in anything, her whole being filled with a deep sense of longing. The cheerful tone that Oliver had deliberately adopted to make her feel better was making her feel much worse, because she knew that, old friend that he was, he was worried about her, and had written all their old slang expressions to cheer her up. Things that Oliver had written like *Oh Gahd!* made her homesick for that other world, the theatre, that world from which she had been so suddenly removed by her pregnancy.

She went back to Oliver's letter.

She is a fantastic actress, Coco. Really brilliant. There is nothing she can't do, and she has taught me so much, which I needed, to be taught, I mean. I am enclosing the programme and some of the notices for the new musical we did together last week. It is by Jolion

Stephens, the son of the man who owns the theatre. He never stops composing. Quite something. I am the one in the tweed suit smoking the pipe. Elsie is on the left! Ha ha! this is a very dull letter.

Write soon and tell me how you are feeling. Meanwhile, back to rehearsal for me. Acting, acting, acting. That is all I have done since I got to Tadcaster, and honestly, Coco, I have never been happier. Anyway, enough of that, this is a very dull letter. Lots of love to you, Oliver.

'Damn you for sending this letter, Oliver. It has made me more mizzy than ever.'

Around and about her Coco could hear the click, click, click of the nuns' low-heeled metal-capped shoes as she lay staring at the ceiling above her. She could hear a young mother in the bed next to her quietly crying because, she had previously told Coco, she missed her little boy at home. She could hear ambulance bells ringing, or was it a fire engine? She could hear all of these things and they were real, but most real of all was the awful ache she was feeling, an ache brought on because of missing everything, because of missing Oliver and the theatre, but most of all because of missing Coco.

She missed herself as she had used to be, only a few months ago. She missed madcap Coco who kept everyone else amused. Kooky Coco who liked to wear crazy clothes, who had more opinions to the inch than Oliver had brains in his head, who took up acting because art school was a bore. That was the person she missed most of all.

'No, no tea, thank you, Sister.'

She lay back against her pillows, Oliver's letter still in her hand. She would never now be young again, she knew that. Never feel carefree, not for the rest of her life. There would always be someone else to worry about, miss, or think about. Having a baby meant that you were never going to be alone again, that there would always be someone else in your life, that you could never be properly selfish. Meanwhile Oliver was having the best sort of time, *acting, acting, acting*, as he had put it in his blasted letter. Coco realised that she would do anything to be with him, on stage, or on location, anywhere except where she was, alone in a grim, out of town nursing home with the goodly nuns swaying past at regular intervals, and other girls in other beds nursing their un-wanted babies.

'There is a visitor for you, Miss Hampton.'

Coco looked up from the programme Oliver had sent her, and to her horror saw her guardian, looking outrageously smart in a navy blue suit, sailor boy hat complete with petersham ribbon banding, and matching accessories, sashaying down the ward, while a flock of nuns, suddenly looking strangely like black and white doves, flew ahead of her, or moved behind her, their wimples providing a somehow equally chic backdrop to Gladys's fashionable façade.

'Darling.' Gladys bent down and kissed Coco on her cheek.

'Gladys.'

'I knew about you, but not from whom you might think.' Gladys, quite composed and smelling beautifully of Miss Dior, sat down on the small bentwood chair provided by the nuns for the single visitor and crossed her elegant legs.

'Who did you know about me from, or from whom do you know about me, in other words?'

Coco, as was her way in conversation, started straight in. She had no time for shilly-shallying. Besides, she knew from Gladys's composed expression that she must have known for years and years – well, months anyway.

'Quite by chance, darling, met your gynaecologist at a cocktail party in Norfolk. What a dish! Anyway, you don't think, I mean, you didn't think we hadn't guessed? Silly old thing, of course we had guessed, ages ago. All that not coming home, what do you think that is always, always about? Well, nearly always, especially with single girls. It's always about being preggers, darling. Just a fact. With single girls.'

'Well, it would hardly be with married ones.'

'I've brought you some magazines, to cheer you up. Locked up in here I suppose you only get given the Lives of the Saints, or the Bible, don't you?'

'Not quite.' Coco snatched up *Vogue* and started to turn the pages of the magazine as if she was a starving woman let loose in a food shop. 'Oh, look at that.' She turned the magazine back towards Gladys, a look of fainting ecstasy on her face. 'Look, Glad!'

'I know, darling, I already looked. Too divine. It would look wonderful worn at a spring ball, don't you think? I always say that Victor's clothes are to die for.'

Victor? Oh God, *Victor*, not the man whose child she was expecting. Coco shook her head and turned another page. Anything to get away from someone called Victor, even if it was the great fashion designer Victor Stiebel.

'I thought it would cheer you up, to bring you some magazines, and, you know, let you know that we know, and it is fine by us, all that sort of thing. Your life, do as you wish. I am sure your mother and stepfather, and your father, when anyone can find him, will feel just the same as we do, darling. Your life is your own, of course it is.'

'No, no. Please don't tell them—'

Coco looked horrified, and Gladys noted this with some pleasure. It had always worked, ever since she was a small child; a little mention of her parents and Coco would quickly come into line.

'Oh, very well, darling. Might be as well not to,' she now conceded. 'I mean I know your step-pa and your ma are in India at the moment, visiting a great many maharajahs, and after that they are to go to South America, to that frightfully 'in' place – I can never remember its name – and then on to buy polo ponies, and so home. Or at least home to France, not to England, because as you know your stepfather loathes England.'

'Just as well they are in foreign parts,' Coco agreed. 'Not that it matters, really, because

340

they're not interested in me, are they, Glad? So why would they mind, now we come to think of it?'

'Oh, I think they would, darling, really I do. My heavens, that is a lovely cocktail dress, I do agree.' Gladys moved closer to Coco and stared at the photograph in *Vogue* which had held Coco's attention. 'God, I dread to think how many pounds I have put on since I moved to the country.'

'No, no, you look wonderful, so slender, Gladys, really you do.'

'Nice word that – slender – so much better than thin, I always think.'

Coco was still flicking desperately through *Vogue* as if any minute now she would find some photograph of something that would fit her, despite her pregnant state. Feeling Gladys staring over her shoulder, cricking her neck to see the pictures she was looking at, she stopped suddenly.

'Sorry. I will give it to you in a minute, Gladys. It's just that I haven't seen a magazine like this for so long, being in here, and all. Just haven't caught sight of so much as a jacket or skirt, let alone a ball gown.'

'That's what I thought. Now, that is not the only reason for my visit here this afternoon, and I would like *Vogue* back, if you don't mind, darling, when you've quite finished devouring it. No, I do have another reason for my visit, I'm afraid.'

Gladys leaned forward and lowered her voice.

'You see, Coco, I am very much afraid that I am badly skint, done my money, come here on the scrounge to ask you for a bit of a loan, darling. Can't ask you-know-who, can't ask hubby, because he's skint too, poor old soldier.'

Coco nodded, without thinking. Ever since she was a child she had always bailed Gladys out, at one time or another, but most of all when her mother had sent the cheques which enabled both Coco and Gladys to dress quite beautifully, but hardly left anything at all over for the house-keeping and feeding poor old Harold, who had been forced to put up with a permanent egg and ham salad if Gladys had fallen for something particularly ravishing.

'Of course, Glad. How much do you want?'

'As much as you can give me, Coco. You know how it is, up and down from Norfolk to London whenever I can, seeing friends, living off dog food with Harold. Things are not what they were when you were growing up with us, you know, Coco. Those were the days when Harold was always out at a business lunch, and I had the flat to myself, not to mention going to the hairdresser twice a week, and ladies' luncheons and cocktail parties every night. No, that is all finished, what with Harold's shares gone down to minus pounds, in their thousands, and having to sell all our paint-ings, and I know not what.'

Coco quickly wrote Gladys a cheque. Gladys looked at the figure with some satisfaction, as she always had, but said nothing before putting it away in her own handbag.

'Thank you, darling. I'll pay you back, of course.'

They both knew that she never did, and never would, but even so they smiled and nodded and shortly afterwards kissed, both obviously relieved that everything they had to say to each other had been got over so quickly, and all over a nice copy of the newest *Vogue*.

Shortly after their small negotiation, Gladys left, her high-heeled shoes stalking back down the ward, past the other more poorly dressed mothers and fathers perched on their own bentwood chairs, making her look like some chic navy blue bird of paradise. For a second each little cluster of relatives and the occupants of the beds that she passed ceased talking, looking up and after her. Of a sudden it was as if Gladys was a dummy in a shop window stepping out to walk among them and remind them of some other life, a life about which they might have only read, guessing at its exotic qualities, removing all its realities, seeing only the glamour.

Coco lay back on her pillows and stared at the ceiling once more. She must be mad with guilt about having been foisted on her guardians because she had just signed over most of her baby money to Gladys to waste on trivial, passing fads such as hats or shoes, or having lunch with her girlfriends. That was how conscious she felt that

Gladys and Harold had been so kind as to take her in as a small child and spare her from being brought up by her parents, that was how guilty, that she had willingly surrendered some of her much needed money to her guardian.

'Would you like a cup of tea, Miss Hampton?'

Coco smiled and nodded, and when the tea came she thought it had never tasted so good, for the simple reason that as she sipped at it, it came to her with terrifying force that Gladys was a very selfish woman. Only a very selfish woman could, after all, take money from an unmarried mother such as Coco. And she had been all too happy to do so, when she must have known that there was someone else who needed it more than either of them, someone very small who would soon be needing every penny that Coco had managed to put by. Yet, because she owed so much of the warmth and kindness of her childhood to Harold and Gladys, Coco had been helpless to do anything else, which was clearly why Gladys had been so happy to take it from her.

The safe arrival of a baby is a bottle of champagne. It is a bouquet of flowers that lasts and lasts. It is a happy house filled with music, it is a beautiful day by the sea, it is a tree filled with blossoms, it is the smile of its mother when she sees it for the first time.

So Coco had been able to write in her diary, even after the long, long, and often agonising delivery of Holly Healey Hampton into this world.

The baby was small, as had been predicted, but perfectly formed, with a particularly pretty, bow-shaped mouth. Of course Coco thought Holly was beautiful. It was inevitable. She also knew that, whatever happened, she would always love her.

She left the hospital on her own, unaccompanied, carrying the Moses basket in one hand and her suitcase in the other. Just after the birth the nuns had tried to make up to Coco for the fact that she had no visitors. Their efforts had been so sensitive and so touching that Coco had finally found that she did not want to leave the warmth of the nursing home and their tender but unsentimental care. Nevertheless it had to be done. She had to strike out on her own. She and Holly had to go home and face real life together. Happily the birth had been normal, even more happily the baby was perfect, and in the face of these glorious facts nothing much mattered at all.

After such a long time in hospital Coco returned to a flat that was cold, damp and inches thick in dust, and until she could make a nursery of the spare room the baby's only cot was the Moses basket that the nuns had sewn as a present.

But nevertheless there was an instant comfort in familiar things, and cleaning the place and making it look good again took Coco's mind off her loneliness, off the fact that no one she knew had cared to send her either flowers or cards. No one she had met either on a film set or at drama school had kept in touch.

She had thought her isolation was due to the

unwanted pregnancy, but now she had to face the fact that the truth was that she was simply unwanted. She was nothing but an embarrassment, an embarrassment that not even her own generation could, or would, bear to face. And yet, looking down at Holly cradled in the Moses basket, tucked up under the blankets that she herself had knitted, against all the odds, Coco felt herself to be the luckiest person in the world. And if Holly had been an embarrassment, so now was Coco. So be it, she resolved, as she began to clean the flat. They would be embarrassing together.

'No need to ask why her second name is Healey, is there?' asked Oliver, who had driven down the week after their arrival back at the flat, with the sole intention, or so it seemed to Coco, of swamping the nursery with presents and walking up and down with Holly in his arms singing to her, for all the world as if he was the father. 'It was either Holly or the car, and Holly won.'

'How's it going, then?'

They both knew what 'it' was, and it certainly was not just the play that he was currently starring in with Elsie Lancaster.

Coco poured them both a beer and sat down opposite Oliver.

'Should you be drinking that?'

'Beer is fine, very good for – you know.' Coco's hands flapped vaguely in the direction of her bosom.

'Yes, yes, of course.'

Oliver was trying not to notice how ungainly, frumpish, and distraught Coco was looking, trying even harder not to remember how she had been before, stylish, carefree, and devil may care.

'Do you really think you should keep Holly, Coco? I mean, can you manage? On your own, here, in London, in this flat? Quite an expensive flat too, isn't it?'

'Oh yes, very expensive, but I shall go to work and make money, don't you worry.' Coco sipped at her beer without interest, pushing her hair back with one tired hand. 'The guardians know all about Holly, by the way, and they're not telling, you know, they're not telling anyone. Apart from anything else, if they tell the parents, bang goes the allowance. So I know Holly and I are quite safe, because as long as I keep shelling out to Gladys every time she comes up from Norfolk, or is it down? I don't know. Anyway, as I say, we should be all right, as long as I give her some of my allowance.'

That was indeed one of the many reasons why Coco had given Gladys a sizeable slice of the allowance that her mother sent her, and they had both known it.

Harold and Gladys, in darkest Norfolk, would not have cared if Coco had been delivered of twins. On the other hand, if Coco's parents ever found out they would cut her off without a penny, and this despite having taken care never to have seen Coco for more than a day a year when she was a small child, and now that she was older never seeing her at all. They remembered her at Christmas, of course, and usually telephoned, although this year they forgot, her father having taken up travelling with his newest lady friend, and her mother and stepfather being involved in the international social round in such an energetic way that the presence of a daughter would prove to be not just a hindrance, but an embarrassment.

Coco explained all this to Oliver in her laconic manner. Oliver shook his head in disbelief.

'Isn't it funny, when you come to think of it, Coco? Don't matter who you live with, or what you do, so long as you never get found out having done it. I mean your and my parents, they have not exactly been angels, have they, Coco? I mean, getting through the pearly gates might prove to take a little longer than they hoped, I should have thought, but so long as they did not give birth to a baby outside holy deadlock, then no one cares a tiddly damn what they do within it, do they? I mean to say.'

Oliver sighed and looked at the ceiling for a second as he thought about it. He had been dying to see Coco and the baby, had driven down from Tadcaster on a Sunday at a speed that seemed as if it was faster than sound in the particular car that he had taken care to hire.

Not only that, but he had spent all that week's pay packet on toys and clothes for the baby, and yet now that he was here he found himself not just wishing but longing to be anywhere rather than sitting with Coco and all the now quite awful complications of her life.

It was no good pretending. He just wanted to run away, and forget that he had seen his beloved old pal Coco like this, flat shoes, no make-up, her hair caught up in rubber bands, no beautiful jewellery, no amber bracelets, no floating scarves. Seeing her like this was to realise that it was very, very possible that Coco had made a complete hash of things, to put it mildly.

'Want a sandwich, Ollie?'

Oliver thought of Elsie, so different from Coco, so beautifully slender and lithe, so full of life, always thinking of what she could do to make life more exotic. Of a sudden he wished with all his heart that he was back with her spending Sunday in their own special way, cooking, making love, with no hint of bottles or nappies, no pram in the hall, no baby crying to be fed, no distressed young mother looking at him a little hopelessly.

'I should love a sandwich. Can I come and help you?'

Coco shook her head, and laughed suddenly. 'No, Ollie, it's all right, really – they're already made. Your favourites, ham with mayonnaise, and egg and cress.'

'Then why ask me?'

'Just to see your face fall at the idea of having to help make them. Why else?'

They both laughed and for a second it was just like the old days, so long ago, nine long months ago, with no baby, no worries, nothing but the theatre, and Oliver feeling monstrously jealous of Coco's always seeming to be about to film in faraway places with strange-sounding names. Now that jealousy appeared as being absurd, and while he had struggled not to feel envious before, he now struggled not to feel impatient. Coco had enjoyed everything she could want, her whole career before her, and now look at her! It was madness to keep the baby, but there it was, she had, and he could do nothing about it.

Again, as Oliver made half-hearted conversation with Coco, he sensed an underlying tension, because they were unable now to find many subjects about which they could either agree or disagree, since Coco had not seen any recent films or plays which she could tear to shreds or praise to the skies in the way that had been so much a part of her attraction for Oliver before. His mind shot once again back to Tadcaster and, inevitably, Elsie.

They had now done a play and musical together at the Stephens Theatre, and both play and musical had done extremely well at the box office, filling the theatre not just with locals but with people from out of town who appeared happy to travel to see what was fast becoming, by provincial standards, a famous young theatrical partnership.

Acting with Elsie gave Oliver the thrill of his life, more even than living with her. Living with her was a thrill too, of course, although slightly less of one now that she had moved Portly Cosgrove into the flat.

'So really,' Coco was saying, when Oliver's thoughts returned to her, and her situation, 'I am very grateful to you for sending me to the nuns and the nursing home. Really, I am, Ollie. Very grateful.'

Oliver put on the expression of a modest man who had no need to be thanked for what he assumed anyone would do for a childhood friend, and then waited for the rest of the visit, the sandwiches, the beer, the effort at conversation to creep by, which they did so slowly it was almost agonising. Finally he stood up, feeling horribly guilty because he knew that when he left Coco he would be leaving her completely alone.

'Not going so soon?'

'I have to, love, really. I have to get back. We are giving a supper party for the cast. You know, Sunday night, and all that.'

Coco looked up at Oliver. He was already so much part of what she had, deep down, in her heart of hearts, wanted to be part of, the casual, free and easy world of the theatre. So much part of it that she knew he did not even realise it, did not even appreciate that he now looked like an actor, talked like an actor; so much that he was already taking it all for granted, the whole glorious, chaotic world of the theatre, that world without tedium, with its own exotic timetable, its own seasons, it own beginnings, middles and ends.

She felt so envious of him it was like a bitter taste in her mouth. It did not take much for her to imagine just what kind of supper party to which Oliver would now be returning. Unfortunately she could see it all, quite vividly. The cast crowding into some small flat, talking non-stop, everyone on intimate terms, a casserole laid out with endless rice and salads, none of which anyone would take much notice of, but all of which would be eventually eaten, once the wine had been drunk, cigarettes lit and stubbed out, arguments begun and forgotten.

At last Oliver felt it was all right to take his leave. He had always loved going to visit Coco in her eclectic, beautifully artistic two-bedroomed flat, with the roof garden high above that was open to all the tenants to use whenever they wished. Now, however, he could not wait to return to Tadcaster, to Elsie, who would by now be putting the finishing touches to the buffet for the party.

''Bye, Ollie.'

'Give the baby a kiss for me, won't you?'

'Sure.'

Oliver kissed Coco, and then fled.

For a minute Coco watched him from the upper window that gave on to the street as he walked out of the block of flats towards his hired car, and then she turned away and picking Holly up started to walk the floor with her, despite the fact that there was no need to nurse the baby, since she was neither crying, nor hungry.

Picking her up, unwrapping her from her homely pale blue knitted blankets, was obviously disturbing, but such was Coco's need for some kind of human contact, that she cared less. In fact the baby never woke, but nevertheless moved against Coco's shoulder making minute little infant sounds, her eyes still tight shut.

As she walked up and down her living room Coco tried hard to grasp the reality of her baby, and failed, because the truth was that the only reality she could feel at that moment was Oliver, driving off, leaving her quite alone.

Chapter Eleven

It was not that Oliver did not like Portly, because he did. No one could, in all reality, *not* like Portly. He was too naturally affable. He had no desire to hurt anyone. He wanted only to help everyone. He helped Elsie all the time. He helped Oliver too. And of course Elsie was devoted to him, that much was clear, which was why, Oliver realised, he did not want Portly around. Nothing to do with Portly, of course, but everything to do with Oliver. The fact was that, for no precise reason that he could name, Oliver was furiously jealous of this tall, affable man with his gentle manners. Most of all, of course, he was jealous of his seeming hold over Elsie, their past together. It was as if they had grown up together in some other country, which in a way they had, a theatrical country, a place where they had become passport carrying citizens long before Oliver Lowell.

Having finished reading his favourite cartoon in the *Daily Mail*, Oliver now stared across at Elsie with something approaching the kind of courage he did not feel.

He did not want to get on the wrong side of Elsie, but nevertheless the question had to be asked. How long was Portly going to stay? And why was he with them, anyway? Following these thoughts, Oliver plucked up his courage and asked Popeye the question that was so much on his mind at that moment.

'How long is Portly going to stay with us?'

'Oh, I don't know how long Portly is going to stay, Oliver. As long as he wants, I suppose—'

Elsie stared at her reflection in the sitting room mirror with some satisfaction. She had added just a few lighter streaks to her hair, and she was quite pleased with them. As she had hoped – they did indeed make her appear older – which she was going to have to be, in Bartlett's next production, which was the reason she had decided to put them in.

'You must know a bit – how long?'

'No, I don't, really I don't. I mean, you saw the state of him when we bumped into him at the café, you saw the state of him yourself. We couldn't just leave Portly there.'

'I don't see why not?'

'Because,' Elsie said with every evidence of patience in her well-trained voice, 'he was the first person to really help me when I changed categories, he really was. He helped me to get my first real starring role. Without Portly I would still be going up for coughs and spits and twirling in front of producers in the vain hope of getting minor roles. He really did help me.'

355

'Help you? He cheated you!'

'Portly did not cheat me, Oliver, Donald Bourton cheated everyone. Portly knew nothing about what happened, why should he?'

'They were partners, weren't they?'

'Of course they were partners, Ollie.' Elsie stared at the beautiful colour of the new lipstick that she had just put on her mouth. 'Diana Dors pink, that's what I call that,' she said out loud to herself. Then she turned back to Oliver. 'Of course they were partners, we all know that, but Donald was always in charge of the business side. He brought Portly in to the production company. A lamb to the slaughter, that was what young Portly was—'

'Saw him coming, more like.'

'Donald Bourton was much older than poor Portly. Anyway, Portly paid back everyone that Cosgrove and Bourton owed, every penny, from his own pocket, that is why he is so broke. Because he did the decent thing and made sure that every single person was paid what they were owed, and how many managements can you think of as being that decent, Oliver?'

'I don't think managements are capable of being decent, Popeye, do you know that?'

'Well Portly was, and is. That is a fact.' Elsie was beginning not only to feel, but to sound, impatient. She just would not have Portly thrown out of the flat, particularly not just when he was beginning to look, and obviously feel, much better. She would never get over the shock of seeing him in that café looking so pale and thin he had hardly been recognisable. 'Anyway,' she continued, turning from the mirror to face Oliver. 'How many managements have *you* known, sweet lummox, may I ask? Come on, how many have you known, when they were at home?'

Oliver looked sulky, and putting his hands behind his head he stretched out the full length of the sofa so that Elsie could not possibly have joined him there, even if she had wanted to.

'That's not the point—'

'This is priceless. Ollie, you are priceless. You have known just one management, just one, and now all of a sudden you are an expert! I have known upwards of – well, I would hate to count – and believe you me, Portly Cosgrove is the only one who ever cared a tuppenny damn whether I lived or died.'

Elsie thought back to when Dottie had to be fooled into thinking that the play script was a radio script, and how Portly had met her in Fullers. How they had cast about trying to think of how Elsie could be offered the part, and how she might be able to accept without Dottie's say-so. How they had both finally agreed that offering Dottie a part was the only way to get her to agree to his casting Elsie. She shook her head. No, no one was ever going to tell her that Portly Cosgrove was less than she knew him to be.

'Anyway,' she gave Oliver a lightly disparaging look before turning back to the mirror, 'anyway, *you* wouldn't understand Portly, really you wouldn't, Oliver.'

'Why not?' Oliver was pretending to read a book.

'Why not? Because Portly is a gentleman, Oliver Lowell, which you are most definitely not. What was it you told me the other day your father was when he was at home—'

'I can't remember, I can't remember what I told you,' Oliver replied at once, with complete truth, his heart sinking as he was reminded of his double existence, his make-believe background, which, for some reason that he could not understand, he had, on the spur of the moment, decided to keep up with everyone at the Stephens Theatre.

'Well, whatever he is, he is certainly not any Portly Cosgrove. He is at least as common as you, isn't he?' Elsie gave a short, sarcastic laugh. Portly's vaguely patrician background had always impressed her, most particularly since he never, ever referred to it. He just was, or came over as, one of nature's gentlemen.

'Coming on all grand, are we, now?' Oliver stood up and walked over to Elsie. 'And since when were *we* so posh, Miss Elsie Lancaster?'

'Oh, I'm not posh. I know that, but then, I don't pretend to be, whereas you, on occasions, well, you would honestly think that you were at least a Vere de Vere, which you certainly are not.' Elsie smiled across at Oliver, her eyes momentarily straying from her own image. She had a good smile, but she had to give it to Oliver, he had an even better one. Oliver had a brilliant smile.

'Did you know that this famously grand Portly Cosgrove is not coming back until after lunch, Miss Lancaster?'

'Oh, isn't he?'

'No.'

'What do you want to do then? Your choice – it's either trying to find me some nose scissors, or staying in and—'

'Nose scissors, definitely. Nose scissors are my choice.'

Elsie just managed to keep a straight face before shopping and lunch were put on hold in favour of something rather more passionately interesting.

Portly returned with a huge bouquet of flowers for Elsie, and not only that, but he also returned with lunch. Being acutely aware of Elsie's kindness in taking him in, from the first Portly had made sure to absent himself after breakfast until well into the early afternoon, after which he always tried to return with something, or some things, that would make him once more welcome.

Living with lovers was probably not always easy, but living with Elsie and Oliver was perfectly beautiful, not just because he himself was also in love with Elsie, but because they were his sort of people. They took life as it came, just like the porridge that Portly enjoyed making for them all for breakfast, sometimes with sugar, sometimes with salt, but always with verve.

'Shall I make us all a spaghetti bolognese?'

Oliver and Elsie, filled with that languorous but hungry state that follows energetic love making, nodded happily at Portly's suggestion, and he hurried equally happily towards the small kitchen, the fresh ingredients in his shopping basket just waiting to be cooked up into a perfect sauce.

'The perfect spaghetti bolognese is made like this,' Portly announced as he finally emerged from the kitchen.

Oliver nodded, and sat down, not at all interested in the recipe. He was much more interested in eating than hearing about the ingredients of a dish which, at that moment in time, everyone every- where seemed intent on serving. Elsie followed suit and sat herself at the small, square table. She was more interested than Oliver in the perfect bolognese sauce, although also, admittedly, raven- ously hungry.

'Go on, Portly,' she told him, 'tell me. I'm inter- ested in your sauce, even if Ollie's not.'

'You must have perfect meat, the best steak minced in front of you in the shop. It cannot be butcher's mince, nothing like that, that would be far too fatty.' He put a hot plate at each place setting and carefully ladled perfectly cooked, al dente spaghetti on each. 'So. You begin with some olive oil and butter, about four tablespoons, into which you put a choppped onion and four ounces of chopped bacon, add a clove of garlic and a little salt, crushed together with a knife, a chopped carrot, a piece of chopped celery, and cook until the onion is soft. After which—' Portly, having helped everyone to both pasta and sauce, now sat down to the first silence that any of them had enjoyed all day. 'After which,' he continued, 'you add the minced beef, stir until it loses its pinkness, pop in four ounces of chicken livers and turn them until they are browned before adding a tin of consommé, a pound of skinned tomatoes, a bay leaf, and some salt, pepper, and nutmeg. Cover and simmer gently for thirty minutes. At the end of the cooking, stir in four tablespoons of cream, and serve with grated cheese or pecorino, if you can find it in Tadcaster, which, believe me, you can't.'

Sitting back, very, very eventually, after two helpings of this sumptuous pasta dish, Oliver found that his earlier objections to Portly's residing with them had quite disappeared, never, perhaps, to be aired again.

'Portly, you are to be congratulated. I have eaten spaghetti far too many times in my life before, but never, ever, like this. This bolognese sauce has all the taste of Bologna and none of the King's Road. This is a sauce for Italians, by Italians, and you are a genius to recognise it. Where did you get the recipe?'

'Bologna.'

'How appropriate.'

And as Portly served the best coffee, too, that Oliver had yet tasted, Portly's own special mixture, Oliver found that he could not leave the subject of the spaghetti alone.

'Really, you are to be congratulated, from the bottom of my heart. What are you going to make us tomorrow?'

'Proper English chicken pie. None of that rubbish with garlic and tomatoes drowning out the taste of good, corn-fed chicken. Made with cream, and lemon pastry, naturally. Nothing better.'

Before standing up and announcing that they would leave the dishes, and now go in search of the stubbornly elusive nose scissors, it came home to Oliver, and quite forcibly, that Elsie was quite right. Portly was a very nice person, and it would be terrible not to have him in the flat, in their lives, very much part of their present existence. What was more, Oliver could not wait to sample his chicken pie and lemon pastry.

It was a sunny afternoon and as the three of them sauntered happily down Tadcaster's main street it occurred to Portly that they must be the luckiest people in the world at that moment. Certainly he felt that *he* had to be. He had been at the bottom of the pit, in utter darkness, not knowing which way to turn, and, being an only child without any living family, desperately lonely, all business acquaintances having turned their backs on him.

That had been his state of mind, when, on looking up, he had seen the familiar and to him utterly beautiful face of Elsie looking down at him. The round contours of her youthful beauty had been, he knew, in stark contrast to his own grey, badly shaven face. Her hair, so thick and lustrous, his own lank and dull, his clothes barely presentable, shiny in their effort to look clean, hers glossy with that particular look that newly fashionable clothes assume on the young and beautiful.

It had been a terrible moment, and he of course, realising instantly the potential humiliation, had immediately looked away, while Elsie with her usual élan had pulled him to his feet and instantly embraced him, as if she knew, from the very look of him, that he had, after all, been the innocent party in the whole turgid affair of Cosgrove and Burton, and the ill-fated tour starring Elsie Lancaster, and she had always known it.

'Ah, now they may well have an ink well and pen in here.'

Oliver stopped and stared into the antique shop which, before he had even looked in the window, Portly was sure would be filled with excellent, over-priced, reproduction antiques. He knew at once that it would be the kind of shop which has a few over-polished items and a couple of jars of beeswax polish and the inevitable proprietor sporting half-moon glasses and a superior expression. Inevitably it was, but it also had an inkwell with accompanying plumed pen, very Shakespearean and completely lacking in authenticity. This did not deter Oliver who happily bought it, and turning to Elsie and Portly announced, 'I shall write my first play with this.'

Elsie raised her eyes to Portly, and then turning

to Oliver said, tongue in cheek, 'Well then, listen, Will dear, if you are to write plays for us—'

'For me actually, Elsie. Don't please be deceived, I wish to write *myself* into work – not necessarily *you*.'

Elsie stopped and stared into Oliver's eyes. Seeing that he meant it, she smiled, and putting on her most *faux naïve* expression opened her eyes wide, casting about in her mind for some way to retaliate, to get back at Oliver, finally settling on a plan to turn up her evening performance so much that she would wipe the floor with him.

'If you are to write plays for you and you alone, then Portly had better be—' She turned to Portly frowning. 'Portly had better be my agent. That will even everything up, won't it? After all, if you've been in management, being an agent's a doddle, wouldn't you say, Portly?'

Oliver turned at that. 'Do you think that is wise?' he asked, before starting to write out a cheque for the inkwell and pen.

'Why ever not. After all, the fact is – and it is a fact, Ollie love – I at least am going to need an agent, whereas you, if you are going to write things for yourself, won't, at least not really, will you, not if you are going to write yourself into work?'

When they were outside the shop again Oliver felt it was quite safe to become indignant.

'I will need an agent for my plays, you know I will, Popeye.'

'Well, you can't have Portly, because I have just nabbed him.'

'I have an acting agent, but I *shall* need someone for my plays.'

'You can't have Portly, Oliver. I have just told you, once and for all, he is mine.'

'I don't mind doing actors *and* plays – I had never thought before – I mean about becoming an agent. But now I can see, I could do it, couldn't I?'

Portly looked from one to the other with a pleading but unanxious expression. The truth was that he did not mind doing anything at all, as long as it was for Elsie.

'You haven't enough money to do anything, Portly, you know you haven't, not a single sou.'

'I have my dole money,' Portly protested, keeping a straight face. 'That would be enough to pay for the hire of a typewriter and a desk.'

'You have just enough for us all to live off you, that is all,' Oliver curled his lip in mock disdain.

'I have some. But not enough . . .' Elsie stared ahead as they continued sauntering down Tadcaster's main street.

'I know someone who has quite a lot—' Oliver stopped, his eyes half closed as they sometimes were when he had a bright idea.

'Who?'

'Never you mind, Popeye. But I certainly will write and ask him and see if he can come up with some doh ray me.'

'With your new quill pen, sweet lummox?'

'With the very same.'

That evening, during the interval, when he was quite alone, Oliver dashed off a letter to Cliffie, in biro, because he had not yet quite mastered his reproduction quill pen.

Dear Cliffie,
Some friends and I want to start an agency for writers and actors, but we are quite skint. Have you enough for a down payment – nothing too much, but it should be a London premises, you know, so it has to be quite a bit, I should have thought. Everything is going swimmingly, love Oliver.

He received a letter by return from Cliffie.

Dear Master Oliver,
I enclose a banker's draft for a thousand pounds, which I managed to extricate from Mr Hopkins with some difficulty. In common with your father, he does so hate to send you your allowance, as you know, thinking that you will only waste it on cigarettes and beer and wild, wild women, and so it has been accu-mulating. I hope that it will help things along. As ever, Master Oliver, Cliffie.

Unfortunately Elsie looked over Oliver's shoulder when he was reading the reply.

'Why does this "Cliffie" write to you as "Master Oliver", sweet lummox?'

'It's a very long and boring story,' Oliver told her, turning away. 'As long and boring as they get. They're just nicknames that we all use for each other really, and we had better hurry, or we just might be in danger of being on time to make up for the matinée, just for once.'

He snatched up his jacket and hurried off. Elsie hurried after him, knowing that this was Oliver's way of telling her to mind her own business, both of them leaving Portly, as usual, to clear up the debris from their tea.

'So that is that. We have a cheque, now we have to find the premises.'

'Portly says it has to be London.' Elsie skipped along, barely keeping up with Oliver.

'Portly is quite right.'

'He says otherwise we will just appear as hicks.'

'Which is what we are.'

'Exactly. But we must not appear as such.'

'I shall stay with Tad Protheroe's agency for my acting, of course, because Portly has not got the experience that old Tad has. You can go to Portly, because you have no one else, and I don't suppose anyone else would take you on at this moment anyway.'

'Oh, don't you, is that right?'

Elsie stopped skipping, allowing Oliver to go ahead and frowning at his back as he did so.

'Oh, don't you,' she repeated, but this time to herself. 'Well, just you wait, Master Oliver, just you wait. The Tad Protheroes of this world are pretty soon going to be falling over themselves to sign me up, but they can go jump, because it is Portly I am going to, and Portly who is going to make me into a West End star, see if he doesn't.'

She said all this to herself while ahead of her, by

367

some way, Oliver had gone on talking, not realising that Elsie was no longer by his side.

'No, I don't think anyone but Portly would want to sign you up, Popeye, because, it stands to reason, you have not been seen in the capital, and then you are a girl too, you know, and there are far, far fewer parts for girls, and agents know this, d'you see? On the whole they prefer men, and they don't get pregnant, men don't get pregnant, that's another thing.'

Continuing to follow him at a distance Elsie made up her mind to see Oliver off, not just at the evening performance, but at the matinée too, which she did, and thoroughly enjoyed doing. But then Oliver saw her off at the evening performance, but only by cheating: upstaging her, coming in too early and too quickly – the whole boiling lot.

Nevertheless, despite being secretly infuriated, Elsie said nothing afterwards, pretending, as she would do with any other actor, that she had not even noticed, while mentally making new plans to get back at him, even as she knew Oliver would be doing the same to her. The truth was that the gloves were well and truly off now, and they both knew it.

As far as the idea for the new agency went it took some time, and many brochures depicting premises that were all far too expensive, before they eventually gave up, and decided that the only way to go about finding a suitable office was for Oliver to send Coco to look for one on their behalf. Coco after all was living in London, so she could whip round to see places as soon as they came on the market, whereas for them, from Tadcaster, it would take for ever.

Despite being home-bound, or perhaps because she was home-bound, Coco set out determinedly to find premises for Oliver and Portly. Happily it was a very flat time for rented property, and within a few weeks a former newsagent's shop in a back road in Kensington did indeed come on the market.

It was placed most fortuitously bang opposite a pub, with an old-fashioned apothecary shop on the other side of the road, so it appealed to Coco as being the perfect site. It was filthy, of course, and filled with rubbish and circulars and in need of more than a lick of paint, but that did not matter, what mattered was that although it was not Chelsea it was at least in central London. One day, Coco found herself wishing, they would probably become so big they would move up to the West End, but until then it would do very nicely indeed.

Coco telephoned the news of her find to Oliver, and Oliver instructed her to sign the ridiculously cheap six-month lease on their behalf, and the following weekend Oliver, Portly and Elsie hired a car and drove down from Tadcaster to London early on Sunday morning, arriving outside the new premises at precisely the same time as Coco.

'I say, Coco, where's the baby?' Where's Holly?'

For a second Oliver was ashamed to realise that he felt a huge surge of relief at the possibility that Coco might, after all, have taken his advice and had the baby adopted. It would somehow make so much sense, and free Coco to be herself again, not ground down by motherhood, and all its cares.

'Oh, don't worry, I've left Holly with Gladys. Gladys is acting as official baby squasher until I get back.'

'Oh. Right.' Oliver leaned forward and pecked Coco on the cheek, in vain trying to obscure her from Elsie's view as he did so.

But it was no good. Elsie had seen Coco, who, seemingly overnight, Oliver now realised, had, outwardly at least, returned to her original self, once more sporting amber bead necklaces and bracelets, beautifully washed and shining dark hair, and a slender shape that did not seem to have had anything to do with childbirth, or long months spent awaiting delivery in a nursing home.

'By the way, Coco, I don't think you know Elsie Lancaster, do you? Elsie, this is Coco Hampton, Coco – Elsie.'

The two young women shook hands, and as they did so Oliver found his eyes half closing.

Oh God, oh God, oh God, they hated each other before their hands even touched.

'Shall we go in?'

Coco being Coco, and all too confident of her decision, Oliver saw that she had already bought the tins of distemper and the brushes and all the other paraphernalia they needed, and so, having approved wholeheartedly of her find, and without more ado, they all four set to cleaning up the one big room, and painting quickly over the pre-war dull cream paint.

As they painted Coco talked to Portly. Portly talked to Elsie. Oliver talked to Coco and Portly. Elsie talked to Oliver, but Coco did not talk to Elsie, and neither did Elsie talk to Coco. They avoided each other's eyes, and stepped back and around each other for all the world, Oliver thought to himself, as if they were warring duchesses in a ballroom. Every time Elsie turned towards him and their eyes met he was sure that her eyes were saying to him, 'You have slept with this woman, haven't you?' Or 'You have had an affair with this girl, haven't you? Why else would she be doing all this for you, even down to signing the lease for us?' Or 'Just what is this young woman to you?'

'Right. Well done, everyone. Now there is only the brass plate to get engraved, and a plumber to be called to get the loo working, and a desk and a telephone to put in. After that, Portly, old chap, the world, as my old—' Oliver was just about to say 'nanny' but remembering his story, he quickly replaced 'nanny' with 'mum' and smiled his usual brilliant smile. 'As my old mum used to say, after that the world's your lobster.'

Portly smiled. He could not believe his luck in finding such a bunch of friends, all willing to help him to get back on his feet.

371

'I say, can I buy you all lunch at the pub opposite out of my dole money?'

'Course you can, Portly, love.'

They all trooped across the street and sat down at one of the pub tables. It was early summer, the trees were out, life was suddenly very good. After a few drinks they each chose a plate of food at the counter and sat back down at their table, keeping a clear view of their new premises, of which they already all felt inordinately, and quite ridiculously, proud.

'Coco can join the agency too, can't she, Portly?' Oliver nodded at Portly and towards Coco, a portion of scotch egg poised on his fork.

'Course she can. I need as many people as possible. I would be honoured to include her.'

'That's very kind of you—'

'What work have you done?' Elsie interrupted, addressing Coco for the first time, her voice oddly clipped, the look in her eyes that of a cowboy who had just seen a line of Red Indians on the far horizon. More than anything in the world she hated any whiff of amateurism, and the fact that Portly had readily accepted Coco just because, Elsie was sure, she was Oliver's friend, or ex-girlfriend, or something of that nature, was just so amateur.

'Coco was at the Royal with me—'

Just one look cut Oliver down as effectively as if Elsie had been wielding a broad sword.

'What work have I done? Well, Oliver knows that.' Coco looked towards Oliver and smiled that particularly intimate smile that comes from having been friends since they were small. So small that in order for either of them to see the stage properly from the stalls, Gladys had been forced to bring cushions for them to sit on. 'Ollie thinks I have done too little acting and too much filming and he doesn't think that's acting. He despises it, in fact, don't you, Ollie?'

'She's done two films, and would have gone on but for the arrival of a small person,' Oliver finally put in, and he smiled towards Coco, making sure that she knew that he at least was not embarrassed by the fact that she now had a baby in her life, although she was quite evidently not married.

But at that moment Elsie was less than interested in Coco's baby, although she was, of a sudden, silenced by the fact that Coco had already been cast in two films, which was more than Elsie had ever been. It was a fact. Portly could not turn down an actress who had been in two films, and they all knew it. Elsie nodded, assuming a nonchalance she did not feel.

'Sure. Of course. Two films. Great for the agency, to have someone of your experience on the books—'

'But I don't want to go on acting.'

This time not just Elsie but Oliver too stared at Coco.

'You don't want to go on acting?'

If they had not been plum in the middle of eating both their mouths would have dropped wide open, such was their astonishment.

'No, I don't want to go on acting. That's why I left my previous agent. I don't want to be on tour all the time, or on location, or any of that nonsense, not now I have a baby. I want to be with Holly. I want to design. That is what I have always wanted to do. Acting was just a lark, and you know it, Oliver, just a lark.'

Elsie's eyes lowered themselves, the point finally getting home. This girl had a baby, a real baby, and no wedding ring. Of a sudden Elsie's plate of food seemed to be really so interesting that it might well have been the first time she had ever seen a ham salad.

Meanwhile Oliver was quite sure that he could actually see Elsie's thoughts, so convinced was he of how she would be thinking.

The baby would, by now – following the passionate affair Elsie would deeply suspect Oliver of having had with Coco – the baby would be Oliver's baby. In Elsie's imagination, he would have made Coco pregnant. Even so he said nothing, thinking, in his innocence, that he could explain everything later.

'What was it you said you wanted to do?' Portly looked both interested and disinterested, judging the mother of a young baby to be naturally sensitive on this point.

'I want to do what I have always wanted to do – Ollie knows this – I want to design costumes for the stage.'

'I see.'

Now even Oliver could see the gap widening

and a vast emotional hole in the road opening up in front of him. Why did Coco have to go and be such a damn fool as to mention the fact that *Ollie knows*, not once but twice? Why should he be the *only* person to know? Why not – say – the father of her child? Why not the nuns who had looked after her so well? Why *him* especially?

'You want to design costumes? Well then you won't clash with Elsie, so I can quite easily represent you, can't I? That is if you would like me to?'

Portly smiled his usual affable smile at everyone, relieved. Knowing Elsie, he had been all too aware of what she must be feeling, having to suddenly tolerate the presence of another young woman, someone of her own age, someone who had previous knowledge of her lover, someone who was, if not as arresting as Elsie, at least very pretty, if only in a dark sort of *gamine* way.

'Yes, of course I would like you to represent me,' Coco agreed, after a quick look for confirmation to Oliver. 'I would like that very much, of course I would.'

'No clash,' Portly repeated out loud, looking from one young woman to the other, as if to reassure both himself and them.

No clash?

Oliver looked away, at the same time lighting a cigarette. He was dreading the return journey. No, worse than that, he was dreading getting back to Tadcaster. There would be all hell let loose, and nothing, least of all the look in Elsie's eyes, could dissuade him from this notion. Elsie was going to be mad with rage and jealousy over Coco, whom she was bound to suspect of having been Oliver's mistress. She would be mad with the kind of jealous rage that only comes from having enjoyed the first passionate affair, both on and off stage, she had ever had.

Still, he had no doubt at all that he would be able to convince her of his innocence. After all if he could not prove his innocence, who could? He loved Coco, of course he did, as much as he loved anyone, perhaps more, but as a brother, that was all, just as a brother. And she loved him as a sister, and nothing more, that was for sure.

In saying goodbye Coco quickly bent down to peck him on the cheek, as if to reassure Oliver of her lack of interest in anything but his friendship. She herself could not wait to hurry back to her flat and Gladys.

Naturally, the moment she had met Elsie Lancaster it had been quite clear to Coco that Oliver's girlfriend was ready and willing to scratch her eyes out, and frankly she herself could not have cared less. All she cared about was getting back to the baby and making sure that Gladys had not literally squashed her, in some way or other, because Gladys had never had a baby, and had certainly never looked after one as small as Holly, Coco having come to her, as Gladys said endlessly and often quite pointlessly, ready made.

It seemed to take for ever to drive back to

Chelsea, although of course, it being Sunday, and the streets being quite empty, it actually could not have taken longer than quarter of an hour. Nevertheless Coco found that her heart was in her mouth as she leapt up the stairs towards her first floor flat, her pulse racing as the full idiocy of having left Holly with Gladys of all people dawned on her.

She tried not to burst in the door, because to look as she felt, almost, although probably quite unreasonably, frantic with worry, would be so insulting to Gladys. So, carefully putting her key in the lock, and equally carefully shutting the front door of her flat, she sauntered as casually as she could into the sitting room to be confronted by a sight from her worst nightmare – Gladys rocking to and fro, clutching a cushion to her stomach, tears streaming down her face.

'Well, now you have three people on your books. Me, Elsie and Coco.'

Oliver smiled as brightly as he did not feel at the other two, while Elsie stared moodily across the road at the front door of the new agency.

'Time to get back to the painting.'

As Elsie painted, and it was once more just the three of them, just like in Tadcaster, her good mood returned, and she seemed to forget all about Coco and her baby. As they worked they made excited plans. It was natural. Great plans for the future are only made by those who do not yet have one.

First, they realised, they had to name the agency. Portly, Lowell and Lancaster, or PLL, seemed the easiest and best, because, naturally, Portly did not want any mention of Cosgrove in the name. It would bring back bad memories not only for him, but for other people too.

'What about Coco?' Elsie looked round from finishing her wall and stared innocently at the other two. 'Won't Coco want to have herself included in the name of the agency? I mean, she did at least sign the lease for us.'

'That's just temporary, in case we lost it, after all this looking. No, we're rearranging everything as soon as perfectly possible. Coco gets sent money, you see, at the start of every quarter, by her guilty parents, so she didn't mind at all, but we're paying her back, tomorrow, if not yesterday. So, no, in answer to your question she's definitely not part of the agency, and she wouldn't want to be.'

'Why not?'

'I don't know, because she's Coco, I suppose,' Oliver said, frowning. 'And, well,' he continued after struggling for a logical reason which Elsie might understand, 'well, Coco does not like that kind of thing. Knowing Coco, I'm sure she would prefer to grumble about us in the acknowledged manner of every artist who does not represent themselves. Besides, she has done nothing to deserve it—'

'Except find this place.'

'Oh, she enjoyed that—'

378

'How do you know?'

'Because I know Coco. She likes finding things, that is what she likes best. Old materials, pieces of lace, beads, agencies, doesn't really matter, it is the search that she enjoys most. I know this because I have known her since she was a very small person,' said Oliver, and his eyes took on a mosaic look as if the eyes themselves had made up their own minds, deciding to turn their backs on the subject, drop the blinds on the whole matter.

'None of us is particularly interested in how well you know dear little Coco, or for how long, are we, Portly?'

Portly, sensing danger, nodded and at the same time shook his head.

'Yes, no, maybe,' came his diplomatic reply.

'Typical Portly.' Elsie snorted lightly and rolled her eyes, flinging back her mane of curly hair. She did not say so, because she was far too fond of him, but the truth was that the reason why Portly had been cheated out of everything by Donald Bourton was that he was too nice and too trusting, and they all knew it.

Elsie lit a cigarette and gazed ahead of her at the now quite beautifully white walls of what was to be their very own agency. Portly would not have been so soft if he had been dragged up by Dottie, and that was the truth, the whole truth, and nothing but the blooming truth.

'You think I'm soft, don't you, Elsie?'

'I know you are, Portly,' Elsie told him,

repairing her lips with her newest and favourite pale pink lipstick. 'It's all going to have to change once you're behind the magnificent desk we are going to buy you. PLL is going to have to get a reputation for being as tough as my grandmother's Friday night steak.'

Elsie's thoughts returned once more to Dottie, and despite the brightness of the day, and the fact that they had now put the finishing touches to the one room of their sparkling new agency, she felt her heart sinking. It was always the same. If she thought about Dottie for too long, even the mention of her name would bring about a feeling that Elsie had, somehow, been cursed by her, and that it would only be a matter of time before Dottie would somehow catch up with her, and Elsie would start to know just how real bad luck could be. But until then, she just had to do what people always told those who had been cursed to do – she would just refuse to believe it. She would not believe in Dottie's curse, and that was that.

Even so, for a second, her thoughts stretched back to the tall house filled with resting, out of work actors, to Dottie and her ironing board, to the occasional knock at the front door when a manuscript was sent back to an aspiring playwright, or a script from BBC Radio was delivered.

How would they all think of her, she wondered to herself, as she stared in the little mirror of her powder compact at her perfectly shaped mouth. At best with indifference, or in Dottie's case with scorn, which would doubtless, by now, have turned to venom. Elsie Lancaster, her own grand-daughter, would have joined the 'black hats brigade'. Dottie would have her knife in Elsie Lancaster, all right. She never did not have her knife in someone. Curse or no curse, Elsie knew very well that Medea's murder of her babies would be nothing to what Dottie would be imagining about Elsie. Boiling her granddaughter in oil would be merciful compared to some of the other things Dottie would be prepared to do to Elsie, if Elsie ever had the misfortune to see her again.

And like the Cowardly Lion and the Tin Man in *The Wizard of Oz*, the out of work actors and the resting thespians would now be hiding in terror at the mere mention of Elsie Lancaster until the Wicked Witch of the West retired once more to her kitchen, to the trails of water running down the windows, to the ironing board which would be smacked with the iron every few seconds, to the ironing itself which would be sprayed with water and then, in its turn, smacked with the iron, the iron zip-zapping its way across the material with surprising speed and dexterity, the whole growing into a pile of bitterness, because nothing made Dottie more bitter than ironing. It was as if the ironing was some hideous unending task, a labour set by the devil and imposed by God on innocent women who would never, ever be released from its remorseless hold.

Back in the present Portly was saying, 'Just

think, PLL might well become internationally famous, making huge deals—'

'Managing the stars—'

'Me—'

'Yes, you, Ollie – and Elsie.'

'Me first—'

'Alphabetical order, Ollie. Lowell comes after Lancaster, remember?'

'Both first, darlings,' Portly murmured. 'Now let's go back to the pub and have ourselves a really rewarding beer.'

They sat down once more at the pub table, and there was a long silence as they all drank, and Elsie lit another cigarette.

'These are the good days, aren't they?' Elsie nodded at Portly, her long legs spread out in front of her, her eyes half closed against the smoke of her cigarette.

'Before the real things begin, you mean?'

'Just so. Before reality sets in.'

They all nodded once more in agreement as their eyes strayed across the short strip of pavement and the small side road to their proud new office. As yet there was no letter box, but even so it was already looking smart.

An old tramp wandered past, and perhaps encouraged by the sight of the hole in the freshly painted black front door where they were planning to put their brass letter box he stopped, and within a very few seconds he had managed to relieve himself before wandering on.

The proud owners of PLL stared after him for a

few seconds, unable to quite believe what they had just seen. Naturally Elsie was the first to her feet.

'Oi, oi! Here! You!'

She started to cross the road, but Portly pulled her back, laughing. 'Leave him alone, leave him alone—'

'Did you see what he did? My God, I will have his guts for garters—'

Portly nodded, still laughing. 'Elsie, love – wait, wait! *NO*. Wait. Really.' Elsie stared up at Portly, who had caught hold of her arms in his strong grip. 'Don't you know what that is? Good luck, Elsie. That is good luck, darling.'

'Good luck, my foot—'

'No, really. That is one of the oldest superstitions there is. PLL will now grow and prosper, nay, you watch, PLL will flourish like the green bay tree, see if it doesn't. Really, that is good luck. What just happened brings luck, I know it does. It's one of the oldest superstitions in the world, like coal on New Year's Eve and passing a funeral on the way to the races, all that, but more. A tramp's tinkle is worth a million, that is what they say. Perhaps we should rename the agency? TT?'

Elsie scowled at the now fast retreating tramp, but nevertheless she went back to sit at the pub table with Portly.

'It had better be good luck, Portly Cosgrove, or I shall personally throw a bottle of Dettol all over you, and that's just for starters.'

As he stood up and stretched his long legs,

preparing to go to the bar for yet more beer, Portly paused and smiled down at the two young stars, one of whom was now on his books.

He had a chance to start again, and this time he was going to make sure that no one ruined it. He was determined to make Elsie into a big West End draw. Just the sight of her name on a theatre bill, if he had anything to do with it, was going to put, as the somewhat crude theatrical saying went, 'bums on seats'. Portly was determined on it. In his hands she would become a big draw. Whether her love affair would also stay the course was another matter. For the moment all that mattered was that they were all on the threshold of a bright future. And at long, long last, Portly knew that he himself had grown up.

'Oh, by the way, you two – now we have settled on a name, just as well if I sign you up, Elsie, before you change your mind, wouldn't you say? And Oliver for his plays, if he is going to stay with Tad Protheroe, which is probably a good idea.'

But Oliver and Elsie did not seem to hear what Portly had said. They were too busy thinking about their billing, Oliver kicking himself that he had allowed himself to be persuaded to use his mother's family name. If he had chosen a name beginning with A, or even K, he would have had it over Elsie. Damn, damn, damn! He needed to be billed over Elsie if only to give his ego a small boost, and now he never would be billed above her.

Unless?

He persuaded Tad, when negotiating for Oliver, not to agree to alphabetical order? If he could persuade Tad Protheroe, that would be something.

'I say, Portly, before Elsie signs with you, I'd better remember to tell Tad Protheroe that I shall be with you for plays, hadn't I? Or do you think I should leave him? Do you? Do you think I should leave Tad, after all? Come to you with my acting as well?'

'No, I don't really, better to stay with him. He after all has a reputation, whereas I haven't, as yet.'

'Oh, OK, if you think so.'

'Anyway, I don't want you in the agency,' Elsie teased Oliver. 'I want Portly all to myself, finding *me* jobs, not *you*.'

Following this small exchange, Portly found his heart actually sinking. After all, if Oliver could leave Tad Protheroe with so little thought, then Oliver could leave Portly with equally little.

At first Coco could not make out, between the loud sobs that were shaking Gladys, what exactly had happened, why she was crying. It was all so terrifying. First of all the sight of Gladys, of all people, rocking to and fro, to and fro, tears coursing through her mascara and making a sooty mess on her face, and then the sight of the empty pram in the corner of the room.

The pram with no baby in it, the pram in which

Coco had left Holly safely fast asleep, fearing that the smell of paint in her nursery might disagree with her.

'What? What? Gladys? What has happened?'

Coco did a three hundred and sixty degree turn, spinning round in the middle of the room, while Gladys just rocked to and fro. Finally, ignoring Gladys's moaning sobs, Coco ran frantically through the flat, finally bursting into the little, brightly painted nursery that she had only just finished decorating for Holly.

There Holly was, totally against Coco's orders, asleep in her bassinet, quite fast asleep, appropriately dressed, her breathing just as it should be, eyes shut, colour perfect.

Coco leant against the nursery wall, recovering her breath, and resisting the impulse to pick Holly up and hug her thankfully to her. Instead she stepped back into the outside corridor, her whole body shaking with relief.

Standing for a second by the door she looked back once more at Holly, her knees still weak. What would she have done if her baby had not been as she undoubtedly was, beautifully well, and sleeping peacefully? It was unimaginable, but at last it came to Coco what love was really about. It was about you yourself not mattering in the least, only the other person, in this case a very small person, having any reality.

She went back to Gladys, whom she thought she could still hear sniffling and snivelling in the sitting room, but this time Coco went in with a drink in each hand, one for her, and one for Gladys.

Now, thank goodness, Gladys was mopping herself up, and the sobs that had racked her body were subsiding.

Coco lit a cigarette and waited. Her own mind was quite clear of panic. Nothing bad had happened to Holly, that was all that mattered, nothing else mattered. For some reason that she was doubtless about to hear about, Gladys had suffered a most uncharacteristic crying jag, and that was that. Coco looked at her guardian with some compassion, making up her mind that, whatever happened, she would never let Gladys near Holly again. She could not risk it. Even when her guardian was in London, she would have to get someone else to babysit for her. Besides, Gladys always wanted money from her. Never wanted anything but money, so all in all, now that Coco had a baby, she simply could not afford Gladys too, it was just a fact. Gladys would prove more expensive than any baby, if you let her.

'Thank you, darling.'

Gladys popped the inevitable cheque into her handbag, and smiled through her freshly remade-up face, now all pale powder and dark lipstick.

'I am sorry if I gave way just then, darling. But you see, coming here, being with you, made me realise just how much I miss London, and the shops, and all the other things that made my life such a happy one. I hate Norfolk, all the people so stuffy. All those *we've been here for a thousand years*

387

types, and really, I don't fit in, not anywhere. And here you are, so lucky, just a nip from Selfridges, and a tuck from Harvey Nichols and Woollands, and Harrods, and Peter Jones. I mean, I used to be so well known in Peter Jones they would quarrel amongst themselves to serve me, really they would.'

Coco nodded, and turned away. Just for a tiny moment she had actually thought that Gladys was going to say how lucky Coco was to have a healthy baby, how beautiful Holly was, and how much she, who had never been able to have babies, envied Coco. But no, good for Gladys, she remained as determinedly shallow as she had always been, and doubtless always would be.

As if she had guessed something of what Coco had been thinking, Gladys, drawing carefully on one of Coco's cigarettes, now said, 'I never wanted babies, you know. I could never have gone through a pregnancy the way you have just done. So brave of you, really, darling, so brave, but not very practical, wouldn't you say?'

'I don't think that anything worthwhile is ever very – practical, Gladys.'

'You always were a bit of a romantic, weren't you, Coco?'

'Not really, no.'

'Yes, you were. Even the way you dress, that's romantic, all amber beads and so on. Always had your own style, even when you were a small thing. Never could get you to wear conventional clothes, always liked to dress like something from an old painting, Harold always said.'

'Well, never mind that. Now I have to earn my living, so you had better go, Gladys. I have to start drawing some costumes.'

'I thought you were still acting, Coco? All those films you were doing? Surely—'

'No. Acting's not me, Glad, not at all. I'm too egotistical, really. I don't want to become someone else. No, I want to design, and design I shall. As a matter of fact,' she took out a letter from her handbag, 'yesterday I had my first commission, right out of the blue. A company I wrote to and sent some drawings that I did when I was in the nursing home, have commissioned me to design their opening production of *The Merry Wives of Windsor* just based on what I sent them, which is rather flattering, I must say. So I am afraid, you are now going to have to toddle, because, as always in the theatre, they want them yesterday, you know?'

Gladys nodded sadly. 'I suppose I must go back. Back to Norfolk.'

Coco kissed her. 'And Gladys, no more cheques to be had from me, not now I have Holly, I am afraid.'

'But – what about telling your parents? You don't want me to tell your parents, do you, about Holly? Who, by the way, was really very good when I put her back in her nursery because I wanted a fag. Contrary to what you said, she hardly murmured. But where was I? Oh yes, your parents. You don't want me to tell them, do you? About Holly?'

'Oh – do.'

Coco picked up Gladys's coat and handed it to her, and with a gentle guiding movement started to walk her to the front door, because she could never quite believe, not since she was quite small, just what an overt blackmailer Gladys always had been, never seeming to mind Coco's knowing that she was extorting money from her.

'No, really, tell them. Tell anyone you like. I don't really care any more, Gladys, really I don't. It doesn't matter who knows. All I care about now is Holly. You see when I came back just now, and saw you crying, for an awful moment I thought you were crying because of something having happened to Holly—'

'I was feeling depressed. So would you, if you had to go back to Norfolk. I feel as if I have been exiled from civilisation, for ever.'

'Very possibly you do, and it is quite understandable, but as I was saying, Gladys, the point is that when I thought that something had happened to Holly, and it hadn't, I realised that no one matters much to me now, apart from her. That is how much she means to me.'

'How strange, and Harold and I were so awfully sure that once you found out how much work a baby was, we were quite sure, positive, that you would have her adopted straight away.

That is what we both thought, that the work that a baby brings would drive you nuts.'

'Well, that is how wrong we all can be. And, to finish—' Coco opened the front door. 'As I just said, I don't mind at all if either or both of my parents know about her, or about anything to do with me, or my life really, because she is what matters, not them, but her. She matters to me now more even than you and Harold, which I am sure you don't mind. And if my parents do decide to dock my allowance because of Holly, then I shall be only too happy to do without it, the allowance. After all, Gladys, it's only money. Money does matter, but not as much as Holly. Holly is what matters most to me now.' Coco leaned forward and kissed her guardian affectionately, but it was very much a farewell kiss and they both knew it. 'Do come again, and as soon as you like, Gladys. I always enjoy seeing you, you know that. You've always been so kind to me, in the past, you and Harold, and I owe you a great deal, all my childhood happiness really, and I will pay you back some day, I promise, by making you proud of me, and Holly. We will both make you proud of us, you wait and see.'

Gladys walked away from Coco, frowning, and inwardly starting to seethe. She knew very well what Coco was getting at, and really it was insolence personified. As a matter of fact, she doubted very much that she would come again to see Coco and her silly little baby.

Really! What a way to behave towards her of all people, and after all she had done for Coco. Serve her right that she had given birth to a girl and not a boy. Girls brought trouble home.

But, having vented her feelings at the walls of the lift, at her own reflection in the lift mirror, at the street outside, a lump came back into Gladys's throat, and reality struck. No more cheques from Coco meant no more London. Gladys stared ahead of her. It had started to rain, which meant there would be no taxis to take her to the station. More than that, with the prospect of no more little cheques from Coco, she could not, really, in all honesty, afford to take a taxi. She would have to walk or she would never be able to afford new nylons, and her weekly visit to the hairdresser, albeit to the ghastly, ghastly village barber who only knew how to sheer a horse, or a man, with clippers, and whose idea of a stylish hairstyle was the Windsor Bob. Tears rolled down Gladys's cheeks as she started to battle her way through the light rain towards the bus stop. Gone were the glory days, gone for ever. She could see all too clearly that she was going to end up wearing a Windsor Bob and clumpy shoes with much mended lisle stockings. Oh dear, there was no doubt about it, she did feel so awfully sorry for herself. Why Harold had been such an idiot with their investments heaven alone knew.

Coco had closed the door quietly but firmly behind Gladys as she disappeared into the lift, despite its being only one stop before the ground floor.

'No more cheques to Gladys,' Coco told the now oddly silent flat. 'From now on I am on my own, for ever, and the devil take the hindmost, and all that.'

She stood for a second contemplating her future. She had no idea what 'the devil take the hindmost' actually meant, really, but she was quite sure that it had a one door closing and another door opening kind of meaning, and that being so, she was glad.

Chapter Twelve

Elsie had been quite right in thinking that Dottie would not have just closed the door on her, put her out of her mind, covered all the furniture with black cloth, and sworn never to let her grand-daughter cross the threshold of the house. That would not be Dottie's way. Dottie's way was such that she would brood, and brood, and save up her revenge, and then, when it was least expected, she would strike.

Elsie was constantly expecting this, but never knowing where Dottie might strike she tried to imagine how she would bring about her revenge. It would not be as difficult as someone outside the theatre might imagine. Everyone in the theatre, if they did not know each other, at least knew *of* each other, and everyone gossiped. Time spent in pubs and clubs, in the Salisbury, in drinking bars and theatrical clubs, time on tour or hanging about film sets, all these times were open season for gossip and speculation. And everyone and anyone was game to play. Not to be game would put someone well beyond the pale.

And how distorted the stories became, how the names of the protagonists changed to produce pieces of scandal surrounding the most unlikely people, was the very stuff of the theatre and film world. No story concerning a star ever stayed the same. It was just a fact.

No star who was ever the centre of a story remained at the centre either, so that it was perfectly possible for an actor or actress to be found recounting some mildly amusing or vaguely scandalous story which had originally been about themselves, but due to distortion as it went the rounds, had become about someone quite other.

Not only that but it took only a very little – and Elsie having grown up in the theatre knew only too well just *how* little – to destroy someone's reputation.

Someone had only to murmur 'can't learn the lines any more, love' to the friend of a friend of a producer who was casting and that was it – you would not be used again.

And the worst of it was that you would never, *ever* know why.

Unfortunately this idea of possible revenge took considerable root in Elsie's mind, and she began to spend too much time trying to imagine the kind of destruction upon which her grandmother and former agent might possibly be bent. She found herself waking up in the middle of the night, and staring out into the lit street beyond the cheap curtains of her Tadcaster flat, wondering over and over again how and when Dottie would strike. It was as if Elsie had committed a crime and was now only waiting for the person affected to catch up with her.

One of the many comforting aspects of being the leading lady of the Stephens Theatre was that Elsie was, as well she should be, permanently employed. On the other hand one of the less comforting aspects was that West End managements, film producers, and talent scouts for television companies, never ever bothered to go to places like Tadcaster. It was a pity, but it was a truth. To be seen by a powerful and fashionable management or agency you had to be able to be seen near the West End. To be in Tadcaster, however brilliant your work, meant that you would, very likely, stay buried for ever and ever in Tadcaster.

It was too far for anyone connected to the theatrical thrones of the West End to even wish to be bothered about. This meant that, despite having enjoyed there some of her happiest professional days so far, Elsie knew that she, and Oliver, if he knew what was good for him, had to leave Tadcaster, and the Stephens Theatre, not in a few years' time, but in a few months' time, indeed as soon as it was perfectly possible. Disloyal though it might seem, it was nevertheless a necessity.

Yet they could not leave to go nowhere.

As Portly insisted, it would be madness to leave a happy, secure set-up where you were doing good work, for months, perhaps years, of unemployment and uncertainty. Their only hope was for something other than a revival, or a musical written by Mr Stephens's only and very beloved son, to somehow come their way.

However, knowing that nothing happens in the theatre the way that you would wish, unless you make it happen, Elsie now proceeded to try to encourage Oliver to write a play for her. And him, of course, but mostly for her, because there was nothing much around for her age group.

To which Portly had to sadly agree.

'It cannot be said too often, I completely agree, darling. There are not enough women's roles, and the reason for this is because there are not enough women playwrights to write women's roles.'

Yet, strangely, among all the famous British and American stars, all the theatrical knights and film stars who deigned to appear in West End theatre, Portly had told Oliver, neither Sir Laurence Olivier nor Sir Anyone Else could fill a theatre if the *play* was not appealing to the public. Only one actress was able to do that, and no actor. No matter what the vehicle, only Miss Vivien Leigh was known to be able to fill a theatre, on her name alone, no matter what the quality of the play.

Naturally, being an actor himself, Oliver was not particularly impressed by the failure of the male sex to fill theatres on their names alone. Privately he hated to think that the success of his play might be dependent on Elsie Lancaster's appearing in it, but he also knew that he would probably have to reconcile himself to this fact.

Very well, he was still passionately in love with Elsie, and she was not just very beautiful – in his opinion now more than ever – but also immensely talented, but he wanted to show himself off to be as talented as *she* was, and up until now there had been no such opportunity.

On the other hand if he wrote a play just for *himself*, he could not be certain of having even a local hit, such was the mesmerising effect that Elsie Lancaster had on local audiences. It was a galling but indisputable fact that Mr Stephens would only be interested in Oliver's play, however brilliant, if there was a starring role for Elsie in it.

After some struggle, and in an attempt to emulate Noel Coward, Oliver wrote a comedy for himself and Elsie, but not in five days flat, in fifteen nights. Although it was his first attempt at a play, when he finished *Love To Popeye* he could not help feeling that he had, in some way, achieved what he had set out to do, namely to pen a light-hearted piece about two utterly selfish human beings who were, at that moment, nuts about each other.

Love To Popeye was therefore, necessarily, a character comedy, based entirely and endearingly on his own relationship with Elsie. Essentially really a vehicle for two, he nevertheless made sure that there were three additional minor character roles – a cast of five at that time being rumoured to be the only acceptable minimum for audience satisfaction. The two main characters, unsurprisingly, looked exactly like Elsie and Oliver, dressed exactly like Elsie and Oliver, and behaved exactly like them too. The only trouble was that while Oliver, as a writer, was able to happily accept that he was deeply flawed, such was not, it seemed, the case with Miss Elsie Lancaster.

Having read the play, which showed all too clearly that the central characters were both self-involved egoists, Elsie threw it at Oliver, hitting him on the side of the head, just as the owner of their flat, who occupied the flat on the ground floor below, came through the door bringing with her, as was her wont of late, a tray of tea.

Hearing Elsie's language, which was quite obviously not of the kind normally heard in the genteel sitting rooms of Tadcaster, the owner of the flat merely smiled sadly as she placed the tray on the stool in front of the gas fire, at the same time shaking her head more in sorrow than in pity.

'Oh, Miss Lancaster,' she said, pulling at a small tendril of hair that was doing its best to escape from under the scarf that she still wore knotted on the top of her head in the manner of those who worked in the armaments factories during the war. 'I see from the way that you and Mr Lowell are throwing things at each other that you must be rehearsing one of those newfangled kitchen-sink plays. We can only hope that it's not too meaty for Tadcaster, dear, because you know, when all is said and done, Tadcaster is *Tadcaster*.'

After which she exited their little sitting room,

and was halfway down the small, narrow, squeaking oak staircase before both Oliver and Portly, not to mention Elsie, dissolved into laughter.

But, despite time out for laughter, Elsie could not, or would not, leave the matter alone.

'I am not a vain, self-obsessed person, am I, Portly? Come on, defend me! You wait till you read this – because that is exactly how Oliver sees me, as vain and egotistical, and – yes, hard, very hard.'

'Also loving, kooky, and larger than life!'

'No wriggling off the hook, Oliver Lowell, Now, come on, Portly, defend me. I mean you are my agent. I am not vain, am I?'

Unfortunately for Elsie as she asked Portly this all too loaded question she happened to be staring at herself in the pink-tinged nineteen-thirties mirror that hung over the fireplace in the little sitting room of the flat. She was also, at the time, trying out a new lipstick, in a rather darker colour than she normally used.

Having finished putting it on her rounded full-lipped mouth, and waiting for Portly to spring to her defence, Elsie turned her head from side to side in the manner of a woman intent on buying a hat in a department store, admiring both the colour of her lips and the new blond streaks in her hair that she had now been affecting for some time.

Instead of answering her question, Portly started to laugh once more, but this time even louder. In fact he did not just laugh, he rocked from side to side, his ribs aching with the effort to stop. Finally he gave in completely to hysteria, becoming doubled up with mirth, and banging the cream-painted wall behind him over and over again as he laughed.

Elsie turned from the contemplation of her new lipstick, and stared first at Portly and then at Oliver, who, on hearing Elsie's indignant appeal for help, had also started to double up with laughter.

'Well, really, I have no idea what you two can possibly find so funny, really I haven't, but I suppose I will have to play Lareina or else you will both chuck me out of the flat. But, even so, I think it is a bit much, Ollie, to put me in a play like that, warts and all, even down to putting my pop eyes into the title. Really, it is a bit much.'

'Be fair, I have put myself too, Else, I mean, haven't I? I mean to say. And I come off far worse, you must agree. Besides, there is no such thing as putting people into things. You can only ever put a little tiny fragment of someone into things, the tiniest tiny fragment. No one, no playwright, was ever able to put more. For one thing, most regrettably, there isn't the time, at least not on stage, there really isn't. There's hardly time to put more than a hundredth of a whole, real live human being in a stage play of all things, Else.'

'Hark at him, Mr Lecture Us All Playwright, and after penning only one play, and a comedy at that.'

'As long as you haven't put Mr Stephens in the play, we'll be all right,' Portly sighed and dried his eyes on his cotton handkerchief.

'Oh but he has, Portly, he has put Mr Stephens in, and not just put him in, he is recognisable to the last T.'

Portly stared at Elsie. 'Don't tell me that!'

Elsie shoved a copy of the play into Portly's now more than reluctant hands, while looking questioningly over her shoulder towards Oliver for confirmation.

'No, it is true. I have put Mr Stephens in—'

'You're mad—'

'No, I have. And I have made him the kindest nicest owner of a theatre ever created. Believe me, Portly, when Mr Stephens reads this he will not only put the play on, he will do everything he can to get it a number one tour. When he reads how wonderful he is in this comedy – the kindly humorous owner of a provincial theatre who loves everyone – when he reads this he will want to sit in the stalls, not just on Saturday night, but on every other night of the week.'

'I only hope you are right, dear boy.'

Oliver stared at Portly. 'Now, that really is a first.'

Portly stared back at Oliver, not getting it. 'What is a first?'

'You *dear boying* me. Typecasting. Suddenly it's typecasting for an agent, and you've hardly been one for more than two seconds. Pretty soon you will be wearing very large pinstriped suits with very, very large legs, just like Tad Protheroe.'

'If this play is any good,' Portly smacked the play on its cover as if it was a baby and he was smacking its bottom, and so bringing life to it for the first time, 'if this play is any good I might soon be able to even afford a suit – *dear bo-o-y!* And won't that be just something?'

'Read it before you order the suit, Portly, you may hate it. Meanwhile, come on, Popeye' – he turned and jerked his head first at Elsie, and then towards the door – 'time to leave for the theatre.'

For a second after they had gone Portly just stared at the manuscript, not wanting to open it and be disappointed. So much depended on it – so, so much. Besides which he hated to think what would happen to his relationship with Oliver, at present so bright and full of promise, if he, Portly, did not like his play. It would not just be a hurdle, it would be a double oxer. He breathed in and then out. No point in putting off the awful moment. He opened the play. Touchingly Oliver had dedicated it to Portly. And it was very touching, but it would make it far worse if Portly did not, could not, like it. Because whatever happened Portly knew that he had to be honest. There was no point in being anything else. Quite apart from anything else, he was too fond of Oliver not to be quite frank with him. He just so, so hoped that the play would show talent.

The play was funny, sweet, and mad, and written very much in the zany style of the American two-handed comedies that were, and had been for some time, creating success after success on Broadway. Naturally, since Oliver had written it not only about Elsie but for Elsie, Elsie's role was perfectly tailored to her talents. She was also, Oliver quite rightly bowing to her local appeal, centre stage for most of the play. Oliver's character had to be played off Elsie's part. Lareina wore the trousers, as it were, throughout the play, yet everyone else was given more than a good chance, they were given a golden opportunity. From that point of view the play was completely even-handed, and, for those and many other reasons, surely could not fail?

Portly also noted, with some satisfaction, how quickly Oliver had learned his stagecraft, for there was surely nothing like the experience of being on stage in other people's plays to pull an actor/playwright into shape, and Oliver had been pulled into shape all right. Best of all, and apparent from page one onwards, was that the play was funny. It was light-hearted and young, and it could not have been written by anyone over the age of thirty, the piece having that particular lightness that comes before the arrival of the first grey hair, that unfathomable quality which like a youthful bloom can infuse so much early work, that never-to-be-again-recaptured gossamer touch. Nothing about it struck Portly as being worked over. It lay lightly on its pages, and above all, its love of life sparkled and glinted over every page.

Finally, its authentic magic, its lightness of touch made Portly sigh. Having finished it, he sat back in his chair, and as the light from outside the little sitting room faded, and he reached out to turn on the electric light to take its place, he sat and stared ahead of him for some minutes, knowing that, after this, nothing could or would be the same. Oliver had written them a surefire hit. So why did Portly find himself sighing, all alone as he was, and out loud? Because, grown into maturity at long last as he had, he knew that, from now on, they would none of them remain the same to each other.

There is a moment, just after it has been decided that a play is to be presented, when all the world seems to slide to a shuddering halt. For those acting in or directing the play, for all those involved, of a sudden there is no news to speak of. No matter what the outside world may think of its crises, of its wars, or of its peace, they do not touch those who have gone into rehearsal with a new play. For them there are no tragedies or comedies, there is only the one unalterable fact – the first night. For the playwright, for the producer, for the designer, there is only that one moment coming towards them, the only date that is of any interest, that is at all newsworthy, that one night – the first night of their production.

That moment had just happened to Oliver, Elsie, and the rest of the cast and production at the Stephens Theatre in Tadcaster. Naturally Mr

Stephens was beaming. It would be a world premiere. In Mr Stephens's mind there would never be a premiere like it, not ever. There would never be a time when life was so exciting, not anywhere in the world, except in the Stephens Theatre at Tadcaster. No first presentation of a play could be more important than *Love To Popeye*.

'Well now, I really must wish—'

To her horror Elsie sensed that Mr Stephens was just about to wish them all good luck, which in the theatre is considered to be the most terrible *bad* luck, so she quickly interrupted with, 'But first we must tell you, Mr Stephens, that we are all determined to work our legs off to prove ourselves worthy of your belief in us, Mr Stephens. And we want you to know that. In fact we want you to know that hand on heart, Mr Stephens.'

Elsie found that she could not stop saying 'Mr Stephens' but it did not matter, because Mr Stephens did not mind, he just beamed. He had actually quite forgotten what he was about to say, and now there did not seem much point, because everyone was smiling at him and looking happy, so he thought he would not bother to remember.

'I know, Miss Lancaster, seeing that you are the most beautiful young actress of our acquaintance, I know, and who should know better, that you will give this new play, this world premiere, everything that you have, and more.'

At this everyone beamed at everyone else, and Portly crossed his fingers, and turned away. Now there truly was nothing to do but pray. You could never, ever tell with comedy, even less than you could tell with tragedy. You just could not tell, ever, how something was going to go, but most of all you could not tell with comedy.

If the weather was too hot or too cold, if the news from abroad was all of atom bombs and the Cold War, if there was a political march on, or the Motor Show, if it was Crufts Dog Show, or the Queen was opening Parliament, and yet there was not a seat in the house for weeks, then everyone forgot all about nuclear war, royalty, a new Ford motor car, or the winning poodle at Crufts.

But if the stalls and the dress circle were empty, and the word was out that the new comedy in town was a flop, then it would instantly become the fault of the Queen, Parliament, the Motor Show, and if possibly possible Crufts Dog Show too. It was just a fact. A hit meant that nothing could affect seat sales. A flop meant that everything affected them. But, at that particular moment, none of that mattered. They were all just waiting to make sure that they did their best by the piece.

Bartlett Corrigan, who was directing as usual, had imported Frederick Darby and Mary Allen Finlay into the cast of *Love To Popeye*. They were cast to play the older couple, and the all-important part of the maid was taken by Jennifer Polesden, also imported especially for the play, Bartlett being determined to make sure that no stone remain unturned for this first public airing of the piece.

Everyone had been more than happy with the new imports into the company, everyone, that is, except Elsie. For some reason that no one else could understand, Elsie had nearly had a twin fit when told about the casting of Jennifer Polesden.

Oliver was furious with her. Jennifer Polesden was an excellent character actress, and they were very lucky to get her. He lectured Elsie at length on her bad theatrical manners, becoming quite boring on the subject, but Elsie would not be moved, although neither could she influence the decision. It had been taken by Bartlett, and he was producing, and that necessarily was that, and she knew it.

But it did not stop her moaning. God how she moaned about Jennifer Polesden! She drove Oliver mad about the poor woman, until finally he was forced to confide his frustration to Portly.

'It's not as if Jennifer Polesden's going to be any sort of threat, I mean, really. She is not going to be a threat to Elsie.'

Portly nodded at Oliver, his expression at its most sage. Knowing how Elsie had gone on and on about Jennifer Polesden's being cast, he had done a little bit of homework.

'It's nothing to do with the actress herself, dear boy,' he told Oliver, pursing his lips and raising his eyebrows at the same time. 'By no means, no, absolutely not. I am afraid it goes a great deal deeper than that. She is a friend of her former agent. Someone that Elsie now never speaks of.'

'Isn't that a bit pathetic?'

'No, not pathetic, Ollie. No one who ever knew Miss Temple would dismiss her as pathetic, Oliver, believe me. Think Lady Mac-you-know-who from the Scottish play, and you only get a little near to Miss Temple.'

'Bad as that, eh?'

'No, worse. Terri-bloody-fying, if you get my meaning? I have never negotiated with anyone so tough. But she did, to give her every due, make Elsie what she is. She devoted all her energy to her, but of course, once Elsie became successful, she kicked her out.'

Oliver nodded, his eyes becoming matching green mosaics, as they often did when he was, of a sudden, and at last, deeply interested in what someone else was telling him.

There was a short pause, and then he said, 'Now, *that* is something that happens a great deal in the theatre, apparently. Funnily enough I heard Freddie and Mary talking about that only yesterday, after the read-through. Yes, apparently it is quite a *syndrome*, actors' wives, agents, all sorts of people, they like working to make someone into a star, but once they are up there, topping the billing, and all that, they get bored and leave them, or kick them out, only to start the whole thing again with someone else. Interesting, isn't it? It's the journey to the point of success that involves them, not the arrival. All that plotting and politicking towards something which finally really doesn't hold much interest for them at all. I say, hope *you're* not like that, Portly?'

Portly smiled half to himself, and half to Oliver, and his eyes which normally wore a benign expression, gazing out at the world as if they had never witnessed anything but kindness, now changed expression.

If he ever got 'up there' again, he would never abandon anyone, not anyone. He would work his legs off for them, and for himself, and he would make quite sure to thank his lucky stars that he had been given that second, glorious, chance to bite at the apple, or *get near to the fire*, as they called success in America. What was more, he would consider himself the luckiest man in the world.

'No, I don't think you will find that I am like that, Oliver, not for a single, solitary second. I want everyone on my books to be successful, and stay successful. Nothing else is interesting.'

He turned away to go into the kitchen of the flat, his thoughts once more on the lasagne that he was making, on the salad that he insisted on turning with his own, admittedly well-washed hands, coaxing each little lettuce leaf and piece of tomato into marrying with his subtle French dressing.

Oliver lit a cigarette, and smiled. He had really enjoyed seeing that determined expression crossing Portly's face. More than that, he had gloried in it. After all, now that they had the agency, they had to be grown up. It was a fact, a sad fact, but their salad days were over, for ever, and they somehow all knew it. Things had to start moving for all of them, or else, before they knew it, they would be old, and the curtain would have fallen for the last time – on them.

But first the curtain had to rise on *Love To Popeye*. The nerves, the shaking in the shoes, the whitened faces, the colour draining even from lips that had only a few seconds before been coloured with Max Factor lipsticks – it was always the same. The wondering if it was really worth it, each actor or actress asking him or herself the same question. Why had they not taken up market gardening? Or running a corner shop? Why had they decided on acting of all things? Acting that required nerves of steel to just walk on stage and say a line without looking like a complete *ass*. Acting that required a degree of self-belief that was almost incredibly fantastic. Acting that asked of a human being what no one but a raving idiot would imagine could be possibly possible, namely to be in the right play, at the right time, with all the right actors around you, and all the scenery staying upright, and all the lighting cues happening rather than not happening, and with all the costumes fitting and the wigs staying straight, and the audience in a rollicking good mood, not to mention the critics, and every mum and dad and sister or brother rooting for you, rather than hoping against hope that you will fall flat on your artistic face. To ask

411

this was, quite simply, to ask the impossible of life.

And yet, it can happen. It is a fact. And for the cast and author, the producer and management of *Love To Popeye*, it did happen. And it happened so big, and so stupendously, despite the sudden unseasonal heat of the autumnal night, despite the fact that the side doors had to be opened to let in some cold air, and the audience became a sea of waving theatre programmes, and the bar ran out of both warm beer and warm white wine – despite all that, the comedy took off, and ran off, as a comedy has to if it is to win against the audience – all of whom are busy telegraphing their inevitable hostile first night message to the stage: 'Make us laugh – if you dare'.

Of course it helped that Elsie looked beautiful, and that she had no first night nerves whatsoever.

'Why aren't you nervous, Else?' Oliver had wanted to know, asking her in a sudden and purposefully ferocious manner, because his own lips, hands and body were trembling like jellies on an express train, not to mention everyone else's, including, for no reason he could quite think, those of both the stage manager and, if you please, the assistant stage manager.

'Because, Ollie, there is really no point *at all* in being nervous. It is a complete waste of time.'

'How do you mean?'

Oliver's lips had now started to knock together so that they actually made a *burr, burr, burr* sort of sound, as they might if he was freezing cold, and his attempts at lighting a cigarette were failing miserably because the cigarette would keep falling out of his mouth on to the shelf in front of his make-up mirror. He looked at Elsie, standing dressed and made up and now staring into his mirror at him. He hated her for being so composed, her lips not trembling, the expression in her slightly protruding eyes one of barely concealed contempt.

'There is no point in being nervous, Ollie,' she told him in her most bored voice, 'because, love, it dissipates your energy. The only thing to be nervous about is getting the play right. If you are nervous, then you are thinking about yourself and not the play, or the rest of the cast. Try being a little less selfish, and you will be sure to become a little less nervous, see if you don't. Being nervous as an actor is exactly like being shy as a person. If you stop thinking about yourself, the nerves, or the shyness, will vanish. Besides, I have decided to strain every nerve not to be nervous. I always do decide this. That is why I am not nervous. And that is what you should do – decide not to be nervous, and the whole silly business will stop.'

After this, for her, really very deep and searching speech, Elsie had swept out of Oliver's dressing room, her lip curling, her eyes still flashing veiled contempt at him.

It worked, of course, and almost straight away. The fact that Elsie had made such a show of despising Oliver for practically falling to pieces in front of her meant that he almost immediately found that level of indignation that is entirely necessary if an actor is to pull himself together and not make a cracking ass of himself just because it is a first night, and just as if the play is not going to be played on any other night.

In the end Oliver bounded on stage giving every impression of not caring a tiny damn if the audience liked him, or his play, or indeed anything that was happening once the curtain rose. He played his own piece as if he was back in the nursery playing only to Cliffie, who, thank God, had elected not to come until the play was 'run in', as he put it.

That neither Elsie nor Oliver would ever be able to remember the first night of *Love To Popeye* in any detail was quite normal. Actors remember certain aspects of a first night – missed cues, or fluffed lines; spectacular moments – but not the whole performance, and most particularly not if it is a success.

Bartlett would always remember it because it was the first time a cast that he had produced rose to the occasion in such a way as to make both the play and his production look even better than he could have hoped.

Mr Stephens remembered it because he had never realised, before he saw himself portrayed on stage by Frederick Darby, that he was so warm-hearted, so kind, so lovable or, indeed, so delightful.

As a result of *Love To Popeye* he would say afterwards, 'I am not nearly as nice as that young man Oliver Lowell made out, you know, really I am not' – while busily writing out a cheque for yet another local charity.

And yet even his wife noticed that, perhaps as a result of seeing the play over a dozen times, he became, if anything, more like his character on stage – even, eventually, affecting the same kind of suiting as the actor who had played him, and sporting the same kind of rather elaborate fedora which he raised to his fellow citizens every few seconds, eliciting smiles from many who thought of him now only as '*that nice man in that play*'.

And yet, despite all its success, everyone involved knew that nothing would come of it for any of them unless someone from some West End management, some spy from the great metropolis, or some international agent, came to view what they had now all come to consider as their little comic masterpiece.

It is always called 'luck' because whatever else can it be called, at the end of the famous day, when someone's secretary, in an idle moment, reads a newly arrived script and decides that she will induce her boss to put it on? Whatever else can it be called, for goodness' sake, when a bored man's car breaks down, and he makes his way to a matinée of a play that he knows nothing about and finds it funny and enchanting, and decides there and then to back a new and more expensive production, take it on tour, and bring it into the West End?

Of course it was just luck that Denholm Heighton's Jaguar 'motor car' as he always referred to it, developed a fault, and rather than wait at the garage he strolled off and bought himself the last seat in the stalls at that day's matinee. Despite being in a particularly foul mood, he was won over completely by *Love To Popeye* and, perhaps more importantly, fell wildly in love with Elsie Lancaster.

Being allowed backstage after the performance was not a difficulty since Denholm Heighton was one of the most famous names in theatrical management.

'I will take this play on an extended tour of the best dates, and then into the Criterion, or the Comedy, or even perhaps the Haymarket, who knows? It will run and run—' He paused. 'I have to say that I have not always admired Freddie Darby in the past, but equally I have to admit that I now take it all back, because I love him in this. And the way he plays the scene with the fedora – well, it is perfection. I could write the reviews now. As for you, Miss Lancaster . . .' He turned from Oliver to Elsie, and his smile sent up the temperature of Elsie's dressing room another few points. 'The whole of London is going to be at your feet, my dear, within a very few months, of that there is no doubt at all.'

Elsie smiled what Oliver always called her *I*

think I am going to be sick smile at Denholm Heighton, but murmured, 'How sweet of you. We didn't actually think we were quite on song this afternoon.'

'I am now going to book a room at the White Hart Hotel, and stay for the evening performance. Who do I negotiate with?'

'Portly Cosgrove represents us, and Mr Stephens is the management, as you know, but Mr Stephens is leaving all the business side to Portly.'

'Cosgrove.' Heighton stopped by the door. 'That name rings a bell – has *he* been in management?'

'No – at least I don't think so, no.'

Elsie smiled, but this time it was not her *going to be sick* smile, but her best and most dazzling smile. Her *you will not remember anything when you wake up from this* smile.

'No,' she told Heighton. 'Portly Cosgrove is quite new to management. Quite new. Mr Stephens is a businessman in his own right, but he prefers to leave the fine tuning to Portly Cosgrove.'

'Don't speak to me of fine tuning – blasted Jaguar!' Heighton frowned, momentarily. 'What was his name again, did you say?'

'Portly Cosgrove.'

'Good, well, tell him to be here after the performance this evening, and he can come and dine with me at the White Hart Hotel, and we can see if we can't reach an agreement by midnight tonight. How fortuitous, really, that my wretched

417

motor car broke down. Lucky for me, and I hope, very soon, it will be lucky for you too.'

He slapped Oliver on the back, quite lightly.

'You are a very clever young man. This play will be a great hit, you know, I am certain of it. It will run and run, and change all your fortunes.'

He did not add that it would change his too, because they all knew that he was so successful his fortunes did not really need changing. For Denholm Heighton *Love To Popeye* would be just another hit, whereas for the rest of them, it would be life changing.

If Denholm Heighton was right, never again would Portly have to put newspaper in his shoes, never again would Elsie carefully count the change from the loaf at the bakery, or spend hours comparing the prices of lipsticks at different chemist shops. Never again would Portly have to balance the budget for their food, making sure that the all-important Creative Leftovers, as he always called them, would carry them through from Tuesday to Friday.

No, their lives were about to change for ever and ever, but would they, Elsie suddenly started to wonder, become any happier? Surely that would not be possible, because the truth was that since the play had opened they had all become as one in their joy at its success. Now, however, they were going to have to share it with more and more people, and, in some strange way, it would become *used*, and worse than that – they, Elsie, Oliver and Portly would become used to the *success* of it, so that it would lose its taste, its reality, its freshness.

Oliver waited until Heighton had visited all the other actors' dressing rooms and was wandering back to book himself into the lovely old hotel that stood in the centre of Tadcaster before turning to Elsie and saying, 'Well, really, I honestly think that the reason managements like this play so much is because of the fact that I have made the theatre manager such a warm-hearted old sweetie! I really do think that. Do you realise what this means?'

Elsie shook her head, picking up a magazine and pretending to read it with fascination, as she always did when she heard Oliver about to embark on one of his extra-long moans.

'This means,' Oliver went on, 'that every time you want a hit in the theatre you have to write a kindly manager into it. I think my next play will have to be called *The Kindly Impresario*. God, honestly, it makes you sick. All those funny lines, everything you do, every single thing we both do – what did he say about them? Nothing. Just went on and on about how brilliant Freddie was. Really, impresarios!'

Elsie read on, not looking up. It had started already, as it always did.

'I hope Portly knows how to deal with him. I mean, Denholm Heighton, you know his reputation? Tad Protheroe told me all about him. He chews up provincial managements for breakfast. I hope Portly gets a lawyer to give the contract

419

the once-over before he puts his monicker on it.'

It occurred to Elsie that a few hours earlier Oliver had hardly heard of Denholm Heighton, but now, of a sudden, he was an expert on him.

Elsie stared at the stunning dress in the photograph in the magazine she was intent on reading. Soon, pretty soon, she might be able to afford that dress, and the one on the next page, and the one after that. It was unimaginable, and yet true. Except she must not imagine it, or anything else. She must just take one day at a time. Anything more would be madness.

'Beginners, please.'

They were no longer beginners. Not even Oliver was a beginner, not any more.

'I must see if we can't get Coco to do the costumes for the touring production,' Oliver mused. 'I'll speak to Portly about that. Because if Heighton is going to overhaul the production, which he surely must, it would be good for PLL if Coco gets to do the costumes for any new touring production.'

Elsie put down her magazine and stared at herself in the mirror. Blasted Coco Hampton. It seemed she was going to follow them everywhere, no matter what. 'You don't know whether or not she has any talent, do you?'

Oliver left the dressing room without bothering to answer. Of course Coco had talent. She was, after all – Coco. Coco had always had talent. When he thought of Coco in her little flat with Holly and all those nappies and bottles, he felt nothing but impatience, and yet the thought of not including her in the success of *Love To Popeye* was simply not a possibility. Coco would do the new costumes, and make a name for herself, and a future for Holly. He would make sure of it, no matter what Elsie had to say on the matter.

'Beginners, please!'

Their second call, and the curtain was about to rise for the second time that day. Oliver closed his eyes. It was all about to happen. The cold draught that always swept through the set when the curtains rose, the murmur of the audience gradually dying to a hush, the sound of a late arrival, Elsie and himself waiting in the wings to go on, as if drawn by a magnet. Gone were the desperate first night longings to become a market gardener, to do anything rather than go on stage. From now on, for him, there would be no other life, not ever.

He started to hum as he made his way towards the small stage. *Hey diddley dee, an actor's life for me.* And in a very few moments the curtain did indeed rise, on the rest of his life.

PART THREE

DANCING TO THE TUNE

Now you must surely hear it! Ah – at last – I see you do!

Kenneth Grahame, 'The Piper at the Gates of Dawn'
(from *The Wind in the Willows*)

Chapter Thirteen

With his feet up on a stool, a freshly arrived play manuscript on his lap, Portly paused in his reading and yet again gazed around his new flat. It might be just a flat to the estate agent, or to the rest of his friends, but to him, newly arrived back in London for the first time for many, many months, with a West End hit supporting three of his people at PLL, it was far from being just a flat – it was a palace. In a converted house just off the lower end of Sloane Street in the heart of London, it had one large room and a small study on the ground floor. From the central room a staircase led to the first floor where there was a bedroom and a bathroom. Naturally with the flat had come Mrs Todd the hall porter's wife to clean it for Portly, and, equally naturally, after only a few weeks she was already running his life.

'Now then, Mr Portly,' she was even now calling to him from the kitchen, 'you can say what you like, but coffee made with added chicory is a a great deal less wasteful.'

'And disgusting to drink, Mrs Todd. Quite disgusting.'

Thankfully the telephone beside Portly's newly purchased chair was ringing, which brought a merciful end to a fairly tedious conversation, embarked upon when Mrs Todd had discovered that Portly had thrown out the perfectly awful coffee she had brought in for him the day before.

'What do you think?'

Because the voice at the other end belonged to Oliver Lowell there was absolutely no need to announce himself.

'I've only just begun it, Mr Playwright, sir.' Portly managed to sound soothing and amused at the same time.

'You've had it since yesterday—'

'I know, Ollie, but you know I have had rather a lot of negotiations on my hands these last weeks.'

'You have had it two whole days, Portly, two whole days. I could have written a whole first act in two days.'

'Yes, but you are a genius, Oliver, while I – I am only a mere mortal, and a slow-reading mortal at that. Besides, Bernard Shaw said that anyone could write a first act.'

Portly smiled into the telephone. It was difficult for Oliver to understand that it took some people, namely Portly, just as long to read a play as it had doubtless taken Oliver to write it, if not longer.

'How much longer, O Lord?' Oliver was moaning and smoking a cigarette at the same time.

Portly could hear him blowing out the smoke less than quietly.

'Give me a couple of days, Ollie, you know how slow I am. As it is, I have to leave here for the office in a couple of minutes. We are snowed under with work over there, you know. Very gratifying, but it does take a bit of time to organise.'

'Oh, all right, I will ring back on Friday morning, but you'd better have a verdict by then, or else.'

'Or else what, Mr Playwright, sir?'

'I will leave you for the fat woman in the cupboard.'

'Not the fat woman in the cupboard? You couldn't leave me for her!'

'Yes, I could.'

At his end Oliver put down the telephone and hearing this Elsie called from their bathroom, 'Well? What did he say?'

'He's only just begun it!'

'But he's had it since yesterday!'

'Exactly, but you know old Porters – he's a very slow reader. Can't help it, he's just very slo-ow.'

'Dear old Portly, he would be.'

Elsie stared at herself in the bathroom mirror. She was looking more beautiful day by little day, but this, considering the huge success she was scoring in *Love To Popeye*, was only, surely, to be expected?'

She was the toast of the West End. The critics had fallen over themselves to praise her. She was a hit, a hit, a palpable hit. And Oliver was still nuts about her, so that was all right. And yet, there was something missing.

'I think we should go shopping, don't you?'

Oliver shook his head. He could see that Elsie was feeling fidgety and bored, but he could not bear the idea of going shopping, not while he knew that Portly had his new play, and might be at that moment sitting in his flat, reading it, and not laughing.

'You go, Else. I don't think I could stand to see the inside of a shop again for quite a while, not at the moment, not with all this on. Worry. All this worry on.'

Elsie nodded absently, pulling on a high-waisted, black and white redingote coat over a pencil slim skirt and white silk pinch-pleated long-sleeved blouse.

Months into the West End as they were, she found, unsurprisingly, that she liked going shopping more than ever now. Not just because she could afford to buy so much more than she had ever been able to before, but because she liked to see people nudging each other as she passed them, supremely elegant and entirely recognisable.

The hiss of the '*Did you see who that was?*' as she passed was beautifully satisfying.

If it was not for the success of the play, shopping in London might have become boring after Tadcaster, where she had always been recognised, but the truth was it was not boring, because, if anything, Elsie was far more famous in London than she had been even in Tadcaster.

Everywhere she went shop assistants tried not to notice who she was, as did rich customers in the more exclusive stores. Just stepping out on to the pavement from a taxi cab, as she was now doing, had become something of a hurdle, since the moment she stood paying it off she would instantly become surrounded by a crowd of autograph hunters.

It was all Portly's fault, of course. Following the entirely successful provincial tour, Portly, the naughty thing, had insisted that Denholm Heighton put Elsie's face on all the theatre posters, on all the buses, and all the trains, all over London, the result of which was that strange thing called 'overnight fame'. And that was before the West End opening night, when contrary to all the gloomy predictions from the cast and the management, the play elicited just as many hurrahs, as much applause, and as many ecstatic reviews as the provincial tour. One famous critic even swore that he would give everything he had to have dinner alone with Miss Elsie Lancaster. But best of all, and most of all, the advance business at the box office was stupendous – so good that it even had that old shark, Denholm Heighton, quietly purring. Elsie could have sworn that she once or twice even saw Denholm actually smiling – his lips parting, his teeth showing – which for a powerful impresario was quite something, really.

'Miss Lancaster, may I help you?'

The black costume and sparkling lapel brooch

of the woman with the blue rinse now confronting Elsie told them both that she was the vendeuse of the couture fashion department, and as such made it her duty to know all about success. And boy, was Elsie successful at that moment!

'Certainly you can help me. I want some couture clothes, of the kind that will not date, if you see what I mean?'

Of course the vendeuse saw what Elsie meant. Indeed, as she turned towards the cupboards in which beautifully made confections of the most alluring kind were hiding, their sleeves stuffed with tissue paper, their gorgeous materials covered so that not even an inch of light could destroy their radiance, Elsie could have sworn that she could hear the woman purring with inner delight.

The thing about Elsie was that she had been very strictly brought up, never allowed to spend anything on herself unless it was completely necessary. She had been at great pains to point out to both Oliver and Portly that, this being so, she knew where she wanted to spend her money now – on herself – and for no better reason than that she *could*.

Nothing had ever been wasted in Dottie's household, and so Elsie, with an alarming perversity that astonished both Oliver and Portly, was now setting about determinedly spending money, as if it was indeed water dripping through her fingers.

And of course she could, because thanks to

Portly's late night dinner with Denholm Heighton she was not only on as big a salary as any of the biggest stars in the West End, but she also had a percentage of the box. That was just how confident Portly had been that he and Mr Stephens had their hands on a hit, and that was how determined Portly was that no one should ever again do to him what Donald Bourton had done.

'Take it or leave it, Mr Heighton,' he had said, not once or twice, but many times, as the clock in the old oak-panelled back sitting room of the White Hart Hotel in Tadcaster had ticked on, and on, and on, and Heighton had become more and more hunched, like a poker player with a good hand who knows that, good though his hand might be, it is not really going to be quite good enough. He had winced at Portly's outward confidence, at his expressed determination to find a new management the very next morning should Heighton not clinch a deal before the end of the evening. And yet, successful and rich though he was, he had been finally unable to command his feet to take him to the door marked exit. He liked the sweet smell of success. He enjoyed its seaside aroma too much to be able to walk away from *Love To Popeye*.

'This is ridiculous – you are asking too much, and you know it.'

'Of course, but then I also know that I have at this golden moment a rip-roaring hit, and at least one fantastic new star, if not two, not to mention a playwright of extraordinary promise. If you were me you would be demanding quite the same terms, and *you* know it.'

Of course Portly had been right, and of course Heighton, finally, did know it. He also knew that at any moment he chose Portly could now waltz into the door of any West End management and demand the same terms, so desperate were they all for something entertaining, cheap to put on and easy to take out on tour – not to mention the very real possibility that a good comedy with a small cast could possibly transfer to Broadway for American production.

So Portly had his wicked way with the negotiations, which meant that Elsie could now stand in front of a wall of mirrors and revel in the sight of herself turning this way and that in a dress from the Dior Young Collection, a pale frost-blue poult-de-soie dinner dress with ribbon streamers, and a flowered bow.

'Madame looks sensational in this, it is truly, truly a dress for madame. Her skin tones so perfect with the colour, and her figure, just perfect too!'

Elsie smiled at the vendeuse. She was quite right. She was perfect for it. She widened her now famous 'popeyes' at the smiling woman. They both knew that Elsie would not ask the price; that would be too vulgar for words.

Besides, Elsie already knew that the sky was practically the limit as far as her wardrobe was concerned, because Denholm Heighton had agreed to pay for at least one outfit in return for the pages of interviews that Elsie had given when the play opened. The resulting publicity had been enormous, not to mention the attention given to Coco Hampton's designs – some of which were quickly taken up by the glossy magazines, and some of which were even now being copied by the cheaper clothing manufacturers.

Because that was what a success in the theatre brought – it did not just bring money, and fame, it brought everyone to your door, all wanting to touch your hem, share the dazzling light that your success had brought you. In effect success meant that Society adopted you, for however long, and you bathed in its golden glow, hoping against hope that the light would not dim, or move off you on to someone else.

'Now what I really do quite desperately need is a coat and skirt for spring, perhaps something from Chanel?'

'I have just the thing.'

As the vendeuse and her assistant bustled away to the outer room Elsie pulled a little face at herself in the mirror. She could hardly remember a better moment than this, and it was all the more sweet in so many ways for not having Oliver with her. By now he would be becoming impatient for her to choose something, not really caring what she looked like in any outfit, his mind only on his new play, and what Portly might think of it. Whether or not Portly would find the wretched thing amusing. Whether or not Portly would consider that Oliver had lived up to the promise he showed in *Love To Popeye*.

'This will I think please madame as much as it does us, I believe. It is quite exquisite, you will agree.'

The vendeuse draped a coat and skirt over the willing arms of her assistant, her long fingers with their deep red nail varnish lovingly demonstrating to Elsie the perfection of the cut of the two-piece.

'Here you will see that the coat and skirt are made of the lightest of tweeds – Madame Chanel does not like working with heavy tweeds – and the collar has a delicious detail here – a crochet edging – then we have gauntlet cuffs, here, and of course this season's detail – flap pockets.'

Elsie thought it might be time to look a little choosy, so she put her head on one side and nodded, less than enthusiastically.

'And?'

'And . . .' The vendeuse nodded sharply to her assistant. 'And – next we have Dior again. A natural shantung two-piece, belted, flared at the hips, giving a beautifully lean look to the skirt.'

Naturally Elsie tried on both, and ended up buying both. She also bought a black wool dress for, as the vendeuse put it, 'late afternoon'. It had a wonderfully nipped in waist, and the moulded torso did, Elsie had to admit, show off her slender shoulders to perfection.

'Send them, would you, please?'

434

'Of course, madame. And madame, may I say, on behalf of myself and my assistant, what a pleasure it has been to serve you? To be able to fit someone young and beautiful is, believe me, a great, great pleasure, for such is not always our lot, alas!'

Elsie smiled genuinely for the first time, signed a cheque for a staggering amount, and walked slowly and deliberately towards the lift.

She felt as though she had just devoured a whole Fullers chocolate cake, not just a slice. She felt surfeited, satisfied. She had in one short hour spent a fortune, and in that same hour, in her mind, she had defeated Dottie. When she was young Dottie would have a fit if she bought so much as a pair of nylons with her earnings. Yet Elsie had just spent enough on clothes to supply the whole of Tadcaster with nylons, not to mention head scarves and perhaps even belts. She should feel guilt, but she did not. She felt only exuberant euphoria. She had earned every little nip and tuck of those couture clothes. She had earned them for standing backstage in draughty wings watching other performers, trying to learn from them. She had earned them for dancing endlessly, and often pointlessly, in front of bored theatre managers, without so much as a cup of hot milk to fortify her young body. She had earned them for every time she had been given the thumbs down by yet another producer. She had earned them for being 'too old' or 'too young' or 'all wrong'. She had earned them by learning her lines, by heart, every time, before every first rehearsal. She had earned them with her hair, so tightly curled and put in papers that, all through her childhood, she had only ever been able to sleep on her front. She had earned them by not growing too tall, or staying too small. She had earned them with her beautiful 'popeyes', and her perfectly shaped mouth, and her pearly white teeth. So, most happily, she felt not a shred of guilt nor a thread of remorse about buying those clothes. They were hers, because, damn it, she had *earned* them!

But more than that, and in a way even better, she knew that whatever she spent on clothes darling Portly would only agree most whole-heartedly. In fact he would urge her on to buy more and more.

'You must not go around looking ordinary. When you are older, and respectably retired, you can look ordinary. But now, now you must always and everywhere look, and be, a star, or you will let down your public – Elsie Lancaster's public.'

With this in mind Portly would never ever countenance Elsie's taking public transport, and anyone making use of Miss Lancaster's services for whatever reason would be required to send a car for her. Miss Lancaster was not expected to put her nose out of doors unless she was accompanied by a chauffeur of some kind, or hidden from the view of her adoring public by a taxicab at the very least.

At first, hearing Portly playing the powerful agent, throwing his weight about on her behalf, Elsie had been a little inclined to feel embarrassed, but after a while she had come to see the sense in his attitudes. If you were treated as a star, you stayed a star; if you were treated as a nobody, that was how you felt. Conversely, if you felt yourself to be a nobody, that was exactly how people would treat you. It was essential for Elsie, for the play, for all future plays in which she might appear, that she maintain an outward display of stardom.

'People only respect you if you insist that they do,' was how Portly put it.

On his side Portly had decided to keep their relationship to that of avuncular agent and beautiful star. It was better for business. So it was that, out of the office and business hours, their relationship grew into something more intimate, and more relaxed, than anything either of them could or would enjoy with anyone else.

Elsie put her key in the lock of the door and turned it. In some ways she loved her new, fully furnished, and really very pretty Chelsea house, but in other ways she felt uneasy in it, and not because of the grandeur of the furnishings, the inclination to small chandeliers and shiny chintz. It was because of Oliver.

Sharing a flat with an actor had not been easy in Tadcaster, but in Tadcaster she had also shared her life with Portly, who was always, by cooking and generally being his usual benign self,

437

lightening the atmosphere. Now, in London, there was no Portly, only Oliver, and Ollie, as writer rather than actor, was a gloomy so-and-so at the best of times, always staring into the middle distance and moaning about the focal point of some scene that was currently eluding him.

Elsie began to creep up the stairs to her bedroom. They had separate bedrooms, to allow Oliver to work in his in the mornings and afternoons, and when they returned from the theatre, without disturbing Elsie.

'I don't understand you, Portly Cosgrove, really I don't. I mean, I gave it to *Tad* to cast an eye over, you know, in case there is anything in it for anyone on his list, and he loves it. He hooted. He said as much to me, "I *hooted*". He said that. Actually, now I remember it, he also said, "I found it killing, Oliver". Those were his actual words. He found it *killingly* funny.'

Overhearing this Elsie closed her eyes. Judging from the defensive tone Oliver was taking on the phone, Portly had not found Ollie's new play at all funny, which meant that there would be murder, at home and at the theatre, for weeks, and weeks, and weeks.

But there was worse to come, and not just from Oliver.

At the theatre that afternoon, having suffered Oliver's moaning about Portly all the way there, Elsie found out exactly what was missing from her life at that moment. Oddly it was not something

438

that anyone else would have put at the top of their list of necessities for a balanced existence, but once she heard those footsteps Elsie found out what was missing from her life all right – it was fear. And if she had been in any danger of taking her new life for granted, that particular danger would now have been very much a thing of the past.

It was the ring of those shoes in the corridor, that way of swaying from side to side to side as she walked, that put the dread back into Elsie. It was Dottie's walk, the walk that any lodger who was late with his rent would come to dread more than a bad review. It was a fact that no one else walked like Dottie.

Then, all at once, there it was, the unmistakable cry that Dottie always gave backstage. 'Darling, Jenny, darling. Marvellous, really, marvellous, *darling.*'

Dottie was visiting Jennifer Polesden, and seeing that Jennifer's blasted dressing room was right next door to Elsie's larger, more starry one it was really very easy for the old friends to make sure that Elsie and her dresser could hear them. It was at the end of a matinée, so they must both have known that Elsie would be about to rest between shows on her newly acquired silk-covered chaise longue, surrounded by her favourite white and blue flowers, and attended by her adoring dresser.

Seeing Elsie freeze suddenly and put her finger to her lips while pointing to the lock on the dressing room door, her dresser crept quietly over and turned the key. Then, together, as if performing a duet, and as all backstage people know to do, they both picked up the drinking glasses, more normally used for visitors' refreshment, and put them to the wall.

The dialogue in the next door dressing room came through loud and clear. It was all there, as always, in place, almost as if it had already been written, as if it was carefully scripted, the ticky tacky criticism of intimate dressing room talk.

'. . . takes that *far* too fast, darling, and really you know – Freddie, in the second act, he can hardly be *heard*. No, really.' (Pause to light cigarette). 'No, when I tell you,' Elsie could hear Dottie's loud actressy tones, 'when I tell you, Jenny, that the woman next to me complained that she could not hear him at all, she could not *hear* Freddie, and she was only four back in the dress circle – darling, only four from the front, you know.'

'I *told* Bartlett that he should call a rehearsal – I *told* him that last week, he should call a rehearsal, we are all getting sloppy, I said that. We are mistiming, we are, really.'

And so it went on, the clamour of the nit-picking and the fault-finding, everything that was said interspersed with exaggerated sighs and 'Oh, *don't*, darling' until finally, the real taboo subject was aired.

'Are you going next door, Dottie? Tell me, are you going next door to see Elsie? I *must* know. Because you know, if she knows you're in, she *will* ask.'

440

'You must be joking.'

'I am sure Elsie would love to see you, darling. She has behaved very well. Personally I have nothing to find fault with. The consummate professional is Elsie, really, completely professional.'

'And so she should be! The sacrifices I made for that girl – but really, I would rather drop dead, darling, really I would. There is nothing Miss Elsie Lancaster and I have to say to each other any more, but nothing. Not a *thing*. I actually thought she was quite disappointing this afternoon, as a matter of fact. Probably getting tired, so long into the run, but she was not as good as I had been led to believe. Not bad, mind you, but definitely not as brilliant as that review Osgood Lamsden gave her. I mean, talk about going over the top! I mean the review, not Elsie. One thing Elsie does not do is go over the top. But really, I expected more. And no, I will not go and see her. Had to come and see you though, Jenny darling, really. And you must come and see me at the house. Sea air, do you good, when the run closes, come and have a weekend.'

Noisy goodbyes outside Elsie's dressing room door signalled the end of the visit, and also the end of Elsie and her dresser listening to the studied dialogue next door. As the sound of *those* footsteps receded Elsie lay down on her chaise longue and closed her eyes.

She did *not* care, she did not *care*, she did not care in the very *least*, she told herself, and the ceiling of her dressing room far above her.

Let Dottie visit whomsoever she cared to visit, let her visit the whole cast, daily, Elsie would not care. All she cared about was that she was in a long-running hit, the money was rolling into her bank and she was able to buy lovely clothes and live in a marvellous flat with thick white carpet and sleep in until eleven in the morning instead of going out to find work; not to mention hire a maid to bring her a cup of China tea and plain biscuit when she woke up.

She turned her head, her eyes searching suddenly for those of her dresser.

'Can you get me a glass of water and an aspirin, Beattie, love?'

As it happened, Oliver's acting agent, Tad Protheroe, was not the only person who found Oliver Lowell's play killingly funny. So, to Oliver's amazement, did Denholm Heighton, and unfortunately for Portly he telephoned Oliver almost immediately to say that, no matter what, he wanted to put it on as soon as Oliver and Elsie came out of Popeye.

Now Portly was faced with a dilemma which he had seen arriving on the far horizon for some few months. Either he advised Elsie *not* to do her lover's play, at least until Oliver had rewritten it extensively, or he allowed her to go into the play, take it on tour, and suffer what Portly was sure would be an ignominious flop, at a time when her star was riding so high it might as well be the evening star itself.

'You don't like it, do you?'

Elsie faced Portly across his new leather-topped desk. He was still in the same old building, opposite the apothecary shop, where the tramp had performed his untimely christening – a christening that was proving, even now, to be as lucky as Portly himself had predicted.

'No, I don't like it, Elsie, you know that. I like it as little as I loved *Love To Popeye* the moment I read it. Popeye is unselfconscious, artless, and light in touch, and this one is quite the opposite. I don't even like the title. *The Magic of Love* – it's just too *Spring in Park Lane* for me, you know. Just nothing works, Elsie, not for me. Although, of course, I may be wrong.'

They both knew that he was not wrong. They knew it, because without her saying so Elsie quite obviously hated the play just as much as her agent. But Oliver was her lover, and Portly only her agent, and more than that she was in love with Oliver, and she was not in love with Portly.

'Oh, heck, I'll do it. After all – you know – Denholm wants to put it on, I mean he wants so much to put it on. He thinks it is killingly funny. He said as much to Oliver.'

'OK, then whenever you want to come out of Popeye, at the end of your twelve-month get-out clause, I will put the thing in motion for you to tour. Of course you know Oliver will be in it with you, again, don't you? I mean he *will* be in it? You don't mind that, do you?'

'No, you know I love acting with Oliver in his

443

plays. It means I can get a rewrite done without leaving the rehearsal room.' Elsie pulled a wry little face, and Portly smiled, despite the fact that he actually felt like groaning.

He could not tell Elsie that she was making a big mistake, because there was no point. There was no point in his saying so because he knew that she knew it already, but had no idea of how she could avoid it. She was only doing the play to please Oliver. Yet in pleasing Oliver, if it was a flop and she was starring in it she would doubtless also displease him to such an extent that she would become the focus of his frustrations. More than that, as people in the theatre so often did, Oliver would wish, ever after, to dissociate himself from Elsie because of the flop, a flop that she had only agreed to do to please Oliver.

'You are sure that you are not saying yes when you actually mean no?'

'I am quite sure. I love Ollie's work, you know that, all two plays of it.'

Portly watched the elegant figure of his brightest and most glamorous star sashaying into the street outside and stepping into a taxicab to be taken across town to lunch with a producer at the Caprice. Mario would now know Elsie Lancaster, of course. More than that, everyone would know her. Everyone now *did* know her. What they did not know, but Portly did, was that she was just about to bomb in a vehicle which she did not like, and for no better reason than to please her lover.

444

What Elsie did not also appreciate was that Denholm would, at that moment, send her out on tour in anything written by Oliver and starring herself, simply and solely because his backers would willingly stump up the cash. None of Heighton's own money, after all, went into the productions he put on. What was more, Heighton would not care a tinker's curse if the play failed, because after a long run Popeye was being transferred to Broadway with an American cast. As far as he was concerned, if the new play succeeded, all well and good, but if it failed it mattered not a fiddle. It would just be written up in the debit column and go to help any tax problems that Heighton Productions or its backers might be disenjoying at that moment.

So, that was truly that, really. But none of this could be communicated to Elsie, Portly's brightest star. He knew that his role would be to stand back and watch the hurt caused by failure, and hope that Elsie would be up to it.

Whether or not Oliver would be up to it was quite another matter. Oliver was after all the all too tender-hearted playwright, but he was also pig-headed and stubborn, not to mention immensely conceited, and at the same time sensitive to a degree. He was, in effect, the consummate creative artist.

Portly sighed and lit a cigar from his new box, a present from Elsie, who was almost criminally generous.

'Nothing to be done,' he told his new telephone,

and waited for his new secretary to come back with a tray of coffee from the café two doors down. 'Nothing to be done, nothing to be done.'

The realisation that there was very little you could do, Portly was learning, was half the art of representation. Knowing when to step in and when not to, when to do nothing at all, except perhaps breathe, was another all-important lesson. All he could do at that moment was wait and see. He hoped he was wrong, but he somehow doubted it. In his unalterable opinion, *The Magic of Love* was about as funny as a tax form – or Denholm Heighton.

'It's not funny, Master Oliver, really it's not. It doesn't need rewriting, it needs abandoning, for ever.'

'*Cliffie!*'

Ever since he was a small boy, Oliver always had liked to protest both to Cliffie and at him, but the truth was that Clifton was too practised at dealing with him to pay any attention whatsoever.

'You don't mean that. Please, Cliffie, say you don't mean that.'

He had always said that.

'I do, Master Oliver, I mean that very much, I am afraid. Your new play is not funny. I don't know why it's not funny, but it's not, and there it is.' The look that Clifton was now giving Oliver was so serious that he might have been bringing him news of a fatal disease, which, in a way, he was.

'The trouble with comedy is that you can never prove it is funny until it is rather too late. I mean, you didn't think *Love To Popeye* was that good, and look how long it has run for! It will soon be all set to celebrate its first year in the West End, against all your predictions. It will be going to Broadway, too.'

'All I said about Popeye was that although it was delightful, it was lightweight. I thought it was funny, but immensely lightweight.'

'Well, what else is a comedy meant to be if not lightweight – deadweight?'

What they were really arguing about was that Clifton was disappointed with Oliver for writing a comedy, and scoring a triumph with it, instead of joining some weighty organisation and playing Hamlet.

'Your problem is that you only want me to play Hamlet and nothing else. That is all you want of me, to stay in toga or tights spouting the Bard, and that is really not me. Besides, any amount of people can score in Shakespeare, and do, while very few can write and score in their own comedies. It is just a fact.'

'That is true, Master Oliver. I do feel that you would make, indeed you might still make, a great Hamlet, a Hamlet for your generation. Remember it was me who told you to get out into the provinces and prove yourself in modern plays.'

'I know, I know.' Oliver looked suddenly crest-fallen. 'I owe you so much, Cliffie. It's just that I so hoped you would like *The Magic of Love*'

'I even hate the title.' Clifton sighed. He feared for Oliver, and yet he could not exactly say why.

'You as well? What about my father?'

'I wouldn't tell him, not yet. Best not.'

Plunkett Senior had not left Yorkshire for some time now, unlike Newell who attended the first night in London, going round to Oliver's dressing room afterwards and giving his verdict as 'too lightweight for me, I'm afraid. I like plays with some meat on them.'

Seeing Oliver's face not just fall, but crumble, at his middle brother's sarcasm, Clifton, who had brought Newell to see the play, had taken Oliver aside.

'Never mind your brother, Master Ollie. I know it's rather obvious to say this, but he is just jealous.'

And Newell had been, quite openly jealous. After his first visit as Clifton's guest, he had brought friends to the play and laughed his head off – so loudly that Oliver could not fail to hear him – before leaving the theatre without bothering to go round to Oliver's dressing room afterwards.

It was quite deliberately hurtful, and in due course Oliver, much as he did not want to, began to appreciate it as being precisely that, particularly since Newell proceeded to do it not just once, but upwards of at least half a dozen times.

'He's just *frighting* you.'

Oliver had never heard this term used before, except by Elsie, but once he understood what it meant he realised that, in his own way, that was exactly what Newell was trying to do.

He was making sure that Oliver knew he was there, and then by not bothering to go backstage and make himself known, he was leaving his younger brother in a state of growing uncertainty, not just about his acting performance, but also, perhaps more importantly, about his play-writing.

Like Elsie with Dottie, Oliver told himself to forget all about Newell, put aside the question of why he did what he did, and get on with immersing himself in something other than *Love To Popeye*'s long run. He started writing *The Magic of Love* just at the precise moment when he was at his most confused. First hurt by his brother's behaviour, and then confused as to what kind of man Newell might actually be.

He had been coming out of a Soho restaurant with Elsie when he had seen the two figures. Unhappily he was not alone in his sighting; Newell had seen Oliver too. There was, quite simply, nothing that either of them could do. And Oliver, being Oliver, unable to think of anything to say in such circumstances, after his first glassy-eyed reaction, and not knowing the form – if there indeed was one – had simply dropped his eyes, followed Elsie into the taxi and driven off with her.

'I do wish men like that wouldn't be so public about everything, really,' Elsie had grumbled, while Oliver remained silent, completely confused, staring ahead of him into the darkness of the London street, unable to quite believe how he had seen Newell, and what it meant.

It was in this state of secret, puzzled depression, a state of mind that was anxious to conceal what he had seen, even from himself, that he had started *The Magic of Love*, which might account for why it had singularly failed to entertain anyone.

It was not that Oliver had ever put Newell on a pedestal, the way that he had his eldest brother, Richard, but, Oliver being the youngest, Newell was, when all was said and done, an older brother by some way, and an older brother is usually, in the nature of things, a figure to whom a younger brother inevitably looks up.

In fact, without realising it until now, or without allowing himself to admit it until now, all the time that Oliver had been growing up he had never really liked Newell, principally because Newell had always made such fun of him, overtly accusing the younger boy of being effeminate in his love for the theatre, and his hatred for blood sports.

Now it was obvious, even to Oliver, why Newell had always been at such pains to ridicule and hurt him, going out of his way to be sarcastic. It had to be because Newell was trying to distract attention away from himself and his own inclinations.

So it was that Oliver had sat down and written his second play, to clear his head, and at the same time to try to find an answer to the confusions brought about by family life. Forcing himself to write a play to make people laugh, he had also forced himself on to his artistic back foot, trying too hard, as people in a confused state of mind so often do, to be observant and acerbic. Worst of all, in his effort to turn away from everything he knew, Oliver had somehow forgotten to be funny, and that was what the audience coming back to see this second play wanted more than anything. They wanted Oliver Lowell to be funny again. They looked to be entertained by another *Love To Popeye*. They did not want him to force his newly confused vision on them. They wanted his lightness of touch, and he was unable to give it to them.

To begin with, in the provinces, because it was the same team as *Popeye*, the audiences came in their droves, and the play was a sell-out, which might have been gratifying if they had liked it, but they did not like it at all. In fact, they hated it.

Naturally word spread that *The Magic of Love* was a hopeless flop, and theatre managers everywhere panicked. It was not long before even the provincial critics could not find anything good to say about it. Unsurprisingly, after scenes of frightful tension both on stage and backstage, *The Magic of Love* closed, long before it came within even driving distance of London.

With its closing, Oliver packed up his things,

left Elsie and the flat and headed for the south of France where he spent three months in total inebriation. Elsie, on the other hand, having hated the play, and, worse, hated herself for doing the play, and even for a while hated poor old Portly for not telling her *not* to do the play, took up the first film offer that came her way, and prepared to leave for Rome.

Their affair was over. *The Magic of Love* had killed it, as Portly had predicted to himself that it might. No theatrical affair involving a leading lady and her playwright and co-star could survive a fantastic flop, and Oliver's second play had been just that; a huge flop, the kind of flop of which people speak ever after in hushed tones, and murmur, 'Oh, you weren't in that, were you?'

Portly felt sorry for everyone who had been involved in the endless tensions, arguments, and dented egos that a flop involves. Inevitably of course Denholm Heighton had deserted Oliver, quickly finding a new playwright and a new play upon which to concentrate his enthusiasm, and was even now searching for stars to do it. From his point of view of course Denholm could afford to stay calm. Popeye had made him a fortune, on both sides of the Atlantic. Tomorrow had dawned as brightly as ever for Mr Heighton, as Portly had always known that it would.

Even Portly himself did not remain untouched by the disaster that *The Magic of Love* turned out to be, because Oliver not only left Elsie, he also left Portly.

452

Before she set off for Rome, Elsie was broken-hearted but scornful, not least of Oliver's decision.

'His own agency, and he's left it. Only Ollie could leave himself! As to the play – well, Portly love, we were asking for trouble, weren't we? I mean imagine calling a play *The Magic of Love* and expecting your affair to survive it.'

She gave a short, sarcastic laugh, and then, whistling a far from happy tune, left for Rome and her first filming experience, which only Portly realised that she was actually dreading.

'He'll be back,' Portly told his new, glamorous, and really rather grand secretary, and anyone else who would listen, 'Oliver will be back. He will bring his plays back to PLL, you'll see.'

But neither Portly, nor anyone else, really believed it. Probably because Oliver Lowell was, for the time being anyway, finished. He had become increasingly difficult through the provincial tour, so much so that, by the end of it, he had acquired a reputation.

Also, and damningly, Denholm Heighton had informed the whole of the all-powerful Betterton Club that Oliver Lowell was impossible to work with, and that, as he well knew, was quite enough to keep Oliver in the cold for a good few years.

Furthermore, rumour had it that Oliver Lowell, having broken up with Elsie Lancaster on the ill-fated tour of his second comedy, was now having an affair with a famous French actress, a lady not just noted for her insatiable amorous appetites, but infamous for them. Oliver Lowell was her third lover of that year, or was it month? It seemed that between affairs the actress in question was in the habit of retiring to a clinic for the specific purpose of recharging her sexual batteries, before returning to the fray to take up her amorous adventures, and of course filming, once more.

So it was that everyone lunching and dining at the Caprice or the Ivy sighed and shook their heads over poor young Oliver Lowell. Such a bright young talent, and with such potential, but obviously success had come too easily, and too soon. There was very little anyone could do to help such impetuous, headstrong characters. He might go on, of course, or he might not.

Worse than that, he might stay as he was at the moment, and that, everyone was quite agreed, would be fatal. Someone had seen him out of his *skull* outside the Salisbury, and only the other night – such a terrible, terrible shame. Now, how about asking Mario whether the lobster salad was up to snuff?

Then on to discussing or destroying the next reputation, because that, after all, was what lunching and dining, or being a member of the Betterton Club, was all about. It was all about the shadow of reputation upon which a shallow first success so depended. And Oliver Lowell now had neither reputation nor success. He had quite destroyed both.

Chapter Fourteen

Coco looked across at her small daughter with some pride. Holly was now a healthy three-year-old with beautiful dark blue eyes, straight dark hair, and sturdy limbs, not to mention a mischievous expression. Naturally, since Coco was a single mother, for all the time of Holly's growing from babyhood to toddler the little girl had been the absolute centre of her mother's existence.

First thing in the morning Coco would stroll through to Holly's nursery, knowing that the small arms would already be being held out and Holly would be jumping up and down and waiting for Coco to take her back to her bed, where they would lie together for some time in a contented half-sleep, listening to the growing sounds of life from below the windows of the flat. Buses passing, doors slamming, cars starting. Despite the earliness of the hour, outside London was already awake and bustling, but for half an hour they did not yet have to be part of it. It was a blissful time, full of the particular warmth and peace of the early morning, which, because she knew that it was inevitably doomed to be shattered, was particularly precious to Coco.

Until Holly came into her life Coco had never given motherhood a thought. Mentally and physically, because she was an only child, she herself had been the all-consuming and completely fascinating centre of her own existence, rattling along in fits and starts, always hoping that, contrary to outward indications, her boredom at school, her dissatisfaction with her appearance, she might, one day, make something of herself and her life.

But now that Coco had actually started to make some progress, not with ridiculous and very tedious film acting but with designing for the theatre, now that everyone had started to mark her out – now that she was becoming *the* Coco Hampton – Coco had found, to her astonishment, that Miss Coco Hampton meant a great deal less to Coco herself than little Miss Holly Hampton.

It seemed, to Coco's astonishment, that this was what motherhood was all about. It was about the centre of your existence shifting and becoming wrapped around that other small being, so that whenever you were away from your baby, even for a few hours, your mind stretched back to him or her, envying whoever was looking after them for that short time, resenting the fact that the chubby arms would be held out to anyone else.

And too, Coco whose whole life, until Holly was born, had been concerned with her appearance, now found that she stared only into baby shops, saved up only to make Holly a new dress or coat, did not care how many times she was forced to remodel her own clothes to make them seem what they were not and never could be now – new and fashionable.

Of course when it came to designing her small daughter's clothes, Coco could not put aside her own strong preferences, nor could she make up clothes in any other way than how she would design for some star such as Elsie Lancaster, or Margaret Seymour. So, while Holly rested in the afternoons before their walks to the Park, Coco would toil on the small creations that she delighted in making for her daughter.

Without her realising or even intending it, Holly's clothes, sewn with such love and attention to detail, became miniature works of art. Tiny coats with hand-made crochet collars and cuffs and matching tam-o'-shanters and gloves. Silk dresses in Kate Greenaway styles with matching parasols. Small Chanel-style jackets and skirts in navy blue, with piqué collars and mock white gardenias pinned to the tiny lapels.

Naturally Coco pushed Holly proudly out into the Park wearing these tiny examples of her own designing. Equally naturally all the Hyde Park nannies stared at Holly, not really approving of her, since not only was she being pushed by her mother, but she patently looked so different from the other little girls in their Hayford coats with their muslin collars, and bonnets with bunches of flowers pinned to the side. All, that is, except for one nanny, who stopped and asked Coco the single question none of the other nannies could bring themselves to ask – where was it exactly that Coco bought Holly her clothes?

'I don't buy them, I make them.'

The nanny, tall, dark-haired and very correctly dressed in a brown and cream uniform, nodded, her expression serious.

'You should patent your designs, my dear, you could make a fortune. I would buy them for our nurseries, because as you know, the Prince – whom you might well have read about in your newspapers – the Prince adores to dress his children in original designs.'

She stooped to look more closely at Holly, who was immaculately presented in a pale yellowy mustard dress, pinch-pleated, round-sleeved, with small brightly coloured butterflies decorating the shoulders and the tip of her tiny parasol.

Coco did not know exactly to which prince the nanny with her chic pram was referring, and since this must have been obvious to Nanny Ali, she leaned forward and whispered in Coco's ear.

Coco, despite her preoccupation with the theatre and its ways, registered the name immediately. Prince Ali was a famous man, not just for his immense wealth but also for his love of beautiful women, not to mention his taste. His fabulous homes in London, Paris and Geneva were admired by everyone. He had recently become a most popular figure in England by dint of his buying a world-famous painting, and presenting it to the nation.

'Here's my card, my dear. Write to me at this address, and I will invite you to lunch or tea. I have to seek permission from the Prince's secretary first.'

After that Nanny Ali walked her beautiful charges off towards Kensington Gardens and Peter Pan, leaving Coco to contemplate what they both knew might be a whole new career.

It was difficult to know what she should write to Nanny Ali. Coco tried several times, and finally wrote, *Thank you very much for your invitation to lunch or tea. I should be delighted to come at any time. Yours sincerely, Coco Hampton.*

The reply came very soon after she had posted her letter.

We should be pleased if you would take luncheon with us at twelve thirty on Wednesday.

There followed the same address as on Nanny Ali's card, an address which Coco, with her London upbringing, knew to be the cream of all addresses – namely, a road so filled with large, exclusive, detached houses that it was only really affordable to ambassadors, or foreign dignitaries, and princes.

Perhaps because she had made what she herself considered to be a great deal of money from *Love To Popeye* and was now on the list of designers employed by Denholm Heighton and other West End managements, Coco did not feel nervous about her lunch with Nanny Ali. But neither did she not feel nervous. Theatre design was very much a fashion. If she was *in* now, she could as easily be *out* next week, which poor Oliver apparently was at that moment. And although she had designed and costumed *The Magic of Love*, and so could have been fatally associated with that tremendous flop, that was the one element, the only element of the whole production, which, everyone was agreed, had been successful in the whole sorry mess. Coco now had a definite stamp to her designs. No one could look at her work and mistake it for something that someone else had done. She had always drawn beautifully. Now what she drew could make her money. To that extent she could not have been happier.

And yet Nanny Ali's interest in Holly's clothes had awakened in Coco the realisation that she could, if she was lucky, become successful at something which would give her, and Holly, far greater security than theatre design. Children grew and grew, so there was necessarily a never-ending demand for new clothes for them, and, like children's books, and prints for nurseries – like everything made with children in mind – successful clothes would not just be part of their lives, but would become as much a part of their children's children's lives as being taken to the pantomime, or being read to from Beatrix Potter or Alice in Wonderland.

Standing in front of the address to which she had been directed, however, Coco could not help feeling overawed. It was a vast house, painted white with black railings and black double front doors, themselves decorated with large, highly polished brass knockers. Large green curved awnings covered all the downstairs windows, and an immaculate green sward of grass fronted the narrow stone terrace from which rose the flight of steps that led up to the front doors.

Within seconds of Coco and Holly's arriving at those same doors, as if they had been watched by unseen eyes, one of the doors opened slowly and quietly to admit them.

Coco did not have to tell Holly that she was in a very luxurious place. The small, beautifully dressed child seemed to sense it at once, staring round the huge hall with its indoor fountain and marble statues, and finally up at her mother as if to say, 'Is this really where we are meant to come today?'

'I've left Holly's pram outside. I hope that is all right?'

'Madam.'

The dark-faced butler bowed, and without a word he preceded Coco and Holly up the main staircase to a door which opened on to a long corridor leading to another door, and so up to what must eventually have been the third floor of the house.

Here the corridor widened, and the thickly woven wool carpet turned from an elegant maroon to a deep blue. The butler pushed open yet another pair of double doors, beyond which

Coco guessed, before she even saw into the large, high-ceilinged room, lay the nursery.

It was another world. Here, although there was only one nanny, there must have been at least six nursery maids, all uniformed, and all wearing suitably humble expressions, because, it did not have to be said, here Nanny Ali ruled. Here also was not just one rocking horse, but two or three, and not only one doll's house but many, not to mention dozens of dolls, and a cluster of fawn-coloured pug dogs with black masks weaving in and out of both the humans and the toys, their curled tails stretching out in greeting to the former, the bells on their collars singing out their happy familiarity with nursery life.

Just as Coco was swiftly coming to the conclusion that this really might be too much of a display of wealth, another door opened, and into the room trooped Prince Ali's children – all seven of them.

'I am very glad you could come,' Nanny Ali announced to Coco and Holly, and then she said to the nursemaids, 'This is the little girl I told you all about. Look at her beautiful dress and matching parasol, do.'

The nursemaids, all English, and all looking very much as though they must be country girls with their rounded cheeks and shy manners, now did as Nanny Ali had commanded and crowded round a smiling Holly, turning her this way and that, gasping, cooing, and generally making noises of such approval that even Coco, who was very critical of her own work, could not help glowing with pride.

'We,' said Nanny Ali, speaking for either herself or the Prince, Coco was not sure, 'should very much like it if you could be kind enough to design clothes for the Prince's children. We would like it very much. They are all very different; the children are not at all alike, as you can see.'

Coco was unsure to what religion and state Prince Ali, the darling of the Continental magazines and newspapers, belonged, but certainly his offspring's looks varied as much as, perhaps, his taste in wives. Some were dark-haired and blue-eyed, some were red-haired and brown-eyed, all were girls.

'I know, I know,' said Nanny Ali, as she saw Coco eyeing their very different looks with some interest. 'Prince Ali, like a certain famous English king, has had rather a difficult time of it as far as his wives are concerned. He has not, as you can see, for some reason, yet produced a son. Not that he does not love all his children,' she added graciously, 'but we think he would enjoy a change, some time soon. However, you can now see, Mrs Hampton, why it is that I was interested in your designs. We long to dress their Serene Highnesses in different clothes, but different designs are difficult to come by, even on the Continent. After all, since their father is a prince, we do not want them looking like everyone else, do we? It is normal, since there are seven of us, to

463

want the princesses to stand out from other people's charges. Nor do we want seven little girls looking precisely the same, do we?'

'No, of course not.'

Coco did not bother to correct Nanny Ali's manner of address. She herself, since signing up with PLL, had always taken care to wear a wedding ring, and, in private life, settled for being addressed as 'Mrs Hampton'. Not because she was ashamed of being an unmarried mother, because she was not in the least ashamed – rather the reverse, in fact – since it would have been all too easy to give Holly away – but because she liked to save other people from embarrassment. It was just easier all round, for everyone, if they imagined that she was married. It meant that their own, necessarily private sense of morality could remain unexposed.

'Could you design for us, as you have for your own daughter, Mrs Hampton?'

'Yes, I could.'

'Would you like to design for us, Mrs Hampton?'

'Yes, I would.'

'We would want the designs to be completely exclusive. We would not want anyone else to be seen wearing whatever it is you have in mind for the princesses.'

'Of course.'

They both knew that what Nanny Ali meant, put more plainly, was that she did not want to see Holly wearing the same designs as the princesses.

'No, I do understand, of course I do,' Coco added.

'Very well. Shall we take lunch, and then – well, we can talk more?'

Nanny Ali liked Coco. She liked any young woman who said little and looked a lot. She knew, instinctively, that here was a young woman after her own heart. She did not need everything spelled out. Shortly afterwards they went in to luncheon in the nursery dining room, which, from the look of it, was rather more than just a room in which children, nanny and maids ate their meals.

This room too had a high ceiling, and once again the staff in attendance seemed to out-number the children and their nursemaids, with Coco and Holly a new and for once comparatively ordinary addition in what was, after all, an Aladdin's cave of nurseryland.

The nursery china alone would have graced a normal household table only on the greatest occasions, with brightly feathered peacocks and jungle animals depicted in glowing colours, the whole decorated with so much gold that it caught the sunlight shining through the long windows with an effortless display of wealth. Indeed, there was so much gold everywhere – on the footmen's uniforms, on the pug dogs' collars, in the decorations on the salts and peppers, on everything that was in everyday use – that the house might well have been built above a gold mine, so much had the precious metal made itself felt.

The food was classic English nursery fare in

both style and taste, and was perfectly delicious. Chicken coated in a subtle saffron sauce, parsley potatoes, garden peas, lightly flavoured custards with poached fruit, and jugs of freshly made lemonade.

Holly, sitting as still as a mouse, fed herself as neatly as was possible for someone who had only recently learned the art, while turning every now and then to look to Coco for reassurance. It was a memorable occasion, but for one reason more than any other.

'Oh dear,' Coco murmured to Holly, much later as she pushed open their flat door. 'Guess who is going to buy *who* a pug?'

On the next visit to 'the palace', as Coco had now nicknamed the vast house, she took with her two or three samples of the dresses that she had, some weeks before, had in mind to make for Holly, but now had to be sacrificed for the sake of the little family's finances.

'Oh yes, Mrs Hampton, this will be truly perfect for the princesses. Just the right kind of detail and sophistication. His Royal Highness will be very pleased, I am sure.'

Nanny Ali was talking about the *pièce de résistance* of the sample collection, which was a velvet coat with a stand-up collar, and a small amount of smocking in a different colour just below. Long tight sleeves, a small lace-trimmed velvet purse on a silk cord, and a matching hat which tied at the top in an insouciant bow, made up what they could all see at a glance was a stunning outfit.

'I thought,' Coco told her audience of nursery maids and Nanny Ali, 'that if I made these up in seven different-coloured velvets, the children would be different, but the theme would be the same, if you understand me?'

'Wonderful, Mrs Hampton,' breathed one of the nursery maids, unable to contain her enthusiasm. 'Just like something out of a story book, that is how they'll look.'

Nanny Ali did not seem to mind this interruption, but simply beamed at Coco, her eyes positively radiating an emotion which Coco could not quite translate.

'I think they would look very pretty,' Coco agreed with the nursery maid. 'Very pretty.'

Nanny Ali obviously held the purse strings for the fitting out of her charges, which made both of them very happy, because she promptly put in an order for seven velvet coats, purses and hats and seven little wool suits in varying colours, also with matching hats, not to mention dressing gowns with velvet collars and silk-lined nightdresses with matching lace-trimmed mob caps.

'That will teach Nanny Cadogan and Nanny Westchester to look down their noses at us when we visit Peter Pan,' Nanny Ali murmured as she wrote out a cheque to cover the cost of all Coco's materials.

Of course Holly did not know it, but security for both her mother and herself now beckoned.

Despite the success of Popeye, life as a theatre designer held out no certainties for a young mother and her daughter, and just lately, due to the success of the 'kitchen sink' school of drama, there had been a lull in demand for any but either the most distinguished or the best connected of theatre designers. And British films were not, as yet, open to women designers, being, as Coco had observed, very much still a male-dominated club.

'I would so like it if this could become a regular thing for us, Holly darling,' Coco murmured to Holly as she bathed her that night. 'It would take care of so much, the expense of the flat, your clothes, and nursery school, all that.'

Coco thought, with sudden guilt, of how much money she had managed to waste on herself in times gone by. It seemed an unimaginable amount now that she had Holly to support, but none of that would matter if only she could keep on supplying 'the palace' with clothes for the princesses.

Once she had put Holly to bed, Coco's evenings were always spent sewing and listening to the radio. She would not have a television, simply because she knew that if she did she would only watch it, instead of sewing. Tonight the evening's concert was interrupted by the sound of the telephone ringing. Coco stared at it. She had placed it carefully on a high kitchen stool, so that it would not be missed, and she now mounted the stool and put the telephone on her lap, hoping against hope that it would not be Gladys wanting a bed for the night, or angling for some other favour. Mentally she started to prepare a list of excuses which would get her out of seeing Gladys, or, worse, putting her up.

It was not Gladys, which was a relief, it was Oliver, and he too wanted a favour, but he would not say what it was on the telephone.

'Can I come round?'

Coco looked at her sewing machine. She had wanted to finish what she was making that night, but if Oliver came round she never would. Moreover, he would keep her up late, moaning – actors did so like to stay up late moaning – and that would mean that Coco would be tired for Holly in the morning.

'Oh, all right, Ollie. But I can't be late.'

'What a welcome,' Oliver grumbled, half an hour later, as he pecked Coco on the cheek. '*Oh all right, but I can't be late.*' He raised his voice to a falsetto as he always did when imitating Coco. 'I mean to say, Coco, I have not seen you since I went abroad, you know? And how long is that?'

Coco shook her head. Since having had a baby she felt so much older than Oliver. It was as if she had sat some terribly difficult exam that he had not taken, which, in a way, she had. In mother-hood.

'Heavens, Ollie.' Coco stood back and examined him in the light of her electrified oil lamps. 'You do look – brown.'

He looked terrible, actually, so telling him he looked tanned was the best that Coco could do. Not to tell Ollie something about his looks would have been to cause an emotional upheaval, since Ollie, like most actors, seemed to need to be told about his looks every half an hour, on the dot, or else he became rapidly convinced that no one in his immediate vicinity loved him.

'Where's Holly?'

Oliver looked round the room with one sweeping glance, and then down at Coco, this time with accusation in his eyes, as if Coco might have given Holly away, or eaten her for dinner.

'In bed fast asleep, where do you think, at ten o'clock at night? Would you like a glass of wine?'

'Oh yes.' Oliver sank down into a chair and stared up at Coco. 'God it is good to see you, Coco. Must have been an age.'

Coco nodded absently, her mind still on her sewing. She knew that Oliver had been having a bad time of it and that as a consequence she would now no doubt be subjected to a catalogue of moans about the lack of suitable scripts, the shortage of suitable parts, and the complete absence of suitable managements to put on his plays. She therefore placed a glass of wine in his hand and sat down at her sewing machine again, thinking to sew and listen.

'No, no, Coco, you cannot paddle away at your old granny sewing machine while I am talking to you. That I will not allow, really, it would be like talking to the bad fairy in the Sleeping Beauty, or

470

something. Besides, no one can sew and listen, and I want you to listen to me, very carefully, really I do.'

'Oh, I can listen, Oliver, really I can. Besides, I am afraid that I must. You see, I have a commission now to make dresses and coats for these little foreign princesses, and I really must get on with them.'

Oliver did not seem to register the importance of this new security in Coco's life. Instead he groaned.

'No. Please. Please, listen to me, Coco, please! I have something so important to ask you – please.'

'Ask away. I am listening.' Coco frowned down at the paper toile that she was cutting out.

'No, I insist you put down your bloody sewing. No, you must, you must sit down, there, opposite me, and listen. I have something so important to ask you.'

Oliver was loveable, but just so demanding. Even so, reluctantly, Coco did as he asked, and sat down opposite him. Oliver took a draught of the wine she had handed him, and stared first up at the ceiling, and then at Coco, and then at his shoes. Coco was silent, dreading that he was going to ask her for money, which now that she had a baby she really could not spare.

'Will you marry me, Coco?'

As always when returning to his delightful new flat Portly rang the bell for the hall porter and asked him if there had been any letters for him.

'Just the one, Mr Cosgrove, from Rome.'

Again, as always, when it was a small paper-thin airmail letter, it was from Elsie. She seemed to have been travelling backwards and forwards from Italy for the past eighteen months.

Portly darling, she had scrawled in cheap ball-point, the letter having obviously been written on location, *I really must have some proper work to do when I come home, a play or a review or something, darling. Nice though it is to be paid to do nothing, I now feel I have been doing nothing on location for ever! Please, please find me something, even television would be all right. Lots of love Porters, Elsie.*

Portly folded the thin airmail paper carefully back into its original shape, and placed it in his desk drawer. Of course Elsie was completely right, she did need to do something other than film on location in foreign parts, because, nice though the money was, the best part of what she did would, as they both knew, end up on the cutting room floor. Her original stage appearance in *Love To Popeye* was now well forgotten, except by a very few. Such was the ephemeral nature of success in the theatre, even the most glittering success faded into the mists of yesteryear within a very short time, leaving the participants flailing around trying to find the next way forward for their careers.

Since his telephone at the office never, ever stopped Portly found that he usually did most of his more constructive thinking at home, alone, in the flat. The past two and a half years, since his

472

return to London, had proved to be both rewarding and stimulating. Thanks to handling Elsie, PLL had taken off, and was now very much in the forefront. They had moved offices and were currently housed in a building in the King's Road. Here actors and actresses, playwrights and screenwriters could happily call in, knowing that Portly and Constantia, his secretary, would always be pleased to see them, and more than that, would always have news of some kind for them. This was not difficult, because subtly, without anyone's realising quite why, the worldwide focus of attention in both films and television was beginning to switch from America and Italy to England, or more specifically to London. And as if to make an international audience feel more at home in the capital, more and more Italian restaurants with shining tiled floors in complicated designs were opening up everywhere, and film actors and actresses, pop stars, and theatrical knights, flocked there to meet producers and directors, every one of them all too aware that the London scene was not just changing, it was positively buzzing.

Somehow, without particularly concentrating on it, PLL had become *the* agency to which television producers in particular had begun to turn for both writers and actors. While this was very flattering, the truth was, as Portly well knew, that asking actors to appear on television was one thing, but getting them to actually do so was quite another. English actors still curled their lips in derision at what they considered to be this horrid upstart medium. They would not be caught dead appearing on television. They would rather be out of work. The theatre was what counted. Films and television, but television in particular, were below the salt, they would tell Portly, who listened with his usual courteous expression on his face, while mentally remaining unimpressed.

The truth was that British actors and actresses were terrified of television. If they forgot their lines in front of a theatre audience, it mattered, but it did not shatter their careers. If on the other hand they did the same thing in front of what was now millions of people staring at their televisions in their own homes, they could become not famous but notorious overnight. No one knew how to handle television, not the producers, nor the directors, nor the performers. It was dismissed by everyone as merely a medium for panel and variety shows. So, it sometimes seemed to Portly, he alone saw the potential in television, live or filmed. He alone saw that it could be both an exciting and a stimulating medium for play-wrights and actors, if only they could be brought to see it too, instead of coming out with a lot of hackneyed abuse at the very mention of it.

Because of this, the fact that Elsie had mentioned television in her letter from a film set in Rome was exciting. Portly knew that Elsie was far too down to earth not to know that her star was no longer in the ascendant, that although she was fondly remembered for *Love To Popeye*, that play, and her performance, had long passed out of the forefront of people's minds.

With all this in his head, the next morning Portly arrived even earlier than usual at his office, and seizing the trade papers started to look through them with an eye to one thing, and one thing alone – finding Elsie work in television. If he could get Elsie to do television, then, gradually, bit by little bit, he would be able to get a whole host of his other actors to follow. Elsie Lancaster on television in a scintillating play, or even in a series, would be quite something. Moreover, it would start a general feeling of unease, because, if Elsie was doing television, why not any other well-known young actors?

As he spread out the trade papers on his desk and sipped at an excellent cup of Italian coffee, sent up from the downstairs café, an item caught Portly's eye. It was small, but significantly placed, and when he saw the names involved Portly realised that there was even less time at his disposal than he had imagined. Now he really did have to find something for Elsie.

OLIVER LOWELL SIGNED TO PLAY
THE MESSIAH

Young, rugged Oliver Lowell has been signed by the Kass Organisation to play Jesus Christ in a film entitled *The Messiah*. Louis Kass, head of the Kass Organisation, said yesterday that he was proud to be associated with such a fine project. He was also pleased to have found a fine upstanding young man such as Oliver Lowell to play the title role. 'He has put his past behind him,' Mr Kass told a press conference, 'is about to marry his childhood sweetheart, and is looking forward to a golden future.'

*

'I can't marry you, Oliver, I can't, I just can't!'

Oliver was on his bended knees, which, if his offer had been a genuine one, might have been quite appropriate, but since what he was proposing was in the name of business, simply because he needed to have a wife to please the publicity people at the Kass Organisation, at that moment he looked to Coco not only inappropriate to a degree, but also absurd.

'It's in name only, Coco, really. I mean, I shan't make any demands on you, really I won't. It will just be in name only. And I'll pay you, I'll help out with Holly. Think about it, I'll be *able* to help you, because soon I will be earning trillions from the show. It's going to sell all around the world.'

'I can't marry you, Oliver. Apart from anything else, it would be awful for Holly. What on earth would she make of it?'

'It's just a piece of paper, Coco.'

'Ask someone else. There must be some actress, someone, you could ask. Goodness, you've been having affairs with enough of them.'

'I have not—'

'I do read the papers, Oliver. I am not com-

476

pletely blind to your recent activities. Not for nothing have you been dubbed "Lover Lowell" by Express Newspapers. And what was it I saw you called in the *Daily Mail*? Oh yes, "loose-living Lowell of the film star looks, the one-time escort of glamorous French actress Ginette Morceau". Really, Ollie, whatever happened to Shakespeare? You must be making Clifton blush for you, let alone your father and brothers.' Coco glanced up from the paper toile she was working on and gave Oliver a mock reproving look.

'They all know, Cliffie and everyone, they know not to believe *anything* that they read about me. Besides, I have not had nearly as many affairs as they say I have.'

'Big gi-normous huge great *deal*, Ollie, and while you're at it, pull the other one. It has all of Bow Bells on it, really it has. *Mon dieu*, if you are not the biggest spinner of fairy tales around I do not know who is!'

'All right, all *right*, I admit, I have had *some* affairs, since Else and I split up, but after all, I would do, wouldn't I? I am only a man, Coco. I had to get over Elsie, and the play, I mean to say, I had to get over all that. I mean, Elsie, she did behave dreadfully towards me, really she did. The whole thing was a disaster. Couldn't have been worse.'

'At the moment *you* look like a disaster, I mean really, you should see yourself, *have* you seen yourself? You are a wreck, really you are. You've lost all your patina. You were much better off when you were with Elsie. She gave you a bit of polish, really she did.'

Coco looked down at her childhood friend, who was still for some stupid reason on his knees, with the light scorn that all friends who have known each other as children are able to reserve for each other. It was as if no years had passed and Oliver was still the last to scramble into his seat in the dress circle, his knees knocking with fear in case they were discovered.

Now he scrambled to his rather larger feet.

'Oh, please, Coco, just *marry* me, and then forget about it!'

'No, no, *no*.'

'If you don't I will kill myself. I mean it! Don't you realise, I will lose the part, Kass won't let me play the Messiah if I'm not to all intents and purposes a happily *married* man. He does not like the recent publicity that I have had. They have taken a straw poll of all the syndication people, all the Christian organisations worldwide, and it seems that whoever plays the Messiah must be a happily married man. Not even a confirmed bachelor will do. So, please, please, marry me, Coco.'

'I would kill you, if I married you, really I would.'

'Coco. Just sit down.'

'I am sitting down, Ollie, in case you didn't notice—'

Oliver took the paper toile from Coco's hands and put it to one side in order to better command her attention.

'Just for a minute, Coco, consider. Consider what a difference it would, it *will*, make to your and Holly's lives.'

'It will make a huge difference, of course it will, a huge and horrible difference. I do not want to be married, Ollie! *You* have never wanted to be married, the whole thing is the most awful idea, and you *know* it. We have both always agreed marriage just makes people – well, horrible. It's like being locked up in a Ford motor car with all the windows up, and I didn't say that, *you* did, if you remember, once when we were having lunch together at Ramad. And – and we both agreed it would be terrible for our careers, that once you married that was it, everyone gave up on you. It's just not *on* for people like us. We are emotional gypsies.'

'Gypsies get married—'

Coco stood up, but Oliver pressed down on her shoulders so hard, she finally gave in and sat down again.

'What about Holly? You're not thinking of Holly, Coco.'

'I am thinking of Holly. She would hate having a man who was pretending to be my husband around the place, really she would.'

'Holly might need a father–husband person in her life.'

'Having a baby, being a mother, is different.'

'I don't see why.'

'They are not – marriage.'

'Having a baby is pretty serious, Coco.'

479

'If I had a husband as well as a baby—' Coco looked at Oliver, frowning.

'Yes?'

'Well, quite honestly I think I would feel like jumping in the Thames, Ollie, I would really.'

'Well, all right, let's try again. Just tell me what possible difference a silly little bit of paper will make to us? After all, we're old friends. We have known each other since we were children. There is nothing new to learn *about* each other, after all, is there?' Oliver pointed a triumphant finger down at Coco, scoring a point as he well knew. 'Besides, I can trust you, Coco, I can trust you to treat the whole thing as a joke, or a business arrangement, whatever you will, whereas if I marry some actress I don't know, well it won't be the same at all, will it? I mean, will it? I mean they could split on me to the Kass Organisation, they could go to the press, or they could divorce me and demand alimony, whereas I know that I really can trust you, don't I? Please, please, for the sake of world sales, marry me.'

'I don't see why this stupid man Kass has to have his star *married*. Why? I mean to say?'

'I told you, his sales people have got this thing that whoever plays Jesus the Messiah has to be whiter than white, and all that. By marrying me off before filming starts he reckons I will keep out of trouble, and besides, there will be the publicity – all good for the film, and all that. I mean you can see, from his point of view, just what he means, you can really, at least I can. Worldwide sales

480

would be affected by the Messiah going off for flings in wild foreign places, or being found drunk outside night clubs, you know. I mean I can understand that.'

'You can understand it, because you desperately want the part. It will make you even more famous. Or rather it will make you famous rather than infamous, which is what you are rapidly becoming. That is why you want to jump to and do what Kass wants, and start pretending to be a good boy.'

'Oh please, Coco, it is only a little thing, really it is. Just a quick visit to Wandsworth reggie office and out again, no fuss, just the press, and that is that. Besides, you owe me, you know you do. You always said that you would do anything to repay me for finding the nursing home where you had Holly, you did say that.'

'Did I? I suppose I did.' There was a small silence as Coco remembered just how kind the nuns had been. The days and weeks that she had spent lying in bed waiting for Holly to grow had been lightened by their goodness, and it was true it *had* been due to Oliver, completely due to Oliver. 'Well, I am *not* getting married in a register office, that is one thing. They are so depressing.'

Oliver paled. 'You mean you want to get married in a church?'

'Yes, if I am to be married, it has to be in church. I will not go to a register office, Oliver. I hate those places. I would rather be shot.'

'But getting married in church is very serious,

481

Coco, and I am a left-footer, you know that. Not a good left-footer, I will agree, but too much of one to go into a church and take vows and not mean it, and all that.'

'Take it or leave it, Ollie, I am not dressing up to go to a register office *mutter parlour*.'

'No, I am sorry, I couldn't do that, Coco. I couldn't marry in church just for a lark and – and because I want a part. I don't mind a register office, but not a church.'

'You had better ask the Kass Organisation, hadn't you, Oliver?'

'How do you mean?'

'They may insist that you marry in church, and then what?'

Oliver's feelings of propriety were now really under fire. It was one thing to marry Coco in a register office, but to go down the aisle, all proper, as it were, seemed just too sacrilegious for words.

'I don't think they will mind, Coco, just so long as I tie the knot with someone, put paid to the gossip-column tittle-tattle about all my affairs, and all that.'

Oliver stared at Coco, realising of a sudden that if they were talking like this, Coco must have given in to the idea of a marriage of convenience with him.

'So, whatever happens, you will marry me?'

He must have been right because Coco replied, almost absently, 'Oh, very well, but in name only, Ollie, nothing more.'

'And whatever else would it be, Coco? I have

never wanted to get married, and nor have you. This is simply a business thing, you know that, just a business arrangement.'

'I will not go and live with you, and if *you* have to live here with us for a while as cover, you will have to *behave* yourself. And I don't want you living here with some girl or other, or anything like that. I don't want you embarrassing Holly, do you understand?'

'I do. I do.'

Oliver gave a great sigh of relief. He would agree to anything at that moment, and anyway, in due course, after the film was over, and Oliver was free of the Kass Organisation, they could just get quietly divorced.

'And you are not to keep arriving back here *drunk*. If you are the worse for wear you are to book yourself into an hotel and sober up *there*, and that goes for anything else, for that matter. And I will probably want *that* in writing, do you hear?'

Oliver nodded happily. He did not dare tell Coco that he had already signed a contract with the Kass Organisation which included a clause stipulating that he would tie the knot before the start of filming.

'I'll agree to anything you ask, Coco, really I will. I am just so grateful to you.'

'I should think so too.' Coco gave a sharp nod and turned back to her sewing machine.

'I will arrange everything tomorrow – straight away, get it over and done with, once and for all.'

'Yes, you can do all the arrangements. I want

nothing to do with anything. And I don't want any publicity either, thank you. And you can call the Kass Organisation – you can tell the Kass Organisation that they can Kass off – ha, ha! No. They can have their marriage, but no photographs, no press. Our wedding must be completely private. I must keep Holly out of the papers. I don't want her being teased when she goes to nursery school, or anything. People have long memories.'

What Coco did not want to admit to Oliver was that she was not actually thinking about Holly and her nursery school at that moment, but about Nanny Ali. She was worrying that a precipitous wedding might appeal as odd to those at 'the palace', where Coco was already supposed to be married.

Whatever happened she did not want anything endangering her new commissions for the Prince's children. Oliver and his demands were just a nuisance, but Coco's commission for Prince Ali's children would give her, and Holly, a much needed basis upon which Coco could build for the future, something positive, which was more than the sporadic designing offers that she received from theatrical managements could guarantee her at that moment.

Just then the telephone rang.

Coco picked it up, seating herself on the tall kitchen stool as she did so. It was someone calling from Australia, person to person.

'I am afraid Coco Hampton's not here at

present. Could you call back in an hour?' Coco told the operator, putting on a different voice, and then she quickly put the phone down, and sighed. She could not believe that she had just agreed to marry Oliver. It was a nightmare.

'Anything the matter, Coco?' Oliver looked suddenly concerned.

'No,' she lied.

Chapter Fifteen

Elsie had put on weight. It was inevitable. All that time spent in Italy eating pasta and enjoying long film lunches in the shade. Portly looked at her with some affection. The weight she had put on actually suited her. It gave her a more mature look, although she was even now moaning about the need to lose it.

'Actually, Elsie, you have never looked better. Being away from everyone and everything has benefited you.'

'*Benefited* me, really, has it, Portly? Really, just listen to you, you're so avuncular! I shall start calling you Uncle Porters from now on.'

'No, you shan't. I am not your uncle and never will be. And God forbid that I should be landed with such a naughty niece.'

Portly placed a plate of his best chicken pie in front of Elsie, and then he stood back and surveyed the rest of the table, making sure that she had everything she might need. Salts and peppers, butter for her potatoes, wine in her glass.

'You are not to start slimming today,' he

warned. 'I have spent hours making this pie and I expect you to do more than eat it, I expect you to enjoy it.'

Elsie smiled. She had a good smile that reflected in her large eyes, but not as good as Oliver's, which they both knew was the smile of the century. Obedient to Porter's command, because she dared not be anything else, she picked up her knife and fork, and started eating. As she did so, she found herself suffused with a melancholy that was as pervasive and powerful as any she had ever felt. As Portly bustled about serving fresh peas and tiny early potatoes before finally sitting down opposite her, the very familiarity of his concern, his all-embracing kindness took her back to the dear days of their life in Tadcaster. Portly cooking, Oliver spouting some rubbish or another, Elsie deeply concerned with something as world-shattering as the colour of a new lipstick, or the length of a new skirt. She remembered the early mornings which were filled with nothing more important than the purchase of a fresh, warm loaf from the baker, the early afternoons that were filled with nothing of greater relevance than the purchase of a perfect pen, or a length of ribbon, or an old-fashioned button. She remembered how much Oliver had loved her, endlessly and seamlessly, how they had sometimes never stirred from their shared room until lunchtime, and how Portly had absented himself until it was time to cook, when he always seemed to prepare the perfect meal for any particular moment or occasion. Late lunches, early suppers, informal teas, midnight feasts, Portly always seemed to have the ideal menu waiting for them all.

'This is a bit like Tadcaster, isn't it? Except now we are all so successful, it's not a bit like it, is it?'

Portly did not want to think about Tadcaster. While he had, at the time, been ecstatic to be invited to live with Elsie and Oliver, it had nevertheless been an uneasy time for him, a halfway house between the utter failure that he had experienced after being cleaned out by Donald Bourton, and the prospect of success to come.

'How do you think the asparagus goes with the chicken? It's the first time I have done it like that.'

'It is perfect, Porters old thing, perfectly perfect. But what I want to know is, now we are all successful, do you think we are *happier* than we were? I mean – before? Do you think we are all happier? We are a tiny bit famous too, aren't we? Not very, but just a bit?'

Elsie knew that Portly would understand exactly what she meant.

'I don't think we are particularly successful yet, Elsie. Soon we may be, but we have, as yet, to confirm our position in the field, as the saying goes.'

'I have more money in the bank than I ever dreamed of, really I have. It's actually burning a hole in my pocket.'

'Very possibly, but you mustn't let it burn a hole, because you are going to need that money, you know. For the bad times ahead, for the times when you change categories, when something is a flop, when you are ill, for those times. You will need that money more than you will be able to credit it.'

'I never think of tomorrow.'

'No, nor should you have to. That is why I am here, to look after your money for you, Elsie, take care of it for that inevitable rainy day.' Portly looked very serious as Elsie realised the import of what he was saying to her.

'You are going to look after my money for me?' For the first time uncertainty crept into Elsie's voice, and she stared at Portly, trying not to look panicked.

'Yes, I would suggest that I do. I would like to look after your money for you, and make sure that the future is quite safe for you, so that you need not give it another thought. Keep your thoughts for the scripts I send you, and let me look after your doh ray me.'

Alarm bells started to sound in Elsie's head. Of a sudden the memory of all the dust-ups over the sinking of Cosgrove and Bourton came back to her, together with Dottie's voice saying, over and over again, 'Never, *ever* leave your money with your agent or your accountant. Don't matter if they tell you they're keeping it for tax, or keeping it for a rainy day, *always* insist that it goes straight to your bank, and I don't mean that it must go to your bank today – I mean it must go to your bank yesterday.'

'I, er – I, er, I'm not sure that I want to bother you

with my money, Porters, darling, really I don't.'

'I am, Elsie. I know you actresses. Once back in London – bang – it will all go, just like that. Much better for me to manage your money for you, invest it soundly, give you a dress allowance, all that kind of thing, make sure that you have a nest egg for a future which might one day not be quite so roseate. I am doing that for all my actors and actresses, and they all see the sense in it.'

Portly did not usually mention other actresses in front of Elsie, but of course now that he had she became distracted, both curious and jealous, all at the same time.

'How's Juliet Tatami doing?'

Juliet Tatami was currently a very fashionable musical star. Half Oriental, half English, she was both beautiful and talented, and now moving into legitimate theatre, as they both knew – although Elsie was pretending *not* to know.

'Juliet is about to be signed up for a television series, starring opposite George Ludlum.'

'Oh, *George* – he was on *The Roman Legion* with me last year. Send him my love, won't you?'

They both knew that Ludlum and Elsie had enjoyed a brief and completely satisfactory affair. Refugees from boredom on the film set, they had gone everywhere together, and parted a few weeks later with, as the song went, no regrets.

'George has signed with the agency, did you know that?'

'No, I didn't. Goodness, Portly, you *are* fashionable now.'

490

'Goodness has nothing to do with it, Elsie, and you know it.'

A small silence followed, and then Elsie, who had been deliciously seduced as always by the beauty and lightness of Portly's cooking, asked him, 'Do you think Juliet Tatami has sex appeal, Portly?'

'As far as producers and directors are concerned? Yes, quite definitely. As far as I am concerned, I really would not like to say. I represent her, she is a good actress, a nice person, that is all I know, really.'

'Now you're being diplomatic.'

'What else would you have me be?'

'Anything but that. Anything but *safe*.'

Elsie was now feeling suspicious of Portly and his relationship with Miss Tatami.

'If I say she has no sex appeal then you are going to ask yourself, "What kind of agent is this? And if he says that about Juliet Tatami what does he say about Elsie Lancaster?" If I say she has bags of sex appeal, you are going to say to yourself, "He is favouring Juliet Tatami more than me", so either way, I am doomed.'

Elsie laughed. They both knew that Portly was right, and could not be much righter. Whatever he said in answer to a demand from Elsie to rate another actress's appeal would be the wrong answer. It was just a fact. Better by far to talk about herself and revel in eating the perfectly delicious-looking queen of puddings that Portly was now placing in front of her.

'I am never going to lose weight with you as my agent.'

More laughter, and lunch continued in much the same way as it had used to do in the days gone by in Tadcaster, the mood happy and relaxed, each person knowing each other completely, faults and virtues alike, yet trusting and loving each other as friends, sharing common interests and dislikes, able to see each other's point of view.

It was only later, when she had gone back to her newly rented flat with a large bundle of television scripts under her arm, that Elsie remembered that Portly had taken charge of her money, and that, for some reason she could not name, she had allowed him to do so.

Once she reached home, Elsie tried to push away Dottie's awful warnings about such matters, the fund of terrible stories that she had always related to anyone and everyone who would listen. About how so-and-so had gone to Broadway, leaving precious tax money with his agent, only to return and find it gone. About how a certain famous actress had left all her savings in the agency account only for the agent to go bankrupt. All Dottie's stories were true. Elsie knew this, she had always known it. Dottie might be the nearest thing to Medusa on a bad day, but she never, ever lied about such things, and Elsie knew that she would ignore her at her peril.

She put her head in her hands. To have to tell Portly of all people that she did not want him to hold on to her money was such a terrible prospect, it was almost inconceivable. It would be tantamount to telling him that she did not trust him. She opened the first of the television scripts that he had given her, and frowned. One glance at even the layout told her that they looked very different from a play script; so much so that just at first it did not seem as if what the actors did or said really counted for much. Gradually her eyes grew accustomed to the appearance of these very different scripts, and equally gradually the fascination of the potential of live television started to grow on her.

Relatively speaking it was still quite a new medium which had not, as yet, been used in all the ways in which it perhaps could be used. Of a sudden, as she read on, Elsie realised that the possibilities for this new type of playwriting and acting could be endless.

The ability of the camera to get in so close to an actor that it could see what he was thinking meant that an actor's technique had to look as natural as a person in the seat next to you on a bus or a train. That was how intimate it was.

And yet it was live, so that, unlike film, it was not completely in the hands of the technicians. It was, Elsie suddenly saw, a new and better form of theatre for the actor, since the smallest gesture could suggest everything, the least expression convey a million thoughts. On stage the same gestures and expressions would have to be magnified at least three or four times to be as effective, and yet might fail to be so.

493

For some reason Elsie had never brought any of these thoughts to bear upon her art, probably because all the time that she was growing up in the boarding house Dottie had never had a television, and refused to consider the new medium as having any possible artistic merit.

'I would never keep a television,' she would announce every now and then, as if Mr Logie Baird's invention was a tiger or a rhinoceros, needing a cage and exercise, not to mention vast quantities of food.

However, despite never watching it, Dottie nevertheless felt quite able to heartily despise the medium. She thought both television and film were rubbish, and said so, often and loudly. Theatre, theatre, theatre, was all that had mattered to Dottie, and indeed to Elsie, until now. Now it was quite different. Now she wanted nothing better than to try it.

Now, seeing how television could be, how daring its drama could be, just how innovative, made theatre seem old-fashioned and out of date, not to mention almost hopelessly amateur. Theatre, by its nature, had to be large of gesture, loud of voice, all the time striving to make its effects. Live television on the other hand could produce a form of drama that could be as light or as dark as it wished, using only the lightest of strokes; and yet at the same time, in terms of storytelling, it could be just as effective as a film.

As she stared ahead of her Elsie realised more and more the advantages of this new medium. For a start, from the actor or actress's point of view, working in television would be so much more comfortable. No more endless and often pointless tours, playing to fifteen people on a snowbound, foggy night. No tatty digs, or flats, and no endless repetition. In television all the time would be spent on rehearsals, on getting your performance polished and right – to play for just one first night to millions of people in the comfort of their own homes.

Elsie picked up the telephone and dialled Portly's number.

'I want to do it.'

Portly, busy as usual in his kitchen, quickly turned off his radio.

'You want to do which, Elsie?'

'All of them, any of the scripts, I don't really care, I just want to do television.'

'Good. Leave it all to me. If I have anything to do with it, you will be in a series within weeks. More than that, you will be in a *hit* series.'

'Which one?'

'The Edwardian one, of course! Playing the maid.'

'That's a series, the one with the maids and butler and things, that's a *series*?'

'Yes, Elsie darling, didn't I tell you? That is just the opening episode. The scripts are all being written as plays in their own right, but it is nevertheless a series, and you are going to play the maid who is in love with the son of the house, and no more to be said.'

Elsie put down the telephone. She had seldom heard Portly so buoyant. She picked up the receiver again.

'Who else is going to be in the series, Porters old thing?'

'I am putting Juliet Tatami up for the other maid.'

'I thought you might be.'

'And rumour has it that Howard Grey has already been cast as the butler. That the part was written with him in mind.'

'Oh yes – Howard. He used to stay with – he used to stay with us. Even Dottie liked Howard Grey, which is saying something.'

'Don't know what else is happening, but I will keep you up to date, darling, don't worry.'

They put down their telephones without saying goodbye, their newest affectation with each other, which they both found vaguely amusing. Then Portly danced round his kitchen for a few seconds. If he could get Elsie Lancaster and Juliet Tatami on television, then the world would be at his feet, because all the others would soon see the sense in it, conquer their nerves, and follow suit. And what Elsie did not know, and Portly would not tell her, was that Portly had a contact in the producer's office, so he knew that the director was aching for Elsie to be signed for the part of the maid, that he would do anything to get both Elsie and Juliet signed up for the series.

'We live in exciting times,' Portly told himself and his small, fashionably neat kitchen, because at that moment there was no one else to tell.

Elsie on the other hand was not in quite such a joyful frame of mind. She wanted the series all right, and she wanted to play the part of Cosette the little English maid with ambitions to be a music hall star as much as she wanted to go on breathing, but she did not want Juliet Tatami playing the Cockney scrubber with the heart of gold. Juliet might steal some much needed thunder from Elsie, and that would never do. No, she would have to talk Juliet out of doing the part, and into doing something else, and the way to do that was not to talk to her directly, but to get through to her none the less. She thought for a few minutes, and then she picked up the telephone, knowing exactly how to go about pulling Miss Tatami off the scent.

'David, darling, *Elsie* here.'

'*Elsie*. Darling.'

David Miller was Juliet's best friend, but not her lover. That particular position, Elsie suspected, was being currently occupied by Portly. She had nothing to go on, of course, and she knew that if she tried to wheedle confirmation about this particular affair out of Portly, it would get her precisely nowhere. Portly was always the soul of discretion. Unfortunately.

On the other hand, David, Juliet's best friend, was the opposite. David could be relied upon to be completely indiscreet. Within five minutes of Elsie's telling him that she was going to turn the series down, because she had heard the rest of the scripts were rubbish, he would be ringing Juliet and urging her to do the same, because he had heard that the rest of the series was a complete letdown. Meanwhile Elsie herself would ring Portly and suggest that he put David up for the part of the footman, which if he was offered it David would immediately accept, because he, unlike Juliet, was not in demand, and grateful for any offer that came his way.

Having effected all this, Elsie picked up the script and started to read it once again. Her part needed to be larger, of that there was no doubt.

But just before she began to pick the play to pieces, looking for sections where the role of Cosette could be enlarged and made more effective, she could not help reflecting that, whatever she liked to think to the contrary, she was still very much the young Elsie Lancaster – the survivor. More than that, she was still very much Dottie's granddaughter.

Dottie's wheeling and dealing had been something that Elsie had grown up with. She knew how to do it. She had learned at Dottie's knee that it was a dog-eat-dog world, and that it was everyone's duty to go for what they wanted and expect everyone else to do the same. Earning your living in and out of the theatre was all about endurance, and nothing to do with goodness, and if her upbringing had not taught her that it had taught her nothing. Besides, she was only doing to Juliet Tatami what she would do to Elsie. And then some.

* * *

Following his first call from Australia, Coco had been rung by Aeneas Mayo almost the moment that his aeroplane touched down. He sounded as excited at meeting her again as she felt at hearing his voice. In fact just listening to him brought the pre-Holly days back to Coco, those days of long ago when there was no one for whom she had to get up, no one about whom she needed to worry, no one whose slightest sound in the night would wake her as if it was the loudest alarm bell in the universe.

Those other days, the pre-Holly days, had been the saving for the Austin Healey days, the days of total immersion in her own personality, in her appearance, in her presentation to the world, and they seemed to have gone for ever, never to return, until she started to dress to go out to meet Aeneas Mayo. Standing in front of her mirror, of a sudden, Coco felt as she had done then. And certainly to look at her figure you would never really have guessed, she told herself, that she had had a baby. She was as trim as she had ever been, and in a blue velvet suit with frogging on the jacket and wearing a pair of long, black leather boots she felt not just young again, but herself again. The person who had been missing for so long, Coco Hampton, was back – perhaps, she suddenly thought, never to disappear again?

The Italian restaurant where they had agreed to meet was as full as all Italian restaurants in London at that moment seemed to be, so full that just at first Coco felt giddy at the sight of all those people, all fully engaged in the growing politics of swinging Sixties London. As she stood waiting for the head waiter to indicate the correct table, girls passed her wearing startling new geometric hair cuts, and gymslips with blouses with long pointed collars and elaborately cuffed sleeves. Men in dark silk Italianate suits and shirts with gold pins pulling the collars together swung past, all too confident and seemingly rich, everyone smoking, laughing, drinking. For Coco, coming as she had from the nursery quiet of her day-to-day existence, it was as if she had been dropped into a strangely exuberant foreign land. She felt out of place, old-fashioned, wrong-footed. Her long hair brushed into a bow at the nape of her neck, her velvet suit, seemed strangely out of place among so many gymslips, as if she had, for that evening, stepped down from a painting for a few hours – to visit the future.

'Coco!'

'Aeneas!'

He was so late that she had begun to think that he had forgotten all about their date, and had actually been contemplating going back to the flat, when, of a sudden, he emerged from the crowded floor, and arrived at the table.

'I am so sorry! God, that director! He just adores to keep everyone waiting, won't let anyone go. And the last scene – he made me do twelve takes. Imagine? *Twelve takes*, and what for? Nothing! It will be sure to end up on the cutting room floor, as well as making me late to meet you.'

Unimaginably Aeneas was just the same. Living and working in Australia had given him, if anything, an even more easy-going manner, not to mention a tanned skin, and hair that was streaked by the sun.

'You look wonderful, Coco.'

'So do you, Aeneas.'

Of a sudden Coco was an actress again, unselfconsciously complimenting Aeneas on his appearance the way that actors and actresses who are friends so often do, and much as the proud owners of motor cars inspect each other's vehicles they now openly looked over each other's chassis with interest and appreciation.

Coco had been in dread that everything would have changed between them, that the casual banter that shared experiences on a film set promote would no longer be possible, but it was far from being so. No sooner had they sat down together than everything started up again. The jokes, the exaggerated stories, the non-stop chatter about everything and nothing, it was all there once more, as was the old Coco. She was well and truly back, thank heavens. It was just as if nothing at all had happened to her since she last had dinner with Aeneas.

'Listen, I'm called all week, but free Saturday. Have lunch?'

'Can't Saturday—'

'Because?' Aeneas managed to look droll, hurt and curious, all at the same time.

Coco pulled a face. 'Getting married.'

Now Aeneas managed to look not just hurt, but amazed.

'Not married married, just married.'

'There's a difference?' His expression had gone back to being both droll and curious.

'Yup.' Coco leaned towards him. 'An old friend of mine, remember? Oliver Lowell—'

'Lover Lowell?'

'Yup. Him. He has to be married or the Kass Organisation won't cast him as the Messiah.'

Aeneas did not shout with laughter at that, he exploded with it. 'My God! Can you credit it?'

'I can believe anything to do with Oliver,' Coco grumbled, raising her eyes to heaven.

'So will you be free after you're married, Mrs Lowell?'

'Of course.'

'Dinner, Saturday night?'

'Love to, really. I'll book a babysitter.'

'That part of the Kass Organisation plans for you, too?'

'No.'

'Some long term thing?'

'No. A very, very short term thing, filming, after you went to Australia. I was missing you.'

There, it was out. She looked at Aeneas, who merely nodded.

'I know. Happened to my sister, but she's happy now.'

'Really? What happened?'

Aeneas smiled. 'Oh, nothing. She remet some-

502

one she had once been in love with, and they lived happily ever after.'

Coco's eyes dropped, and she looked away. Aeneas touched her hand.

'Cigarette, Miss Hampton?'

'Love one.'

'I've never forgotten you, Coco Hampton.'

'No?'

'No.'

'We've both been through a lot really, haven't we?'

'But, somehow stayed the same.'

'Yes, we have, haven't we?'

The truth of this suddenly dawned on Coco, and seconds later on Aeneas. It was as if they were both looking at an old photograph, from that time long ago, when Aeneas had somehow got her through filming, and all that. She remembered his suede jacket and his boots, he remembered her amber bracelets and their mutually madly glamorous aura.

'Meet you after the marriage, because it certainly is not going to be a wedding.'

'That has to be one of the best lines ever.'

They kissed in the doorway of the flats, and Coco thought how funny it was that when they were kissing as themselves they didn't have to fake it. She started to laugh as they broke.

'What?'

'Nothing really. I'm just so astonished we're not kissing each other's chins!'

* * *

There was a long silence in the dining room of the Plunkett manor house. To say it was long in normal terms would be an understatement, because this particular silence was actually more than long, even in terms of that particular household. It was a marathon of a silence, a silence that to someone coming fresh upon the scene might have appealed as a solemn silence, a silence to mark a national remembrance, or the passing of a loved one – which in the minds of those intent on reading their newspapers it might as well have been, since all those concerned were at that moment reading an account of Oliver Plunkett's marriage to his childhood sweetheart, one Coco Hampton. A wedding to which, as it happened, none of them had been invited.

John Plunkett was the first to raise his head, lower his newspaper and speak.

'I see that the Tories lost the by-election at Brimfield.'

From this mild remark Richard and Newell knew at once that their father was firmly marking their cards as to how he expected them to treat the front page news about their brother and his new wife, 'Lover Lowell's Lover' or the 'Messiah's Missus', depending on which newspaper they were concentrating upon.

'They should never have fielded Dandy Holbroke. He is simply not *Yorkshire*, far too London. He was just not right, was he?' Richard asked the still sepulchral dining room.

Another long silence, during which neither a

504

cup nor a fork, neither a spoon nor a piece of toast, was taken up or laid down, until, finally, from John Plunkett, in answer to Richard's open question, came a very heavy-sounding *no*. It was a final no, a no to end all nos, a no which to all those in the dining room, his butler included, sounded ominously like a door shutting firmly, and for ever.

After clearing breakfast Clifton hurried off to telephone Master Oliver as soon as he could. It took him some time to get hold of his former charge, who sounded surprised and somewhat put out that Clifton wanted to know why he had been photographed getting married, and not told anyone of this fairly major event in his life.

'Oh, sorry, Cliffie, I meant to send you all a telegram, but it happened so fast. Tell everyone that it's not a real marriage, would you? Nothing like that. It's the Kass Organisation, they won't let me play the Messiah if I'm not married, you know? Ridiculous, but there you are anyway. You understand, Cliffie, so you explain. It's just a reggie office marriage, in name only, no um – consummation or anything, and all that, just to keep the Kass Organisation quiet. Nothing more to it, really, and when I come back from filming in Israel we'll just wait a bit and then get an amicable divorce, all very friendly, and all that.'

'I see.'

'Good I got the part, don't you think, though, Cliffie? I got it over all the rest of the usual mob. They all went up for it. And I say, Cliffie, you'll like this, I only got it because I am working class! You know, father was a carpenter, and all that. I thought you would like that. I'm playing it deep, deep Yorkshire, because the director is convinced that the Messiah would have had a rural accent. So, wish me luck, Cliffie, and send all the rest of them my best, and I'll be back in about two months. No, six weeks. Well, you know films. It all depends on the weather.'

'Well, good luck, Master Ollie, and I hope I see you when you get back.'

'Course you'll see me, Cliffie, who else?'

Oliver put the phone down, yawned yet again, and wandered off back to his bed. It was only as he lay back, head against the pillows, eyes firmly on the ceiling above him, listening to Coco bathing and singing to Holly, that it suddenly came to him that Cliffie had not sounded quite himself. If he had the energy, which he assuredly did not, he would have hauled himself out of bed and gone back to the telephone, but since he was still tired, and it was Sunday morning, he fell back to sleep again, and only gave Cliffie another thought when he finally arrived in Israel, and for once remembered to send him a postcard.

With Oliver's departure Coco was once again free to occupy her own flat with Holly, ask Aeneas round to dinner, pursue her sewing for 'the palace', and finally call on Nanny Ali and her charges.

Once again the doors of every room were

506

opened by uniformed servants, and once again the myriad royal children were presented to her. If Coco had been worried by the unwanted publicity surrounding her marriage of convenience to Oliver Lowell, it had rather the opposite effect on Nanny Ali.

'How exciting to marry an actor, my dear, and take him as husband number *two*. Such a handsome fellow he looks in his pictures. But, my dear, will he take you away from your sewing? Gentlemen can be strange in that way, very possessive.'

Coco thought of telling Nanny that her marriage to Oliver was only one of convenience, and what was more she had not had a first husband, but then seeing the excited expression in the other woman's eyes she decided that discretion was far better. Let her think what she liked. It was immediately obvious that Nanny Ali was convinced that Coco led an exciting life, and could not have cared less about how many husbands she had enjoyed, as why would she not, living as she did in a household with a man who had enjoyed many, many wives? Instead of blurting out the reality of her situation, therefore, Coco took out the first of her commissions, and held it up to the light for Nanny to see.

Nanny took the first of the seven velvet, smocked coats, with their matching purses, and held it up.

'But it's exquisite, a work of art.'

'There are six more of them, all different colours.'

Coco started to unwrap the rest of the coats, keeping a firm eye on Holly who was being given a gentle ride on a rocking horse by one of the many nursery maids.

'It's all right, my dear, Rose is very careful.'

Coco, who was unused to having to trust anyone else with Holly, nodded, but her maternal eye remained vigilant. She had never forgotten finding Gladys in a storm of tears the one and only day she had been left to babysit for a couple of hours. Holly may not have been planned but she was totally wanted.

Perhaps because of this the heartache that she felt when she received a bouquet of flowers and a note from Aeneas, although certainly more than she would have wished, was also less than she would have imagined before Holly had arrived.

Can't do Thursday for dinner, will be in touch v.v.soon. Aeneas.

She expected to hear nothing more from him. She knew how it was with actors, particularly handsome actors. Women were like taxis; there was always another one along in a minute. She therefore put the whole matter out of her mind and went back to her sewing. There was nothing else that a sensible person could do. After all, her security depended on her sewing now; she had not been offered any work in the theatre for some time, therefore her 'palace' commissions were more important than ever. Seven taffeta dresses to make, followed by seven tweed dresses and matching coats. All worked in the best materials, fabrics that were a joy to cut and sew, which she would never be allowed to use in the theatre, not with the ever vigilant eye of managements keeping the costs down. Nanny Ali was quite different. She seemed to like the costs going up.

'My dear, just wait until the next birthday party we give. It will put the noses of those snooty Peter Pan nannies right out of joint when they see our little princesses in their beautifully made dresses. They will turn emerald green with envy, and serve them right. And they will never, ever again look down their noses at us for being foreign. No, not ever.'

She had sighed with contentment, imagining the scene, and Coco had returned home, her feelings momentarily lightened. Hours later Aeneas phoned and those same feelings were not just lightened, but heightened to a point that she would not have thought possible. He was coming round, soon, soonest; there had been yet more delays in filming but he had not stopped thinking about her, not for a minute, not for a second. Moments later Coco was waltzing round the flat with Holly in her arms, Clarence the pug trotting happily behind.

Portly was furious with himself. He had made certain rules when he took up the reins at the agency, and one of them was that, whatever happened, he would not, ever, have an affair with anyone whom he was representing. Throwing caution to the wind he had finally broken one of his own golden rules and succumbed to the charms of Miss Juliet Tatami, and as a result, it seemed to him, he had now lost both a potential star and a beautiful girlfriend. For this reason alone he could have kicked himself good and hard.

How it had come about was fairly bewildering. One minute she had been only too keen to do television, seemed very taken with the first script of the Edwardian series – as was Elsie Lancaster – and the next minute she had turned on it, and him for even suggesting it. As actresses were wont to do, she had then decided that her agent was entirely to blame for putting her up for television rather than film, and had left the agency for an altogether more powerful organisation whose leading partner had been only too happy not just to poach her, but to have an affair with her too, following which he had done a deal with the Kass Organisation and had Juliet cast as Mary Magdalene in the new film *The Messiah* which was being shot in Israel, and starred Portly's ex-friend and writer, Oliver Lowell.

It was altogether horribly humiliating, and made Portly realise, as always, that there was no one else to blame but himself, and he had as usual mismanaged everything to a degree which was – well – humiliating was the only word for it.

The fact that Oliver had suddenly upped and married Coco Hampton did at least mean that Oliver would not be able to take the usual ruthless advantage that star actors took on location, and have an affair with Juliet himself. But this was small comfort compared to the discomfort of knowing that both Oliver and Juliet were now lost to the agency, probably for ever. Not to mention Coco. Because Coco, now married to Oliver, would surely drop Portly?

'What a mess of potage,' Portly told Art, his new Irish wolfhound puppy. 'Worse than a mess of potage, it is a cauldron of potage, and I hate myself more than ever, Art, because I just don't seem able to learn from past mistakes. What sort of person am I? I mean to say – what?'

At that moment the telephone on his desk rang and Portly, reluctantly, picked it up. It was only when he was at home with Art that he found he could have really intelligent conversations, man to wolfhound conversations that covered the whole territory, so refreshing after the kinds of business conversations that he had, by rote, at the office.

'Portly, it's Coco Hampton.'

They both paused at that announcement.

'Don't you mean Coco Lowell?'

They both laughed.

'No, I do not mean Coco Lowell, Portly, and I must come round and see you, if you don't mind, just to straighten a few things out.'

'Wouldn't you rather I came to *you* – you know, because of the baby?'

'No, no, really, I would rather come to you. Besides, I really need to be somewhere neutral to say the things I have to say, I don't know why.'

'All right, pop in a taxi and come round. I have just finished putting the finishing touches to a rather splendid bread and butter pudding, which I think you will enjoy, unless of course you've passed the pudding stage?'

'Can't wait.'

Coco fairly bounded through the door, and like all nice people she did not bother to push the over-friendly Art off her beautiful hand-made silk skirt, but sat down in one of Portly's large squashy chairs and stroked Art's majestic if puppyish muzzle with every display of enjoyment.

'New person?'

'Very new person.'

'We have a new person too.'

'Really?'

'Mmmm.' Coco took hold of the drink that Portly was offering her. 'Yes, a pug.'

'Name of?'

'Clarence. Pugs have to have pompous names, because they are so full of themselves. They all think they are mastiffs, really they do. I bought him for Holly, really.'

'Of course.'

'And to annoy Oliver. He doesn't know which end he hates most, the back or the front.'

'How *is* Ollie?'

'Delicious drink, Porters old thing.' Coco smiled happily, ignoring the question. 'Goodness, it is nectar. Don't tell me what you put in it. It is nectar, the drink of the gods, and I am in heaven.'

'I hear you married him.' Portly poured another cocktail from the mixer, this time for himself. He sipped it thoughtfully, having never tried this particular combination before, and then nodded happily. Coco was right, it was nectar, quite definitely. 'Yes, I heard you married Oliver. Quite sudden it was, I heard.'

'Yes, I did. But it is only a marriage of convenience, you know? I owed Ollie, you see, Portly. When I found I was preggers with Holly I did not know which way to turn so I went to Oliver and he was very good and found this nursing home filled with gentle nuns, and so I owed him.'

'Which was why you decided you should marry him?'

'Yes, but not to please Oliver, to please the Kass Organisation. It was touch and go, you see, for Ollie, whether or not he would get the part of the Messiah. And when his agent— what's his name, the one who took him on when he walked out on you and Tad Protheroe after *The Magic of Love* . . .'

'Patrick Bates,' Portly prompted, through gritted teeth.

'Yes, him. He found out and rang suggesting that Oliver should get married, and that would put an end to all the problems. And he couldn't really ask anyone else, could he? I mean, could he? After all, first of all, I owed him, and second of all, well, there was no one else he could trust, not after he broke up with Elsie. By the way do you know what has happened to poor old Elsie Lancaster?'

Portly nodded. Yes, he did know what had happened to *poor old* Elsie Lancaster. She had been cast in a new television series and just about to start work when the whole thing had been postponed for another three months because the company was unhappy with the scripts. Portly explained this to Coco in as short a way as was perfectly possible, making quite clear, as he always did with all his actors and actresses, that a postponement was not a cancellation.

'So what's she doing until the series starts?'

Coco's voice had taken on the pleasant tone of a young woman who, although not wishing any harm to come to the individual being discussed, was nevertheless not wholly displeased at the idea that she might be having a tough time.

'Elsie's in Tadcaster, acting her socks off. I am going up to see her next week. She will be giving us her Blanche Dubois, very interesting too, I should have thought, particularly since she is about twenty years too young for it.'

'Back in Tadcaster? That's a bit of a come-down, isn't it, after films?'

'She wanted to get back to the theatre.'

'Yes, but *Tadcaster*, bit genteel for our Elsie, isn't it?'

'We owe Tadcaster a great deal, all of us. After all, if it had not been for Tadcaster we would never have had our first hit. No, we owe them a lot, Coco.'

'You bet, but I mean – *Tadcaster*.'

*   *   *

Although Elsie could not have known it, Coco was quite right about Tadcaster. Elsie had returned to it expecting to find it the same, which it was, the only problem being that although it indeed was exactly the same, she was not. She had changed. She was no longer the same Elsie Lancaster, straight out of working in a café, she was Elsie Lancaster straight out of filming in Rome, not to mention a long West End run in *Love To Popeye*.

And although she rented the same flat, because Oliver was no longer there, and Portly was no longer there, her feelings of isolation increased even before she went back to work with a new company, all of whom deeply resented a West End and film actress's returning to Tadcaster when, in their quite audible opinions, she could be working anywhere.

It was tiring, and it was tedious, and it made her feel that they might be right. Not even dressing down and leaving all her chic clothes behind in her London wardrobe disguised the fact that Elsie Lancaster was, to them, a star, and as such had no business coming back and playing about on a stage which, in their openly held opinions, should be reserved for people of lesser fortune.

'Portly!'

Elsie had been terrible in the play, but of course Portly could not tell her. As he surmised, she was yards too young for the part, and worse than that, those very qualities that made Elsie a star were completely obscured in the part of a neurotic woman obsessed by her past. Not even a brilliant make-up or the most professional acting could ever get over the fact that if a part did not fit an actress it was as calamitous as a badly fitting suit. The part of Blanche Dubois hung off Elsie, the hem trailing, the waistline sagging, the whole making up the sum of a total disaster which nothing could save.

Naturally Portly was far too discreet to tell Elsie this at the time of visiting her dressing room. The critics might tell her; he would not. Instead he took her out to dinner, and then they went back to the dear old Tadcaster flat of so many, many memories for a nightcap.

'Down memory lane, as my old nanny used to say.'

Portly looked round the magnolia-painted room with its comfortable pre-war chintz furniture and its prints of bunny rabbits at play. The coffee table made from an old chest, the tiny kitchen with the red and white formica cupboards, were all perfectly the same.

'We were all so happy here, weren't we, Elsie?'

Elsie nodded and turned away. 'Very.'

'I spent my whole life cooking for you two, while as far as I remember you two spent your spare time looking for the perfect pen, or nose scissors. Never been so relaxed, and never will be again, I don't suppose. No worries, except where to find garlic, or a bottle of good red wine. No money worries – not really – no telephones ringing, just the performance in the evening, and waiting up for you two with the hot chocolate and the ginger dunkers.'

'Not like that now, is it, Portly darling? Now we all have money, and worries. *We are dancing faster and faster to the tune played by others*. Remember that line in Popeye? And how true it has turned out to be.'

Perhaps it was one brandy too many, or perhaps it was just that she must have known, in a way, what a disastrous choice a return to Tadcaster had turned out to be, but halfway through her second brandy Elsie looked at Portly with eyes now bossed with the effects of alcohol and moaned. 'How could Oliver have married Coco Hampton, and not at least warn me? Bad enough she already had his *baby*, but then to go and marry her, and not *tell* me.'

Portly shook his head, holding up a hand to stop her. 'No, no, you've got that all wrong, Elsie. Coco's baby is not *Oliver's* baby. Coco's baby is someone *else's* baby. He must have told you that, surely?'

'Oh yes. He lied to me about that, yes. So if it was not his, why did he go and marry her, then?' Elsie's lipstick was smudged, and she swayed to the side of her chair before straightening.

'No, really. It is not Oliver's baby. It's someone she met filming, and has never seen since. His baby. Not Oliver's. Really. The baby is not Oliver's baby, that I do know. No, Coco and

517

Oliver are only *friends*, that is all, just friends.'

'Oh really, so that is why he ups and marries Coco, is it?'

'No, really. Besides, Oliver hasn't married Coco because he loves her.'

'Oh, no, of course not, he's married her because he likes her costumes.'

'No, really, Elsie, they really are just friends. No, it is only a marriage of convenience, because of the Kass Organisation. They didn't like his bad press – you know, "Lover Lowell" and all that. They wanted him married before he began filming *The Messiah*.'

'How do you know all this, Portly?'

'Because Coco came round and told me. They're getting annulled or divorced as soon as filming is finished.'

'A marriage of convenience, you say?' Elsie knocked back her brandy and attempted to pour out another, but Portly quickly removed the bottle, so she lit up a cigarette instead.

'Imagine *Oliver* doing anything convenient. It must be a first, the first time Oliver Lowell ever did anything convenient in his whole life, the very first time.'

Elsie started to laugh, but hearing the quality of her laughter, and seeing her eyes filled with tears, Portly's heart sank. Like it or lump it, for better or for worse, Elsie was still in love with Oliver.

Chapter Sixteen

Coco threw down the newspaper, but not on Oliver's bed, on his head.

'Well done! Just so many congratulations are in order, aren't they, Ollie?'

'Please, Coco, I haven't even woken up yet, please!'

'You certainly have not woken up, you have not woken up to the fact that you are a crass idiot, that is what you have not woken up to, Oliver Plunkett! My God, isn't it enough that you have made me *marry* you, and now look!'

'What? What on earth are you talking about?'

'Read, Ollie, just read about yourself, you great banana, see what you have been up to with your life – in the newspaper.' Coco changed her voice to that of a newsvendor crying his wares. 'Read all abaht it, in today's *Daily Vomit*, read all abaht it!'

Oliver switched on his bedside light, just as Coco threw open the curtains of the spare bedroom in her flat. She had sewn and smocked those curtains with her own hands, and they did not at all suit Oliver's occupancy of the room, seeing that they were flowered. He looked pretty silly in the room. A great brown-skinned six foot three hulk spread about the place, as if he owned it, which he jolly well did not.

'Read all abaht it,' she went on, purposefully, 'read all abaht Juliet Tatami having an affair with the Messiah!'

'*What?*'

Oliver shook out the newspaper and started to read the appropriate paragraphs, after which there was a long and deathly silence before he croaked, 'But I *didn't* have an affair with Juliet, I promise you, Coco. How could I, how could I when I had just married *you*?'

'Oh, pull the other one, it has got Big Ben on it, Ollie. Of *course* you had an affair with Tatami. Who else would you have had an affair with – the man playing Joseph? Geoffrey Blumenthal? Or Dame Sarah Codrington? Besides, you're not married to me, that is just a joke gone through for the Kass Organisation, and you know it, so why on earth would you *not* knock off Tatami, please tell me? There is no possible reason why you would *not* knock her off, is there?'

Oliver threw the newspaper across the room.

'The truth is, Coco, I always intended to respect my marriage to you, until this week when we decided to divorce. I always said I should be faithful to you, and that is one truth. And the second truth is that much as I don't expect you to believe me, I did not fancy and do not fancy Juliet, and what is more, *she* made a pass at *me*.'

'And?'

'And I turned her *down*.'

'You turned her down?'

'Yup.' Oliver flung aside the bedclothes and grabbing his dressing gown he started to walk up and down the room. 'Which is obviously why she has done this to me. She has tried to scupper me with tittle-tattle to the press, to upset my position with the Kass Organisation. Kass will go *crazy* with this. It will affect the sales worldwide, it will affect the Americans, you know. The Americans like their Messiahs clean-cut and above-board – they don't want them having affairs. God, this is terrible, just terrible.'

And it was, because of course the press had a field day with Lover Lowell's rumoured affair, following on his marriage, with the actress playing Mary Magdalene.

Portly at once suspected that his rival Patrick Bates was somehow responsible, because agents always suspect other agents as a matter of course. Juliet Tatami could not of course be contacted, and promptly went into hiding before re-emerging to play another fallen woman, this time in a film set in ancient Greece, which was immensely convenient because the press, being too lazy to follow her out to the remote Greek island where the preliminary filming was taking place, were able to continue the story without fear of contradiction. Useless for Oliver Lowell to contradict the rumour, because, as they all knew, contradictions simply furthered the story. So, all in all, no one except the press was happy, least of all the Kass Organisation who promptly claimed that Oliver Lowell had contravened his contract with them, and put all payments to him on hold.

'Not much new there,' Portly told Elsie, who was still having a lousy time in Tadcaster, 'since, in my experience, all payments from the Kass Organisation are *always* on hold. However. Nasty for Oliver, poor old chap. And for Patrick Bates,' he could not help adding a little gleefully.

'Poor old chap, my foot,' Elsie murmured, as she put down the telephone.

She at least was in a good mood. The television series was at last scheduled to go forward. Pretty soon she would be free of a cast that loathed her, and back in what she had now come to think of as proper work.

The same could not be said for Oliver. Following the back-stabbing delivered to him by Miss Juliet Tatami, he found himself so much in the wilderness that even he became frightened. As far as he could gather his father and brothers had put him in Coventry for marrying Coco without telling them. Coco was fed up with him, and quite obviously hated him living in her flat, and not even his agent wanted anything to do with him. In fact, since the undesirability of one client at the centre of a scandal tended to rub off on the others, Patrick Bates had, very politely and firmly, asked Oliver to leave.

And to cap it all, as if it needed capping, *The Messiah* was now being recut for the American market with the emphasis on Joseph rather than the Messiah, so, as his now ex-agent remarked before giving him the boot, 'Oh, and they're probably going to retitle it *Joseph and Mary*.'

Oliver realised that the possibility of Portly's taking him back on his books as a playwright was so remote as to be laughable, particularly since Elsie was still very much with PLL. Yet, remembering just how affable Portly's essential nature was, Oliver did eventually telephone him and ask himself round to the office in the King's Road, if only after downing a couple of very strong beers.

He was unsurprised to find that Portly was now successful enough to be able to afford a personal assistant. Tall, blond, and really rather grand – and probably, if Oliver only knew it, as tough as Portly was not – Constantia was perfect assistant material.

She eyed Oliver with a serenely indifferent expression, smiling politely. They both knew who he was, but nevertheless she asked his name, and he, having given it, was told, not asked, to sit down, while she went to see if *Mr* Cosgrove was free to see *Mr* Lowell.

For Oliver the wait was long and hard, and inevitably, as he waited, his past sins, as well they should, came up before his eyes.

He had been arrogant and selfish, he had been cold and ambitious, he had made the wrong choices about everything and everyone. He would not be at all surprised if Portly refused to see him.

'Mr Cosgrove will see you now, Mr Lowell.'

523

In a way it would have been comforting to find that Portly had not altered at all, but Oliver saw at once that his old friend and partner had changed. He had grown tougher-looking, and the expression in his eyes was not that of a man prepared to take Oliver back into the fold without a fight.

'Portly.'

'Oliver.'

Because he was an actor Oliver realised straight away that Portly was not even prepared to shake his hand. He did not ask him to sit down, forcing Oliver to ask him, in a humble voice, if he minded if he did.

'No, do.' Portly's eyes shifted towards both his smart white telephones, and then back to Oliver. 'In a bit of trouble, are we, Oliver?'

'More than a bit. I am in a lot of trouble, as you probably heard.'

'I did, Oliver, I did. Been kicked out by the man with the receding hairline?'

This was the nearest that Portly could bring himself to naming his arch rival, Patrick Bates.

'Well, yes and no, Portly. I mean, it's not that much of a blow. He was doing nothing much for me before, and even less now – in fact, nothing at all. I might as well be dead, quite frankly. As a matter of fact I feel as though I am dead. Every morning I wake up feeling surprised that I am still alive.'

Oliver stared at a space just behind Portly's head. He was as near to tears as he had ever been, fighting back the humiliation, and feeling as wretched as he had ever done, even when Cliffie left him at his first boarding school all that time ago.

'What do you want to happen?'

'What do I want to happen? I just want to get my confidence back, Portly. I don't care where, or how, I just want a job, acting preferably, because my muse has deserted me ever since *The Magic of Love*. Coco's going mad with me in the flat. You know how Coco is, doesn't like clutter – and boy – am I clutter! My family won't speak to me because I married her without telling them, and they won't listen to Clifton, you know – well, forget it.' He lit a cigarette. 'Suffice it to say I am vermin, to everyone, really I am.'

'You look terrible,' Portly told him, sounding quite affable.

'I know.'

'What sort of acting do you want, Oliver?'

'Anything.'

'Classical?'

'Could do with it. Anything, a cough and a spit, even a toga part, although I do rather hate them, but never mind, I would do a Roman, if pushed.'

'How about tights? Hamlet? Black tights?'

There was a long silence. They both knew that Oliver hated the idea of wearing tights, but he had little choice, which was another thing that they both knew.

'Our Clifton has always said that I would make a good Hamlet.'

'Your Clifton has impeccable taste. And you are the right age too, Oliver.'

'Very well. But who would want me? East Marchand Repertory?'

'No, London. The newly based, altogether in need of star names Royal Company, no less.'

'I thought they were only going for ensembles, as in the Berliner Ensemble?'

'Don't be daft, Oliver, you know the Royal – always giving out to no good effect what they definitely do not mean to practise. Now that you are not simply famous, but just a mite scandalous too, the Royal will jump at you, I am sure.'

'Will you put me up for it?'

'Of course. But I happen to know they will be thrilled to have you, no doubt of it. *Thrilled*. They need a name to kick off the London Season, really. The part is yours for the asking.'

No more to be said. The old friends stood up. The past was behind them. Oliver's throwing over Elsie, and leaving the agency, blaming everyone but himself for a play that he should never have written, let alone allowed to be put on, could not of course be forgotten, yet the miserable experience could be built upon.

'Thank you, Portly.'

'That's all right, dear boy.'

Oliver walked towards the door. Dear boy! They had both used to laugh about agents and producers *dear boying* each other, but then they had both used to laugh a great deal about the people it seemed they had now become.

'Oh, and by the way, Ollie. Sorry about Clifton.'

'Sorry?'

'Yes, you know, sorry that he is not well.'

'I didn't know he wasn't well. He was perfectly fine when I last saw him.'

'Oh? I heard at the Betterton – you know your brother Newell is a member now? We meet quite often.'

'Doesn't surprise me. The Betterton would suit Newell down to the ground, I should have thought.'

'I heard from him that Clifton was not at all the thing. Thought you at least would know about it?'

'No, no, I didn't know. We talked on the phone the other day, but he didn't say anything.'

'Doesn't sound too good, according to Newell.'

Oliver fled down the stairs. It was always the same, in his view. Life took with one hand and gave back with the other. Portly had taken him back, which meant that life must be on the up. On the other hand, Clifton was not well. Could there never be a time when it all evened out into a sunny day with nothing to do but be busy doing nothing the whole day through, as Elsie and he used to sing, walking hand in hand through the streets of Tadcaster?

Elsie. He stopped to think about her for a minute as he passed her photograph in the foyer. God, how he had loved her, and so passionately. He never thought he would love anyone as he had loved Elsie, but then she had seemed to turn on him, and side with everyone else, during the tour of *The Magic of Love* – she had seemed to become someone else, not his darling old Else, someone quite different, someone intent on hating him, blaming him for the embarrassment of the tour, for the empty auditoriums, for the lack of laughter, for the cast turning on her, for everything.

He walked quickly down the King's Road. None of that mattered now. Now he was going to play Hamlet. The part that Clifton had always wanted him to play, the only trouble being that, judging from Portly's expression, Clifton might not be there to see him.

Back in the agency Portly nodded at the beautifully grand Constantia, who gave him her best Giaconda smile.

'I knew he'd do it. I told Antony Mansion last night at dinner that he would – before he'd even walked up the stairs to see me this morning.'

'Of course.'

'I am something of a genius. Admit it, I am.'

'Of course.'

Constantia swayed out of the door, throwing a casual but beautifully tailored smile over her shoulder at Portly. She had a fine figure, a tall, slender young woman with a great deal of *savoir faire*, Portly thought with sudden emotion. She was a great choice for the agency, and perhaps not just for the agency.

'Cliffie.'

Oliver hugged Clifton quite unselfconsciously, and started to give the performance of his career, because even his untutored eye could see that Clifton was deathly pale.

'Good news, Cliffie. Portly has heard from the Royal. They want me.'

'Good news, indeed, Master Oliver.' Clifton looked bravely happy.

'I am now officially signed to do Hamlet, if I have read the runes right.'

'Master Oliver, just what I always thought. You will be perfect. Which company did you say – the Royal?'

'The Royal.'

Clifton breathed out and for a minute or two he did not have to act. His whole life had been spent in trying to hone Master Oliver to become the sort of actor Clifton knew he could be, and now, at last, it seemed he was coming within reach of just that.

'No more shoddy films then, Master Oliver?'

Clifton did not approve of film acting. To him it was not acting at all. He only approved of the theatre. The theatre was what mattered.

'No more shoddy films, Cliffie. Just theatre, theatre, theatre, from now on. One thing, though – thanks to you, I don't have to bone up on Hamlet. I don't only know Hamlet, I know all the other parts. Remember me playing the ghost – my first stab at it – how old was I?'

Clifton's eyes now seemed to brighten as he looked back to the golden years of the past.

'Oh, you must have been all of six years of age. Very good, too. You were very spooky.'

'You were a brilliant Hamlet too, Cliffie, You looked great in tights, which is more than I will!'

They both laughed, and Clifton sipped his whisky. With the impact of the alcohol he seemed to acquire a little more colour.

'Your legs are not your best asset, I will agree, Master Oliver, but neither are they anything to be ashamed of. How is young Miss Coco, by the way? Happy to be married?'

They both laughed again.

'Oh, you know Coco, nothing but *angst* and *drang*, if not *sturm*, too. She hates me being at the flat. I drive her dotty. Nothing must do, but she wants me to move out and go and find a place of my own, but I can't, not while we're meant to be married, I mean to say.'

'I'm having tea with Miss Coco tomorrow, before I go back to Yorkshire.'

'Are you? Why?'

'Oh, you know, we have tea from time to time, or drinks or lunch, always have done. She's my type of girl, you know, Master Oliver. Spirited. I like a spirited woman. Nothing of the doormat about her, and that is the truth. And she makes me laugh, always has done.'

'She never told me that you two met – for these lunches and teas and things.'

'Well, she wouldn't, would she?'

'Why not?'

'She just wouldn't.' Clifton smiled. 'Looking forward to your Hamlet, though, Master Oliver, truly I am. I shall keep going until then.'

Oliver ignored this direct reference to Clifton's shortened future and leaping up went and ordered them both another drink.

'Rehearsals start tomorrow.' The expression in Oliver's eyes became opaque. Hamlet was one of what the older generation of actors called 'the big ones', his first *big* one.

Over tea the following afternoon Clifton met Coco.

'I just don't want Master Oliver to give up on his acting. He's a better actor than he is a writer, Miss Coco. His writing is fine, if he will only stop being so lightweight, but his acting, at its best, is sublime. Truly it is. I know that he will be the Hamlet of his generation.'

'Come and see Holly, Cliffie. She has grown so, so much.'

They walked off towards Coco's flat, arm in arm.

The following morning, before leaving early for rehearsal, Oliver seemed to spring at Coco from behind her own front door.

'I didn't know that you were seeing Clifton – that you have been seeing Cliffie?'

'Of course. Cliffie and I have been friends ever since I was – oh, I don't know. But whenever he brought you down to London and you had to go to the dentist, or like when you were having your tonsils out, Cliffie took me out to tea, usually at Fortnums. He used to buy me strawberry milkshakes and chocolate cake, and then I used to go home and be sick all over Gladys. It was a perfect arrangement. Actually, you did know, you know, Ollie, because I always used to tell you. I think you just forgot.'

'You know he's not well?'

'Really? He seemed quite well to me.' Coco turned away, starting to tidy Holly's toys.

'No, apparently Newell told Portly at the Betterton that Cliffie is not at all well. God, supposing something happens to him? I mean, I don't know how I shall get through Hamlet without Cliffie, Coco?'

Oliver walked towards the door, grabbing his duffel coat which he had flung across a sofa.

'You will get through Hamlet *for* Cliffie, Oliver, because you are an actor *because* of Cliffie.'

'I don't know if I can get through Hamlet if something happens to Cliffie during rehearsals, Coco. Will I get through it? If something happens to him? He looked at death's door when I saw him.'

'Of course you will, Ollie. Gracious heavens, Hamlet is all about death.'

Elsie was facing the television director with all the courage that she did not feel. There was no way that anyone at that moment could have told that they were about to embark on the most successful television series ever put out by a British company. The only thing that anyone in the studio that day could have said with complete certainty was that no one, but no one, knew anything about the medium into which they had just flung themselves. Everyone was hazarding the most enormous guess.

Did close-ups work? Was it better to avoid trick shots, mirror shots, long shots, shots shot through earrings? Was a straightforward attitude to the scripts the best? Should they just tell the story, or should the camera work embellish it? It was all a monstrous adventure, and as the cables flicked and spun across the studio floor, and the wheels on the cameras creaked, in her state of supreme uncertainty Elsie found herself wondering if anyone at home would be able to hear what she said. She had never feared 'drying' in the theatre, but now she feared drying as she had known older actresses and actors to fear it. She trembled, not just on the outside, but on the inside, at the very idea of it. Supposing she dried in front of perhaps fifteen or sixteen million people? Supposing she fell down the stairs? Supposing the door stuck as it had during rehearsal? Supposing old Arthur Mayne, playing the night porter – supposing he dried completely, as he had just done? It was all a nightmare, but not a nightmare from which she could expect to wake up for another thirteen episodes.

'Arthur darling?'

'Yes, Elsie darling?'

'Don't worry, just stand by me and if you go, I'll just carry on as if you haven't.'

'I've got some of it written on my hand.'

'So have I, darling.' Elsie held up her hand.

'Yours?'

'No, yours, darling.'

They both started to laugh.

'It'll be all right, darling.'

'It's not war, is it?'

'No, it's not war, but it could cause pestilence and death.'

They both looked thoughtfully towards the cause of Arthur's constant drying – the director. The untalented bully who had picked on the old actor constantly throughout rehearsal. So overt had been his harassment of the older man that in the end Elsie had been forced to pick on *him*, throwing her script at his head and causing the rest of the cast to shun her at every possible moment.

'We stand shoulder to shoulder, Arthur.' Elsie went on. 'The two musketeers, nil thingy carbor-thingy and all that.'

'No, we will not let the bastards grind us down,' Arthur agreed, putting a trembling finger up to his stick-on moustache which he was terrified might be about to unstick itself during the performance, as it had done at rehearsal.

Afterwards, long afterwards, the first episode of *Golden Days* would go down in the annals of British television history as being the most exciting event of the television decade. Naturally it did not feel like that to the participants, all of whom would really rather have been enjoying a bad bout of measles than being ground into the dust by the experience.

'I don't know why they have to do it *live*? Less and less drama is being done live.'

Portly's words ran round and round Elsie's head as she dashed in and out of the Edwardian sets, as required by the script. In the event, to the relief of both of them, Arthur Mayne, playing the old night porter, did not need to use either his own or Elsie's hand as a prompt, but sailed through his part with all the aplomb of an actor who is completely at home with live television.

The euphoria at the end, when it was all over, almost made doing it live worth it. Almost, but not quite, for Portly, having been in close attendance on the performance, although now convinced that it might be a long-running hit, was equally convinced that the series should be pre-recorded. As he saw it, putting it out live was merely an unnecessary strain on the cast, and a completely capricious whim on the part of little Mr Hitler, the director, who clearly subscribed to the widely held belief that a terrified actor is a better actor.

'Live drama on television is far, far too much strain, particularly on the older actors.'

This was to say the least of it, for as the series, put out at the unlikely time of ten o'clock at night, met not just viewer approval, but viewer delirium, the actors concerned, none of whom except Elsie had been previously famous, now found themselves unable to snatch a cup of coffee in a café without being mobbed by ever growing armies of *Golden Days* fans.

Realising that they had a hit on their hands of fantastic proportions, agents around London found themselves booking lucrative personal appearances for any client who had a part in it. The success of the series was such that fame came not just to the actors and actresses portraying the major characters, but spread its wings over every single member of the cast. And so it was, as happens following the successful recognition of a hit, that whether it was Arthur Mayne as the night porter, or dear old Howard Grey as the butler, everyone in the series had become a star overnight.

However, despite the scale of the success of *Golden Days*, Portly, while happily booking his actors and actresses in and out of episodes, was feeling uneasy. It was a feeling that he now actively dreaded, the *everything is too quiet* feeling.

He tried to put his feelings behind him, he tried to talk himself out of them, but they just would not go away. Something was going to happen, although what exactly it was he could not have even told himself. All he did know was that whenever these feelings occurred he never awoke in the morning without a presentiment of bad times just around the corner.

Portly could not have known it, but Clifton was never going to make the first night of Master

Oliver's portrayal of William Shakespeare's *Hamlet, Prince of Denmark*. The news was conveyed to Oliver by Clifton himself.

Dear Master Oliver,

As you know I have not been quite myself lately, and so it is with great regret that I realise I will not be able to attend the first night of your Hamlet. However, I will be there in spirit, and will come to see a subsequent performance, just as soon as I am up and about again.

As always, Master Oliver, Cliffie

Cliffie's absence meant that, perhaps because of the nature of the tragedy of Hamlet, because it was all about the death of a father, and because he remembered how ill Clifton had looked the day they had met in London, Oliver found himself succumbing to a true state of pre-mourning for his childhood father figure. He did not become Hamlet, he *was* Hamlet. It was inevitable. Cliffie had taken so much of his own father's place, had coached Oliver so endlessly in the part, that as rehearsals gathered pace the dividing line between the Prince of Denmark and Oliver Lowell became virtually invisible to everyone, including himself.

In the ghost Oliver now saw only Clifton, the white, strained face not of the murdered king but of darling old Cliffie, the only man who he could honestly say had been able to show him that kind of unconditional love that is so reassuring to children. The kind that singles children out in their own eyes as being somehow more special than the stars that light the skies.

All in all, as he stepped on to the stage that now famous night, Oliver Lowell was no longer himself. As a result he was nerveless, and not so moved by his own situation as an actor that he could not stand outside himself and move the audience. Because that, as he knew from Clifton himself, was the essential ingredient of a successful performance. If he himself was moved, he would never, ever move the audience.

Even as, quite unknowingly, Oliver indeed became the Hamlet of his generation, it seemed to him that he was able to look down on himself from high above the stage and study his own characterisation. And here it was at last, the detachment that is so necessary to all artistic achievement, present and correct. He saw it himself, as his spirit seemed to move over his body, high above the apron stage, yet all the while he could feel that his body was truly leaden with grief. He mourned his father, he avenged his father, he threw Ophelia away from him, he grieved for his tragic friend – *Alas! poor Yorick*. Alas, poor Clifton. He wondered at the fleeting nature of life, he was torn apart, yet all the time there was Oliver Lowell, high above his own acting performance, watching so carefully, making sure that each cadence was given its full poetic value, that he never, for a second, lost the attention of that other animal, the one that made up the fourth wall: the audience.

As the lights dimmed on the last dreadful

538

seconds of Shakespeare's greatest tragedy, there was that extraordinary stunned silence that so often follows a great acting performance, as if the audience has been holding its breath until at last it comes to and howls its approval.

After taking his calls, Oliver staggered back to his dressing room. For a few seconds he stared at himself, as actors do, asking himself the one and only relevant question – *Was I good enough tonight?* Because, no matter what they said, it was tonight that mattered. He had barely enough time to answer his own question with *nearly* before his door was opened by his dresser, and the world and his wife crowded in to pay court to him, whilst, unbeknownst to Oliver, his own father, John Plunkett, correctly dressed in his evening jacket and bow tie, walked off, unaccompanied by anything except his thoughts, to buy himself a lone drink at the Savoy Hotel.

As his familiar waiter placed the glass in front of him John Plunkett looked up and said, 'Well, Laurie, tonight I saw a great actor.'

'Did you, sir?'

'Yes, I did, Laurie. In fact I saw a very great actor.'

'That is nice, sir.'

'Yes, I saw a great, great actor. I saw Hamlet as Shakespeare must have written him.'

All alone at his table once more John Plunkett raised his brandy glass.

'To Oliver Lowell née Plunkett.'

*   *   *

Elsie had been at the first night, of course, although not with Portly, but escorted by Howard Grey from the cast of *Golden Days*. Howard had been lost in admiration for Oliver's performance. Elsie had too, whilst also hating the interpretation of the actress playing Ophelia.

It was only natural for her to see herself as being able to be better in the role. Not taking *that* speech so fast, not making *that* over-large gesture there. Even so, Elsie had to admit, the actress concerned had not been *that* bad. How could she be against Oliver giving the performance of his life?

After the performance, since it was a fine evening, Elsie and Howard decided against taking a taxi and walked home instead, talking about the play. Howard told her all about previous Hamlets of his generation, and those before that, and then reminisced richly on the usual disasters that had happened to him as a young man acting in repertory theatres all over the country.

'But of course television is going to change all that,' he said, without a trace of sadness. 'It will make the actors' lives much, much more secure, much more comfortable, and yet at the same time it will not be the same. Just think, no more repertory theatres with notices saying *Evening Performance at 7.30 Tonight – Tides Permitting.* No more entrances through the fireplace, none of those kinds of larks, but none of that honing either. Touring and repertory theatre is such a very honing experience for an actor, I always think, don't you?'

Elsie hesitated before answering. She did not want to hurt Howard's feelings but she felt that she could have done without Dottie's honing – or could she? She laughed suddenly.

'My grandmother always said that – "tides permitting". Of course I had forgotten why – that the tides used to really come up into the dressing rooms.'

'Oh they did, darling, they did. And we never minded because it was all back to the café for tea while you waited for it to go out. The tide I mean, and very nice too, this time I mean the tea. Nothing like that hot cup of tea and those sticky buns that kept you warm between matinée and evening performances.'

'No, I suppose not. I used to have a twist of paper with sugar and lemonade powder in it. Dipping a finger in that kept me going all through rehearsals, until at last, it was time to go home.'

Elsie's tone was matter of fact rather than nostalgic. She did not have much time for theatrical nostalgia; when you had to bring home the bacon to help keep the home fires burning there was truly very little time for sentimentality, which, from what Howard now said, he seemed to appreciate.

'I sense you regret a childhood in the theatre. I on the other hand only joined the profession in my teens, and have no regrets. It is the only life, the one and only life. The smell of the size, the excitement backstage, the costumes and the wigs, there's nothing like it, darling, not to my mind. I

541

have had such a happy life, and then to come to this, fame at my age in *Golden Days*. Imagine! And money too. It doesn't seem possible to be paid this much to do so little, and at the same time become a *face* too. I am truly blessed.'

Since they had reached the apartment block where Elsie now lived, Howard leaned forward and kissed her affectionately on both cheeks.

'Good night, darling Elsie. Good night and thank you, a thousand, thousand times, for taking me tonight. I was all for a cup of cocoa and an early night with my lines, and just think, I would have missed the Hamlet of a lifetime, truly I would. I can't thank you enough.'

He waved a hand, first at Elsie and then at a taxi, and seconds later was gone, still waving from the back of the cab. Elsie waved back, feeling both happy and exultant, and at the same time infinitely sad, although she could not have said why.

Chapter Seventeen

Coco stared ahead of her at nothing much. Well, it *was* at something actually, it was at a picture she had painted years ago when Gladys had taken her to Cromer for a short seaside holiday. She remembered the day so clearly; sunlight on a bright sea, Gladys asleep beside her in a deckchair. That was the moment, more than any other, that had made Coco decide that she would never want to lead what was usually termed 'a normal life'. She would always want to spend it in some way other than just being married to a stockbroker or a banker, like Gladys. It was as if she herself had become part of that same sea, part of that same sky, caught up in that carefree moment of nature at ease in its summer guise, and it was then, just past her tenth birthday, that Coco had made up her mind that she never, ever wanted to be ordinary. Now she was twice ten, and more, and only thinking about it to keep her mind off Oliver crying.

Oliver's crying did not embarrass her because Oliver, after all, was a boy, and boys always did cry more than girls, but more than that it did not embarrass her because she loved Oliver. She had always loved Oliver, but now she loved him as an actor and as a man, as well as a person. At last, seeing him not acting Hamlet, but being Hamlet, she had seen the purpose of Oliver, and it was to be a great actor.

'Lover Lowell' was just not Oliver, nor was working for the Kass Organisation in some toshy Biblical epic. The real Oliver was all about real acting. And now he was crying, but the tears were real, not just acting.

'It's just the strain of the last weeks. I'll get you some tea.'

She went to the kitchen, and by the time she came back Oliver had recovered himself.

'It's the strain,' Coco said again, as she handed him the tea, and with a cool hand pushed his thick hair back from his forehead.

'I'm sorry, I didn't want to give way like that—'

'Oh toshy tosh, it's good to cry. In eighteenth-century England men cried *all the time*. Stood up in Parliament and blubbed like babies. It's normal to cry, really it is. What are we given tear ducts for otherwise? It was having the empire that stopped all that. Couldn't cry in front of foreigners and so on, so everyone had to stop up their tear ducts and put on the famous stiff upper lip. But now we have lost the empire, we can cry again. So that's a relief, eh?'

Oliver sipped the sugary tea and nodded, still not trusting himself to be able to speak.

'I never thought he would write to me like that.'

Coco nodded, understanding. She had just read the letter, and while to someone else it might not have appealed as particularly moving, Coco understood exactly and precisely why it had moved Ollie to tears. It was written on writing paper headed *The Savoy Hotel*.

Dear Oliver,

I write to tell you that I attended the first night performance of Hamlet, Prince of Denmark tonight. It was as moving a performance as I have ever witnessed. To say that I think you have the makings of a great actor would be to lie. You are a great actor.

I remain, as always, your loving father, Pops.

Oliver pointed at the letter again now.

'He has never put that before – *never*.'

'What, about being a great actor?'

'No. You know, that.' He pointed to the word *Pops*. 'He has never put that before. It makes up for all that time disapproving of my acting, or what I thought of as disapproval. Having a mass said for my soul every month, and all that. As if I had gone to the devil, which I suppose in his mind I had.'

Coco put a hand over Oliver's hand, and smiled. 'You have come of age with your performance, but so it seems has your father. Just think, he might even have forgiven you for marrying me.'

'He thinks the world of you. You know that.

545

What was it that he always called you? "Oh yes, sparky little thing, Coco, very sparky".'

'Guess what – I'm coming to see your performance again tonight.'

'Really.' Oliver was miles away.

'Yes, bringing a friend and all that.'

Oliver came to suddenly, sitting up. 'Boyfriend? That new boyfriend of yours, are you bringing him?'

'Perhaps. Soon. Maybe. I don't know. Tonight I am bringing a friend, just a friend.'

Oliver sat back. He did not know why, but as long as Coco was married to him he did not want her to have a boyfriend. It would muddle everything up, and besides, he would be sure not to like whoever it was. Bad enough that Coco had already had a baby by whoever it was she had met filming that time. Although the fact that she could not even remember his name was somehow reassuring.

'Do you want us to come back and see you afterwards?'

'Yes, and come out to dinner. If I like your friend. If not we'll come back here and have scrambled eggs.'

Oliver looked at his watch and then sank back among his pillows. Two o'clock in the afternoon and he still had some sleep to catch up with before he left for the evening's performance. By four o'clock he would be unable to eat or drink anything, his whole nervous system geared only to leaving for the theatre, but until then he must sleep.

'To be, or not to be: that is the question: Whether 'tis nobler in the mind to suffer The slings and arrows of outrageous fortune . . .'

Oliver took the soliloquoy at a brisk clip compared to Hamlets of previous generations, as if the question was tearing at him, not as if he was thinking it over.

'To die, to sleep; To sleep: perchance to dream . . .'

In the interval Clifton turned to Coco and said, 'You know, I sometimes think those are the most solemn words ever written in any play. Surely they must be?'

Coco nodded. And Oliver had said them so beautifully, substituting heartbreak where, in other characterisations, poetry had been the sole aim of the actor. So much did he move the audience that each night you could have heard a pin drop.

Going backstage afterwards she went in front of Clifton into Oliver's dressing room.

'You were brilliant, Ollie, and even your old teach thought so.'

Oliver stared. 'My old teach, Coco? *Cliffie?* I didn't know he was in tonight? Cliffie, *here*? Where is he?' Of a sudden Oliver stopped looking like Hamlet and started to look more like his father's ghost.

'Master Oliver.'

Clifton stood in the doorway of his protégé's dressing room, his eyes filled with pride, and of course, seeing him quite hale and hearty, Oliver could not resist hugging him.

'Coco wouldn't say who she was bringing. She wouldn't say. My God, it's good to see you. And you were in, tonight. I was good tonight.' Oliver stepped back suddenly and stared at Clifton. 'And you are – I mean you look – quite all right. Are you quite all right, Cliffie?'

'Never been better, Master Oliver.'

'But I thought – I thought – well, last time I saw you, you didn't seem very *well*, Cliffie. A bit white around the gills.'

'Bad bout of flu in the winter, that's all.'

'I heard – I heard – well, I heard that you were not at all the thing. But you are, you are quite sure you are all right now?'

Clifton smiled. 'Never been better, and now I am going to take you both out to dinner.'

Later, Clifton was pleased to see that Oliver ate like ten men. All in all, it was most satisfactory.

The following morning Clifton rang Coco.

'Can't talk for long, Coco, just about to catch my train.'

'I know, Cliffie, and I am just about to make Master Oliver his brekker, but before I do, do tell me what you used to give Oliver such a fright about your health that time.'

'Oh, just talcum powder mixed in with the normal daytime make-up. Nothing too heavy.'

'And all it took was one lunch at the Betterton with Newell and all London was convinced?'

'Hardly all London, Miss Coco, but I knew if I gave Master Newell the impression that I was not at all well, word would get back to Master Oliver—'

'And he would stop fuffing about and give the performance of his life, which was what happened.'

'He's been doing bad work. It can mean you lose depth. Bad work is infectious. The new people in America – I expect you've heard of the Method, Miss Coco – they do this sort of counterfeiting all the time, with some very good results, I hear.'

Coco shook her head as she put the phone down. Dear old Clifton, he would never falter in his ambition to see Oliver become a great actor. Except, supposing now that Oliver knew that Clifton was *not* going to die, maybe he would not *be* Hamlet any more?

'Come on, Holly, let's go and take Ollie his breakfast.'

Seeing Oliver's Hamlet had made Elsie fall in love with him all over again, and what was more it had convinced her that he was becoming just as good as she had always been. If she had not been so much the professional it would have put Elsie off wanting to act with him ever again, as it would many a lesser actress, but, far from doing that, it made her frantic to partner him once more.

The second series of *Golden Days* was being hurried into production when Howard Grey suddenly died. It was a terrible blow to the series and a worse one to the cast, all of whom had loved and admired him. It also meant that the series had to be rewritten, and new characters brought in. Inevitably Elsie found herself suggesting that a younger man be brought in, a younger butler, with whom she, as the maid, could fall hopelessly in love. She then urged an understandably reluctant Portly to put Oliver up for the part.

'I am not sure that I can see Oliver as a butler, Elsie. I mean I am not at all sure he is not too much the nob to play a butler.'

Elsie laughed. 'Oliver's not a *nob*, as you put it, Portly. Good God, he's the son of Yorkshire confectioner or something, born and bred.'

Portly stared at the telephone receiver in his hand. 'Whoever told you that?'

'He did.'

'Oh.' Portly did not want to go on, but he knew that he was already too far in to go back. 'Oliver is John *Plunkett's* son, Elsie. I thought you knew that?'

'John who?'

'Never mind. The point is that he is the son of an old landed family, old as the hills. The butler, Clifton, whom you met – that's not his father, they just always pretended that he was, when he was briefly at Ramad and all that, so as he could be like the rest of them, and people wouldn't be preju-

550

diced. You know how it is now – if people know you're grand, well, you've *had* it, darling.'

'Oh. I see. Oh. Well, he never bothered to tell me, probably didn't think it mattered, that it would matter, to me, which of course it doesn't, not now, because why should it?'

It was Elsie's turn to stare at the telephone receiver in her hand. Suddenly she felt such a fool. All those jokes about Oliver's not being able to understand what a gentleman was, all that – it must mean that he had been laughing up his sleeve at her all this time. What a fool she had been, never noticing that Oliver's accent was really too slapdash impeccable to be just a trained Ramad version; and his careless ways, his confidence, everything about him had really always been far more exaggerated than could have been perfectly possible if he had been raised in comparative poverty. He would have been more uneasy, less sure, or more assertive anyway.

'Well, look, I mean to say, all the better,' she went on bravely, 'I mean who better to know how a butler goes on than someone who has grown up with one? But for the interview with the producers, I agree, he will have to go on being Clifton's son. Never do to be a whatever – grand or anything. I agree. Butler's son, even better.'

So, for the interview conducted by the producers over lunch, Oliver once again became Clifton's son, and of course he got the job, because, as well he might be, he was totally convincing as the son of a butler.

Elsie and he remet at the read-through. Life on *Golden Days*, now it was a success, had changed for everyone. For the cast, who all wore new clothes even for read-throughs, for the crew, who all now seemed to be driving new cars, for the company who made the show. But most of all it had changed the producers, all of whom now strode about with the air of wartime officers who had won a great battle, which indeed they had, the battle of the ratings.

Perhaps because of this they now sat at a special desk, just a little removed from the cast, as officers might remove themselves from the men at a briefing. It was at this little desk that, like the military, they made special announcements which they read out to the cast in solemn tones.

Having avoided each other at the outset, carefully taking coffee at the refreshment table at different times, Elsie now caught Oliver's eye as one of the producers stood up behind the desk to announce how thrilled they were that, fresh from his great success as Hamlet, Oliver Lowell had joined the cast to play the part of Wright, the new young butler.

During lunch in the canteen, where once again the producers ate in a partitioned-off room, well away from contact with the actors, Elsie made equally sure to put her tray down opposite Oliver's while announcing, 'My tray is going to marry your tray and have lots of traylets.'

'The Traylets – not a bad name for a girl singing group,' Oliver mused.

'Got over Hamlet then, Oliver?'

'Not really.' Oliver sighed before pushing a piece of ham towards a limp lettuce leaf, concentrating on it, rather than Elsie.

'You were great, Oliver. Truly. The Hamlet of your generation.'

Oliver looked up at that, as well he might since Elsie had never, ever praised him to that degree before.

'Did you see it? Why didn't you come round, if you saw it? Why didn't you come round when you were in?'

'I couldn't, we had to get home.'

'We?'

Elsie was surprised to see the familiar spark come back into Oliver's eyes.

'Who is we?' he asked, once more.

'Oh, just Howard Grey and myself – we had to go home and learn lines, or at least Howard did. Remember the first series was live, Oliver. Not funny.

'Christ, of course, *not* funny. I must say I'm glad this isn't live, but I'm also sure that a lot of the fun will go out of television if everything is going to be recorded. No more opera singers falling into the orchestra pit, no more drunken entrances, shame, shame, I say.'

'Huh. Define fun.' Elsie lit a cigarette and smiled bleakly, remembering the terror and the horror of both the cast and the production team.

'Personally, I don't fancy making an entrance through the chimney like Santa Claus, which happened last week on *The Blue Smoke*. You know it was Portly who helped get this recorded? He fought like a steer to get us recorded and, thank God, he won. I am quite sure that it killed Howard Grey – an actor of his age going out live like that – such a strain, poor soul. No, as far as I am concerned you can keep the thrill of going out live, Oliver, and settle for less dangerous practices.'

'Do you think I will be *accepted* as Wright, Elsie? I mean, do you think the audience will accept me? After all, Howard Grey, he's a pretty hard act to follow, wouldn't you say?'

'You're tailor made for the part, Oliver, as well you should be, considering your background – the son of a sometime confectioner turned butler. I mean to say, you're *tailor made*, old love.'

Elsie rolled her cigarette between her teeth and narrowed her eyes as she said this, while staring out of the window at nothing much. This small display of acting did not fool Oliver.

'You know, huh?'

'Yup.'

'Who told you?'

'Portly, of course. He had to, if I was to – if *he* was to put you up for the part.'

'He might have kept it to himself.'

'And you might *not* have kept it to yourself, Oliver Lowell, you truly might. All that time I spent thinking that we were twin souls when in reality you were a toff – a nob – not a bit of blood, according to Portly, that is not stained bright sky blue.'

'By the time I went to Tadcaster I was convinced that I was a man of the people. I had forgotten my background. I had to just get on with it. Now, I must go and study. Coming?'

'No. Don't have to.'

Elsie stared up at Oliver, a cheeky look coming into her eyes as she pulled a little face.

' "One Glance Lancaster", surely you remember, Oliver?'

'Oh God, of course. You never have to learn lines, do you? You just read them, and there they are.'

'Precisely – there.' Elsie touched her temple, at the same time giving a lazy smile. 'Watch it, Oliver, I shall soon be wiping the floor with you, Hamlet or no Hamlet.'

'Don't I know it.' Oliver hurried off.

Elsie watched him, and for a few seconds she felt pleasantly sad, as if she was listening to a Strauss waltz on an old gramophone, and then she stood up.

'Watch out, Oliver Lowell, here comes Elsie Lancaster.'

Portly watched his wolfhound romping between the trees in Kensington Gardens. It was a fine spring morning, so good that it threatened to become an equally fine spring afternoon and evening. He felt more than content, he felt happy, and having called Art to have his lead put back on he headed back to his flat, and from there to his office. A normal day lay ahead of him, not that there was such a thing in the life of an agent. Telephone calls, lunch with Coco about her new commission to do the scenery and costumes for a musical, then tea at the Ritz with a dear old actor laddie who wanted to start up again, and was hoping for a part of some kind in *Golden Days*. After which it was back with Art to the flat, change into evening dress, and off to the Awards Ceremonies with Oliver, Elsie and Coco.

He was therefore experiencing the usual frisson felt by those accompanying potential winners, but in his case, and he trusted in Coco's case too, there was something extra as well, an additional excitement that had nothing whatsoever to do with prizes.

Six hours later Coco called at the office.

She looked, Portly was relieved to see, quite, quite stunning.

'Coco.'

'Portly.'

'You look – stunning.'

'As a matter of fact, I do feel quite good.'

'Did you design that for yourself?'

'Who else would design it for me, Portly?'

'You are the crème de la crème, chérie, and I must be the luckiest man alive to be escorting you to the Awards Dinner.'

'Actually, Portly, you're not escorting me, if you remember, you're escorting Elsie?'

'Oh God, so I am, I'm escorting Elsie.'

'And Oliver's escorting me.'

Portly had the feeling that he was in the wrong play, that he was having the actor's nightmare, that he was standing on the stage not knowing any of the lines.

'We're meeting up with the other two – at the Savoy.'

'Yes, of course, so we are.'

Coco had, courtesy of Nanny Ali's commission, been able to create a most elegant gown for herself. And if she said it herself, her design displayed exactly the right amount of restraint and cut, which, teamed with an extremely expensive fabric – blue silk gazar – showed off her slender figure. The gown was cut across the bust in a straight line, the V beneath it meeting at a point in the middle, and continuing in a straight line to the hem, which was ankle length. Two bows to the side of the Regency-style bust line held a tiny cape of matching ostrich feathers. Naturally she wore shoes dyed to match her dress, and an evening purse of the same material, also trimmed with ostrich feathers. The whole effect was of a tailored gown which, as it should, suited the wearer to perfection.

Elsie too had been costumed by Coco. For her perfect blond beauty, and knowing that she was more than likely to walk off with the Best Actress Award for her role in *Golden Days*, at Portly's request Coco had designed an evening gown in eau de nil silk satin which would catch the light quite beautifully. The skirt was full and fell quite simply from a wide belt in the same material, but the bodice had been hand-embroidered by Coco with tiny stitches and decorated with pastes in the same colour, which caught the light as Elsie moved towards them and kissed them both warmly on the cheeks, just as if she had not seen them both the day before.

'Darlings,' she murmured, smiling.

'You look wonderful, darling,' Portly murmured automatically, but his glance at Elsie was, as far as Coco was concerned, far too brief.

'Doesn't – Elsie – look – fantastic,' Coco prompted, but Portly did not seem to think more was needed, which meant that Coco had to turn to Oliver. 'Doesn't Elsie look fantastic? She must win – surely she must win. You both must.'

Oliver swallowed hard. He wanted to win. Not that he minded Elsie winning, but he did not want Elsie to win if he was *not* to win.

His father had rung him just before he left for the hotel.

'Much enjoyed the series,' he told his youngest son, his head some way from the receiver as it always was when he was talking into the telephone. 'I have to say that I have never seen a butler done better. Every now and then I thought there might be little touches of Clifton? Just hope he can't see it, you sly devil. But there you are. Good luck for tonight, old chap. Hope you win. We'll be toasting you, you can be sure of that.'

Elsie breathed out. She knew that she looked fantastic, thanks to Coco's dress, which was fit for at the very least a duchess. She also knew that Oliver was mesmerised by her, because when they had met up he had not said a thing, which she knew of old meant that he was enraptured by how she looked.

'Else.'

Oliver had not called her that for – well – years.

'Yup?'

'You look twenty-four.'

That had been their shorthand. Twenty-four carat gold.

'Get on. It's just because you've only seen me in a maid's uniform for the past God knows how long.'

'Do you think we're going to win, Else?'

'Yup.'

'Why?'

'Because we're bloody talented, sweet lummox, that's why.'

Oliver stopped and stared. Elsie had not called him that for God knows *how* long. Not since God knows when. Not since God was a boy, he didn't think, not since then.

Of course none of them could eat dinner, as people never can when there are prizes in the offing, even when the food is worth eating, which is not normally the case. Elsie went to the loo several times and returned with her make-up yet more freshened. Coco, who was after all not involved, became more and more excited, not, as it happened, for Elsie and Oliver themselves, although of course she wanted them to win, but for Portly. What a coup it would be for him, she suddenly realised, a little late in the day, if two of his actors walked off with the best acting prizes. As the lights were dimmed and the first announcer strode on to the stage Coco crossed her evening-gloved fingers and waved them discreetly at Portly, while at the same time a waiter's gloved hand slid a note into Elsie's palm.

Please come at once, Dottie is dying and asking for you. She is at the Beeches, Kitchener Road. You may remember it' The note was signed *Richard Clough.*

Elsie stared first at it, and then across at Portly. Dimly the words started to work their way into her brain, finally becoming fact. Her grandmother was dying. Dottie. Of course, her grandmother, Dottie. She was dying.

She rose slowly from her place.

'What are you doing?'

'It's Dottie, she's dying.'

'You can't go now – you just can't.'

'I have to. It's over an hour's drive, I have to go. An hour and a half. It will take me an hour and a half, at least. Got to go. Can I take the driver?'

'Tell her, tell her, Portly,' Oliver hissed across the table to Portly. 'Tell her she can't go now, Portly.'

'She's *dying*, Oliver.'

Portly, who knew just what Dottie had once meant to Elsie, nodded. 'Oliver's wrong, of course you must. Take the car,' he whispered, while at the same time trying to listen to the compere. 'Of course you must go. If you win, Oliver can go up

560

for you, and explain. Of course you must go.'

This notion obviously assuaged Oliver's affronted feelings, and, clutching her evening bag, Elsie quickly left.

'How awful,' Coco murmured.

'Terrible,' Portly agreed, but his eyes had reverted to the stage.

He was not as concerned as he might be, because if Elsie won Best Actress Oliver could collect for her. She had been heavily photographed arriving in her chauffeur-driven car. It was a pity, but if she won, Fleet Street had the pictures. Besides, he quite understood why she had to go.

But, God, Dottie of all people, to be dying at that very moment, it did not seem possible. Dottie had once meant everything to Elsie. She owed it all to Dottie. Never said so, but Portly and she had both known it, from way back when, from when she had been sacked from that first show.

Arriving outside the Beeches Nursing Home, Elsie did not wait for the chauffeur to open the door for her, but burst out of the car into the rain, pulling the beautiful pale green evening coat with its high collar around her as she did so.

Unhappily it was raining hard, and she had forgotten her umbrella. The chauffeur ran after her holding out a large black gamp, but not so soon that it could prevent Elsie's hair, Elsie's coat and Elsie's dress from becoming soaked.

'Oh God, oh God,' she sobbed suddenly. 'Poor

Coco. She will be devastated, the beautiful coat and dress she made specially.'

The chauffeur sought to comfort her as Elsie turned at the door. 'Don't worry, Miss Lancaster, it will dry out, really it will.'

'Thank you, thank you so much.'

She ran towards the night desk, towards the smartly dressed night porter. She had only been at the Beeches once before, when one of Dottie's 'boys' had been taken ill of a heart attack and subsequently died.

'Miss Dottie Temple – I have been called to see Miss Dottie Temple. Dorothy Richards? Mrs Richards?'

She kept repeating various names under which Dottie might have booked herself in, but the night attendant looking down the register kept shaking his head.

'Sorry, Miss Lancaster, there is no one here of that name.'

'But there must be, there must be, truly there must.'

She glanced back at the chauffeur, shrugging her shoulders, and he smiled reassuringly.

'Perhaps Mary Martindale then?' Elsie suddenly suggested, remembering one of several names Dottie had sometimes used when she was still acting, when Elsie was tiny.

'There must be some mistake, I am afraid, Miss Lancaster.'

The night attendant looked apologetic. He recognised Elsie, from *Golden Days*, of course, and

562

she could see from the expression on his face that he would dearly have loved to find this mysterious Mary Martindale or Dottie Temple, if he could, but he patently could not.

Elsie turned back to her chauffeur. 'I don't understand. I mean you saw the telegram, didn't you?'

'Yes, Miss Lancaster. As a matter of fact, it's here.' He produced it from his uniform and they both stared at it.

'Please come at once, Dottie dying, et cetera, et cetera. Signed Richard Clough. There you are, it's all there. The Beeches, everything.' Elsie pushed the relevant piece of paper across the desk to the attendant.

'Perhaps Richard Clough could help you?'

Elsie nodded. Of course, Richard Clough, one of the oldest residents at Dottie's house. Old Richard Clough, sometime actor and director, of mixed attitudes, to say the least. Someone of whom Dottie used to murmur, as she slapped down the iron on yet another sheet, 'I'm not quite sure about Clough's credits, really I am not, but it's easier to go along with them than not.'

'We'll go back to her house. There must be someone there who knows something, surely?'

Back through the rain which was now coming down in stair rods, following her instructions, the large car made its way slowly back to Elsie's childhood home.

Of course it looked smaller, as childhood homes always do. And of course it looked even smaller because she was arriving at the front door in a large car with a chauffeur, dressed to the nines in an Awards dress and coat, all of which made the paint on the front door look even shabbier, not to mention the one geranium in the pot by the front door, and the boot scraper with all its bristles missing.

Elsie smiled at the chauffeur as she raised the door knocker and then let it fall. 'I just can't believe this.'

He smiled back at her. 'I'm sure there's an explanation.'

There was.

Hours later it seemed to Elsie that it was something from a nightmare, like the actor's nightmare, and that she would wake up from it and laughingly turn to Oliver – why did she think she would turn to him? – and say, 'My God, what a nightmare I've just had, I dreamed I was at an Awards dinner, and I had a telegram that Dottie was dying, and when I went to the house she opened the door to me! And she was laughing, and laughing, and that awful old actor who lodged with her, you wouldn't know him, Richard Clough, old Clough, he was behind her and he was laughing at me too, except he didn't have his teeth in. God, what a nightmare.'

But it was not a nightmare, it was all true, and Richard Clough was not the only one with his teeth out. The chauffeur had stared at this sight from some hell hitherto unknown to him, and he backed off down the steps as he heard Dottie screaming with laughter and saying, 'Only you could be so stupid, Elsie, only you could be taken in by such a stupid trick!'

'I think we had better go, Miss Lancaster,' the chauffeur had called quietly up to Elsie.

Elsie had wanted to move, but she had found that she could not. Her pale green satin evening shoes seemed to be glued to Dottie's top step, just beside the boot scraper with the bristleless brush.

'You always were an idiot, Elsie.'

Even after the door slammed in her face, Elsie stood rooted to that same top step facing that same front door up to which she had used to reach with the door key tied around her neck on a string.

That was how much Dottie hated her. Enough to drag her away from her first big night, to pull her out, as she had used to pull her out of the coal hole when Elsie dashed down to it to cry her eyes out when she had lost a part.

The chauffeur touched her on the arm.

'Come on, Miss Lancaster, you don't want to bother with folk like that, they're not worth bothering about. Jealous, that's what they are. Just jealous. Get back into the car, and have a good sleep while I take you back to town. Nothing like a good kip to put everything into perspective, that's what I always say.'

'It doesn't matter. Not really.'

'No, of course it doesn't, Miss Lancaster.'

565

He folded the long trains of her beautiful dress and coat into the car after her and, going round to his side of the car, he slammed his driver's door with some force. As he said later to his wife, 'You wouldn't credit it, not unless you'd seen it, really you wouldn't.'

Oliver was waiting for her at Elsie's own flat. They had both decided on a party back at her flat, whatever happened, whoever won or did not win.

It seemed that they had both won, and pretty soon after Elsie arrived back from her abortive trip, the newspapers too arrived so that they could both stare at pictures of themselves on the inside pages, Elsie in the beautiful dress that Coco had made for her, and Oliver accepting the second award on her behalf. So there he was smiling, holding two awards, and now, as Oliver poured a drink for the chauffeur, Elsie found herself staring at the statuettes in bewilderment, turning over and over in her mind what the night had brought. Triumph and disaster, hand in hand, typical of the theatre; even of life.

She still could not believe that Dottie hated her enough to play such a cruel practical joke on her, one that she must have known would mean that Elsie would miss her big moment. But that was how craven Elsie had been: she had been prepared to leave and go to Dottie's bedside and hold her hand as she left this world, in place of receiving what might be the only award she would ever win.

It was chilling, but it was real. She had known and seen enough of theatrical jealousy to realise that it could eat into the soul to such a degree that it destroyed it. Dottie and Richard standing there laughing and mocking her, doubled up with laughter, had been a sight from hell.

'Oh, by the way, how was your grandmother?' Oliver suddenly asked.

'Sorry?'

'I said, how was your grandmother?'

Elsie could see the chauffeur out of the corner of her eye and thought she could feel him blushing for her.

'She's dead. Quite dead.'

'Oh, I am sorry.'

'Yes, it is a pity,' Elsie agreed. 'But there you are, these things happen.'

Some minutes later, murmuring his congratulations, the chauffeur took his leave.

'Good night, Miss Lancaster.' He looked at her evenly.

'Good night, and thank you again.'

'Sorry, again, about your grandmother I mean.'

'Yes, it was a pity, wasn't it?'

'Still, all in all – a merciful release.'

'Yes, it was, wasn't it?'

'Next year. You'll win again next year.'

'Of course.'

Elsie closed the door behind him, as Oliver

called excitedly from the sitting room, 'Want to hear the news, Else? I mean the bits that you missed when we all came back here?'

'Portly and Coco have gone home together,' Elsie joked.

'Yes, you're right.'

'Portly and Coco, gone home, you mean *together* together?'

'Yup.'

'But they can't—'

'Why not?'

'Because – because – they're not suited, that's why.'

'Just as well they went home with other people, then.'

'Who? Who? Who? Oh come on, do tell.'

'We-ll.' Oliver was determined to drag out the news which he knew would be of foremost interest to Elsie. 'Portly seems to have a deep desire to get engaged to the lovely Constantia who is, let's face it, just so *Portly*, and they will make a formidable couple, so organised it will be absurd, but also utterly right, don't you think? Just so long as she lets him do the cooking. So, that's all right, tick.'

Elsie put her head back on the sofa, closing her eyes. It was just so nice to hear Oliver rattling on in his usual artless way, a bit of gossip, and then a sip of champagne, some more gossip and more champagne. She let it all wash over her, closing out the earlier scenes of the evening, the nightmare.

'I do love you, Ollie – you're such a chatterbox,' she murmured.

'And Coco was picked up from the reception by Aeneas, who is obviously besotted, so they have gone back to Coco's flat, and I don't want to be a gooseberry, particularly since I am in the process of divorcing her and could be spotted by the Queen's Proctor, or she could – so would you mind if I stayed here for the night?'

Elsie opened her eyes and looked at the clock on the mantelpiece. 'Don't you mean for the day?'

'Well, both, really.'

Elsie closed her eyes again. 'No, of course not. You can stay here for the rest of my life. Just keep on talking, Oliver, just keep on. It's just so lovely to be home again, with you, that's all that really matters.'

Aeneas was protesting, vociferously.

'I don't understand about the Queen's Proctor.'

'Well, if you're divorcing, which I am, divorcing Oliver for non-consummation, you have to be careful not to be spotted by the Queen's Proctor and had up for collusion, or something like that.'

'You mean this Proctor person is a voyeur?'

Aeneas followed Coco up to her flat on the first floor, carefully putting lights on and off, just as they had been careful to leave their taxi at the back entrance.

'Yes, that's it, he spies on people for the state, filthy beast. No, it's quite serious actually, but don't ask me how it all works.'

'I don't care about how the Proctor works, only how you work.' Aeneas tiptoed after Coco down the corridor. 'I love you, Coco Hampton, and tonight you looked like an angel from heaven, that is what you looked like, like an angel from heaven.'

Coco turned back to look at him. They had waited long enough to make love, until Aeneas had finished filming, and Coco had finished her collection for 'the palace', and now the time had come, it was somehow so right.

'Do you think if we had got together, um, earlier, it would have been better, Aeneas?'

'Not at all. No.' Aeneas shook his head. 'There is always a perfect time and a perfect place, and just now, I would say that we have both.'

EPILOGUE

THE CAROUSEL

Play orchestra play, play something sweet and light and gay, for we must have music, we must have music!

Sir Noel Coward, 'Play Orchestra, Play'

John Plunkett was preparing for his son's second wedding. He was, although he would not admit it, even to Clifton, excited. It was going to be a London wedding, which was a little bit of a pity, but on the other hand he liked London. Taking time out to see old friends at the Betterton Club, catching up with the gossip and so on, and so on, was pleasant; but more than that, his youngest son had achieved such fame, quite a bit was rubbing off on his old father, which made visiting the Betterton even more stimulating. The triumph of *Golden Days* was indisputably the greatest television success of its era, and might indeed prove to be so, some were saying, for many eras. It had, overnight, made watching television somehow acceptable, even for members of the glorious and ancient Betterton Club.

However, there was only one thing that still really puzzled John Plunkett, and that was Clifton's refusal to see how like Clifton himself Master Oliver looked in the series. Each week, when the series went out, the conversation was always the same.

'Master Oliver has somehow assimilated you, Clifton, d'you know? I swear it. Magnificent performance, really it is. I thought his Hamlet was the tops, but this – well this is really quite *something*. Everyone is saying so. All my friends keep ringing and saying "It's a young Cliffie, to a T."'

'Can't see it myself, sir. To me, as you have always said, Master Oliver is a throwback to his ancestress on the upper landing. His mother's great-grandmother.'

'Yes, but don't you see, Clifton, that's it? That's the actor's art. They assimilate someone so well, they even start to look like them. He looks like you, moves like you. Uncanny.'

'Really, sir.' Clifton looked enigmatic. 'I just can't see it myself.'

He turned away. He had plans for Master Oliver in the breaks between making the series, big plans that he must discuss with Portly Cosgrove. Back to the theatre – perhaps a sparkling Benedict, certainly a Romeo would not be out of the question – he was still not too old.

Clifton went off to his pantry cheerfully humming. Everything had turned out a lot better than he had thought it would when Master Oliver was born, which was when the likeness to Clifton had, for some reason, first manifested itself.

Not that Mr Plunkett had seemed to notice, only hesitating slightly when he was first shown the baby, before saying to his wife and

574

Clifton, 'Little chap looks just like your great-grandmother, Amelia, the one on the landing, doesn't he, really? Spit of her, I would say, absolute spit.'

Which all in all was exactly like John Plunkett, always and ever the gentleman, which was why Clifton was so very proud to serve him. As to Master Oliver, he was marrying a great actress in Elsie Lancaster, and it had to be said that they were not only going to make a match of it. The general feeling was that both of them had *met* their match.

THE END

Charlotte Bingham would like to invite you to visit her website at www.charlottebingham.com

COUNTRY CASUALS

£3000 worth of *Country Casuals* clothing to be won

Do you feel like a complete new wardrobe?

Enter now and you could be one of six lucky winners who each win £500 worth of fabulous clothing from Country Casuals

One of the UK's leading fashion labels, *Country Casuals* offers affordable, versatile yet exclusive collections. Renowned for high quality and contemporary sophistication, *Country Casuals* combines elegance with innovative fabrics for a classic but distinctly modern look.

And now available at selected *Country Casuals* stores nationwide is the new Petite Collection, specially designed for women 5'3" and under in sizes 8-16.
For details of your nearest Main or Petite collection stockist, or to request a copy of either brochure, contact *Country Casuals* Customer Services on 01845 573 120 quoting reference CC/BOOK/02 or log onto www.countrycasuals.co.uk.

HOW TO ENTER:
Simply write your TITLE/NAME/ADDRESS/POSTCODE/HEIGHT/DOB/TELEPHONE NUMBER and, if applicable, e-mail address on a postcard, completed in BLOCK CAPITALS, and send it to:
Marketing Department, Country Casuals Ltd, 16/21 Sackville Street, London W1S 3DN
or enter online at www.countrycasuals.co.uk. Closing date for entries is Sunday 26th May 2002.

...ou do not wish to be contacted by Country Casuals in the future please state 'NO FUTURE CONTACT' on your postcard.

...ions: **1.** Closing date for entries Sunday 26th May 2002. **2.** The winners will be the first 6 entries drawn. **3.** Winners to be drawn by Sunday 30th ...within 28 days. **4.** Prize voucher is valid on full price clothing only for 12 months from date of issue, at the designated store. **5.** No purchase ...ternative will be offered. **7.** The competition is open to residents of the UK and Republic of Ireland (excluding employees and families of The ... Reed Group PLC). **8.** Entrants must be aged 18 or over. **9.** No responsibility can be accepted for lost or misplaced entries and incomplete ...nly one entry per person. **11.** For a list of judges, winners and results, send an SAE to Country Casuals, Marketing Dept, 16/21 Sackville ... judges' decision is final and no correspondence can be entered into. **13.** All entries become the property of Austin Reed Group PLC. ...rld Publishers reserve the right to withdraw the offer, terminate the promotion or declare void any entry in the event of actual fraud in ...mplies acceptance of rules. **16.** The winner must be willing to have their name published and featured in regional press at no charge.